John Lescroart is the *New York Times* bestselling author of twenty-four novels, including *Damage*, *Treasure Hunt*, and *A Plague of Secrets*. His books have been printed in sixteen languages and published in more than seventy-five countries. He lives in northern California with his wife and two children.

Praise for the novels of John Lescroart:

'No one, attorney or not, can write a trial scene better than John Lescroart'   *New York Journal of Books*

'The master of the legal thriller'   *Chicago Sun-Times*

'John Lescroart is a terrific writer'   Jonathan Kellerman

'Unusual in his ability to combine courthouse scenes, action sequences and well-drawn characters that come together in a fast-paced text'   *Wall Street Journal*

'John Lescroart is one of the best thriller writers to come down the pike'   Larry King

'A master'   *People* magazine

'Succeeds on every level'   *Publishers Weekly*

'High-class . . . first-rate'   *LA Times*

'Brilliant'   *Washington Post*

'The courtroom dr   *Independent*

D1321709

By John Lescroart

Sunburn
Son of Holmes
Rasputin's Revenge
Dead Irish
The Vig
Hard Evidence
The 13th Juror
A Certain Justice
Guilt
The Mercy Rule
Nothing But the Truth
The Hearing
The Oath
The First Law
The Second Chair
The Motive
The Hunt Club
The Suspect
Betrayal
A Plague of Secrets
Treasure Hunt
Damage
The Hunter
The Ophelia Cut

JOHN LESCROART
THE OPHELIA CUT

headline

Copyright © 2013 The Lescroart Corporation

The right of John Lescroart to be identified as the Author of
the Work has been asserted by him in accordance with the
Copyright, Designs and Patents Act 1988.

First published in Great Britain in 2013 by
HEADLINE PUBLISHING GROUP

First published in paperback in 2013 by
HEADLINE PUBLISHING GROUP

2

Cataloguing in Publication Data is available from the British Library

ISBN 978 0 7553 9322 0

Typeset in Granjon by Palimpsest Book Production Limited
Falkirk, Stirlingshire

Printed and bound by CPI Group
(UK) Ltd, Croydon, CR0 4YY

Headline's policy is to use papers that are natural, renewable
and recyclable products and made from wood grown in sustainable forests.
The logging and manufacturing processes are expected to conform to the
environmental regulations of the country of origin.

HEADLINE PUBLISHING GROUP
An Hachette UK Company
338 Euston Road
London NW1 3BH

www.headline.co.uk
www.hachette.co.uk

To Lisa Marie Sawyer,
MY LOVE AND MY LIFE,
AND TO OUR CHILDREN

Violence and injury enclose in their net all that do such things, and generally return upon him who began.

Lucretius

Prologue

ANTHONY XAVIER RICCI never set an alarm clock because he never needed one. When his eyes opened in the darkened room after a fifteen-minute afternoon nap, he didn't move for a couple of minutes, letting full consciousness creep up on him. The clock next to his bed read 4:30.

Ricci was thirty-one years old and after eight years in the NYPD, a sergeant. He lived alone in the basement of a beautiful brownstone in Brooklyn. A couple of windows up front by the sidewalk let in a good amount of light and kept his spacious living room from feeling like a cellar. Ricci was proud of his place and kept it pin neat. Over the past three years, he had accumulated some very nice things: a Persian carpet in bright yellows and blues, and several strikingly colorful, contemporary paintings that were already worth more than he'd paid for them. He'd also bought a brown leather sofa, two low, modern armchairs, and an antique wood marble-topped coffee table. On the wall opposite the paintings, built-in bookshelves held his library, his CDs and collection of LPs, a turntable and a pair of out-of-date but excellent JBL speakers, and a large flat-screen TV. Not many of New York's Finest lived so comfortably at his age.

In the back half of the apartment, he'd recently redone the kitchen – stainless steel stove and refrigerator and granite countertops. A high-tech wine cooler that held thirty-six bottles hummed quietly next to the sink. Abutting the kitchen was the bedroom, where he was just opening his eyes.

He'd needed the nap. The previous night he'd been out with about twenty other cops, dinner at Mario's to celebrate the retirement of Captain Greg Sheppard, his boss in Vice for the last five years, and a well-liked figure in the department. They'd closed the bar at 4 A.M., and then this morning Ricci had been up at dawn for his weekly seven-mile run, after which he'd done his laundry, picked up his dry cleaning, done some grocery shopping, had lunch with his cousin Victor and Victor's wife, Bette. But he had big plans tonight as well – some business and then dinner at home and perhaps bed for the first time with the lovely Andrea Bernardi, whom he'd been seeing for a month; she was coming over at 8:00. The nap was a hedge against fatigue.

He showered, shaved, weighed himself – rock steady at 180. In ten minutes, he was dressed in Dockers, tennis shoes, a Knicks sweatshirt against the light September chill. He'd also be grabbing his bulkier generic gray hoodie before he ventured out, and a knit cap to pull down over his hair, cover his ears, though not so much for the cold.

Sitting on his bed, he turned his cell phone back on and on a whim decided to take a look at his photo stream. In a minute he'd traveled back six months and was staring at a picture he'd taken of Teri Wright, a fellow cop and former girlfriend.

A twinge of regret seeped into his consciousness. What had he been thinking when he let her go? Andrea was a beauty, sure, with a fragile Anne Hathaway look about her. But all of his past girlfriends were beauties – it was the Golden Age of the single straight man; the pickings were endless.

Teri, even among the stiff competition, was still near the very top. Now he stared at her smiling face on the screen of his phone. Much more Scarlett Johansson than Anne Hathaway, with a sexual energy and vibe that was even more powerful because of her maturity. Andrea wasn't yet twenty-five, still with (he guessed) a lot to learn; Teri was thirty-two and, from his experience, had pretty much mastered it all. And there had been a sweetness to it, too, combined with an ability to laugh at herself. And to make him laugh, which was much more rare.

Ricci was a serial monogamist; in general, he loved the chase and the first few weeks, sometimes even months, of sexual intimacy, but after a while the excitement and desire, even with a Teri Wright, always tended to pale. He told himself that that was just who he was. He usually didn't worry about it, although now flipping back through some more pictures of Teri – that topless monokini shot when they'd been on their weekend at Turks and Caicos . . .

Lord.

He felt the beginnings of arousal.

Maybe he should call Teri again. It hadn't been the easiest breakup – lots of tears and anger, but there was no way she could deny the chemistry they'd shared. What about their true love? The commitment they'd talked about? That breakup day came back to him now; it had been pretty ugly.

Nevertheless, he thought it was entirely possible he could get her back. He could just give it a little more time, let things play out with Andrea over a couple more months, then give Teri a call. She'd no doubt be resistant at first, but he was confident he could wear her down. It was definitely an idea. Let time work its healing magic, then move in.

Shaking himself from his reverie – he had work to do, after all – he got out of the photo stream, left the phone facedown on his bedside table, grabbed his hoodie, and headed out.

Ricci kept a small storage locker about five blocks from his house. There were perhaps eighty units in a low-rise brick building at the back end of a public parking lot – $8 ALL DAY – although on a Saturday evening at a little past 5:00, the lot held only three cars. With his key, he unlocked the left-hand side door and let himself into the building. Turning on the overhead lights, he walked about a third of the way down to his locker. As usual, there wasn't a soul in the place.

After working the combinations both on his own Master Lock and a built-in dial on the locker itself, he had the door open. Inside, the contents of the four shelves were arranged as neatly as he kept things in his home. The top shelf held a shoebox full of hundred-dollar bills – $33,700 worth. He kept the exact updated count of deposits and withdrawals on a lined sheet of paper taped to the inside of the door. On the next shelf, he kept stored several boxes of ammunition and one of surgical latex gloves. The bottom two shelves held the guns – some registered (not to him, of course) and some not, of several different calibers and makes – that he'd picked up in the course of his work over the years. Seven, all told.

Moving quickly, he pulled out his new favorite, a Ruger LCR revolver – five .357 Mag rounds and a barrel under two inches for easy concealment. Flipping open the cylinder, he slid the bullets home, snapped everything back into place. Five rounds were plenty. Hell, one was plenty for his needs, but he generally took two shots for certainty. If he needed more than five, he'd probably wind up dead.

Putting the gun in his hoodie's front pouch, he grabbed a couple of latex gloves, checked the shoebox for luck, just to see that the pile of bills looked all right. Checking both ways one more time, seeing no one, he closed the locker, twisted the first dial, and hooked in his own Master Lock.

James Di Marco didn't want to let the summer get away without one last barbecue. Now here it was, the last weekend in September, and the forecast next week was rain, possibly sleet, the temp going down to the thirties. So yesterday he'd bought four fat rib eyes and started them marinating soon after he'd woken up this morning. They were going to be outstanding.

4

The Weber was perfuming the entire Coney Island neighborhood with the smell of cooking meat, while James and Carla and the Jensens from down the street sat out in the backyard with their second pitcher of margaritas. Everyone was in slacks and sweaters, but nobody was cold. The sun wouldn't be setting for at least another half hour, and they had positioned themselves to enjoy its last rays.

At forty-five, improbable as it was, James felt that his life had turned around at last. He didn't kid himself that this was through his own efforts, although he had learned how to play the game better, learned how to take advantage of opportunities he routinely couldn't identify when he'd been younger. He wasn't part of Mr Tedeschi's inner circle, of course, and not being related by blood, probably never could be. But he'd worked his way up as Mr Tedeschi had transitioned out of the stolen goods and drug business to an emphasis on the flesh trade, from driver and deliveryman to manager of an entire block of apartments, a euphemism for massage parlors, in Queens.

And this was where James had begun to realize the bonus that Mr Tedeschi had made available to him. It was simplicity itself, and though he knew that technically it was skimming, certainly as sins went it was more or less venial: reporting just a little less than he actually collected from the girls, he'd been doing it so long and so successfully now that he'd come to believe that Mr Tedeschi actually, albeit tacitly, condoned it. This was how his lieutenants augmented their earnings, improved their lifestyles, and he didn't begrudge them for it. Over the years, the additional income had allowed James to keep Carla happy with a yearly cruise, some nice jewelry, and, perhaps most of all, this second house a few blocks from the beach.

Out in the backyard, he heard the front doorbell ring. Tipping up the last sip of his margarita, he stood up from his chair, put his glass on the patio table, and asked, 'Anybody want anything while I'm up?'

From the hallway, he could make out the outline of the caller through the glass of the front door. The sun was low and glaringly bright behind the man's figure, but as he got closer, James saw that it was a friendly-looking, young white guy. Opening the door and squinting in the sunlight, James said, 'Help you?'

'I sure hope so,' the young man said, flashing a winning smile. 'Sorry to bother you, but I'm looking for James Di Marco.'

'You found him.'

Still smiling, he said, 'Mr Tedeschi says to tell you, "Thou Shalt Not Steal."'

In an instant, Joe's face started to go dark with fear, and also with understanding.

Ricci didn't hesitate. 'Oh, one last thing,' he said, pulling the Ruger out and up. In one smooth motion, he stuck it under James Di Marco's chin and pulled the trigger twice.

Forty-five minutes later, the gun locked away in his storage unit, the surgical gloves and the spent cartridges thrown into a trash container in the subway station on the way back, Ricci went down the four steps leading to his apartment, took out his key, inserted it into the lock, and started to push open the door.

The minute he turned the knob, a pair of strong hands took hold of him from behind and pushed him forward into the door, which slammed open in front of him, and then he was thrown down onto the floor, his face into the Persian rug, three men holding him down. When he stopped struggling after only a few seconds – resistance was obviously useless – a calm and measured voice said, 'There's four of us here and we're all armed and very dangerous, Tony. You are, by the way, under all kinds of arrest. But we're really here to talk to you, which would be easier and so much more pleasant if you were sitting up. You think you want to do that?'

Ricci raised his head and saw a man sitting at his kitchen table with an open bottle of wine and a couple of glasses in front of him, one of them half-filled. 'Sure,' he said, 'I'll sit up. Let's talk.'

'No funny stuff.' The man reached under his jacket and showed a gun. 'No kidding.'

'I get it.'

'Good.' The man nodded to his comrades, and the pressure behind him went away. 'One of you get the door, please.'

Ricci slowly got to his feet. He looked around, and sure enough, there were three other guys, all about his size, complete professionals. 'What do you want?' he asked the man at the table.

'Have a seat,' the guy said, indicating the other kitchen chair.

'Who the fuck are you?'

The man broke a tight smile. 'Oh, yeah, the introductions.' He dug into his pocket and pulled out a wallet, which he opened to reveal a badge. 'We're a little posse of federal marshals, Tony. My name is Frank Ladoux, and I predict that you and I are going to be good friends for a long time. Please, have a seat. Can I pour you a little wine? You're going to want, maybe need, something to drink pretty soon, I expect.'

'I don't know what you're talking about.'

Ladoux tsked. 'Tony, please. A little respect.' He leaned forward, picked up the wine bottle, and filled the bottom of Ricci's glass. 'Come on, take a sip. It's your bottle after all. It'll make you feel better.'

Ricci picked up the glass and drank. 'Okay, now what?'

'Now you're going to tell us how much you know about Martin Tedeschi.'

Ricci hesitated, scanned the kitchen, came back to Ladoux. 'He's a wine collector and business guy out in the Hamptons. He throws a lot of parties.'

'Parties where you've provided security.'

Ricci nodded. 'Sometimes. So what? Half the force moon-lights.'

'Maybe they do, but they don't usually become pals with their hosts, do they?'

'I'm not pals with Tedeschi.'

'No?'

'No. If that's what this is about, you got the wrong guy.'

Ladoux shook his head. 'You disappoint me, Tony. You're a cop. You know what it's like to make an arrest. You don't do it without preparation and evidence up the ass. Isn't that right? So here we are, a team of four – and believe me, the team is much bigger than that – and you're acting like you think we don't have everything we need and then some. Of course we do. You're done, dude. You have only two ways to go: one, you roll over on Mr Tedeschi or, two, starting tonight you go to jail for the rest of your natural life, which won't be too long.'

Ladoux poured himself a glass of wine, took a sip, and put the glass down. 'Listen, you are the break we've been looking for for at least two years. We know you're majorly connected to Tedeschi. We've got pictures, we've got tapes, videos, you name it. We know you've been working for him for five years and know everybody who's anybody in his organization. We're going to want you to testify against these people so we can put them away where they belong.'

Ricci barked a laugh. 'And, even assuming that what you think you know is true, I'm going to do this why?'

'Because otherwise . . . I thought I'd made this clear . . . other-wise, you're in prison forever.'

'For what?'

Again, Ladoux shook his head, smiling. 'I'll be honest with you, Tony. We don't know for sure yet how many people you've hit, although the deposit list on the door of your locker ought to give us some leads on timing.' Ladoux nodded. 'The locker? Oh, yeah, we know about that. In fact, we got its contents in evidence right now, collected by my colleagues right after you left, oh, about twenty minutes ago.'

Stalling for time, Ricci picked up his glass and drank up its contents.

'Here. Let's pour you some more of that. I've got your attention now, don't I? We were talking about the number of people you've hit, and the good news for us is we don't need a lot of bodies. We just need one.'

'You're saying you've got proof I've killed people?'

'Honestly, Tony, I'd have to call it an embarrassment of riches.'

'Because I have a locker?'

'It's more what's in the locker, but that's a start. Seven guns that'll match ballistics with who knows how many dead people. Thirty grand plus in cash. Ammo.' Ladoux held up his hand. 'Now, I know what you're thinking. That it's all circumstantial. There's probably no record you even rent that locker. Except we've been filming it round the clock for the past four months, and it's pretty obvious it's yours.'

Ricci sat back. 'I want to talk to a lawyer.'

Ladoux clucked. 'Shit, Tony, I'm giving you a chance to live here, and you're pissing about finding yourself a lawyer. You get a lawyer and go to jail to await your trial and Mr Tedeschi has you killed in your cell. I promise you this will happen, and you know it's true. So let's stop this nonsense talk about lawyers. I am offering to protect you forever. You testify for us and then you start a new life. You don't get that?'

But Ricci crossed his arms and sat back in his chair. 'I never killed anybody. I want a lawyer.'

Ladoux looked over at his colleagues, who'd found themselves seats in the living room. 'Can you believe this guy?' He reached into his pocket pulled out a cell phone, came back to Ricci. 'It's amazing the clarity you can get with the video on these things, Tony. Take a look at this. No, come in closer. Get a look.'

U.S. Marshal Ladoux pushed a button and the screen came up. Ricci saw himself walking along a sidewalk. With a rush of blood in his ears, he realized that this was the block where James Di Marco lived. He watched himself stop at the front gate, walk up the short little path, knock at the front door. He waited, the door opened, and then the camera zoomed in on him and Di Marco. Ladoux was right. The clarity of the zoom was excellent.

Ricci couldn't take his eyes off the screen. It seemed to take forever, though he knew that the whole thing hadn't lasted thirty seconds. There was a moment of discussion, then he pulled the gun and stuck it under Di Marco's chin. In his kitchen chair, his whole body reacted with a jerk at the clearly audible reports of the gun as Di Marco went down.

Turning away now, they got Ricci directly facing the camera, his face nearly filling the screen. Out of zoom, finally, he broke into a lazy jog.

Dumbstruck, Ricci shook his head in disbelief. 'You had a guy tailing me?'

'Tony, we've had a dozen people tailing you round the clock for the past four months. I told you, this is a big operation and you're in the middle of it. When the word got out you were at your locker earlier, we kicked it up to high gear, and, I must say, you didn't disappoint.'

'You just shot the video knowing what was coming down? Thinking I was going to do the guy? When you could have stopped me and saved his life? What kind of fucking guys are you?'

'I told you, we're fucking serious guys. Really. Any one of us. And we needed you to actually shoot the poor fucker. You can understand that, I'm sure.' The marshal sipped wine and tsked again. 'Hey. Get over it. The world's a tough place. Whoever he was probably deserved it. And we got what we needed, too. That's what counts.'

Ricci came forward, poured himself more wine, drank half of it. His hands were shaking.

'So look,' Ladoux said, 'let's cut the bullshit about how you never killed anybody. We got you killing somebody. You're going down for this, unless you want to play ball with us. And I mean you're going down now.'

Ricci reached again for the wine. 'How'd you get on to me? You mind if I ask?'

'You remember you dated Teri Wright? A fellow police officer.'

'Shit. Teri?'

'Maybe you want to let 'em down easier in the future. She was a little bitter. And then she got to thinking about all the great stuff you've got around this place, all the extra money you had all the time. It got her thinking with her cop's brain. Where was all that coming from? And, of course, she also knew about you moonlighting for Tedeschi. She knows that you're working in Vice; she knows he's running lots of girls. It all started to fit – she didn't know exactly how – but she came to us.' He spread his hands in low-key triumph. 'And then there was today.'

'So what do we do now?'

'Well, I'm afraid now you disappear.'

'Just like that?'

'Pretty much. We get you out of here tonight, right now, and into a safe environment, and then we get your initial testimony and get you set up in a new place with your new identity. And then when we need you to come back in to testify, you're available for us. A case this size, it might be years. In the meantime, you got a life.'

'What about after I testify?'

'That is up to you, but you'll probably want to stay in the program.'

'Forever?'

'Up to forever. But it's your choice. You got family? Relatives?'

'No. Couple of cousins, but nobody especially close.'

'That ought to make it easier, the choice I mean.'

'And you set me up with a new identity, just like that?'

'Couldn't be easier. I'll show you. What's the name of this wine we've been drinking? It's delicious.'

'Solaia,' said Ricci. 'It's Italian. Wine of the year a few years ago in *Wine Spectator*.'

Ladoux put his finger into his wineglass and motioned Ricci to come in closer to him. 'Anthony Xavier Ricci,' he said, touching his wine-soaked finger to Ricci's forehead. 'I hereby christen you Tony Solaia. Where do you think you want to live from now on?'

Tony Solaia reflected for a moment, then nodded and said, 'I've heard good things about San Francisco.'

PART
ONE

1

Moses had wanted to see Dismas Hardy alone.

He'd unexpectedly dropped by Hardy's house on Thirty-fourth Avenue, and now the two men kept up a brisk pace as they walked along Geary toward the beach on this overcast November Sunday afternoon. Moses McGuire didn't like to worry his only sibling, Frannie, Hardy's wife. And he was, himself, worried to distraction.

That morning San Francisco's second newspaper, the *Courier,* had run an article by a columnist named Sheila Marrenas. It was part of a series on unsolved crimes in the city. This one revisited an event dubbed the Dockside Massacre, in which six years ago, five people, including the city's head of Homicide, Barry Gerson, had been killed in a gunfight on Pier 70.

For McGuire – and, he would have thought, for a lawyer like Hardy – it struck a little too close to home.

'They don't call her Heinous Marrenas for nothing,' Hardy said. 'Nobody reads her, Mose. I wouldn't worry about it.'

'I read her. Lots of other people read her. She mentioned you by name.'

Although that sent a little shiver of apprehension down Hardy's spine, he suppressed it. 'She mention you?'

'No.'

'Abe, Gina, anybody else?'

'Freeman.'

'David remains dead, if I'm not mistaken. He's not about to talk. Is that it?'

McGuire went on for a few steps, then stopped. 'Tell me it doesn't get inside your head,' he said.

Hardy pulled up, took in a breath. 'It's never *not* inside my head, Mose. It never goes away. Not what we did. We had no choice about that. But the idea that it might come out. I live in fear of it every day.'

'You ever think it might be better if we just . . . I mean, as it is, I read an article like that, I'm just waiting for the other shoe to drop.'

'Should we maybe bring it out into the open? Here's the easy answer to that: never in a million years. You shouldn't even begin to think anything like that. It would ruin a lot of lives, including yours.'

'All right. But this living under the constant threat of exposure—'

'—is far better than living with the alternative, and don't you kid yourself.' Hardy started walking again, and Moses fell in beside him. 'You feel guilty?' he asked after a few steps.

McGuire shook his head. 'No. That's why I think it wouldn't be so bad. If people knew what really happened, they'd see we had no choice. It was pure self-defense.'

'True, but probably better not to let other people make that decision. We know it. We live with it. That's enough.'

'It's wearing on me. That's all I'm saying.'

'It wears on us all, Mose. I wish it hadn't happened, but talking about it isn't going to make things better.' Now it was Hardy's turn to stop. 'You don't think I haven't had nightmares? I'm watching a damn ball game and suddenly I'm zoned out, back there on that pier, taking the hit to my Kevlar. I'm not wearing that vest, I'm dead right now, you realize that? You don't think that makes an impression?'

'That's what I'm saying. We keep it a secret, we're basically saying it wasn't the right thing to do, and we know it was.'

'No. Completely wrong. What we're basically saying is that, right or wrong, we can't tell anybody – not ever – because nobody would understand, and our worlds, as we know them now, would end.' Hardy hesitated, then went on. 'This is your damned twelve-step program talking. I don't care what they've been telling you all this time, having every issue out in the open, in the bright light of day, so you can talk about it and analyze how you feel about it is not the solution to every problem. Sometimes the solution – trust me here – is you just shut up and suck it up.'

As always, with any even minor criticism of his A.A. program, McGuire became defensive. 'Talking about issues has saved my life,' he snapped. 'Maybe you ought to try it. You might surprise yourself.'

'I hate surprises.'

'Yeah, well, there's a time and place for everything.'

'Not necessarily,' Hardy said. 'And even if there is, here and now isn't it.'

In the middle of the afternoon on the second Tuesday in November, the head of San Francisco's Homicide detail, Lieutenant Abe Glitsky, got back from a staff meeting. The light on his desk phone was blinking, and he punched into a voice message from his best friend, Dismas Hardy, inviting him to a dinner that evening at Sam's Grill, where Hardy had reserved a four-top booth. Glitsky, he said, was needed. Cryptic, but that was Hardy. Glitsky should show up with bells on at six-thirty.

Glitsky usually made it a point to eat with his family, but upon hearing this message, he realized that he couldn't remember the last time he'd been out for fun. Come to think of it, he hadn't laid eyes on Hardy in almost a month. The face time they got had taken a bit of a hit over the past couple of years, a victim of the difference between their home lives, Glitsky and Treya with their second round of young children, ages five and seven; Hardy and Frannie empty nesters, pretty much over all that.

Glitsky picked up the phone, about to call Hardy to say he couldn't make it, not enough notice, but instead paused, sighed, and hung up. Ten seconds later, now thinking he'd call his wife and ask whether she'd mind if he went, he picked up the phone again, then looked at it as though it were a foreign object and replaced the receiver.

Treya worked as the private secretary to the district attorney, Wes Farrell, whose office was down two flights of stairs in the Hall of Justice. If Glitsky took the longest possible route – down his hallway to the elevator, then back down her hallway – she was about two hundred paces from where he stood.

The inside stairway was quicker and got him there in under a minute.

'Hey!' Treya brightened and stood up behind her terminal as Glitsky came through her door. When she looked at him, her smile faded as quickly as it had bloomed. 'What's wrong?'

'Is something wrong?'

'I don't know.'

'Well, something made you ask.'

'It's just you show up out of nowhere with that frown on . . .'

'That was my "everything's fine" frown.'

'Here's an idea. Maybe you could work on an "everything's fine" smile, the way other people do.'

'Smiling's not really my thing. Sometimes I feel bad about that, but it's useful in my work.' He came forward and stood across her desk from her. 'Okay, heads up. Ready?' He flashed his teeth, returned to deadpan. 'How was that?'

'Maybe worth practicing, slow it down a little. It could fly.'

'I'll work on it.'

Treya's expression softened. Like her husband – Jewish on his father's side and black on his mother's – Treya came from a mixed heritage that showed in her face: black, white, perhaps some Pacific Islander somewhere back in the gene pool. Five feet ten, big-boned, and strongly built, she could project a formidable presence. Now she reached across her desk and touched her husband's cheek. 'Meanwhile,' she said, 'to what do I owe the pleasure of this personal audience?'

'I got a call from Diz. He wants me to meet him at Sam's for dinner. I thought I'd run it by you.'

She didn't hesitate. 'Sounds like a good idea to me. You don't have to ask.'

'I know. I just thought you and the kids . . .'

'Please. One night? Go have some fun. You stop seeing your friends, they stop being your friends. And you don't want that with Diz. Is it a special occasion?'

'No. Just hanging out, I gather.'

'Go.'

'You're the best.' Coming around the desk, he kissed her. 'I owe you one.'

In the booth at Sam's, Glitsky's three prospective dinner partners sat over their drinks. Dismas Hardy had started early on his first martini at the bar with his law partner, Gina Roake. She sat next to him now, nursing her Oban Scotch, into which the one ice cube had long since melted. Across the table from them both, Moses McGuire turned his club soda around in his glass.

'Is that really when you stopped drinking? That day?' Gina asked him.

McGuire nodded. 'Not exactly, a little later, but six years ago.'

'That's worth celebrating on its own,' Hardy said.

'Speak for thyself,' Moses said.

'Has it been that hard?' Gina asked.

Moses grunted, possibly under the impression that he was laughing. 'Only every day.' Then, to Hardy, 'And while we're at it, I'm not sure celebrating is the right word, Diz. Commemorating, maybe.'

'I like commemorating.' Gina's mouth was set as she took another sip. 'I guess I'm here more to commemorate David.'

'I'll drink to David,' Hardy said, 'anytime. But let's not forget that there's the quick and the dead, and we're all still here among the quick, so call it what you want – commemorating or celebrating – I'd say that's worth raising a glass. Figuratively, in your case, Mose, since you probably don't really want to raise a glass of real stuff to your sobriety, either.'

'Thanks for reminding me.'

Hardy nodded. 'I live to serve.'

At that moment, Glitsky pushed aside the booth's curtain, filling the entire opening. 'Is this the place?'

'He arrives,' Hardy said.

McGuire pushed his chair back to give Glitsky room to sit next to him, but the lieutenant didn't move. He stood where he was, in the doorway, obviously surprised by something. His face morphed through a catalog of expressions, none of them his 'everything's fine' smile. He chewed the inside of his cheek.

McGuire moved his chair back another couple of inches. 'Grab a chair, Abe,' he said. 'Take a load off.'

The scar through his lips beginning to stand out in relief, the lieutenant took another beat before his shoulders gave slightly and he blew out through his mouth. 'This is not a good idea. I can't do this.'

'Abe!' Hardy said.

But with a shake of his head, Glitsky had already stepped back and pulled the booth's curtain closed behind him.

In truth, they were there neither to celebrate nor to commemorate. After his talk with Moses on their walk to the beach two days ago, Hardy had thought it would be a good idea to gather all the surviving principals of the massacre so that he, Gina, and Glitsky could gang up on Moses and help him reaffirm his commitment – all of their commitments – to their lifelong vow of silence. Even Abe, with his abrupt and unplanned departure, had unwittingly underscored the urgency of the commitment. He wasn't even going to talk about it with the only people who knew.

Gina, her hand protectively on McGuire's arm, leaned toward him across the table. 'If you really need to talk about it – find a place to put it – you can always come to me.'

'Gina,' Hardy began with a warning tone, 'I don't think—'

She stopped him midobjection. 'No. Moses has a point here. We don't have to keep it bottled up forever. I've wanted to talk about it a hundred times. All of us, it's got to be the same. Then something like Marrenas's column comes around, and the pressure builds up. I don't see anything wrong with being each other's safety valves.'

Hardy shook his head, far from agreeing. 'And then we get kind of used to it being something we talk about. I don't even want that here, in our private little booth.'

'All right, Diz, then don't. You've got my permission. You do it your way, which you're going to do anyhow. What I'm telling Moses is, if he wants, I can be there for him. For this.'

With a somber look, McGuire put his hand over Gina's, gave her a nod. 'That's all I'm saying.'

Hardy looked from one to the other. 'I'm wishing Abe would have stayed. He's got the right attitude. He'd vote with me.'

Gina gave him a tolerant smile. 'That would still only make it a tie,' she said.

Glitsky lived in an upper duplex just off Lake Street on a block that ended at the wooded southern border of the Presidio. At a little past midnight, the only light in his living room came from the streetlamps outside through the bay window in the front of his building.

In a bathrobe, he sat in his reading chair, hands gripped in his lap. Subliminally, he registered his home giving up the occasional tick or moan – the heat going on and off, one of his children turning over somewhere behind him in the back of the unit, wood creaking as the ground shifted a millimeter along one of the city's fault lines.

A muted rustling of cloth preceded evenly spaced footfalls, and his eyes went to the hall leading to his bedroom until a silhouette appeared. Treya. 'Are you coming back to bed?'

'I didn't want to keep you up.'

'That's not working out so well.'

'Was I making noise out here?'

'Just sitting there?'

'I don't know. Sighing or something.'

'No. That wasn't why I couldn't sleep. I felt you not there.' She lowered herself onto the couch across from him. 'Do you want to talk about it?'

He lifted one arm off the chair, let it drop back down. 'There's a reason the four of us haven't been in the same place for six years. I'm not making this up, you know.'

'No. Of course. I never thought you were. I remember it all pretty well myself.'

'I mean, I'm a cop, Treya. I don't get in shoot-outs with other cops. Even rent-a-cops like those Patrol Specials. And Gerson winds up dead. The head of Homicide. We killed him. We killed all of them.'

'They killed people, too. Don't forget David Freeman.'

'I don't. Not for a minute. I never said they didn't deserve it. All of them. And if Diz and Gina and Moses had come even two minutes later, they would have gotten me, too. I get it. I really do. We had no choice, okay, but that doesn't change the fact.' Now he did sigh. 'I don't know what they were thinking, throwing a party at Sam's. McGuire, okay, I can see. He's always a wild card. But Diz and Gina? They're lawyers. They should know better.'

'Maybe they want just to put it behind them. They think it's not an issue anymore.'

Glitsky blew out a frustrated breath. 'They can't think that. They know otherwise. There's no statute on murder, and those were murders.'

'They were homicides, Abe, not murders.'

'That doesn't really matter. We didn't stick around so we could have a nice fair trial about it.'

'They were—'

His voice went harsh. 'We can't acknowledge it, Treya. Any part of it. It never happened. How can they not see that?' He raised both hands and gripped his head as though it were a soccer ball. 'Lord. My brain is going to explode.'

She crossed over to him, sat on the chair's arm, put her hands over his. 'Take a breath,' she said. 'It's all right.'

He settled back against her. 'How do they know they don't have booths bugged at Sam's?'

'Or maybe microphones in the sand dabs,' she said.

'You laugh, but it's not impossible.'

'Pretty unlikely, you must admit. I really think they just wanted to put it all behind them. You know Diz. He likes to have events, mark passages.'

'This shouldn't be one of them. This should be something he takes with him to his grave. And McGuire . . .'

'What about him?'

'God forbid he ever goes off the wagon.'

She pulled his head closer against her. 'This is exhaustion speaking. Why don't you just call tomorrow and talk to Diz?'

'Not on the phone.'

'No. Perish the thought. Think of the bugging possibilities. Go meet him in the middle of Crissy Field.'

'You're making fun of me.'

'Only a little. Come back to bed.'

Moses McGuire sat at the Formica table in the kitchen of his apartment, nursing a Guinness pint glass filled with water. With his dinner at Sam's, he'd had cranberry juice and then club soda; after dinner, coffee. While Hardy and Gina had their Frangelico nightcaps, he went to straight water. He and Susan didn't keep any alcohol except some wine in the apartment, but Moses wasn't much of a wine drinker, so that wasn't usually a problem.

Not that the thought didn't cross his mind.

But he knew the danger he faced if he ever gave in to the constant urge and poured himself a real drink. He knew how he got – social, friendly, garrulous. Words came out of his mouth that should have stayed in. He'd almost mentioned the shoot-out six years ago, at least twice, before barely stopping himself. Twice was too much. Too many other lives were at stake, both of friends and of family. He couldn't risk it anymore, and so, cold turkey, he had hooked up with Alcoholics Anonymous.

Goddamn secrets, he thought. If he didn't have secrets, particularly that secret, he could be drinking right now. And most of the time, truth be told, he could bear the craving. But after the *Courier* article, in spite of the best efforts of Diz and Gina, he hadn't been able to shake his nerves. He wanted a drink – fuck, he *needed* a drink – to calm them. Susan was asleep. There was no one here at home to spill his secrets to. It was safe.

He checked his watch. If he could survive dry for four more hours, he could make the six A.M. meeting.

On the other hand, one little half glass of wine wasn't going to hurt him. Was it?

As he pushed his chair back from the table, he heard a key turn in the front door, then a whispered 'Hey? Is somebody up?'

His twenty-three-year-old daughter, Brittany.

Moses came around the corner into the living room. 'Hey yourself. Just your old man. What are you doing here?'

'I missed my room. Is that okay?'

'Of course.'

'My apartment is nice, but it doesn't always feel like home.'

'No. I know the feeling. You could move back in here, you know.'

She sighed. 'I don't think so. It's just some nights.'

'Okay. But the offer's good anytime. So where have you been?'

'Out.'

'Anyplace specific?'

She half shrugged. 'Just out, Dad, with some guy.'

'Does he have a name?'

'Not really,' she said. 'It doesn't matter. And you don't have to feel like you need to protect me.'

Moses felt his jaw tighten. God forbid he should worry about his daughter. 'No protection implied, just a mild fatherly interest. You show up here, needing the comfort of your old room, I think something might have made you unhappy.'

'No. I'm happy. I'm fine.'

'I'm glad to hear it. Even gladder to see you. How about a little hug, no questions asked?'

Her shoulders rose and fell. 'I don't see how that could hurt.'

2

On the first day of February, a Wednesday, the guy pushed through the door to Peet's coffee, having shown up now four days in a row.

All Brittany could guess about him was that he was some kind of professional – the coat and tie and clean short haircut proclaimed that. Good hair, thick and almost blond; then again, the more she saw of him, the more she realized that this guy, looks-wise, was pretty much good everything – an honest-to-God cleft in his chin, a killer smile, no apparent body fat.

One of the blessed golden few.

Brittany was at the back of the shop today, selling beans by the pound, whole or ground. The last three days she'd been up at the front counter, taking orders for drinks on the premises or working the machines, and he'd come in with a couple of other suits around his age and ordered his latte and then sat with his back against the wall, where she saw him surreptitiously glance at her a few times.

Which meant, of course, that she was sneaking the occasional look at him, too.

Yesterday when he'd ordered, she said, 'Sure. Can I please see your ID?'

He went to reach for his wallet, then stopped, cocked his head. 'Excuse me?'

'Just teasing. But I almost had you, didn't I?'

He paused, looking straight at her, and said, 'You could have me any time you want. But in the meanwhile, I'll go with my regular latte.'

'One latte, coming up.'

Now, one step inside the store and alone this time, he scanned the front counter with the drink servers, and his expectant expression faded. Brittany found herself fighting against waving to get his attention, but she needn't have bothered. She was with another customer, grinding French roast, and when she turned around, he was next in line at her counter.

'Are you allowed to go out with customers?' he asked.

'Not when I'm working.'

'I meant when you weren't working.'

'I don't think there's a rule against it. Who would the customer be?'

'That would be me.'

'Ah. I have a rule, though, that I don't date people until I know their name and they know mine.'

'That's a good rule. I'm Rick Jessup.'

'Brittany McGuire.' She reached a hand over the counter and shook his. 'Hi.'

'Hi.' He let go of her hand and hesitated. 'So . . . ?'

'So?'

'So would you like to go out someplace?'

'I'd consider it. Yes. When?'

'Today? Tomorrow? Friday?'

'Do you drink anything besides lattes?'

'Occasionally.'

'Do you know the Little Shamrock, out on Lincoln?'

'Sure.'

'How about there on Friday around seven?'

'Done. I'll be there.'

At a quarter to five that afternoon, Rebecca Hardy – known as the Beck to family and friends – two years older than her cousin Brittany, sat on a stool at the city's oldest bar, otherwise empty except for a solo dart player in the back room. On the other side of the rail, Brittany's father, Moses, shook some bitters into a shaker, then turned around, grabbed a flat bottle filled with light green liquid from the shelf behind him, and measured out a careful portion with his jigger. 'The return of absinthe is a beautiful thing,' he said. 'And I might add that in spite of my own rather checkered history, I'm proud to see the younger generation of my family embracing it. In fact, embracing cocktails in general.'

'Cocktails rule,' Rebecca said, 'especially Sazeracs. I could drink them all night. In fact, don't tell my dad, but I have drunk them all night. Not, however, recommended.'

'No, you want to be a little careful. Especially with the hard stuff.'

'I've learned. Or at least I'm learning. I think.'

'It's a process.' McGuire upended the shaker and emptied its strained contents into a flat-bottomed cocktail glass. He added a lemon twist and set the drink on the bar. 'Enjoy.'

She picked up the glass, held it out to him in a quick silent toast, then took a sip. 'Perfect,' she said. Then added, 'I should have known.'

'Known what?'

'That you'd make this perfectly.'

McGuire's craggy face cracked, showing off his teeth under the oft-broken nose. 'Sweetie, after forty years of bartending, I like to think I've got a basic handle on the profession. Drinks-wise, anyway. It's the other stuff . . .'

'What do you mean? What other stuff?'

His face went sober and he raised a hand. 'Nothing.' Then shrugged. 'Nothing to do with bartending, anyway.' He added, 'Daughters.'

A smile played around Rebecca's mouth. 'Uncle Moses, your daughters are great.'

'Right. I know. That's what everybody tells me. But Erica's in Thailand, as you may remember, having dropped out of UCLA with no apparent plans to return, or to work, or anything, and Brittany . . .'

'Brittany's good.'

'I know, I know.' He added, 'But she's making minimum wage, Beck. With a bachelor's in engineering, and she's working in a coffee shop.'

'At least that's a job, Uncle. Do you know how many people don't have jobs? Me, for example.'

'You're in law school, Beck. That's different. You'll get a job when you graduate. I mean, a real job.'

'Not necessarily.' She sipped at her drink. 'It's all different now. Having a law degree doesn't mean you automatically have a job. And Brittany's got résumés out. Something will come up. She's looking.'

'Mostly for guys, it seems to me.'

'Well, the line *is* long,' Rebecca admitted, then brightened up. 'But the wait is short.'

McGuire winced. 'That's what I mean,' he said.

Rebecca reached out and touched her uncle's hand where it rested on the bar. 'I know, but really, I wouldn't worry about her. I see her all the time, and she's fine. She's just searching a little bit right now. At twenty-three, that's her job, right?'

'Says her much older and wiser cousin.'

'Older, anyway.' Rebecca checked her watch. 'Aren't my parents supposed to come down here today? It's Wednesday, right?'

'Wednesday it is.' Date night was a sacred ritual at Chez Hardy. Dismas and Frannie arrived at the Shamrock for a civilized drink or two right about cocktail hour, then usually repaired to one of the city's restaurants to round out the evening. 'And see,' McGuire said, 'that's what I mean. Your parents inviting you along on their date night. Brittany would never want to come along with her mother and me, assuming we ever had a date, which we don't have too many of.'

'Except,' Rebecca said, 'that my parents didn't invite me along to wherever they're going next. They invited me to join them for a drink here. The end.'

'But you'd go with them if they asked, wouldn't you?'

'Well, sure. But they won't.'

'Still,' McGuire said, 'there's your difference.'

Brittany wasn't on as much of an existential search as the Beck had implied to McGuire. In the eight months since she'd graduated from Cal Poly, she'd shredded her way through six different suitors. These did not include any number of casual hookups, to which her father was not privy. Brittany had played this unlucky half dozen as if they had the potential to become actual boyfriends. The longest-lived of any had been one of her mother's cello students, Ben Feinstein, a sweet, funny, smart, handsome guy who loved poker and bike riding and music, and whom Moses thought was a great guy. Ben had lasted three whole weeks before Brittany decided she needed to move on.

She didn't want – her phrase – to waste the pretty.

Brittany could get away with this attitude and behavior because she was distractingly beautiful. She was tall, just under five eight, and both so slender and so buxom that her father more than once had heard her crueler friends refer to her as Barbie. That voluptuous figure would have been enough to attract a host of men even if Brittany were not blessed with the loveliest Black Irish face in the kingdom – fair, finely pored skin like Venetian marble over perfect cheekbones, jet-black hair setting off luminous green eyes. A strong aquiline nose and naturally pouty lips gave her countenance an edge that would forever elevate her above mere prettiness.

Sometimes, catching her in an unexpected light, Moses would find himself stopping short – his wife was lovely and he himself wasn't ugly, but Brittany's face was insane. Her junior year, a casual shot of that face in full smile had lit up the cover of Cal Poly's admissions brochure, in the wake of which she'd turned down three offers to come to Hollywood for screen tests, all of them, to Brittany's mind, flighty and not serious. She might be pretty, she'd told her father, but she was a serious person, majoring in engineering, after all, carrying close to a four-point. These people wanted to use her face, and her face alone, basically to sell soap.

She was a lot more than a pretty face, and if none of these people could see it, to heck with them.

Now, possibly a little bit drunk and before any crowd had come in, Brittany sat at the end of Little Shamrock's bar, baring her soul to her long-suffering father, who loved his girl to distraction, although – as he'd told the Beck – he worried about her, about her choices, about her life.

Lord, how he worried.

She was going on about the new guy, whom she'd laid eyes on, by Moses's count, a total of four times. 'Even across the counter, I could feel the chemistry. I think he could be the real deal.'

Moses sat on the high stool that he pulled behind the bar when it was slow. 'The real deal,' he said with minimal enthusiasm. 'Really?'

'Sometimes you can just tell.'

'If I remember correctly, wasn't Ben the real deal for a while there, too?'

'Ben's a great guy, Dad. That just didn't work out.'

'Brit. It didn't work out because you dumped him after . . . what was his name?'

'Paul.'

'Paul, right. Who lasted how long? A month?'

'Well, this is different.'

'Okay. I'll keep an open mind. What's his name again?'

'Rick.'

'And what does he do besides drink lattes?'

'What do you mean?'

Moses had to keep himself from rolling his eyes. 'I mean, does he have a job? A life? Anything? Do you know where he lives? Or works? Is he married?'

'No. I'm sure he's not married. No ring, and besides, he doesn't act married.'

'Married people act different than other people?'

'Guys, yes, quite a bit, actually. You can tell, or I can. And he's not.'

'Okay.'

'I don't know why you're being so negative.'

Moses slumped on his stool. 'Because your poor father cares about you, that's why. You meet a guy three or four times and suddenly decide you need him in your life. You don't know him at all. He could be an ax murderer and you'd have no idea.'

'Come on, Dad.' Brittany sighed. 'You don't have to be so dramatic. Look. He wears a coat and tie. He's got friends his own age, and that can tell you a lot right there. He's got a sense of humor, and he's incredibly good-looking. What more do you need?'

'Depth, intelligence, sensitivity, taste?' At Brittany's dismissive glance, he said, 'Just throwing out some random possibilities.'

'You don't know him.'

Moses couldn't hold back a laugh. 'This just in, Brit. *You* don't know him.'

'I'll find out.'

'Yes, I'm sure you will. That's what I'm worried about.'

'You don't have to worry. I'm a big girl, Dad. Really. All grown up and everything.'

'I know you are.' He let out a sigh. 'Here's the deal, Brit. I'm not worried about this guy in particular. I'm just concerned about . . . about you getting hurt, I suppose, more than anything. You're all grown up, granted, but you're still my baby. Is it so bad a thing that I want to make sure you're all right?'

'No. I love that. I love you.'

'I love you, too.'

Brittany drained her cosmo. 'Maybe I shouldn't tell you all this stuff. Maybe it's TMI.'

'Not to me, it's not. I want to be in your life. I'm glad you feel you can confide in me. I just worry about all the drama. In the long run, drama's not as much fun as people think.'

'Better than boring.'

'Maybe sometimes. Not always. And the opposite of drama isn't necessarily boredom. It might be contentment. You could try to look at it that way. Go for something good and solid.'

'Maybe Rick will turn out that way.'

'Maybe,' Moses said. 'That would be nice.'

'But you don't think so.'

Moses shrugged, then sighed. 'He could be anything. What I'm saying – granted, I'm old, but – is you might want to find out a little bit about somebody before you start talking about him as "the real deal." He's a guy you don't know at all. How can you even consider that he might be the real deal? You're setting yourself up for disappointment, and I hate to see that. Over and over again.'

She nodded. 'It'll stop when I find the right guy. That's what I'm going for.'

'There's more to life than that, and I know you know this, but it's not just all about the right guy.'

'Don't try to tell that to Mom.'

'All right, all right, although a little unfair. Your mother and I have been very lucky.' He took in a breath, let it out. 'But what about in the meantime, while you're looking for this perfect right guy?'

'The meantime is what we call life, Dad. Sometimes it's a little scary, sometimes there's drama. I'm okay with that. Really, I am.'

Moses crossed his arms.

'What?' she asked.

'Nothing,' he said. 'You're right. I'm too protective. It's your life. You should live it the way you want to. I just don't want to see you get hurt.'

At this, Brittany's whole being seemed to relax. Her head canted to one side, and a soft smile gathered around her mouth. 'I'm not some fragile Ophelia. You remember what you always used to say to us when Erica and I were younger and got upset, that line from "Try to Remember"?'

Moses nodded. 'The one about the heart being hollow if it hasn't been hurt.'

'Beautifully rendered, Dad. Yes, that's the one. See what it does? It turns a little bit of hurt into a good thing.'

'As long as it's only a little bit,' Moses said.

'Any more than that,' Brittany said, 'I'd kick its ass.'

'That's my girl,' her father replied, 'but you'd have to get in line.'

3

For no apparent reason, Dismas Hardy decided to get serious about losing a tenth of his body weight. Sixty years old, he'd always been a fair-weather jogger and occasional aerobics guy on the street or in one gym or another, but like Jiminy Cricket, he wanted to live to be a hundred and three, so he thought he needed a hard-core approach, something that could punish him and reward him at the same time.

This approach also fit his personality, which had its competitive side, to put it mildly. He had not lost too many cases in his professional career; he was an expert thrower of darts and a skilled snorkeler and scuba diver; he tended to win at chess, at poker, and at Scrabble (except against his son, Vincent, a fact that galled the shit out of him). He related to the Jimmy Buffett song 'Last Man Standing' – and he often was. The private investigator he used, Wyatt Hunt, was almost twenty years younger and a jock of the first order, and Hardy always whipped him at darts and sometimes beat him at basketball and racquetball by sheer force of will.

So he wanted a challenge that would get his BMI down a couple of points, turn back the clock so he would feel the same as he did when he was thirty-five.

Not that he was worried about dying or anything.

But today he was having second thoughts about the regimen he'd decided upon. He stood on the packed sand outside the Dolphin Club, on the shore of the bay in Aquatic Park. Out in front of him, choppy green water stretched across to the breakwater about a quarter of a mile away. Buoys demarcated a swimming lane in the enclosed area.

He wore a wet suit against the fifty-four-degree water, the same temperature as the surrounding air. It was a few minutes after ten, the hour when the club opened to the public; the fog had not yet lifted.

A fit guy somewhere in his thirties appeared next to him wearing only a blue Speedo. Hardy glanced sideways, fighting down his pique at young guys in general and thinking that by no stretch was fifty-four degrees reasonable for swim trunks, but the guy didn't appear to be suffering at all from the elements. Instead, shifting easily from foot to foot, he offered Hardy a smile. 'Better not to think too much about it,' he said. 'Just wade in.'

'I'd like it better if there was someplace to jump, get it over in a hurry.'

'First time?' the young man asked.

'Is it that obvious?'

'You were standing out here when I started getting changed. Most of the regulars, they just go for it.'

'I'm going to. I'm waiting for a command from on high.'

'Hey, don't let me rush you. We've all been there. But it's too cold to just stand here, so if you'll excuse me.' And with that, the guy took five or six springing steps and then dove flat into the water and was off in an efficient crawl.

'Show-off,' Hardy said to himself. Then he stepped forward, gasping as the cold water came up under his wet suit. In a few steps, he was hip-deep.

He threw himself forward in a racing dive and starting swimming.

Though the younger man swam twice as many laps inside the buoys as Hardy did, lapping Hardy in the process, they finished at about the same time. Hardy, his teeth gripped to keep them from chattering, had just sat down in the locker room, still in his wet suit, when the door opened behind him and Adonis appeared again. 'How'd it go?' he asked.

Hardy nodded, shook his head, nodded again. His cheeks were numb, so he wasn't sure how much of a friendly grin he was mustering. 'Could be warmer.'

'You'll get used to it. I never thought I would, and now I don't really even think about it. Get in, start moving, pretty soon you're almost toasty.'

Hardy looked up with a rueful eye. 'I'm a few light-years from toasty.'

'You'll get it,' the man said, then after a moment's hesitation, he stuck out his hand. 'I'm Tony.'

Hardy took the proffered hand, a vise grip that stopped short of being intimidating. 'Dismas.'

Tony cocked his head. 'The good thief?'

'That's him. The name doesn't ring a bell with most people.'

'Yeah, well, Anthony Solaia – that's me – I was an altar boy in first grade. I was all about the saints back then, especially Joseph and Dismas, numbers one and two to make it into heaven.'

'I always thought Dismas was first.'

'Before Joseph? I don't think so, dude. Joseph, after he died, just waiting in purgatory or wherever they held them all that time? They had to let him in first. Besides, married to a virgin his whole life as part of the deal, never complaining, he had to have figured they owed him. He would have made a fuss.'

Hardy broke a small grin. 'We'll ask when we make it up there, get it straightened out.'

Though he'd been warned, Hardy nevertheless paused in front of the address on Mission Street that his daughter, Rebecca, had given him. For all the world, it looked like another of the derelict buildings that had become so depressingly common in the greater downtown area over the past few years. What once might have been a beckoning storefront window was now painted a dull matte black, as was the front door, which yawned partially open into a darkened reception area. Hardy was thinking that this was a great spot, all right, if you wanted to get mugged.

But yes, this was the address.

While he was standing there taking in the ambience, a mixed-gender posse of seven young people appeared from around the corner and, with no hint of hesitation, pushed through the half-open outer door and entered. Hardy fell in a few steps behind them, entering the dim anteroom in time to see the last of them disappear as the inside door clicked shut.

Hardy walked over to that door, looked around, and – feeling foolish and somehow conspicuous in his business suit – knocked three times. At eye height, a two-inch-diameter circle of red light opened in the center of the door. An eye appeared briefly in the peephole, then a disembodied voice intoned, 'Yes?'

'Fiddle,' Hardy said. The password.

The door clicked again and swung open. Barely visible in the dim red light behind the door, a leather-clad, sweet-faced young man sat on a stool. 'Welcome to Burning Rome,' he said. 'Watch your step going down.'

It was good advice, and not entirely unnecessary, since the stairway descended into even darker blackness before a landing midway led to the next flight of stairs, perpendicular to the left. A solitary red lightbulb shone above this second stairway, casting its minimal glow onto the steps, and as he walked down, Hardy became aware of a bass line emanating from behind the door at the bottom of the stairs.

When he opened that door, to his surprise, he found himself in an attractive place. It was a well-lit, classy speakeasy rather than skuzzy garage, with a high ceiling and brick walls on all sides. A substantial dark wooden bar stretched from one end to the other; John Mayer sang through the sound system at a volume far below the assault level Hardy expected.

Hardy made his way across to where his wife and daughter sat, looking similarly lovely – two redheads in leotard tops, fitted jeans, and boots. Mother and daughter were facing each other, turned toward the bar, wineglasses in front of them, and neither saw Hardy until he appeared at the table and said, 'You've got to love a place where you need a password to get in.' He hung his jacket over the back of the chair at the tiny table in the middle of the teeming room. 'Although I think "fiddle" is a little obvious, don't you?'

Frannie leaned over and kissed his cheek, and the Beck answered, 'It changes every day.'

'They really don't let you in if you don't know it?' Frannie asked.

The Beck's face took on a puzzled look. 'Why would you not know it? It's on their website.'

'What if you aren't near a computer?' Hardy asked.

The quizzical expression remained. 'Then you Google it on your phone.' She put a hand on her father's arm. 'And don't say, "What if you don't have a phone?"'

'Okay, I grant you everybody has a phone, but what if you can't get Google on your phone?'

His daughter looked to her mother. 'He's joking now, right?'

Frannie patted Hardy's hand. 'He's smart in other ways,' she said.

'I'm just thinking about the hordes of poor people walking by on Mission, unable to slake their thirst for want of a password.'

'Slake,' Rebecca said. 'There's a Dad word.'

'And a fine one it is,' he said. 'Maybe they should make it tomorrow's password. Meanwhile, I'd like to order something slake-able. Do waitresses come around, or do I go to the bar?'

'Either way. The bar, though, if you want the complete experience.'

'Which is?'

'One of their signature cocktails. The mixologist here is amazing.'

'Mixologist,' Hardy said. 'There's a daughter word. Is a mixologist different from a bartender?'

'He invents drinks, Dad. Makes his own bitters, infusions, garnishes, like that. I think you'd like some of them. He does a thing with gin and bitters and basil that you would positively love.'

'Basil the herb?'

'Is there another kind?' Frannie asked.

'What if I just want a single malt or a simple martini?'

'He cures his own martini olives. They're awesome. But watch out for the pits.'

'Yikes,' Hardy said. Then to Frannie, 'We can't tell Moses about this place. He'd go postal here in a heartbeat.'

By this time, a cocktail waitress who was only slightly prettier than Scarlett Johansson had gotten to their table and, with a devastating smile, put a napkin down in front of Hardy.

'Macallan Twelve.' Hardy, striking a blow for purism, added, 'Neat.'

On his way back from the bathroom, Hardy passed the mixologist station at the end of the bar, with its substantial line of young and even younger people waiting for service. He'd been here for only one drink, and already the crowd had thickened to the point that he could barely see through to the back wall. Someone had cranked up the volume on the sound system. The place was definitely starting to hop. Glancing over to his right, Hardy caught a glimpse of the dervish behind the rail mixing up a shaker of something, then stopped and did a double take as he recognized the young jock from the Dolphin Club, Tony.

Small town.

Crossing to his table, excusing himself through the throngs, he got back within earshot of his two women and yelled at them, 'When did they lower the drinking age to fourteen?'

Then his eyes drifted back to the entrance just as the door flew open and a couple of men appeared, quick-stepping over to the nearest corner. A couple more appeared right behind them. Hardy, knowing cops when he saw them, stepped back to see what was going on. A third pair came in and headed directly for him, and for the office behind the bar.

The first IDs came out as the uniforms started through the front door. By this time, no more than seven or eight seconds after the first uniform entered, Rebecca put her hand on her father's arm. 'What's happening? Who—?'

The question was answered for her by a fullback in plain-clothes who, seeing that the cops had the people they had come in after, had stationed himself by the door. He blew a whistle that stopped every conversation in the place, then bellowed over the music, 'May I have your attention, please. San Francisco Police. This bar is closed. Please stay calm and make your way to the exit.'

'Stupidest thing I ever saw in my life,' Hardy was saying to Frannie as he cut into his duck at Prospect, one of their favorite new places to eat. 'Total overreaction, the idiots. So there are sales to minors? You wait until the bar's closing, and you arrest anybody you want. They're lucky somebody didn't have a heart attack, or people didn't think bomb or fire, or a gang of kids didn't decide to mob them. You know how easily the whole thing could have gotten out of hand?'

'I thought it was out of hand from the beginning.'

'And you're right.' He chewed, swallowed, blew out a heavy breath. 'Pack of fools.'

Frannie put down her fork. 'Can you believe how they stormed in and took the place over? You'd have thought everybody in there was a major criminal.'

'Well, see,' Hardy said, 'you put your finger on it. Gateway activity. Have a drink before you're twenty-one, next thing you know, you're robbing a bank or kidnapping somebody. It happens all the time, as the day follows the night.'

Frannie shook her head. 'I mean, as if there isn't serious actual crime, they decide they're going to bust kids for underage drinking?'

'We won't stand for it,' Hardy said. 'It frays the fabric of society, don't you know? And don't forget, they also get to close down the bar and arrest the bartenders.'

'That benefits who, exactly? Unemployment's at – what? – fifteen percent, and this puts more people out of work. Who does that help?'

'That's a good question.'

'I know. But really, why? I can't believe anybody in charge of anything could have let this happen.'

'Didn't just let it happen, Fran. *Made* it happen.'

'That's plain scary,' she said. 'They could have arrested the Beck if she didn't happen to have her ID on her.'

'No, they weren't arresting the kids, and thank God for that. The guys my heart goes out to are the bartenders. Felony conspiracy, for Christ's sake. How are they supposed to know somebody's underage? People get carded at the door out front when they give the password. Inside, the bartenders pour them their drinks, and guess what? The IDs are bogus. Whose fault is that? And now those poor suckers are downtown getting booked for conspiracy to sell alcohol to minors. It's a travesty.'

'Especially with you being a bartender and all.'

'Damn straight,' Hardy said.

4

LIKE HUNDREDS OF other law entities across the country, Hardy's firm had changed dramatically over the past few years. The commercial real estate market and all of its ancillary parts had ceased to be a meaningful source of income, and in its wake, dozens of other businesses failed. Construction and development money, business money, money that had been the lifeblood of the firm, had almost completely dried up. From a high of nineteen lawyers four years ago, Freeman Hardy & Roake was down to seven, mostly those who did plaintiff litigation, along with a mixed bag of criminal defense, including DUIs, shoplifting, minor drug busts – bottom-rung legal work. Not helping matters was the fact that of the firm's four original name partners, Freeman was dead; Farrell had to remove his name after being elected San Francisco's district attorney; and Roake was pursuing a more than halftime career as an author.

That left Hardy.

And wouldn't you know it, he often thought, the cuts in staff had not extended to his receptionist/secretary, the perennially sour, long-suffering, humorless Phyllis. She'd been with David Freeman before he'd established the firm, and there was no way Hardy could get rid of her in good conscience. Which did not stop him from contemplating new scenarios for her murder on a regular basis.

Such as this morning, when he came in at eleven-thirty after his swim and she greeted him at the elevator door, arms crossed over her chest, tapping one foot, doing her best imitation of a schoolmarm cornering a child who was unconscionably late for school.

Hardy dredged up a hopeful smile. 'Good morning, Phyllis. And how are you this fine morning?'

'It's barely still morning, sir,' she said. 'Several calls have come in for you.'

'Important calls?'

'I'm sure I couldn't say, sir. This being a law firm, people who call us sometimes want to bring us some business, and that would seem important in the general scheme of things. To me, at least. Ed Benson was one of the calls.'

Benson was the chief clerk of the Superior Court, and his name got Hardy's attention. 'Ed Benson called for me? Did he say what he wanted?'

'Something about a glut of conflicts cases that they're trying to clear. He said he'd consider it a personal favor if you could come down to the courtroom this morning . . .' She paused, sighed, continued. 'By now it's too late for that. I left the message on your cell phone, too.'

Hardy pulled his phone from its holster, glanced at it, and gave her a sheepish grin. 'Sometimes I forget to turn the darn thing on.' He pushed down on the top of the instrument. 'There. And oops, look at that. Here's your message. I'd better go call him before it gets any later.'

It was a classic conflicts case. The public defender could defend only one of the bartenders because whenever two people get arrested together, it is overwhelmingly likely that one will end up pointing the finger at the other. One lawyer, or one firm (in this case, the public defender), cannot represent both defendants. Or, in this case, more than one of the dozen or so defendants. The court would have to appoint a private lawyer for every defendant after the first one. It wasn't just a conflict, it was a cluster.

When business otherwise was slow, these cases could be something of a godsend, since attorneys' fees were paid reliably, if not promptly, by the court. So the judges had no problem having a lawyer in court every day to pick up a conflicts case if there happened to be one. But there wasn't a contingency for a dozen conflicts at once, so Ed Benson was on the phone explaining. 'You read about the ABC sweep last night, Diz? Putting the word out on the scourge of underage drinking the city's experiencing right now.'

'Better yet,' Hardy said, 'I was part of it. Dumbest thing I ever saw.'

'Tell me about it,' Benson replied. 'So now we have a dozen felony arrests, all of them set for arraignment this morning, most of them first offenders, none of them remotely happy, and few if any lawyers down here answering the conflicts call.'

'You want me to make a couple of calls,' Hardy asked, 'see who's around?'

'The more the merrier.'

'I'll see what I can do, Ed. Give me about fifteen.'

After spending the night awake in the slammer and getting booked for felony conspiracy to distribute alcohol to minors, then released on his own recognizance along with the other mixologists, Tony Solaia didn't bear much resemblance to the dashing young swimmer from the Dolphin Club or the dervish from Burning Rome. Now, a little after two P.M., he slid into a booth across from Hardy at Lou the Greek's, an ancient semisubterranean establishment across the street from the Hall of Justice that served the legal community – cops, attorneys, clients, relatives, jurors, secretaries, social workers, reporters. The place opened at six A.M. for the hard-drinking crowd and didn't slow down much until it closed at two A.M.

They both ordered Anchor Steam on tap.

'How am I supposed to thank you for this, much less pay you?' Tony asked.

'You don't,' Hardy replied. 'The city's going to pay us. If these cases go all the way to trial, which I doubt, my firm could bill a few grand. If anything, I'm in debt to you. But my real feeling is these turkeys aren't going anywhere.'

'You don't think so?'

Their beers arrived and Hardy drank. 'We can't guarantee results, but I can't imagine the DA playing hardball. At most, he'll reduce to misdemeanors, you'll do some community service. Case dismissed. End of story.'

'So why did all this happen?'

'That's the question. Somebody trying to make political hay. One of our supervisors, I'm thinking probably Liam Goodman, on his way to the mayor's office. Stupid.' Hardy lifted his glass. 'You look like you could use a little sleep.'

Tony nodded. 'You're an observant guy.' He sighed. 'The good news is I don't have a job anymore, so I can sleep all I want.'

'I wouldn't worry about that,' Hardy said. 'If your bar doesn't open again soon, I can get you a couple of shifts at the place I own. Keep you in cash, anyway, until Burning Rome reopens.'

'If it reopens.' Solaia swirled his glass. 'You own a bar?'

Hardy shrugged, broke a small grin. 'I like to think we're a full-service firm. But yeah, I own a bar. A quarter of it, anyway. The Little Shamrock. Out in the Avenues.'

After Tony Solaia caught a cab home outside the Hall of Justice, Hardy entered the building, passed through the metal detector, and debated whether he wanted to visit Abe Glitsky on five or the DA on three. Deciding to let fate make the call, he boarded the always crowded elevator in the lobby. If somebody pushed three, he'd stop off and see Wes Farrell. Otherwise, he'd ride up to Glitsky's floor.

A minute later, he was walking down the long hallway past the offices where he'd first worked as an assistant district attorney almost forty years earlier. As usual, he was astounded to find that the hallway still looked, smelled, and felt exactly the same.

When the clerk at the window announced his arrival to Farrell's secretary, Treya Glitsky gave the order to let him right in, and the door to his left buzzed. Hardy went through it and stopped again.

This hallway, with its heavy doors leading off to tiny cramped offices on either side, carried an even larger mnemonic charge than the walk down from the elevators. Halfway down, two earnest young women who couldn't possibly be old enough to be working here whispered like conspirators, and perhaps they were. A guy in a business suit stood in one of the doorways and suddenly laughed and just as suddenly cut it off. Behind Hardy, the door opened again, and when he half turned, he was facing Paul Stier, a tough adversary whom he'd trounced in their two trials opposing each other, the most recent only two months before.

Stier pulled up in his tracks, failing to conceal his surprise and displeasure. 'Mr Hardy.'

Hardy inclined his head. 'Paul. How are you?' He held out his hand, and the other man took it perfunctorily.

'Can I help you?' Obviously, it bothered Stier that Hardy, a defense attorney, was standing unaccompanied in the prosecutor's hallway. Probably spying.

'I'm just on my way in to talk to Mr Farrell. We used to be partners.'

'Yes, I know. You can find your way, then?' Meaning: move it along and quit loitering here where you don't belong, polluting our sacred hallway.

Hardy tried to keep traces of apology out of his voice. He had every right to be here, and if Stier didn't like it, that was his problem. Pointing, he said, 'On my way.'

A chilly smile. 'Nice seeing you.'

When he stood in front of Treya's desk in Farrell's anteroom, she looked up from her keyboard, flashed him a genuine smile – 'Diz!' – pushed out her chair, and came around to give him a quick hug. Regarding him at arm's length, she asked him if he was all right.

'Fine, except I just ran into Paul Stier. I think he took our last trial together a little personally.'

Treya tsked. 'How does he think that helps anything?'

'I bet it keeps him motivated. But still . . .'

'They don't call him "The Big Ugly" for nothing, Diz. Don't let him get inside your head.'

'No, of course not. Nothing gets to me. I'm a defense attorney. I have no inner life.' Hardy inclined his head toward Farrell's door. 'Is His Majesty in?'

She lowered her voice. 'I just woke him up and told him you were here.'

'Fantastic.'

'He said to show you right in.'

'Really?'

'His exact words.'

'I'm feeling better already.' Hardy stopped at the door and turned back to her. 'On the wildly improbable assumption that I have feelings at all.'

After almost two years in his official position, Wes Farrell had acquired enough furniture to imprint on his physical office the stamp of his personality. He had never been a believer in the desk, for example, feeling that it created an unnecessary barrier between people. Instead, Farrell had installed a couple of wooden library tables on the room's periphery. Randomly arranged on the table over by the Bryant Street windows were his computer and printer/fax, his landline telephone, and several thick stacks of folders. The table on the back wall held his enormous flat-screen television, with a dozen or so folding chairs in front of it, theater-style. The office was also large into the game theme, with a foosball table smack in the center of the room, a Nerf basketball net hung from the bookshelves, and a chessboard on a small table next to the door, right under the dartboard – the latter a gift from Hardy. Farrell had converted the counter under the book-shelves into a well-stocked, completely illegal (alcohol was forbidden everywhere in the Hall of Justice) wet bar complete with a minifridge, sink, and hot plate, and with spirits, wine, beers, a high-end espresso machine, and an assortment of teas. A few weeks into his administration, Treya had convinced him to bring in some real chairs, a couch, and a coffee table to create two well-defined seating areas – one in chrome and one in leather – in the event that guests wanted to sit down at any point.

When Hardy entered, Farrell was drying his face over the sink. He was wearing brown slacks over worn-down, scuffed-looking brogues, no jacket, and no tie. His white dress shirt had its top buttons undone over his T-shirt, and this Hardy took as a cue. 'Drum roll, please, for today's secret message,' he said by way of hello.

Farrell hesitated only a moment before he put down his towel, nodded agreeably, undid two more buttons, and opened his shirt, under which his T-shirt read: SMITH & WESSON: THE ORIGINAL POINT-AND-CLICK.

Hardy, a longtime fan of Wes's T-shirt fetish, nodded in appre-ciation. 'What happens when you run out of those things?'

Farrell shook his head. 'Couldn't happen. The themed T-shirt market is unending. I get six or eight a day from my legions of fans. If it stops tomorrow, I'm good till I'm seventy-five.' He started buttoning up his dress shirt. 'So how've you been? How're things at the old office?'

'Good and good. Phyllis sends her love.'

'Ah, Phyllis. The things we never thought we'd miss.'

'You miss Phyllis?'

'Actually, no, not specifically. I think I was talking about those carefree days of yesteryear back when Phyllis was the worst thing we were likely to encounter on any given day. Here, every fifteen minutes, we get people who make Phyllis look like Mother Teresa.'

'So you take naps to avoid them?'

'Hey.' Farrell pointed a warning finger. 'I deserve some rest when I get up at four-fifteen, as I did today. And even with the nap, trust me, I've already filled the asshole quotient for the whole day.'

'Having to do, by any chance, with the bar busts last night?'

Farrell squinted. 'As a matter of fact, exactly. Are you on that?'

Hardy nodded. 'Ed Benson called me a few hours ago, begging for conflicts attorneys. Naturally, I volunteered to do my public duty.'

'For which I, public servant extraordinaire, am deeply grateful.'

'But really. You charged these turkeys? Underage drinking?'

'It wasn't my idea, trust me.'

'So who do we both have to thank, then?'

'You are aware, I presume, of our esteemed supervisor, Liam Goodman?'

Hardy sat on the arm of the couch. 'I thought it might've been him. I'm just a little surprised you okayed the warrants.'

Farrell waved him off. 'Don't get me started on politics. Goodman wanted felony arrests, Diz. I'll spare you the conversation we had. As for people knowing it was Goodman behind it, there won't be any doubt by tonight. He's going to be all over the news, local and national, taking whatever credit he can.' Farrell had come over to the foosball table. He took the ball from its spot under the goal and dropped it on the table, lined up a shot, and viciously spun the handle. Score.

Farrell looked over at Hardy. 'As though the city doesn't have enough problems. We had three murders last night, you know that?' Three. I don't even know how many assaults and break-ins and drug deals and muggings and random mayhem, all of it more or less serious, and what do I get a call about? The scourge of underage drinking. Are you kidding me?'

'Twelve arrests,' Hardy said.

'You don't have to tell me. I've already gotten an earful from everybody from the sheriff to the mayor, including my beloved girlfriend. Why was the city moving on this? Why wasn't there any warning? Wasn't this a little bit of an overreaction to a nonissue? Was I really going to prosecute all these people? On the other hand, if I wasn't, why not, since they all broke the law I'm sworn to uphold. Meanwhile, I am as in the dark as anyone except Mr Goodman about the real reason he wants these warrants. All I know is that he does.'

'So what did Goodman do? To make all of this happen?'

'I've got a better one: why did I want this job?' Farrell took a chair across from where Hardy sat. 'But Goodman? He's having trouble getting his name in the papers. This is going to fix that, believe me. My guess is he knows somebody high up in Special Ops with the ABC and talked him into these busts. We're going to find out soon enough.'

'What are you going to do?'

Farrell dredged up a weary smile. 'You mean am I going to prosecute these people to the fullest extent of the law? Shit, no. But I had to go forward. That's the beauty of all this. Goodman's got me completely squeezed. If I decline to prosecute, citing the unnecessary cost in dollars and manpower to my already understaffed and underfunded office, then I'm soft on policing these violating premises that not only serve booze to kids but also deal in illegal narcotics and fence stolen property and are hotbeds of other vice and criminal activities. Since I am in fact underfunded and understaffed, I'd like to concentrate my efforts on people who are doing a lot worse things, and which, if I don't, will affect my job approval rating down the line, I guarantee you. It's a perfect end run.'

'Slick.'

'Fucked.'

'That, too,' Hardy said. 'I picked up a client who's more than a little freaked out about a felony conviction and going to jail. The guy's a bartender, right? There's somebody at the front door checking IDs. You tell me how a bartender is supposed to know how they got the stamp on their hand.'

'I hear you,' Farrell said. 'And we know nothing is really going to happen. But I don't see how I'm going to go up against the ABC and Goodman and blanket say I'm going to dismiss all of 'em. Best possible outcome, from your perspective, is bide your time and all the bullshit goes away.'

'Bide your time long enough, everything goes away, Wes.'

'True. Sorry I can't be more help.'

Glitsky was reading a book at his desk. At Hardy's knock, he looked up, his expression blank almost to the point of non-recognition. After a slight hesitation, his lips went tight, his shoulders settled, he closed the book, and he leaned back in his chair. 'What up, Diz?'

From the open doorway, Hardy said, 'I was just downstairs and saw your wife, which reminded me that you were alive and kicking and maybe I should drop by and brighten up your day.'

Glitsky cocked his head at the windows high up in the wall to his left. Outside, the sky was gray. 'It's not working.'

Hardy came forward a few steps. 'Sometimes it takes a minute for the full brightening power to take effect. What are you reading here in the middle of the afternoon, which I'm sure is against some regulation or other?'

Glitsky seemed surprised to find the book on his desk. 'Steve Jobs. Totally allowed. What can I do for you?'

'Nothing. I just thought I'd say hi. You and I haven't gotten much quality time in lately, maybe you've noticed?'

Glitsky sat back, then said, 'Why don't you shut the door.'

Hardy did, then pulled up a folding chair in front of Glitsky's desk. 'You're still pissed off,' he said.

'More worried than anything.'

'Abe,' Hardy whispered, 'it was six years ago.'

Glitsky sat back in his chair, hands clasped over his stomach. 'That's what worries me, Diz. The three of you there, thinking, "Hey, it's been six years. We're cool. Nobody cares anymore. Nobody remembers." Guess what?' He let out a breath. 'Even you and me, right now. This is a topic that must never come up.'

'It didn't. We never talked about it. The actual event.'

'I'm so glad to hear it.' Glitsky straightened up. His hands went to the sides of his head. 'Diz. Please. Lord.'

'So that night at Sam's—'

Glitsky cut him off. 'It shouldn't be in anybody's consciousness. It shouldn't be the kind of thing that has any chance of coming up in casual conversation, because after all, six years have gone by, and this is ancient history. God forbid your brother-in-law falls off the wagon. I can hear him now, letting on to somebody across the bar—'

'Abe. Mose hasn't had a drink in years.'

His voice in tight control, Glitsky said, 'He's an alcoholic, Diz. He admits that himself. Every day at his meetings. You know how nervous it makes me feel to know that my future is a couple of ounces of Scotch away from being destroyed?'

Hardy crossed an ankle over a knee. 'A little dramatic, Abe, don't you think?'

'No. I don't. It's well within the realm of possibility.'

Hardy sighed. 'I'll talk to him, not that he needs reminding. Would that help?'

'Honestly, probably not. I'm not saying it would come out in everyday life if everything stays the same. But if something changes and he stresses out and starts drinking . . .'

'He's not going there.'

'Famous last words.' Glitsky glared at his friend, arms crossed over his chest. 'Actually, the last thing you should do is talk to Moses about it, put it in the front of his brainpan as something he has to deal with. We've just got to hope he doesn't leak. For that matter, we have to hope that none of us leaks for the rest of our lives. Gina's great, but she writes books. What if she wakes up one day and decides this would be a great plot? What if one of us gets religion and feels the need to confess publicly? It's so easy in the movies – you blow away the bad guys, and they roll the credits and never think about it again. This situation isn't like that. Not even close.'

'Well, while I don't worry about Moses and you do, Frannie bought half a steer and wants me to cook it on Sunday, and we wondered if you guys wanted to come over and help us eat it. Moses won't be there.'

Something like a smile appeared on Glitsky's face. 'You know how long it's been since I've had a hunk of beef?'

'Probably too long.'

'That's the right answer. What can we bring?'

Hardy gave him a grin. 'Just your family and that sunny, carefree personality we know and love so well.'

5

LIAM GOODMAN AND his – at the time – paralegal Rick Jessup had worked with Jon Lo since 2008, before Goodman's election to the Board of Supervisors, back when he was in private practice and Mr Lo needed legal help handling the re-zoning of ten properties that he owned downtown. Six of these multifamily apartment buildings had been residential units – rented almost exclusively to Korean tenants – for over forty years, ever since Lo's grandfather built them in the 1960s. San Francisco's aggressive rent control laws by themselves limited profits in the early years, to the degree that they would have been untenable as investments had it not been for the phenomenal rise in real estate prices. But the prices had kept rising, and it seemed that all was well.

In the late '80s, Lo's father had refinanced and taken over $3 million in cash out of the properties, which he'd then invested in four more buildings, filled with more recently emigrated Korean renters. These tenants represented an influx of capital, true, but some of his tenant families, especially from the earlier buildings, were in their third or even fourth generation. Many of these tenants were paying under a thousand dollars a month when individual *rooms* in private homes or condos right next door often commanded two to four thousand.

But the laws were unambiguous – as long as the tenant resided in the unit, the increase in rent was held at one percent per year.

In 2008, Jon Lo found himself in a cash-flow bind. The

recession and bursting of the housing bubble had wiped out two thirds of the equity in all of his downtown properties. At the same time, several of his tenants – laid off or cut back or simply poorer – stopped paying even the insanely low rent. In theory, Lo could evict these families, but it took forever, was vastly expensive, and sometimes San Francisco judges refused to order evictions. When Lo did get an eviction order, he had to convince the sheriff to enforce it, and that was a whole other cycle of obstacles. In the meantime, he was paying off his father's refinancing, and the monthly rents weren't covering his nut.

There had to be a better way.

Liam Goodman, his lawyer, had come up with the answer. Goodman had explained – though in truth, Jon Lo was more than passing familiar with the practice – that the apartment units should be converted from residential properties to massage parlors. The massage parlors would, in turn, be staffed by recent female immigrants from Korea who had been lured to the United States by promises of big money and clean, steady work as waitresses or models or hostesses; in fact, these young women often arrived owing thousands of dollars to the brokers who had arranged for their travel, documents, and relocation to America.

To pay off this debt, their brokers – or owners in all but name – forced them to work in the massage parlors as sex slaves. They usually worked six days a week, entertaining as many as a dozen men every day, earning for their landlord fifty dollars per trick plus half of their tips (one to four hundred, depending on the services performed), with the remainder going for their freedom, a freedom that could and often did prove elusive.

Bad as it was for the girls, the business was terrific for Jon Lo, and it solved all of his monetary problems. In the city's super-permissive atmosphere, sexual behavior flew under the radar. Officials tended not to care about these so-called victimless crimes. Beyond that, in 2004, jurisdiction for the massage parlors moved from the police department to the city's Department of Public Health, whose mandate to check on general cleanliness in these places of business did not necessarily include reporting signs of suspected or probable prostitution to the police. A used condom might be a health violation, but it was nothing to call the Vice Squad about. Besides, sex in a massage parlor, unless police saw money change hands, went ignored.

In short, it was a good time to be the owner of several massage parlors in San Francisco, and Jon Lo, grateful to Liam Goodman for the legal and zoning assistance in turning his financial life around, had no problem with donating to Goodman's campaign for city supervisor or with urging his fellow businessmen in the Tenderloin and in Chinatown to support that campaign as well.

The proximate cause of the city's sting this week against bar owners and underage drinking had been the third trickledown effect that had begun two months before with an unexpected federal sweep of the city's massage parlors. The sweep resulted in the arrests of one hundred masseuses, most of them Korean. In response, the mightily embarrassed mayor, Leland Crawford – who was shocked, *shocked,* to discover that there was a lot of sex at these locations – called for the formation of a task force of health and police inspectors to step up their surveillance and enforcement of the city's antiprostitution laws.

In the much publicized second event from only a month before, Crawford, accompanied by members of his new task force and a brace of reporters, had waited in the cut, or narrow unnamed alley, abutting the Golden Dream massage parlor, owned by Jon Lo and licensed by the Department of Public Health, while a plainclothes Asian policeman rang the doorbell. When the metal security door opened, the decoy officer duct-taped the lock so the mayor's party could get in, just in time to discover a man in the middle of a sex act in the building's lobby.

Not too surprisingly, this had caused a stir, and in its aftermath, Crawford had all but declared war on sex trafficking in the city. Unfortunately, all the immediate hue and cry came to naught when the inspectors who'd accompanied Crawford could cite the Golden Dream only for inadequate ventilation, for employees who were improperly attired, for using the business address as a living quarters, and for using a bed instead of a massage table. Since no one had seen money change hands and neither party had talked, the blatant sex act they'd all witnessed couldn't be charged as prostitution.

A week later, an administrative law judge – Liam Goodman's wife's former law partner, Morrie Swindell – declined to revoke Mr Lo's permit to operate the massage parlor; and not one woman who worked at Golden Dream, rumored to have been threatened into silence by the owner, would testify against him. By this time, the federal case that had netted the original hundred arrests had foundered as well. The ten massage parlors were still in operation.

In spite of the zero sum change in prostitution in San Francisco, sex trafficking had officially become one of the city's hot liberal issues. Crawford had claimed it as his own; his concern over the victims of this international humanitarian crisis would translate to hundreds if not thousands of votes from women and Asians as he set his eyes on the state capitol. It was only a matter of time before his task force grew some teeth and started negatively impacting the businesses of Jon Lo and his colleagues.

Liam Goodman wasn't afraid to be proactive. He knew that the average voter's span of attention could be measured in seconds, if not less. He also knew that the city's Vice Squad was strapped for both personnel and money, and if he could siphon off a few officers for other duties, the sex-traffic task force would take that much longer to reach a minimal level of competency. Further, if Crawford got elected to Sacramento next year, the mayor's office yawned open for someone with sufficient profile and name recognition. Someone just like Goodman, if he could get his name in the news a little bit more often. And once Liam was elected mayor, the task force would be allowed to atrophy and then go away entirely.

He had been reading the paper last week when he came across a very sad article about a drunk teenager who'd run a red light and killed a young couple in town from Boise for their honeymoon.

Underage drinking, he thought. As a bonus, most of the kids in these upscale drinking establishments were middle- and upper-class whites, so he could crack down without the accusation of racism that hampered any effort to interdict the dope traffic in the city's poorer, mostly minority communities.

Underage drinking. That was the ticket.

Goodman finished giving his press conference at the top of the grand staircase in San Francisco's city hall. Present were reporters from the *Chronicle* and the *Courier* as well as all the local networks and a few cable and Web-based outlets. He had started off with the unfortunate couple from Boise and managed to include statistics on the increase in traffic problems and other crimes involving minors who had been drinking; on bars that served as distribution centers for drug sales; even down to a few riffs on the proliferation of fake IDs and the threat they posed to national security. 'We are a tolerant city,' he had concluded after a robust Q&A, 'and rightfully proud of it. But that tolerance cannot extend to premises and people where illegal activity threatens lives and is a danger to individuals and to public health.'

He was feeling good as he turned away from the knot of reporters to walk to his office. When he saw Jon Lo standing in front of his door, Goodman at first thought that his client had come down to congratulate him on a job well done. But there wasn't any pleasure in Lo's face, no sign at all of approval.

Goodman rearranged his own expression, a quick smile, then all concern. 'Jon,' he said. 'Something on your mind?'

'Maybe inside?' Lo replied.

The suite featured two small anterooms where the clerical staff worked, although this being Friday evening, none was in attendance. Behind those rooms, overlooking Van Ness and peering out to the Opera House, Goodman worked in surroundings that were both traditional and somewhat opulent – red leather chairs and a mahogany desk on a Persian rug, file cabinets, bookshelves, and sideboards hugging the wall space.

Lo went over to stand by the windows, hands clasped behind his back. Short and stocky, in a tailored blue business suit, he seemed to be gathering his thoughts, his shoulders rising and falling, until finally he turned back to Goodman. 'I do, as you say, have something on my mind.'

Goodman nodded. 'I'd like to hear it. I thought it went very well out there, but if there was some note I didn't hit—'

Lo held up a hand. 'It's not about that. That went fine. Everything with the alcohol strategy has been good. This is about one of your people.'

'My people? Constituents?'

'No. The young people working here, in your office. The interns.'

This was a surprise, and Goodman showed it. 'What about them?'

'How many are there?'

'It varies by day, paid and unpaid, part-time and full, but six average. Always at least three, plus my secretary. Why?'

'All men?'

'One woman. Plus my secretary, Diane, and a new temp we've got here from Berkeley. What about them?'

'All right, then, four men. One of them . . .' Lo stopped and drew a breath. 'One of them has been visiting my houses and not paying for services. Worse, when the girls complain, he threatens them. He has manhandled one.'

'Which one of my interns?'

'I don't know. You will laugh, but my girls say they can't tell, the clients all look the same. Truth is, they're afraid. They don't want to make trouble, to be caught in the middle. So when I ask them, they say they don't know. One says she heard it from another. When I question that one, she says she heard it happened, but not to her.'

'Then how do you know it was somebody from this office?'

'Because I know.' Lo shrugged. 'Understand, Liam, that is not why I'm here. I am not asking, I am telling you it is someone from your office, and I cannot let this continue. It is my job to prevent it. It must stop. I don't want my girls hassled like this. They perform a service. They get paid. They pay me my share. Everybody is happy. If you can't find a way to do this and it keeps being a problem, the solution will fall to me. But I would much rather you handle it yourself before it causes bad feelings between us.'

Goodman got the message. He backed up a step and put a haunch on the corner of his desk. 'I'm really not sure I believe this, Jon.' He held up a hand. 'I believe *you,* of course. This is what you hear from your girls, and you bring it to my attention. Which is as it should be. But anybody could say he works for me and try to stiff them.'

Lo nodded. 'Please don't underestimate how serious this problem is. I'm sorry to have to talk to you about this, today of all days, when you should be happy, when the bar sting has worked so well. But I just found out about it myself, and I can't leave my girls unprotected.'

'No. Of course not. If it's really one of my people, I'll find out who it was and fire him immediately. I promise you.'

'That would be good,' Lo said. 'At least that.'

Tony Solaia went home to his third-floor studio apartment on Ellis near Mason, in a building bordering the notorious and dangerous Tenderloin district. He showered, then slept on his Murphy bed for four hours before he woke up hungry and worried.

Even for a studio, the place was small. The side walls were eight feet apart; front to back was twelve feet. A sink in a thin counter hugged the wall next to the refrigerator, so the bed barely cleared them when he lowered it. Above the counter, two wall-mounted cabinets held the glasses and plates and mugs that had been there on his arrival. The other two cabinets held various canned foods and coffee and Top Ramen and spaghetti. The color scheme of the walls and counters was pale yellow, with the occasional brown water spot for accent. Bracketed on one side by a scratched end table and three-way lamp and on the other by the unit's only chair, a mostly black couch of indeterminate fabric sagged under the windows. He had no television. A tiny closet and bathroom took up the rest of the footprint.

Solaia rolled over, put his bare feet on the floor, and stood up. He raised the bed into the back wall and closed the doors over it, instantly tripling his living space. In the bathroom, he peed and brushed his teeth, then took a two-minute shower.

His dinner table folded out of the side wall opposite the refrigerator, and ten minutes after his shower, he was sitting down to a bowl of Dinty Moore's beef stew that he'd cooked on his one hot plate, chased by a sixteen-ounce can of Coors Light. He was dressed in clean jeans, hiking boots, and a stylish Jhane Barnes sweater.

After rinsing the dishes, he sat at the table, pulled out his cell phone, and punched up a number he'd marked as a favorite.

On the second ring: 'Tony. How you doin'?'

'Hey, Frank. I'm doin' okay. Going on the assumption that you didn't see my name in the papers?'

'No. What happened? You make up another fancy cocktail?'

'Not this time.'

'You really shouldn't be getting your name in the paper, Tony. This or any time. No picture, I pray to God.'

'I'm hoping that, too. I don't remember any pictures.'

'Well, there's a plus. Pictures really wouldn't be good.'

'I hear you. I kind of remembered that from the initial briefing. It wasn't something I had control over, but I don't think there were any pictures.'

'Okay.' Pause. 'So what happened?' Tony told him. When he finished, Frank asked, 'Who's this lawyer?'

'Just a guy I met where I swim in the mornings.'

'Does he know?'

'No. I don't know why he would.'

'So why'd he come down and pick you out?'

'Luck of the draw, I guess. I think he's just a good guy who thought he could help.'

'Right. From all the lawyers who grow on the good-guy lawyer tree.' A mirthless chuckle. 'Okay, what else?'

'Well, what else is, I'm out of a job.'

Frank's sigh echoed in the cell phone. 'What do you want me to do about that?'

'Nothing at the moment. I'm in wait mode, see what happens to the bar. Hardy – the lawyer? – he says Rome is probably going to reopen in a couple of days. Meanwhile, I can make a week or two, but if it doesn't reopen, I'll need something else.'

'All right,' Frank said. 'I'll keep my eyes open. Another bar, I presume?'

'I've got experience in bars. That would be easiest. Hardy's offered me some shifts in the place he owns.'

'This good-guy lawyer also owns a bar and says he'll hire you?'

'Strange as it seems.'

'It seems like a miracle, you ask me. This guy have wings?'

'Not that I saw.'

'Jesus. All right.' Short pause. 'So. Did they print you?'

'Sure.'

Another sigh. 'I'll have to talk to somebody down there, then. If they run you for outstandings . . .' He let the phrase hang.

'I get it, Frank. That's why I called. I thought you'd want to know.'

'I've got to know, Tony. Your cover gets blown, guess who takes the hit for it? Your friendly U.S. Marshal, that's who.'

'It wasn't my fault, Frank.'

'It wasn't you pouring drinks for the kids?'

'I poured the drinks, but I didn't know they were kids. They had IDs. They got stamped at the door. Not my fault.'

'No. I guess not. But not the best luck, either.'

'No,' Solaia said, 'no, it wasn't.'

6

BRITTANY WAS STARTING to wonder if this was the way it always would be.

Last night she'd been waiting at the Shamrock, passing the time with her dad and the Beck, and Rick had appeared, dressed up in coat and tie and looking every bit as hot as he did during the week when he stopped in at Peet's. Seeing her, he lit up. He and Brittany and the Beck went into the back room and shot darts and drank some whiskey, and everybody was getting along great, Brittany thinking that the night was going to work out, textbook – she knew she would have her hands and everything else all over Rick Jessup tonight and as far into the future as she wanted to hold on to him.

It got to be around nine o'clock, and she'd had a couple of cosmos and learned more about Rick. On the positive side, he had a real job, chief of staff for Liam Goodman; he wasn't and hadn't been married; he was twenty-seven. Not so good was that he wasn't wild about dogs or cats or country music, although he could tolerate . . .

'. . . Taylor Swift.'

'She's not even country anymore,' the Beck said.

'No,' Brittany put in. 'She is country. She's just not stupid country.'

'Well,' Rick said, 'stupid country is what I mean by country. Which is why Taylor Swift is okay. Because she's not really country. Like' – he turned to Brittany – 'who's this playing right now?'

'Carrie Underwood.'

'There you go. Totally country, totally stupid. "Jesus, Take the Wheel."' Rick was getting into it. 'Give me a break. Drive the damn car yourself! Don't give it to Jesus! How's Jesus supposed to know how to drive? Does she think they had cars back in ancient Israel? I want to punch her.'

'No punching women allowed,' Rebecca said.

'Not unless you have to.' Rick gave the Beck a flat look, dead serious for a split second before breaking into a teasing smile, then continuing, 'But country? Really? Totally LCD.'

'How can you say that?' Brittany cut between them. 'Carrie is not the lowest common denominator. To say nothing of Brad.'

'Who's Brad?'

'"Who's Brad?" he asks. Paisley? Only the best guitar player in the world? And singer and songwriter, while we're at it.'

'Nope. Sorry. He's the tick guy, right? "I Want to Search You for Ticks"?'

'A great song.'

Jessup shook his head. 'LCD.'

'Blake Shelton?'

Rolling his eyes. 'No.'

'Miranda Lambert.'

'Please.'

'Get out! Kenny?'

Rick turned to the Beck. 'What's this with the first names?' Back to Brittany. 'Kenny?'

'Chesney? Hello?'

Finally, Rick let himself grin. 'Okay, beach stuff only, not bad. But that's as far as I'm going. At least until I get another drink. And speaking of that, what's a guy got to do to get a drink around here?'

In the bathroom, washing her hands, the Beck said, 'I'm glad neither of our dads was around to hear him say that sometimes you had to punch women.'

'That was a joke.'

'Really? Not the funniest one I've ever heard. And you didn't pick up just a little tiny bit of condescension?'

'Why? Because he doesn't like country music?'

'No. Just the general attitude.'

'He's got opinions, Beck. That's a good thing.'

'Kind of depends on what they are, don't you think? I can't say I'm really taken by the way he got you to order another round for us all. And you went.'

'I'm a nice person, Beck. I went to get us drinks. Big deal.'

'I don't know. You combine arrogant and impatient, and okay, he's good-looking, but he's a politician, and I bet he's used to getting his way. At least that's the way he comes across. Don't you think?'

'I think somebody might be a little jealous here.'

Drying her hands, the Beck turned to face her. 'Get real, Brit.'

'Your daughter is beautiful,' Jessup said.

McGuire leaned over the bar, close to the young man wearing a suit and tie on a Friday night. 'She is,' he agreed. 'She's a wonderful person. How'd you two meet each other again?'

'I'm a regular customer at Peet's. We got to talking. One thing led to another, and here we are.'

'So where are you two off to?'

'That plan is still uncertain. Hopefully someplace we can talk, get to know each other a little.'

'That's a good start.'

Jessup flashed a confident grin. 'Gotta communicate,' he said. 'That's the key.'

McGuire narrowed his eyes. Was the guy putting him on with this cliché? He simply nodded, saying, 'Can't argue with that.'

'I think it's cool,' Jessup went on, 'that she asked me to come meet her down here. Say hi to her dad on night one. That's not everybody's first move. It's gutsy. I like it. And no guts, no glory, as they say.'

'I don't know if I'm all that intimidating,' Moses replied.

'Not you personally but the whole idea. Meeting the dad. She's obviously proud of her family. I like that.'

'You'll see when you get to know her that there's a lot to like. She's really pretty great. But I'm her dad. What else am I going to say?'

'You might say nothing. You might say she was a difficult kid and still is. You might say I should watch out, she's trouble underneath it all.'

'Nope,' McGuire replied. 'I can't say any of that. I'll let it go with pretty great. You'll see. And speak of the devil . . .' He nodded as his daughter and the Beck made their way back from the bathroom.

'Nice talking to you,' Jessup said, extending his hand over the bar. 'I'll watch out for your girl.'

She and Rick were going to grab a bite before they went dancing and drank some more, although frankly, Brittany was skeptical about whether they were really going to dance, or even eat, before they went back to Rick's place.

Not her place. She didn't do her place with guys.

So they were at the Shamrock's front door, holding hands on the way out, when her uncle Dismas showed up with this guy Tony, who was insanely off the map in terms of hot, and suddenly, Rick seemed like a kid. Next to this new guy, Rick's coat and tie looked pretentious, forced.

Everybody shook hands, and Brittany hugged Uncle Diz and learned that Tony was here to meet her dad and maybe work at the bar part-time. So the Beck – it turned out she knew Tony slightly from Rome Burning – would get to be here and hang out with him, and who knew where that would lead?

There was nothing Brittany could do about it in the moment. She was leaving like *right now* with Rick, and it would be super-awkward, to say the least, to stick around long enough to flirt a little, let Tony know that this Rick thing was new and maybe not even happening in any serious way.

Now it was Saturday morning and she was at Rick's place, in bed with her eyes barely open, and he was coming back naked from the bathroom, and even as he was sliding under the sheets, she was thinking of a plan so it didn't turn into an all-day, all-weekend kind of thing.

He sidled up against her, and she felt his breath under her ear, and she wondered why it always seemed to be like this, where, just when you're pretty sure you've got exactly what you've been craving, you see something else, and you want that more.

Rick set a nice breakfast table with a bouquet of flowers in the middle. There was fresh fruit – strawberries, blueberries, and pineapple in a large white bowl – and orange juice and delicious-smelling coffee already poured into oversize colorful mugs. Humming, he was working over the stove in boxer shorts when she came in from her shower, her hair wet, wearing a robe with a Ritz-Carlton emblem that he had given her from his closet, no doubt for mornings such as this.

She sat at the table, sipped her coffee, picked up a slice of bacon, and took a bite. She stole a look at him, so confident in his underwear with his solid back, six-pack stomach, and ripped abs.

He turned and caught her. 'Are you okay?'

'Good.'

'Only good?'

'Good is pretty good,' she said.

'You're right,' he said. 'Me, I'm amazingly good. You know why? Because you're amazing. Last night was amazing. This morning.' He pointed at the table. 'Help yourself to anything.'

'Thanks. I will.'

'Eggs up in two minutes. I'm a genius with eggs, omelets my specialty. Brie and mushroom.'

'I can't wait.'

He took a beat, narrowed his eyes. 'Is something wrong?'

'No. I just said I was good. You don't remember that?'

'I do.'

'Well, then.'

'Okay. Because if there's anything else you'd like . . .'

She lowered her gaze at him, said in a warning tone, 'Rick.'

'I just want to make sure you're happy.'

'In about one more minute, I won't be,' she said.

'Okay, I get it. I'll stop.'

'That would be the move.'

When he set the plates on the table, he sat down opposite her, still shirtless, his confidence seemingly restored. 'Double your money back if this isn't the best omelet you've ever had in your life.'

'In my life? My whole life?'

'Ever,' he said.

She cut off a piece with the side of her fork and took a bite. 'Wow,' she said.

He beamed across at her. 'What did I tell you?'

'A-plus,' she said, gesturing around the table. 'Everything is great. I mean it.'

They were silent as they tucked in to their food. Then Rick put down his fork, reached across the table, and touched the sleeve of her robe.

'What?' she asked.

'Just this. I knew we'd be good.'

She forced a smile against a pang of guilt and what she realized was pity. Completely misreading her smile as reinforcement of his own complacent state of mind, he let his lips turn up a fraction. 'So what else do you like to do?'

'Besides . . . ?'

And then it hit her what he was referring to, and the eggs went rancid in her mouth, and she bolted up from the table.

'Can you believe the arrogance? I mean, what *else* do I like to do? We have a little sex, and that's all I like? That's who I am? Rick Jessup can go straight to hell!'

Brittany sat on the Beck's bed in her dorm room at Hastings College of the Law. Brittany hadn't been back to her apartment and was wearing the clothes she'd had on the night before.

The Beck sat at her desk, feeling sorry for her cousin, though it wasn't like she hadn't tried to warn her. 'Maybe he didn't mean it that way,' she said.

'How else could he have meant it, Beck? You had to see his face, like he was so hot and wasn't I lucky to go a couple of rounds with him.'

'So it's a couple now.'

Brittany cocked her head. 'Three, if you want to get technical, but not the point.'

'Maybe the point is you shouldn't go home with guys you don't know. Maybe you should get to know them just a tiny bit before you hook up with them.'

'You're right, you're right. I don't know why I let this stuff happen to me.'

'Oh, stop. Yes, you do.'

'I do?'

The Beck leveled a gaze at her. 'Here's the deal, Brit. You

think guys don't like you for who you are but because you're so damn pretty. Maybe you ought to consider leading with your other strengths.'

A brittle bark of laughter. 'Like what?'

'Well, maybe first would be patience. That might address the problem all by itself. You say you don't want to waste the pretty, but you'll have it for a few more years.'

'Okay. Except I'm not patient. It is definitely not a strength. I want everything right now.'

'And how's that working out?'

Brittany shrugged. 'Yeah, but what if I die tomorrow?'

'Not a probability. Even if you did, so what? Meanwhile, in the here and now, you're having days like this one. Is that better?'

Brittany's shoulders settled an inch or two. Her long hair fell across her face.

'Are you crying?' Rebecca asked. Brittany shook her head but didn't raise it. Sighing, the Beck got up from her desk, sat on the bed, and put her arm around her cousin. 'It's okay. It'll be okay.'

Brittany leaned in to her. 'I'm such a mess,' she said.

7

In her jeans and Hastings law school sweatshirt, the Beck sat on the counter in her parents' kitchen. Across from her at the freestanding butcher block, her mother was inserting slivers of garlic into cuts she'd made into a seven-rib roast that was going in the oven.

'You sure you've got enough garlic there?'

'You don't think?' Frannie asked. 'It's two whole heads, at least sixty slices.'

'I was being slightly sarcastic, Mom. Maybe you should just cut off little slabs of the meat and stuff them into the garlic heads.'

Frannie considered. 'Maybe for the leftovers. Your dad might actually like that. And by the way, he was very happy about you coming here for dinner.'

'Which is why he was waiting here with open arms to greet me.'

'He will be. He's trying to be religious about this new swimming thing.'

'Because it's such great beach weather?' A high-pressure cold front had blown in overnight, knocking the temperature down into the forties under clear blue skies. 'Why is he doing this again?'

'He thinks he wants to lose weight, get younger, live forever.'

'So he's going to eat a pound or two of prime rib tonight to kind of kick off the program?'

Frannie inserted another clove of garlic, smiled over at her daughter. 'He's still working out some of the finer details. I think the prime rib was an excuse to bribe Uncle Abe into coming over to spend some time with him.'

'Why would he need a bribe?'

'It's just been a while.' She gave her daughter a look. 'We've tried to get together with them about half a dozen times in the past few months, and they've always had something else going on. Or say they do.'

'You think they've been avoiding you on purpose?'

'I don't know. It seems like they might be.'

'Abe and Treya? Your best friends?'

'I know. I hope not.'

'Is he mad at Dad?'

'I don't think "mad" is exactly the word.' Frannie hesitated, pushed in the last slice of garlic, and slapped the meat. 'Your father thinks it's got to do with the thing.'

Rebecca's face went slack for a second, almost as though she'd been slapped. For the first couple of years after it happened, the thing had been the elephant in the Hardys' living room. Both of Diz and Frannie's intelligent children had been aware of the death threats against them – indeed, the cross hairs in red Sharpie over their faces had been the proximate cause of the final showdown – and they had followed the reports of the so-called Dockside Massacre until the news had all petered out. It had never been discussed, but they all knew, and they all knew that they all knew.

Rebecca pushed herself off the counter. 'Uncle Abe's afraid it could come out?'

'I think that's it.'

'And if he avoids Dad and Uncle Moses . . .'

'Right,' Frannie said.

'But they've been friends their whole lives. Why now?'

'I don't think there's any one reason, Beck. I suspect Uncle Abe just decided that the friendship was a risk. Even after all their history. He's got young kids again. Maybe Abe is thinking that defense attorneys and cops shouldn't be friends after all. It's weird and wrong, somehow. Better to not have the relationship, and then there's no reason to talk about it.'

'But they're coming over today?'

Frannie's solemn nod said she hoped so. 'If something doesn't come up.'

Somewhere just under the surface, Dismas Hardy was aware that he was treading on a path he'd gone down before. And that earlier path had led inexorably to the tragedy of the shoot-out at Pier 70 and all of its aftermath. He didn't know why the reverberations of that long-ago day were reappearing in his life. The situation made him uncomfortable in a way he could not define.

With his law practice slowing down, his partners moving on to other things, his kids out of the house, Frannie settled in to her own work, and his best friend mostly unresponsive to his invitations and overtures, Hardy's day-to-day was not exactly a carnival of excitement. He kept putting one foot in front of the other, but there wasn't much in the way of surprise or delight.

He didn't think about it consciously. He had gotten used to the fact that this was the way life got if something else didn't get you first. He'd had a bit of a crisis about it all when the kids were young – chafing at his responsibilities, acting out against the boredom – but in the here and now, the feeling didn't cause that kind of existential distress. He had gotten past all that. He lived with the simple calm certainty that the big events in his life were behind him.

It wasn't any big deal.

He wasn't bored, wasn't depressed.

But now, suddenly and unexpectedly, it seemed he was making a new friend, as he had before with a guy named John Holiday – a friendship that had turned out disastrously wrong. That path was familiar, with warning signs all along the way. Hardy knew he wasn't going to heed those signs, because the idea that life could still hold promise was seductive, and life was too goddamn short.

The first time he'd gone down this road had been with Holiday, a pharmacist client many years Hardy's junior who had turned into a friend, then – in a surprisingly short time – a good friend. Holiday had been a Tennesseean with a lazy drawl and a laid-back style, to say nothing of a general irreverence for authority that bordered on pathological.

Hanging out with Holiday was, while fun, sometimes dangerous, especially for a married man and an officer of the court such as Dismas Hardy. Holiday drank and partied too much and encouraged Hardy to do the same. Holiday didn't work regular hours; he'd gone into the bar business after getting his pharma license revoked. He absolutely killed women – neither Gina Roake nor Frannie nor even Rebecca, sixteen at the time, had been immune to his devilish charms.

And now Hardy had another client who, in only three or four short meetings, seemed to be turning into a friend of sorts. Tony Solaia was even younger than Holiday, apparently equally foot-loose, certainly equally charming. Also killing time working behind a bar. His Brooklyn accent couldn't have been more different from Holiday's drawl, but it set Tony apart in the same way – he came from someplace else, and he had the air and maturity of someone who had worked at an adult day job before becoming a mixologist. Like Holiday, Solaia was glib, whip-smart, self-deprecating. Whether he represented any kind of danger remained to be seen, but there was a coiled energy in his bearing that suggested the potential for it.

Now, back from a swim where he'd run into Tony and invited him over for Sunday dinner – did Frannie mind setting another place? – Hardy tried a quick hug that his wife ducked away from. They were in the kitchen. The Beck had disappeared into her old bedroom to get in an hour of extra studying.

Frannie kept her voice low and under control, but she wasn't happy. 'Dismas, tell me you're not trying to set our daughter up.'

'I'm not trying to set our daughter up.'

'Do you mean that?'

'I just said it.'

'Yes, but I told you to say it.'

'I know. And I did. And I meant it. And now I stand accused of not meaning it. It seems unfair.'

'I am not in the mood for word games at the moment, if you don't mind. Okay? Because I don't think it's a good idea. We don't know anything about him.'

'I realize that.'

'And yet you bring him down to the Shamrock on Friday night, when it just so happens that the Beck is there, and here today—'

Hardy held up a palm. 'I didn't know she was there Friday night. I wasn't even positive she was coming here today.'

'Although she told us she was.'

'Yes, but traditionally, that has not been an iron-clad guarantee, you must admit. I'd feel better if I got just a little hug. I really would. I'm not trying to set anybody up with anybody. Promise.'

'All right.' She stepped forward, and he put his arms around her.

'Now,' he said. 'Was that so hard?'

Outside, the sun had gone down. Glitsky's young children, Rachel and Zachary, were set up in front of the television in the family room behind the kitchen while the mothers chatted over the sink and the dishes.

The three guys and the Beck sat at the dining room table, the talk finally getting around to Tony's general predicament, the causes and effects of the ABC bust.

Glitsky was unsympathetic. 'You can't sell alcohol to minors,' he said. 'They knew that. They did it anyway. They got arrested.'

'I didn't know it,' Tony said. 'They had IDs.'

'I still can't get the whole thing to make sense,' Hardy said. 'I can see where it puts Goodman's name in the paper, but how'd he even get to it?'

'I heard a rumor,' Glitsky said. 'Anybody here ever heard of Jon Lo?'

Blank stares and head shakes.

'Should we?' Hardy asked.

'Probably not, if you're not running for office. Politically, he's connected. The word is that he was behind the whole thing.'

'No, it was Goodman,' Hardy said. 'He sure took enough credit for it.'

Glitsky nodded. 'Right. It might have been Goodman's idea after all, but the word is it's all because of Jon Lo.'

'Wait a minute,' Rebecca said. 'Liam Goodman the supervisor?'

'Right,' Hardy said. 'You know him?'

'No, but the guy Brittany went out with on Friday – Rick, I think – he's Goodman's chief of staff.'

'And your cousin's going out with him?'

'Went out with him. Once. It didn't go too well. Big surprise. So he must have known about the ABC thing, too, huh?'

'I would guess so,' her father said.

'If I'd known all the trouble he'd made for me,' Tony said, 'I would have kicked his ass when I met him.' He swirled Holly's Hill superb Patriarche red wine around in his glass. 'Who is this guy behind Goodman again? Lo?'

'He's a big donor. Throws a lot of weight around in the Korean community.'

'And Koreans care more about underage drinking than we do?' the Beck asked.

'Not so much, I don't think.' Glitsky, a nondrinker even when Hardy was serving the good stuff, sipped iced tea out of his glass. 'What Lo does care about is massage parlors. This, by the way, is not a rumor. He owns ten of them. To be precise, he's got Health Department permits for ten of them. Last count, he had a hundred and fourteen girls working in them.'

The number clearly floored the Beck. 'A hundred and fourteen?' she asked. 'Those places have eleven employees each?'

'Maybe more, on any given day,' Glitsky said.

Hardy's eyebrows went up. 'Licensed?'

'Every one, in theory. Skilled, highly trained, certified massage therapists.'

The light coming on, Hardy said, 'Lo's the guy who got busted in that federal raid a few months ago.'

Glitsky nodded. 'That's him, but you might remember, the bust didn't stick. Every single girl who got arrested is back at work. They didn't close down any of the parlors. Nobody even got fined.'

'But if they're all certified,' the Beck asked, 'why should they be fined? Or even busted, for that matter?'

Glitsky's lips turned up a half inch, for him a broad smile. He reached over and patted the Beck on the back of her hand. 'Don't ever lose that beautiful innocence,' he said with real affection. 'The sad truth, Beck, is that these women got paid to provide sexual services. They're all essentially sex slaves, and Jon Lo may be one of the biggest human traffickers on the West Coast.'

'So why don't they arrest *him*?'

Tony, who had grown silent during Glitsky's explanations,

let out a short laugh with no humor in it. 'Because he buys protection.'

Glitsky nodded. 'Well, that, yeah. Indirectly, but mostly, nobody cares. At least not enough to do anything about it. Not in this town, anyway.'

'Except the mayor,' Hardy put in. 'His Honor has decided it's one of the big issues that he cares a lot about. If Lo's going to stay in business, he needs a smokescreen to get the mayor's mind off the massage parlors, and that's where Goodman comes in with the ABC.'

'That's the rumor,' Glitsky said.

Tony's face had hardened. 'You're telling me,' he said, 'that this one cretin, Jon Lo, is the reason I'm sitting here charged with a felony, along with a dozen other regular folks who are just doing their jobs?'

'Maybe two cretins,' Glitsky replied. 'Lo and Goodman. But yeah, that's about the size of it.'

Tony turned to Hardy. 'Any chance you can get this into my defense?'

'You're not going to need it,' Hardy said. 'Besides which, it's irrelevant to your charge.'

'It doesn't seem irrelevant to me.'

'Me, neither,' the Beck said. 'In fact, it seems plain wrong. I mean, if this whole sting was made up out of thin air to cover for some bad guy who's into human trafficking, why is he walking around and Tony is looking at going to jail?'

'Tony's not going to jail,' Hardy said. 'I'm not letting him go to jail. But the answer for you, Beck, is the golden rule. He's got the gold, so he makes the rules. That's the way it works. It shouldn't, but it does.'

'Welcome to San Francisco,' Glitsky said.

'Welcome to everywhere,' Tony added.

'But if this is true, why isn't it in the news?' Rebecca asked.

'Your buddy Jeff Elliot could put this in "Citytalk" in the *Chronicle,* and it would be a huge story.'

'How does he prove it?' Hardy asked. 'Without proof, he can't print it.'

'Not to mention,' Glitsky added, 'it might be dangerous. I mean for Jeff. Jon Lo has people who keep his women in line. Leaning on a reporter wouldn't slow those guys down much, I don't think.'

'You think they'd actually hurt Jeff?' The Beck, idealistic law student that she was, shook her head in dismay. 'You know this is going on, Uncle Abe, and you can't stop them?'

'Not before they do it. It's the curse of my job. Though Lord knows I would love it if I could.'

'Aren't they doing bad things to these girls? Keeping them enslaved, or locked up, or beating them up? Can't you go after them somehow?'

Glitsky spread his hands in a helpless gesture. 'The women would have to testify, wouldn't they? And if they do that, guess what happens to them?'

'So, basically,' Beck said, 'the city tolerates this? Is that right?'

'Except the mayor,' Hardy said, 'who's going to crack down on this really soon, unless he makes it to Sacramento first, in which case he'll be too busy with state business to worry about any individual city and these local problems.'

'This isn't local! This is international trafficking in human beings!'

Tony reached over and put his hand over the Beck's, leaving it there. 'It doesn't touch most of us, Beck, that's the point. That's why it keeps working the way it does. These are really bad people who do really bad things, okay, but they do them to people who don't have any power. They're off the radar, completely invisible. So what they do to them is invisible, too.'

Glitsky was giving Tony a piercing look. 'The man knows whereof he speaks.'

'It's everywhere,' Tony repeated, then, to the Beck, 'It's why, in theory, we have the feds.'

Glitsky smiled again, this time his usual closed-mouth effort. 'Who do you think ran the last bust on John Lo's people, Beck? Final score: a hundred arrests, no convictions, not even a fine. As I said.'

'Lo's got somebody inside with the feds,' Tony said.

Glitsky nodded. 'If that were true, it would not fundamentally alter my worldview.'

'This is appalling,' the Beck said. 'Can't anybody do anything?'

'Somebody could kill Jon Lo,' Tony said.

At this, Glitsky lit up a bit. 'And then I could arrest that guy.'

'Except,' Hardy said, 'somebody, probably worse – maybe the guy who killed Lo in the first place, if Abe didn't arrest him – would pop up to fill the vacuum.'

The Beck let out a breath. 'So it never ends?'

Tony shook his head. 'Not really, no. We just keep putting our fingers in the dike. As the lieutenant here says, if somebody goes too far, you reel him in. But mess with the system too much, the flow of the money, bad things can happen a lot closer to home, and that you really don't want.'

'What is it you really don't want?' Treya asked as she came in from the kitchen.

'Sexual slavery,' Glitsky said.

Treya stopped midstep, tutted theatrically, her eyes shining with warmth and humor. She said to her husband, 'Now they tell us.'

About ready to leave the Hardys' place, Glitsky held his five-year-old sleeping son, Zachary, who'd wrapped his arms and legs around his father's body. Three years before, in the street right in front of their duplex, a slow-moving car had knocked Zachary off his Big Wheel, and he'd been in critical condition with a brain injury for a few months. Since that time, he'd worn a helmet against future falls. When Glitsky held him at shoulder height or greater, as he was doing now, it took some management to talk around him. 'So that Tony? How's he fit in, exactly? Is he with Beck?'

'No. He's a client. Didn't have anything going on today, so I asked him over.'

'I gather he's a bartender?'

'Or was. We don't know if Rome Burning is going to reopen. Meanwhile, we're giving him some shifts at the Shamrock.'

'You known him long?'

'No.'

'But before the bust?'

Hardy shrugged. 'He's a Dolphin Club guy.'

Glitsky paused. 'You know what he did before he was a bartender?'

'No. Why?'

'No reason. He just seemed surprisingly conversant with the Jon Lo situation. I thought he sounded like a cop.'

'I don't know about that. But he's a smart guy. He knew who Saint Dismas was before I told him.'

'Yeah, there's a true test of character.'

'You worried about his character?'

'I don't know,' Glitsky said. 'I can't say I'm worried about anything. I just wonder sometimes. You might want to ask him.'

'What?'

'Where he comes from. What he did before.'

'Under what guise?'

'Any guise you want. Gentle persuasion. Naked curiosity. Obnoxious prying. Whatever it takes.'

Hardy took a beat. 'You ever wonder why you don't have all that many friends?'

'Because I want to arrest everybody?'

'That's what I'm talking about.'

'Hey, don't worry about it,' Glitsky said. 'I know I don't.'

'You don't want to arrest everybody?'

'No, I don't worry about it.'

8

THE MOOD IN the office was tense when Rick Jessup got in at ten o'clock on Monday morning.

It didn't help that he was hungover.

What had started out so promising on Friday night had turned into a terrible weekend, with Brittany McGuire walking out on him, then never answering his calls until he gave up.

And started drinking.

After the hangover wore off, he'd go by Peet's today and try to get back to wherever they'd been, or start over, or something.

He was going to get her back, he knew that. It had been only one night and one morning, but as far as he was concerned, no contest, she was the best he'd ever had – best face, best body, best sex. Having had her, he wasn't about to let her walk away. That was not going to happen unless it was he who made the decision.

It wasn't like he was some nobody. You didn't become chief of staff to a city supervisor at his age if you weren't several cuts above. Beyond that, Rick's next step was chief of staff to the mayor, when his boss moved up. Eventually, he'd enter politics himself; in fact, he was already there.

He could make Brittany see that. She just didn't understand. He hadn't made it clear enough who he was, what he could do. How important he was. He wasn't going to have some woman from a coffee shop put him down.

Right now his head was killing him. The staff was all hunkered down, slouching or huddled in the small conference room, nobody talking, nobody goofing off, no one working.

Face tight and posture rigid, the usually affable Diane held up a finger, a signal for him to bypass his own office door and keep coming into the reception area. He wasn't quite at her desk when she gave him a warning look and said, 'He wants to see you the minute you get in.'

'What's up?'

'He'll tell you.'

Sucking in a breath, Rick covered the short distance to his boss's door in a couple of strides, knocked, turned the doorknob, and went in. Goodman, seated with his elbows on his desk, his fingers templed at his lips, said, 'I believe the hours in this office are from nine to five.'

'Yes, sir. I got stuck at my apartment. The disposal backed up and made a mess. I'm sorry. I should have called.'

'Yes, well, speaking of calling, I tried to reach you several times over the weekend. Didn't you get any of those messages?'

'No, sir. I was down in San Jose visiting my sister and forgot to take my phone. I didn't get back till last night.' He tried a sheepish grin.

His boss's accusatory tone was unusual and troubling. The two men had shared many secrets, some of them sensitive, and had always worked more as partners – or co-conspirators – than as employer and employee. Rick wasn't going to show any sign of fear, although his stomach clutched at him. He brazened out in a low-key tone, 'Not my most productive weekend, I'm afraid. So what's going on?'

Goodman sat back in his chair. 'Jon Lo was by here on Friday night. I've asked everybody else, and they've all said it wasn't them.'

'What's not them?'

When Goodman finished telling him, Rick hesitated until he was sure he had his emotions under control. If he was identified or even seriously suspected as the wayward intern, his career was over. The thing to do was remain calm, act as though he truly were Liam's partner and they'd be working on the problem together. 'How do we know it's someone from our staff?' he asked.

'We don't for sure. But it seems a strange detail to make up, doesn't it?'

'It would be more weird if somebody from here admitted it, don't you think? I mean, "Hi. I'm here breaking the law and making threats, and this is where you can find me." Really?'

'Maybe you're right. You put it like that.'

'I'm thinking it's more likely someone who wants to tarnish your relationship with Lo. There's a lot of contributor money out there with those guys, and you're getting a good chunk of it. They take you out of the equation, that frees it up.'

'You're right. It would, wouldn't it?'

'Sounds like it to me.'

'So,' Goodman said, 'I guess I won't have to send over photos of everybody on the staff and see if anyone gets ID'ed.'

With his emotions under tight rein, Rick caught the subtext, both the suspicion and the warning. It was an unmistakable tug on his leash, but he couldn't let Goodman know that he'd felt it. 'I don't see how that would help us,' he said. 'There's just as good a chance that any ID would be false. You'd be giving Lo ammunition.'

Goodman appeared to consider carefully. At last he broke a small smile. 'You're right, Rick. Lo's put the word out. Let's hope that stops it. And listen, I'm sorry I jumped on you coming in here. I know you put in your hours, more than enough. I really don't expect you to punch a clock.'

'I've got it, sir. No worries. I should have called when I

knew I was going to be late.' He straightened up. 'Anything else?'

Sulking at his desk, with the door to his office closed, Rick was thinking that Jon Lo was turning into a real problem. He couldn't believe Lo had gone to Goodman about the indiscretions with some of the hookers. Okay, maybe Rick had let his confidence get the better of him, stiffing the girls because he knew he could.

But so what? Goodman would protect him.

Except apparently not.

Rick had underestimated Jon Lo, certain that Liam would protect him in any dispute with the Korean gangster. He never thought that Lo or his women would dare protest. But Lo had complained, and worse, Liam had sided with him.

Which led to the question: who needed whom?

In the not so olden days, Rick and Liam would often get out of work early and repair to some bar for the evening. They'd gone to Giants and 49ers games together, barbecued at each other's places, done some profitable deals with elements that were perhaps not entirely kosher. Although they had not been actual partners, Rick had been privy to Liam's secrets, plotting and strategizing, growing the business, the Goodman brand.

And now, somehow, much of that seemed to be threatened. This underage-drinking sting was propelling Liam into a trajectory over which Rick would have little if any influence. Rick could envision Lo recommending one of his own people to take over day-to-day operations of Goodman's staff.

And then what would happen to Rick?

What he needed to do was remind his boss that the two of them were bound at the hip, mostly through one of their early endeavors that they called the Army Business. It had turned into Goodman's major source of revenue, accounting for nearly $2 million in billings over a four-year period.

They'd hatched the scheme one day after Rick mentioned an acquaintance of his, a woman in the army stationed at Camp Parks across the bay, who had recently returned from Afghanistan, pregnant and nearing her term. Army policy did not send pregnant women to war zones, and this woman's hope was to get pregnant again soon after her delivery so she could avoid returning to the active theater. She had a six-month window.

The only problem she had was that her husband did not want another child.

As it turned out, Liam knew a wealthy couple who were having trouble conceiving. They were looking for a surrogate mother to carry their baby. They would be willing to pay a hundred thousand dollars for the right person. But they were leery of the type of woman who would agree to do this. They wanted assurances that the price was fair and that, once consummated, the deal would go through as planned. Basically, they thought they'd be much happier and more secure if they had a lawyer on board. If the whole process could get vetted.

Within a month, Liam had contacted all the parties and brokered this first deal, acting as middleman. He pocketed four fifths of the fee – less Rick's finder's cut of three thousand dollars – and gave the remaining twenty thousand to the surrogate mother, who was only too happy to get a small percentage because she wasn't doing it for the money but so the pregnancy would keep her safe at home.

It was a sweet deal all around, the only drawback being that it could be construed as a conspiracy to defraud the United States government, since the army was not only paying the active-duty female soldier but covering all of her pregnancy-related medical expenses as well.

Over the next few years – driven entirely by word of mouth in the city's toniest neighborhoods – Liam and Rick found and provided thirty-two army surrogate mothers for desperate wealthy couples. Lately, with the drawdown of troop levels in Iraq and Afghanistan, the market had all but dried up, but by this time, Jon Lo's businesses and friends had stepped into the breach in terms of campaign contributions and billings, and Goodman's political career had been well launched.

Rick's hangover was gone. And so would be this morning's problems, his sense that his job security was in doubt, as soon as he found an opportunity to remind Liam about some of these less than savory aspects of his early career and rise in politics.

It wouldn't be blackmail. Rick's reminder wouldn't be threatening. The message would be clear and simple – Liam's secrets were safe as long as Rick kept his job.

Satisfied that he'd come to an elegant solution, Rick stepped out into the reception area, turned left, and knocked on Liam's door.

The rain started falling hard just after lunchtime.

Brittany, at her own request, was at the back counter at Peet's. Normally, she preferred the serving counter up front because it made the day go by more quickly. Today she wanted a way to duck into the back room if Rick came in.

She didn't think he would. He'd probably be cool and leave her alone. She'd made it clear that she didn't want any more to do with him. But his phone calls over the weekend had made her wonder – he might be a big enough jerk to come in.

By the time the lunch rush had petered out, Brittany figured he'd gotten the message, so she wasn't prepared when there he was, standing at her counter, looking hopeful and pathetic with his wet hair and his dripping raincoat. Clueless, he started right in. 'Hey. I just wanted to tell you in person that I'm sorry. I didn't mean what I said the way you thought. It just came out wrong.'

'Yes, it did. Do you want some coffee? Because otherwise I've got work to do.'

'I want to see if we can try again.'

'I'm not going to discuss that here. I'm at work.'

'I see that. Can I call you later?'

'I'd prefer not.'

'This isn't fair.'

'It seems fair to me. I really can't talk now. I'd like you to go.'

'I just don't know what I did wrong.'

'That was obvious.'

'But I want to explain.'

'There's nothing to talk about. Really. Nothing. Now you need to go, or I'm going to call my manager.'

Rick put his palms on the counter between them. His face was gray. Rainwater dripped from his hair. 'Listen, I'm begging you here. This isn't right. Just give me a chance.'

'I gave you a chance.' She looked away from him, up to the front counter, and raised her voice. 'Mitch!'

She'd told her manager what she was worried about, and the large black man stepped away from the espresso machines and was by her side, in Rick's face. 'Is there a problem here?'

Rick said, 'I need a minute. One minute, that's all.' He chuffed out a breath. 'I . . . need . . . to talk . . . to this woman.'

Mitch gave him a flat glare. 'She isn't interested. Are you interested, Brittany?'

'No.'

'There you go. Crystal-clear.'

Rick leaned in. 'Listen, I—'

Mitch cut him off. 'You listen, pal. It would be best if you left right now. Brittany, go on in the back room and take a break.'

When she'd disappeared, the two men stared at each other.

Rick wiped his hand over his face. 'This isn't over,' he said. 'I could have you shut down, you realize that?'

'Oh, you're one of the important ones, are you? You work at city hall?' Mitch unholstered his cell phone. 'Let me just call 911 and see if the cops who come know who you are. You want to find out? They come in here every day, so they already know who I am.'

Rick removed his hands from the counter, flipped Mitch off, and turned for the door.

'Have a nice day,' Mitch said to his back.

'I could just have him whacked.' From behind the Little Shamrock's bar at seven o'clock on this blustery Monday night, Tony Solaia smiled into the fathomless eyes of Brittany McGuire. 'You go to the right part of town, the going rate is around a hundred bucks. One good night's tips. Or you could have a crackhead do it for bus fare.'

'You know the rate to have somebody whacked? That's a little worrisome.'

'Bartenders know everything,' he said.

'That's what my father always says.'

'He'd know, wouldn't he?' He pointed at her wineglass. 'Are you good?' he asked. 'Because I'm making the rounds.'

'I'm good.'

She watched him move down the bar, schmoozing, pouring drinks, laughing, a man in his element. Brittany knew how tough a taskmaster her father could be, especially around his baby, the Little Shamrock. Moses tolerated neither sloth nor slovenliness in his bartenders. He demanded perfection first in drink making, then in pricing, the temperature of the water in the rinsing sink, the shine on the glasses, the right type of glass for each drink. God forbid a customer's glass got to empty before the bartender or that night's cocktail waitress offered a refill.

She marveled – it was little short of a miracle – that Tony Solaia had shown up here for the first time last Friday and now was behind the bar working. It hadn't hurt that Uncle Diz had made the introductions.

He was coming back to where she sat. 'Seriously, are you worried about this guy?'

'No. Not really.'

'Which one? Not really, or no?'

'No, I guess. He was more pathetic than anything else. He just didn't get that I don't want to see him again.'

'I can see how that could make a fellow sad.'

'Well . . . thank you. Anyway, I think he got the message today. I don't think he'll be back. We won't have to whack him.'

'Have him whacked,' Tony corrected her. 'You don't whack somebody yourself, although you could. Generally, you have them whacked. It's way cleaner.'

9

SUSAN WEISS HAD a sunroom at the back of the three-bedroom Irving Street top-floor apartment she and Moses had raised their kids in. The girls had named it the Fog Room, and the room's door sported a wooden plank with that name burned into it by some hippie signmakers up in the foothills. Susan, second cellist with the San Francisco Symphony, spent a good portion of her time back there, in rare tepid sunlight or, more frequently, cocooned in fog, teaching her instrument to students ranging in age from four to seventy-one.

Aware of the rule of the universe that cell phones ring in the middle of every lesson, Susan had turned off the sound on hers. But when the phone vibrated in the middle of Ben Feinstein's solo, she took it from her breast pocket and, giving it a glance, tried to suppress a frown.

Her daughter Brittany. More drama.

Susan was sure Brittany knew that Ben's lesson was on Thursdays at four. That was when she'd met him a couple of months ago. Susan also knew – it was hardly a secret – that something romantic had gone on between them for a few weeks and that it had ended badly, especially for Ben, whom Susan adored and secretly wouldn't have minded if Brittany had fallen in love with.

But, of course, Brittany being Brittany, that didn't happen.

Now here she was, calling in the middle of Ben's lesson. Probably not a coincidence, and very unfair to the poor young man, especially if, as Susan suspected, Brittany was playing him along, luring him back for a week or two before tiring of him and dumping him again.

Susan loved her daughter, sometimes to distraction, but this behavior with guys made her crazy.

Ben stopped playing in the middle of Pachelbel's Canon in D. 'Is that important? Do you need to take it?'

Susan sighed. If she even mentioned Brittany's name, that would be the end of Ben's concentration for today. In the immediate wake of the breakup, he'd canceled his next two lessons. Susan had to call him and cajole him back into his routine. Life would go on, she had told him.

And now Ben was trying to let it do just that, and her daughter called.

She shook her head. 'Looks like a sales call,' she said. 'Now, where were you?'

Ben played sixteen bars before the house phone rang in the kitchen. He stopped playing again as Susan held up both hands, certain it was her daughter one more time. Very few people knew the landline number, and everyone understood that lesson hours were off-limits. Calling first the cell phone and then the home phone was a familiar strategy for Brittany, allowing her to get her way and be heard even if it was inconvenient for everybody else.

'I'm sorry, Ben,' Susan said, standing up, frustration oozing out of her. 'This might be important. I won't be a minute.'

She got to the phone on the third ring, saw that it was in fact Brittany's cell number, and picked up. 'Maybe you don't remember that I give music lessons in the afternoons,' she whispered with asperity. 'Can this possibly wait?'

Her daughter's voice was a whisper, fragile as glass. 'Mom?'

The one syllable told Susan that something was seriously wrong. All the anger leached out of her. She felt a wave of vertigo and had to put a hand down on the counter to steady herself. 'What's the matter, babe? Are you all right?'

'Not really,' Brittany said. 'I'm not too good.'

'Where are you?'

'St Francis Hospital,' she said. 'The emergency room.'

That night, Susan sat at her kitchen table, ignoring the cup of tea she'd made for herself five minutes before. She ran her hand down the back of their black cat, Fuji, who had jumped up on the table as soon as she sat down and now, all stretched out, purred like a generator. A fitful, wind-driven rain pattered against the west-facing window.

Her husband's footsteps sounded in the hall. She straightened up, although the events of the day had left her feeling beaten down and bone weary. She was reaching for her teacup as Moses appeared in the doorway. 'She's down and out in drug land. Thank God for Vicodin.' He motioned at the stove. 'Is the water still hot?'

'Should be.'

Susan watched him cross the kitchen, put a tea bag in a mug, and pour slowly from the kettle. They kept a small jug of honey on the counter, and Moses lifted the hand-carved wooden dipper and held it over the mug, letting it drip, then placing the dipper back in the jug. He got out a spoon and stirred with studied deliberation.

A gust threw a torrent of rain against the window. Susan jumped a little, but Moses didn't react in any way.

'Mose. What are you thinking?'

He let out a breath that he seemed to have been holding. The spoon tinkled against the mug as he kept stirring. 'Nothing.'

She said, 'It just took you two minutes to fix yourself some tea.'

'It was a difficult cup to get right.' He lifted it to his lips, blew on it, took a sip. 'And worth all the effort.' He sat down across from her.

'Are you worried?' she asked.

'About whether she's going to be all right? No.'

'It looked pretty terrible.'

He shrugged. 'Head wounds bleed. They look scarier than they are.'

'Also the bump.'

'Yeah, but no concussion. And no stitches, so no scars. She'll heal up.'

'So what are you thinking about?'

'How it happened.'

'Well, we know—'

He held up his hand and stopped her. 'We know what she told us, that's all.'

'You think she lied?'

'I wouldn't rule it out.'

'What do you think happened?' she asked.

Moses tapped his fingers against the mug. 'Her story is that she's talking to this guy and she realizes she's going to miss her bus, so she runs and slips on the wet pavement, falls, and bangs her head.'

'Right.'

'Maybe not so right. How did falling give her two separate head injuries? And why is one such a big bump? It's a goddamn Ping-Pong ball. A bump like that – I've got some experience, you may remember – something flat hit her head. The sidewalk, a building. And where did she get the scratches on her face? Also, did you notice that she'd lost the top two buttons on her raincoat?'

'No. I never looked.'

'You can check any time you want. The coat's in the closet. They're gone, but the thread's there, like the buttons got ripped off.'

'So, a couple of buttons? They popped off when she fell.'

'Popped off? All by themselves? Then explain about her arm.'

'What about her arm?'

'She couldn't stop rubbing her left arm, high up.'

'I thought she was cold.'

'It could have been that,' Moses conceded. 'But when I was back in there, I pulled the blanket down and checked. There's an obvious black-and-blue bruise.'

Susan sipped at her tea. 'What are you saying?'

'I'm saying I want to talk to this guy who disappears, leaving my daughter bleeding on the sidewalk.'

Susan's hand went to her mouth. 'Oh, my baby,' she said.

Moses nodded. 'Just sayin'.'

Moses walked in the rain the seven blocks to the Little Shamrock, where Tony Solaia was turning into a godsend. Moses had called Tony as soon as he got the call from Susan about Brittany being in the ER. The young man had driven down on his motorcycle and shown up at the bar within fifteen minutes, ready and even eager to pull another shift.

Moses had told Tony that he could shut the place down early if he wanted, but at the moment, fifteen visible customers were contributing to his livelihood, with maybe a dozen more throwing darts in the back. Standing outside for a last perverse second, he watched Tony behind the spotless bar, drying glasses to a high shine.

When he stepped inside, Moses hung his waterproof beret and his raincoat on the old-fashioned wooden rack by the front door, then took an open stool. Tony came down and took his order – club soda – after which some regulars came over, asking about Brittany.

'She's fine,' Moses found himself repeating. 'She slipped and fell down. She's going to be all right.'

When they'd all gone back to their places, Tony came down across from him. 'So how is she really?' he asked.

'Sleeping. Drugged. Pretty banged up.'

'That must have been quite a fall.'

Moses crossed his arms and exhaled. 'I'm trying to keep an open mind. Not jump to conclusions. I keep trying to picture it, and it won't come into focus, at least not the way she described it. She's running in the rain, she slips, she falls on her face. She doesn't put her hands out to stop her fall?'

'What do you think?'

Moses ran down the scenario he'd described to Susan and finished up by saying, 'I need to have a talk with Brittany.'

'You think she's covering for somebody?'

'That kind of follows from the rest of what I think, doesn't it?'

'You know who it was?'

Moses shook his head. 'I need a scorecard to keep up with her nowadays.'

Tony seemed about to say something.

'What?' Moses asked. 'You know something?'

'Not really,' Tony said. 'Let her tell you, if there's anything to tell.'

At twelve-thirty, Tony went home, and now, near one, Moses sat on a stool at the far end of the bar. He'd locked the door fifteen minutes ago. Outside, a steady, wind-driven rain continued to strafe the windows. Every minute or two, a lone vehicle would go hissing by on Lincoln. Inside, the only meager light came from a sixty-watt Tiffany lamp on a low table set in the back.

He spun a half-empty glass of ginger ale in front of him. On the bar next to his glass was the Shamrock's shillelagh, a two-foot length of iron-hard Kentucky ash with a fist-sized knot at one end and a leather thong at the other, that Moses had used several times when mediating mêlées in his career as a publican. It was a formidable weapon of persuasion. He had no actual memory of having lifted it from the place where it hung behind the bar and bringing it with him out front.

His mind seemed to be jangling with white noise.

Somebody had, at the very least, manhandled his daughter. The more he thought about it, the more obvious it was. But her assailant was someone whose identity, in her misguided wisdom, Brittany was choosing not to reveal. Moses had a feeling that Tony might know who it was, but he wasn't talking, either.

The inchoate knot in the center of his gut that had accompanied his dawning recognition of what actually happened to Brittany had flowered into a black rage that was threatening to consume him.

Some cowardly punk had hurt his daughter badly enough to send her to the hospital.

He kept having to fight down images of Brittany as a helpless baby, his baby now in pain, with her lovely face swollen, bloody, and battered.

In his younger and even not so younger days, back when he'd been setting some drinking records, Moses had not let his Ph.D. in philosophy keep him from being a serious brawler. His nose was permanently disfigured from all the times it had been broken. He still worked out with a heavy bag a couple of times a week to keep up his hand-eye. As a teenager, he'd fought Golden Gloves; he knew how to handle himself in a fair fight. If your pleasure was street fighting, he could kick and gouge and jam elbows and knees. If a target presented itself, he'd even been known to bite.

Anything to win.

Now he wanted to fight as badly as he'd ever wanted anything in his life. He wanted to pound flesh, to smell copper-fresh blood, to crack bone.

His breath came in ragged gulps.

He would have a drink, goddammit. He *needed* a drink, and it made perfect and absolute sense. What had he been doing, denying his true self for all these years? He was an avenging angel, in a pure and righteous rage, and he wanted a drink.

He went around the bar and took down a bottle of the Macallan from the top shelf. He free-poured to the lip of the glass, then brought it up to his nose to smell it.

God.

The power of the smell slowed him for a second and, the Scotch untouched, he set the glass next to the shillelagh and stared at it.

For a moment, the fury subsided.

He knew who he was. He was Saint Augustine, bringing a concubine to bed so he could deny himself sex with her and thereby, upon conquering the temptation, please the Lord.

Just pick it up and swig it down. Feed the rage. Be who you are.

His hand reached for the glass.

Instead, he grabbed the shillelagh. With an inarticulate roar, he brought the heavy club across in a wild sweep, breaking the glass and sending its shards and the whiskey out into the room. Every swing punctuated by profanity, he brought down the head of the shillelagh time and again with all his might, smashing it against the bar. Again and again and again.

Until, at last, he was spent.

He let the shillelagh fall to the ground. He gripped the edge of the bar, his body sagging with exhaustion, his breathing that of a horse that had galloped to the absolute limit of its endurance.

10

HARDY HAD TWO seating areas in his office. The one in front of his desk was formal, with a Persian rug on which two Queen Anne chairs flanked a lion's-claw mahogany coffee table. The other, off to the side and taking advantage of the corner windows overlooking today's blustery Sutter Street, consisted of two brown leather chairs and a matching love seat.

The office door closed behind Moses McGuire. He stood for a moment, taking it all in. 'I don't think I've ever been here,' he said.

'Sure you have.'

'I think I'd remember. It's pretty fancy.'

'I'm glad you approve.'

'I'm not sure I do. If I were a client, I'd be worried that you were charging me so you could buy this kind of furniture, keep up appearances.'

'If you were a client,' Hardy said, 'you'd be worried about going to prison, and you wouldn't give a damn about the furniture. You'd be thinking you didn't want a cot and a toilet for the next twenty years.'

'There's that, too, I suppose.' Moses glanced around again. 'So where do I sit? Is there a protocol?'

'Whatever makes you more comfortable. Meanwhile, you want some coffee? Water? Anything?'

'I think I'm good.' He eased himself down into one of the leather seats. 'Now I'm better. And where do you sit?'

'Same as you. We're all about equality here. You sit where

you want. I sit where I want. Like here.' He sat in the other leather chair. 'What's brought you down here for the very first time? You don't look so good.'

'I didn't sleep much last night. I was having a wrestling match with the devil.'

'Who won?'

'I think I did, but it was close.' Moses cleared his throat, looked around some more, came back to Hardy. 'I wanted to ask if you could lend me Wyatt Hunt for a day or so.'

'You need a private eye?'

'I don't know for sure. I'd like to talk to him and see.'

Hardy sat back in some surprise. 'You can get Wyatt any time you want. He doesn't work for me exclusively. What do you want him to find out?'

'Who beat up Brittany.'

At once, Hardy's face hardened. He sat forward in his chair. 'When did this happen?'

'Yesterday.'

'How bad is it?'

'She's banged up but okay. She's back at our house, in bed.'

'Conscious, right?'

'Yeah, in and out of sleep. They gave her some pain meds.'

'But you've talked to her?'

'Oh, yeah.' Moses raised a hand. 'And I know what you're thinking: why don't I just ask her who did it? Well, I did. Nobody hurt her. She fell down, that's all. That's her story, and she's sticking to it.'

'But you don't think so?'

'Let us say I am certain beyond a reasonable doubt.' Moses shook his head. 'I want the son of a bitch thrown in jail, Diz. No, that's not true. What I really want is to beat the shit out of him. Failing that, I'd settle for him spending some time in the slammer.'

'I don't blame you. But if Brittany's not going to testify, you realize that's not going to happen, right?'

'I'll talk her into it after she thinks about it a little more. She's smart. She'll give up wanting to protect him.'

'When that happens, she'll give you his name, so you won't need Wyatt. But maybe it's not about protection,' Hardy added. 'Maybe she's afraid of him. Have you thought about that? In either case, protection or fear, she won't help with any prosecution, and you still won't have a name.'

'That's why I want to borrow Wyatt. Just to find out who he is.'

'And then what? If Brittany won't ID the guy.'

'Then I go to Plan B. "B" as in "beat the shit out of him."'

'Good idea, Mose. Then you get to go to jail.'

'Bullshit. I'm justified. Worst case, I'll pay a fine and get back to my life.'

'You know when I just said "Good idea"? That was sarcastic. I meant it's a bad idea. You know why? Because depending on the damage you do, you could go to prison for years, which – grizzled old man that you are – you don't have to spare.'

'I don't think so. He'd have to testify against me, and you want to talk about fear? I'll put the fear of God in him.'

Hardy chortled. 'And because of your vast experience with the law, you're sure that's the way it's going to happen?'

'It's worth the risk.'

'No,' Hardy said. 'It's really not. I understand the anger, and it would be good to get Brittany to press charges if you can. If you can't, you've got to let it go.'

Elbows on his knees, hands clasped in front of him, Moses let his head fall, then slowly raised it to meet Hardy's eyes. 'The reality is, I want to kill him, Diz. I mean literally, whoever it is, I want to end his life.'

'I get it,' Hardy said. 'I don't necessarily blame you, but let's not say those words out loud, all right? That's just anger talking.'

His eyes glassy, Moses blew out a long breath. He pointed at his face. 'This *is* anger,' he said. 'She's my baby, Diz. My beautiful little baby girl.'

'I know,' Hardy said. He reached out and rested his hand on Moses's shoulder. 'I know.'

Bundled up in hiking boots, jeans, and a fisherman's sweater under his Giants jacket, Moses wandered around in the downtown mist for an hour, then stopped into Tadich's for some sourdough and cioppino at the bar. After leaving Hardy's office, he'd come to the conclusion that his brother-in-law was probably right. If he couldn't get Brittany to identify her attacker and press charges, then there was no point in trying to find him.

Hardy was certainly correct in warning him off any direct intervention. That could easily backfire, could cause Moses all kinds of problems, including jail, especially if he involved anyone else, any potential witness against him, such as Wyatt Hunt or Hardy himself.

Half finished with his lunch, he took out his cell phone and called his wife. She picked up on the second ring.

'How's she doing?'

'Okay. She's sitting up with me now in the kitchen, having some chicken soup.'

'How's she look?'

'Good.' With false brightness, Susan was clearly framing her end of the conversation for Brittany's benefit.

'Any change in her story?'

'No. It's about the same.'

'Can I say hello to her?'

'Sure. Just a sec. Here she is.'

And then his daughter's voice, husky and weary. 'Hey, Dad.'

'How's my girl?'

'Better. Still a little tired, but okay. Couple of days, I'll be good as new.'

'You can stay with us as long as you want, you know.'

'I know. Thank you.'

'So, listen, Britt. Do you remember anything more about how it happened?'

'Not really, Dad. It was just all so fast. Running and then slipping and then banging my head.'

'How's your arm?'

'My arm?'

'Your left arm. I noticed you had a big bruise on it when I tucked you in last night. Has that been there a long time?'

Brittany hesitated. 'I don't know. I think it's okay.'

'You don't remember how you hurt it? Maybe you fell on it before you hit your face.'

'I don't remember, Dad. It's all right now, anyway. I'm okay, just sore.'

It hadn't been anything like a real conversation, but Moses played it through again and again, listening in his memory for anything like a false note. The only time he detected a weakness was when he asked about her arm. Maybe he should have been more straightforward, calling her outright on it, ordering her to tell him. But she was in a fragile state, and he didn't want to add to her distress.

Hardy, again, had nailed it. She was either protecting this asshole or she was afraid of him. From the first minute Moses had questioned Brittany's story and thought seriously about what had happened, he had assumed it was the former, but now, with a rushing sound in his ears, came the idea that the guy might constitute a continuing threat.

He might hurt her again!

Moses had not raised his daughters to meekly forgive someone who might hurt them. Both of his girls were independent and strong-willed. He would have thought that Brittany, particularly, would not be inclined to protect someone who had abused or hurt her. If anything, she would fight back, turn the guy in to the police, let justice take its course. But if she was afraid that he would hurt her again, perhaps more seriously, then he could envision her deciding that the better part of valor would be to let the whole thing pass. To Moses, the man who had beaten Brittany now not only had to be punished, he had to be given a message about the future in no uncertain terms.

His brow furrowed, his eyes in a steely squint over a tightly drawn mouth, Moses sat with his fists clenched on either side of his cioppino bowl.

'Is everything all right, sir?'

The elderly tuxedoed bartender slowly came into focus in front of him.

'Sorry?'

'Is there something the matter with the cioppino?'

'No, it's delicious. Perfect, as always.'

'Pardon me for asking,' the bartender went on, 'but you didn't look like you were enjoying it.'

'I've got a few things on my mind.'

'Of course. Certainly. Sorry to have bothered you.'

'No bother. The cioppino's great. You know, on second thought, maybe it could be improved on.'

'And how is that?'

'Let me take a look at your wine list, and I'll let you know.'

He stopped at two glasses of the house red, proving to himself that he was in control. The idea that one glass always and inexorably led to binge drinking or to unconsciousness was ridiculous, and he had just proved it. He hadn't had a drink in six years, and now he'd had just two drinks in six years, an average of one drink every three years, if he wanted to do the math.

He drove his car from Union Square down to Van Ness and found the impossible – a convenient parking place – not a block from Brittany's coffee shop. The lunch rush was well over, with no line at the counter. He introduced himself to one of the workers as Brittany's father and asked to speak to the manager.

Mitch came down from the back room and out into the customer area, where the two men shook hands. Mitch asked, 'How is she? We miss her already. She's a true ace of a person. I'm sure you know that.'

'We like her pretty much ourselves,' Moses said. 'She says she expects to be back working in a couple of days.'

'That's what she told me. So what happened? She says she slipped and fell, running for the bus, and banged her head.'

'That's what she says.'

Mitch cocked his head to one side. 'And yet here you are, her father, just stopping by – what? – to make sure we got the message that she wasn't coming in?'

'No. Not quite that.' He paused. 'I'm not sure I believe she fell. I wondered if anybody here, any of your workers, might have seen what happened.'

'The bus stop's two blocks down.'

'Right. I know.'

'My point is, I don't think anybody saw it from here, or could have, even if we were looking for it.'

Moses stood, somewhat baleful yet imposing, waiting for more. And it came.

'You don't think it was an accident,' Mitch said.

'I don't know. As you can see, I'm looking into it.'

'What else would it be?'

'An assault.'

Mitch's eyes narrowed. 'She dumped a guy last weekend, you know that? He came in a couple of days ago, tried to talk to her, got a little belligerent. I had to throw him out.'

'You got a name?'

After a moment of reflection, Mitch shook his head. 'I'm afraid not. But Brittany told me where he works and what he does.'

Moses trudged up the wide marble steps of the ornate main stair-case under the dome in the rotunda of city hall, a few blocks from Brittany's coffee shop. The setting was elegant and majestic, often used for political photo opportunities. At the moment, from Moses's perspective, his stomach churning and his blood high, the place had a surreal quality. A formal wedding was taking place off to the far right – he half expected to turn and see Susan playing her cello with the string quartet – and sixty or so guests in black-tie finery or designer gowns were roped off from the hoi polloi doing business or on their way to one of the many administrative offices.

At the top of the staircase, Moses followed the signs left to the offices of the city supervisors – San Francisco had eleven of them – and had no trouble finding Liam Goodman's. In the hallway, his hand on the doorknob, he stopped for a last second or two. He drew in a breath, then another one, summoning the battlefield calm that had served him well in Vietnam, in his dozens of bar fights, at the showdown on Pier 70. He willed his blood pressure down, listened as the random lobby noise, the wedding music, faded into silence behind him.

Inside the office, he passed a room where some young people seemed to be working at a conference table. In front of him, an attractive middle-aged black woman glanced up from her computer and gave him a smile. 'Can I help you?'

'I'd like to talk to the chief of staff, please. I'm sorry, his name slips my mind.'

'Rick Jessup.'

'That's it.'

'Do you have an appointment?'

'No. I'm afraid I don't.' Moses could be effortlessly charming when it suited him, as it did now. 'I was just in the neighborhood and thought I'd stop in. My name is Moses McGuire. Tell him I'm Brittany's father. We met at my bar – the Little Shamrock? – last Friday. He'll know what it's about.'

'All right.' She picked up her telephone and spoke into it, then to Moses. 'He'll be right out.'

Moses nodded, moved to one side, stared out through the mist at the Opera House across the street. When he heard a door open behind him, he turned.

'Mr McGuire.' The well-dressed young man advanced on him, the picture of confidence, smile in place, hand outstretched. 'This is a pleasant surprise. Good to see you again. What can I do for you?'

Moses did not take the proffered hand. Instead, he cast a disdainful glance at it and then looked up, meeting the young man's eyes, speaking in a conversational tone. 'You can leave my daughter alone.'

Rick shot a quick look across at Diane. A twitch danced at the corner of his lips. 'I thought I'd been doing that,' he said. 'She hasn't been talking to me.'

'You've tried to talk to her.'

'Okay, you mean at Peet's. I wanted to try to get back together. But she wouldn't talk to me.'

'I heard you objected, and they had to throw you out.'

'That's an exaggeration. I wasn't happy, but I left on my own.' He backed up a step or two.

'That's not the last time you saw her, is it?'

Diane rose behind her computer. 'Is everything all right here, Rick?'

'Everything's fine,' he said. Then, to Moses, 'Although maybe we should continue this conversation out in the hall, let Diane get back to her work.'

'Fine with me.'

'You're sure?' Diane asked with a nervous glance at Moses.

'We're good,' Rick said, then turned to Moses. 'Good. Right?'

'Peachy.'

Rick started walking toward the exit, Moses a couple of steps behind him. Out in the hallway, the younger man turned to him. 'Where were we?'

'I was telling you that Peet's wasn't the last time you saw her.'

Brazening it out, Rick stared into Moses's face for a beat. 'How is she?'

'How would you expect her to be?'

'I'm not sure I know what you mean.'

'I mean when you manhandle somebody, you throw 'em around, sometimes you cause some real damage.'

Rick managed to hold out for some seconds before he looked down and said, 'I didn't mean to hurt her. It was an accident. She pulled away and slipped and—'

Those words marked the end of any doubt about what had happened, and Moses struck with all the power he could muster. Rick, in the middle of explaining, wasn't looking for it and couldn't begin to block the punch. He never even saw the vicious right jab that hit him high on the cheekbone, knocking him onto his heels, his head snapping back and slamming into the wall as a blind flurry of three more punches – left, right, left, carefully aimed, surgically executed – turned his legs to jelly and dropped him.

As blood, a good quantity, started to run out of Rick's nose and mouth, pooling on the floor, Moses looked down at his victim in disgust. Leaning over, he got close to Rick's ear. 'You come near my daughter again,' he said, 'and you are a dead man.'

Straightening up, massaging his knuckles, Moses turned and walked at a normal pace back down the interior hallway, out to the majestic steps, down the imposing wide stairway, where the wedding was still going on, and out into the fog of the late afternoon.

PART
TWO

11

At a little past three o'clock on Saturday, the last day of March, Rick Jessup looked up at the flight of twenty-seven steps that led to the front door of Jon Lo's Victorian home on Divisadero Street. As if the street weren't steep enough, ascending from Cow Hollow up to Broadway. He couldn't imagine why anybody would buy a house that was so torturous to get to. Maybe Lo drove his Mercedes up and down the driveway directly into the attached garage every day and never used the steps. To anyone visiting, those steps were a definite physical and possibly psychological hurdle.

At the top of the stairs, Jessup turned to look back over the roofs of the Marina District and out to the bay, which today was dotted with dozens of sailboats and hundreds of whitecaps. He was standing there, hesitating, when the front door opened. He whirled around.

'How long were you going to wait before you rang the bell?' Lo asked.

'I was just catching my breath and admiring your view.'

'It's the bay,' Lo said. 'The gray bay. Would you like to come in?'

'Thank you.'

Jessup swallowed against his nerves and followed Lo into a lavishly decorated and overly furnished living room that featured the same view as the porch, minus the wind. Lo appeared to be at ease in his castle. He wore pleated light brown dress slacks, tasseled cordovan loafers without socks, a black V-neck sweater.

No sooner had he offered Jessup a seat on the couch than a breathtakingly beautiful Asian woman in a wildly colorful silk blouse appeared bearing a platter: a white porcelain pot, fine china cups and saucers, a selection of teas and cookies. Without a word or even a glance at the two men, she placed the platter on the glass and chrome coffee table in front of Jessup. Straightening up, she put her hands together in a prayerful gesture and bowed, then disappeared as quickly as she'd arrived.

Lo sat across from Jessup in an overstuffed leather chair, his feet on a matching ottoman. 'Please help yourself,' he said. 'All of the teas are excellent.'

'Thank you.' Jessup sat forward, dropped a tea bag into one of the cups, and poured hot water over it. 'I appreciate your agreeing to see me.'

'Not at all. I've admired your work with Liam for quite some time. He speaks glowingly of your talents and follow-through. I understand that you were more or less responsible for coordinating the timing with our friends from Alcoholic Beverage Control, and because of that, my businesses are no longer the mayor's flavor of the month, which is all to the good. So what can I do for you?'

'Well,' Jessup said, 'it's more what I hope we can do for each other. As you might have guessed from the fact that I wasn't comfortable meeting with you in our offices, this is about Liam.'

'I'm listening.'

'Before I go any further, I want to make clear that my first loyalty is to him. He's been my mentor since I graduated from college. I hope to be with him as he continues his political career, whether it's on to mayor or wherever he wants to go. He's a great role model and an even better friend.'

Lo brought his feet down and leaned forward. 'I hear a "but."'

'Yes, you do. The dynamic between me and Liam has changed over the past few months.' Jessup stirred his tea, removed the bag, brought the drink to his lips. Killing time. Putting the cup down, he began. 'The plain fact is that it started with an issue you brought up with him. One of our staff apparently taking advantage of his access to your businesses.'

Lo's mouth turned up into a small smile. 'That's one way to refer to it.'

'It was atrocious,' Jessup said. 'I've interrogated the entire staff but unfortunately haven't been able to get to the bottom of it. I've come to the conclusion that it was one of Liam's political enemies, trying to drive some kind of a wedge between you and him.'

'That's not impossible.'

'No. I think it's actually quite probable. The problem is that I think Liam somehow got it in his head that it might have been me.'

'Why would he think that?'

'Well, this is somewhat embarrassing, but I want to be completely clear and up-front with you. Let's just say I find some of your women amazingly attractive.'

Lo spread his hands, let another smile bloom. 'Listen to me. There is nothing to be embarrassed about. You're a young man. The appetite is there. If that weren't a universal truth, I wouldn't have a business at all. You were perhaps a bit presumptuous and overestimated your position. That can happen in a young man. You acknowledge your error and show respect. I don't see a problem. Is that all you wanted to talk to me about? To reassure me on that score?'

'To some degree, yes. But it leads to the greater issue.'

'Which is what?'

Jessup paused again. 'I fear that Liam may not be as under-standing of the prerogatives of power as you are. I am concerned that he is losing confidence in my discretion and loyalty because of what he thinks I may have done with your girls – and which I swear to you I had no part in – or whether his political ambitions are driving him away from the people who have been his staunchest supporters and allies from the beginning. Now that he's all but announced for mayor, I think his allegiance to me – and, frankly, to you – has become diluted. Again, I don't want to be speaking out of school, but I've heard him make a few comments privately that he wants to build his campaign around a less politically compromised group of supporters.'

'What did you take that to mean?'

'No massage-parlor money. No connection with, forgive me, unsavory elements.'

'That would be cutting his own throat.'

'He thinks not. He's getting a really strong bounce on this underage alcohol campaign, the morality vote. He thinks if he's going to go beyond his supervisor seat, and eventually beyond mayor, he'll have to jettison the people who put him there. Which means you. And, for different but connected reasons, me.'

'You have my attention. What exactly are you proposing?'

'I'm saying I think we can help each other. There was a time, not so long ago, when Liam listened to my political advice. I was a big part of a lot of programs and ideas, and even the alcohol sting, and look where that's gotten him. I used to have credibility with him, and I don't think I'm dead yet, but I've got to get back in his confidence. He's listening to people telling him what he wants to hear who don't have his best interests at heart. What he needs is a straight shooter. And that straight shooter would tell him he's crazy if he thinks he'll be able to fund a campaign without you and your pals and the organization we've all worked so hard to put together.'

'What do you want me to do?'

'I'd like you to tell Liam that you've discovered who it was messing with your business and your girls. You've taken steps. The guy's not going to be a problem anymore. Make up a name if you have to, just have Liam believe it wasn't me. Because it wasn't me, and I can't have him thinking it was. Then I'm back in his camp, where I can exert real influence. I can keep you on his radar, where you belong. He can't win without you, and your interests are going to be in jeopardy without him. Both of you need to be working together. It's win/win.'

'I can see that. But if my money and my support can't convince him, what makes you so sure that you can?'

'I know the man, sir. I know a lot of his secrets, some of which he'd prefer didn't become common knowledge, some of which would kill him politically. If you can help me get this monkey off my back, I'm willing to share some of those secrets, so if he tries to abandon you, you'll be able to bring a fairly strong argument to the table that would convince him to serve your best interests.'

After a long moment, Lo nodded. 'I'll talk to him on Monday and tell him we need to discuss his political future.'

Looking out his picture window, Lo watched Rick Jessup descend the front steps and go left at the sidewalk. Turning back into his living room, he fixed himself a cup of tea. That young man, he was thinking, was a problem.

Lo wondered whether he was using cocaine, if he'd snorted a few lines before gathering the nerve for his really bold end run here today.

He sipped tea, warming both hands around the cup. Lo allowed his mind to settle until it let him know a few things with absolute certainty. First, it had been Jessup who stiffed his girls, slapping around a few of them while he was at it. Second, Jessup was willing to blackmail his boss over past indiscretions. Third, Jessup was mistaken if not truly deluded if he really thought that Liam would decline Lo's campaign contributions going forward. Fourth, if Jessup was willing to betray his long-standing friend and mentor Liam Goodman, imagine how quick he would be to turn on Lo should an opportunity present itself.

He was a vicious, undependable, and therefore dangerous man.

Oh.

Another sip of tea.

As the fifth certainty sifted through his consciousness, its deviousness brought a smile to his face.

Fifth, Lo was now sure that not only would Jessup betray him at the first opportunity, he would not hesitate to turn today's meeting into something other than it had been, spinning it completely around, turning Lo into Liam's betrayer. Lo could almost hear Jessup's words: *I'm telling you, Liam, keep your eye on Mr Lo. He'll co-opt your campaign and end up owning you. Don't meet with him anymore. Don't talk to him. Use me as a go-between so you can deny any connection to him. Otherwise, all you'll ever be is Jon Lo's hired boy.*

Lo raised his cup to his lips and was surprised to find it empty. He went back to the coffee table and placed it on the platter. On the other side of the entrance hall, directly across from the living room, he had a home office with a globe, three hundred books in a dark wood built-in bookshelf, four red leather chairs, a television, a wet bar, and a landline telephone. He picked it up, pushed a memory number, and listened as it rang three times before a familiar voice answered.

'Liam,' he said. 'Sorry to bother you on a weekend, but I believe we have a problem with your chief of staff.'

Jessup was done taking shit from everybody.

First was the issue with Liam losing faith in him, maybe even interviewing other candidates for his job. If Jessup didn't move quickly – which he had just done, and it felt like it had gone pretty successfully – he was going to find himself unemployed.

Which could not happen. Not in this economy. Not with his expenses and expectations. He wasn't going to stop drinking good wine, going to nice restaurants. He wasn't going to give up cocaine. These were not options. Not in his life.

He'd woken up feeling that enough was enough, and he'd made his move, getting things a little way back toward the right track. And sure, it had been risky, going to Jon Lo, but obviously, he'd convinced him, and now Lo would be calling Liam on Monday, setting the stage for reconciliation with his boss.

That, at least, would all work out.

The second thing, while he was at it, would be getting back at Brittany and her lunatic father, who'd blindsided him.

Back home at his place in the Marina, pumped up over the way things had gone with Lo, he picked up the phone and punched in the contact he still hadn't erased. He knew that when she saw who was calling, she wouldn't talk to him, so he sent a text instead: *Brittany. I don't know if you are aware of it, but your father came down to my office. It's not so much that he assaulted me. That was no big deal. But he seems genuinely crazy and dangerous, and I really think someone needs to get him off the street. I feel like I should report this to the police. I'm sorry if he has to go to jail, but what if he goes crazy again and hurts someone else? I would feel responsible.*

Maybe I'd feel differently if I were convinced your father wasn't dangerous. If you convince me that's the case, that can be the end of it. I'll be at Perry's on Union tonight at nine. One drink, neutral territory, lots of people around, totally safe. Or any other date and time you want. I hope to see you there.

When she came in and he saw her again, he realized he truly hated her. What she'd put him through, what she probably put every guy through.

Unbelievable! She couldn't even walk the length of the bar to where he sat without three guys hitting on her as she passed. Here she was, getting to him, awkwardly lifting one hand, pulling out the chair across from him at the small table. 'Hey.'

'Hey. Thank you for coming.'

'Sure.' She tried to arrange her face into a neutral expression, but under it, he sensed a low thrumming of fear.

Good.

'What can I get you?' he asked.

'Whatever you're having.'

Good again, he thought. 'Sazerac.' Bitters and absinthe.

'Bring it on.'

'Save my place. I'll be right back.'

'They've got waitresses.'

'I know, but I'll be quicker.'

When Jessup returned with the drinks, he carefully put hers down in front of her, then moved his drink to the far edge of the table. It wouldn't do to spill one or mix them up.

He sat down, took up his drink, held the glass out to her. 'I won't say to new beginnings or anything like that, but thank you again for coming.'

Sighing, forcing a smile, Brittany picked up her glass and brought it up to his. 'I'm so sorry about everything.'

'Me, too. Really.'

He brought the glass to his lips and watched as she did the same, made a little face, took another sip. 'While I'm being sorry,' she said, 'I didn't know about my dad and you. I didn't even tell him you'd touched me. I told him I just fell down. But he's had some experience with fights and bruises.'

'I gathered that.'

'Did he hurt you?'

'At the time, it was pretty bad. I didn't see it coming.'

'That's my dad.'

'I've been pretty pissed off at him.'

'I get that. I don't blame you. But I hope you don't want him to go to jail. It would be nasty and embarrassing for everybody.'

'Well.' He picked up his glass. 'Here's to your dad maybe not going to jail.'

'Really?'

'Really maybe. A few more toasts, and we may get all the way to really really.'

They both drank.

'The waitress is coming up behind you,' she said.

'One more?' he asked.

'Sure. Why not?'

12

'GRAPE LEAF POTSTICKERS?'

From his corner booth, Abe Glitsky was looking over Wes Farrell's shoulder at the blackboard above the cash register at Lou the Greek's. Today – an unseasonably warm and pleasant Monday in early April – the place was at its usual near capacity.

Glitsky brought his gaze back down to Treya's boss. 'Really?' he asked. 'Grape leaf potstickers? Could that be right?'

His wife, skeptical, squinted up at the board. 'Is that what it says?'

Wes Farrell turned around to check it out. 'That's what it looks like to me. Could grape leaf potstickers possibly be any good? I mean, Chui has worked some miracles before, I grant you, but this one might be a stretch.'

'Well,' Glitsky replied, 'if we're staying for lunch, it's not like we'll get to choose, will we?'

He was referring to the fact – understood by all the regular customers – that Lou the Greek's had carved a successful niche by serving only one dish, the Special, every day. You ate the Special or you didn't eat at Lou's. Which would have been fine if Lou's wife, Chui, made anything resembling standard lunch fare – burgers, fries, sandwiches, hot dogs, salads. But not at Lou's. Instead, Chui found her daily inspiration in the commingling of cuisines from both her and her husband's native lands – China and Greece, respectively. So you'd get Kung Pao pita pockets or sweet-and-sour lamb kebabs, or something equally creative, though not always equally tasty.

And now the ever affable Lou himself was at their table, cutting off their discussion on the merits of the Special, which, according to Lou, was never less than great.

'How is it today, Lou?' Farrell asked, half to hear his reply.

'Great. Your basic dolmas, except healthier. Pork and ginger with soy and garlic filling instead of rice. Really delicious. So' – he pointed down at them – 'three?'

'Sounds good,' Treya said. 'Three.' As Lou was moving along to the next order, she added, 'Uh-oh.'

'What?' Glitsky asked.

'Work.'

Following her gaze, Glitsky saw two of his inspectors, Paul Brady and Lee Sher, standing just inside the doorway, craning their necks to see through the crowded room. 'Looks like,' Glitsky said as he placed his napkin down on the table and stepped out of the booth to wave them over.

Sher was a no-nonsense woman of around forty who played down what could have been very good looks – cropped yet glistening black hair, no makeup, a trim and athletic figure. When she slid in next to Farrell and across from Glitsky, she wasted little time with preamble. 'Sorry to interrupt your lunch, but the call out to the Marina this morning—'

'The cleaning woman?' Glitsky had been in the office when the 911 call was routed to Homicide. The victim's housecleaner had let herself in at a few minutes past eight and gotten the bad surprise.

'Yeah, well, the victim's turned out to be a semipublic person, so the news is likely to go large in the media, and we thought you'd like to know.' She dipped her head toward Farrell. 'You, too, sir, of course.'

'Semipublic?' Glitsky asked.

Next to Glitsky, Brady nodded. He was ten years older than his partner, and his blond hair was starting to go gray, but that was his only visible concession to age. He nodded, picking up his partner's slack. 'Liam Goodman's chief of staff. Kid by the name of Rick Jessup.'

'A kid?' Glitsky asked.

'Twenty-seven. Supposedly a bit of a rising star, or was.'

'Any sign it was political?'

'Not yet,' Sher said. 'Not much of anything yet.'

'Definitely a homicide?'

The inspectors nodded in unison. 'No doubt,' Sher said. 'Blunt-force head trauma.'

'And lots of it,' Brady added. 'Somebody beat him with something hard and kept at it until he was completely dead.'

'Do you have the murder weapon?'

'Not yet.'

'Suspects?'

'No.'

'Forced entry?'

'No.'

'All right.' Glitsky scratched at his jaw. 'Rick Jessup. Why do I know that name? Treya? Wes? Does it sound familiar to either of you?'

'No,' Farrell said, 'but I get the feeling it's going to start to pretty soon.'

'You can bet on that, sir,' Sher said. 'Every TV van in the city was there by the time we left.'

'When did this happen?' Glitsky asked.

Brady said, 'Signs point to last night. The upstairs neighbor heard what she thought was a fight of some kind down in Jessup's place, though she couldn't be sure. Just some bumps, she said, and didn't know what to make of them. She volunteered that it wasn't uncommon to hear noises when Mr Jessup had female guests. When the maid came in this morning, the lights were on, the paper was on the doorstep, coffee hadn't been made.'

'In any event—' Sher began, then looked a question at Brady and stopped.

'No, you go ahead,' Brady said. Then, to Glitsky, 'This is the good part. She likes to do the good part.'

'There's a good part?'

Sher nodded. 'Reasonably. What Paul's saying is it would be nice if it turned out it was last night, because right after the ruckus, that same upstairs neighbor heard the door slam downstairs, and then she happened to look out the window and see a guy leaving the building.'

Glitsky's mouth turned up a quarter of an inch, for him a full-blooded smile. 'You're telling me she saw the killer?'

'She saw somebody. If it was the killer, and if it happened last night, then maybe.'

'Lee doesn't want to jump to conclusions,' Brady said.

'I hear that,' Glitsky said.

'We haven't canvassed around yet,' Sher said, 'but with what we've got so far, the basic description, we're hoping somebody else might have seen something.'

Treya, caught up in it, leaned around her husband. 'What did he look like, this guy?'

'If it was last night,' Sher reminded everyone, 'and if it was this guy.'

'Okay,' Treya said. 'Let's say yes to both.'

Sher threw a questioning glance at Glitsky and, getting a quick nod of approval, went ahead. 'She was looking down on him. After he left the building, he turned around and looked right up at her. He looked dazed. Anyway, she couldn't be sure about the height. She guessed about average, and the same for weight. She didn't think much of it. She's not sure she could recognize the guy in a photo spread or lineup. But it was definitely a white male – jeans, hiking boots, black and orange Giants jacket.'

'Hair?' Glitsky asked.

Brady took over. 'Darkish. Maybe some gray. Definitely not bald. And you'll love this: he was carrying something like a baton or a club of some kind.'

Glitsky made a face. 'A club?'

'That's what Susan said.'

'The neighbor,' Sher clarified. 'Susan Antaramian. She called it a club.'

Rick Jessup's apartment faced east on Mallorca Way, a street only a few blocks long that meandered through the upscale low-rise neighborhood just north of Chestnut Street. Susan Antaramian had told the inspectors that the suspect had turned right, or approximately south, after leaving the building, so Brady and Sher each took one side of the street and began knocking on doors.

Brady had worked his way into the second block without success when he ran into an elderly man – bent over, white-haired, in running shorts and a T-shirt – who was walking a little white Pekingese, who in turn was taking care of business in the gutter as the man waited patiently.

'Excuse me,' Brady said, holding out his badge, introducing himself, and asking the man if he lived nearby.

'Right around the corner. I'm Fred Dyer, lived here thirty-five years. This is about as far as Cosmo can handle. I used to take him all the way down to Crissy, throw a Frisbee for hours, but as you can see, those days are behind him. Behind me, too, I guess. What'd you say you wanted to know?'

'I don't know if you heard about it, sir, but there was an incident in the neighborhood last night.' Brady motioned behind him. 'Down the block there a ways. We're asking people who live around here if they might have seen anything unusual just as it was getting dark.'

'Unusual, like how?' Then, looking down, 'Thatta boy, Cosmo. Good boy.' Dyer produced a plastic bag and leaned down to pick up after his dog. 'Regular as clockwork,' he said. 'Wish I could say the same for me. What do you mean by unusual?'

'Out of the ordinary. Something maybe didn't seem to fit. Or struck you as odd. It doesn't have to be a big thing. Were you out walking at that time?'

'I probably was. Let me think. I like to take Cosmo out before it gets dark but when it's getting close, so he can make it through the night.'

'So you walked him by here last night? This same route?'

The man had his eyes half-shut, dredging for the memory. 'Yep,' he said at last. 'It was last night for sure. I know 'cause I had roast chicken. Sunday's chicken night, and I remember I fed him the skin, like I always do. He loves the skin, but only after I'm done with my dinner, and then we gotta get right outside pretty quick, if you know what I mean. They always tell you not to feed 'em human scraps, but I figure at his age, what difference is it going to make?'

'Right,' Brady said.

Fred Dyer's head canted to one side, then straightened. 'You know,' he said, 'there *was* a guy who passed us, brushed by, really. I nodded and said hi, like I always do, but he just kept going, as I say, in a hurry. The reason he stays with me a little is he was carrying like a . . . I'm not sure what I'd call it. Kind of a heavy stick. Anyway, it was smooth, like a walking stick, except if it was, it was broke off. Which seemed a little weird, like he'd picked up a heavy stick or part of a tree limb and was carrying it around with him.'

Brady kept any trace of excitement out of his voice. 'This man,' he said, 'do you remember, what did he look like?'

'About average, I'd say. A white guy, forty or fifty, maybe. Wearing a Giants jacket, I think. Dark hair, maybe.'

'Did you get a good look at his face?'

Mr Dyer shook his head. 'I can't say as I did. He was just a guy in a hurry passing on the sidewalk. Except for the shined-up stick. You think this could be something?'

'I don't have any idea. I'd like to talk to him, that's all, whoever he is. You didn't know him as a neighborhood guy or anything like that? You'd never seen him?'

'Not that I remember, and I'd know if he lived around here. At least to nod at.'

'Could you ID him if you saw him again?'

Dyer hesitated. 'Maybe.'

'Did you see where he went after he passed you?'

'No. I'm sorry, he was just a guy walking down the street. I didn't pay all that much attention.'

'Of course.' Brady removed a business card from his wallet and handed it over. 'Listen, Mr Dyer, you've been a big help. Would you mind letting me have your contact information if we'd like to get back to you and talk a little more about this?'

'Sure. That'd be fine. It's not like my days are all that full. If I didn't have Cosmo, I don't know what I'd do with my time.'

'We appreciate it. And if you remember any details, anything about his face, his clothes, anything at all, my numbers are on that card. Day or night.'

By about the same time, Lee Sher had made it down almost to the end of Mallorca where it abutted Chestnut, knocking on doors, mostly listening to bells chime or the echo of her knock in empty living units – duplexes, apartment buildings, the occasional stand-alone home.

She stood in a recessed vestibule with two doors. She had only three more doorways to go on Mallorca before she would have to cross the street and head back to the other side until she met up with Brady. She pushed the bell, and a black woman of perhaps thirty showed up behind the half-glass door on her left that led to an upstairs duplex. The name on the mailbox was Anantha Douglas. Seeing Sher, she opened the door a crack and said, 'I'm sorry, but I'm not buying anything. You people have got to stop ringing doorbells and pestering everybody.'

'I'm not selling anything.' Holding up her badge, Sher introduced herself and said, 'I'm an inspector with the police department, and we're canvassing the neighborhood to see if anyone might have seen anything suspicious last night.'

The woman opened the door a bit farther. 'Oh, I'm sorry. I thought you were . . . Is this about the guy who was killed around here last night?'

'Down at the other end of the street. A possible suspect may have come down this far, walking away from the crime scene.'

'What did he look like?'

Sher pretended to ignore the question. 'Did you see anyone unusual outside last night?'

The woman straightened up, her eyes unfocused as she brought her hands up to cover her mouth, then lowered them to her chin. 'Oh my God,' she said. 'Oh my God. He had just killed somebody?'

'We don't know that. We'd just like to talk to him. I take it you saw someone?'

'He was right in front of this building. I was going out to meet a friend for coffee at the corner, and just as I came out the door, I was running late, and I should know that the way these doors are set back a little, you can't see either way up the sidewalk, but I busted out anyway and he must have been just about hugging the building and I walked right into him. I mean, pretty hard.'

'Did you fall down?'

'No. Neither of us did, but . . .' She shook herself at the memory. 'So I'm all like "I'm sorry" and "I should watch where I'm going," and he's standing there. I mean, he's stopped, like he can't believe what happened. And I look at him, and his eyes are all kind of crazy. He's staring at me, and then I see a club in his hand, and for a second it's like he's going to bring it up and hit me with it, but then I back up a couple of steps and ask if he's sure he's okay, and he gets himself under control, like he's been holding his breath almost, and nods and says he's sorry, and he runs his other hand down the side of his face.'

'So you definitely saw his face.'

'Oh, yeah. I looked right at him.'

Sher got a description from the witness, then asked her, 'Do you think you could recognize him if you saw him again in a photo spread or a lineup?'

'I'm pretty sure I could.'

'Would you be willing to work with a police artist to get close to a likeness?'

The woman considered and shook her head. 'Maybe. I could probably pick him out of a lineup, if you needed that. If I saw him again, I mean, in real life. If that would help.'

'It might, if we get to that. Thank you, Anantha. You are Anantha Douglas?'

'Yes, ma'am. But you know, there was something else about his face.'

'What was that?'

'At first I thought he was old, like an old man. But then he looked surprisingly young, like he wasn't old but he'd been through some stuff, you know?'

'How young would you guess?'

'Maybe forty, but not too much older, if that. I could be wrong. I just thought I should say.'

'No. You're right. Anything is important. Can you tell me about the club?'

'Like what?'

'Did it look like commercially made sporting equipment, or a walking stick, or what? What color was it?'

'Darkish brown. Maybe a foot and a half long. And kind of shiny but gnarly.'

'Gnarly how?'

'It was, I don't know, like a branch off a tree that somebody sawed off and sanded until it was smooth. It had like a knot at the end. Also, it looked old.'

'Old?'

Anantha nodded. 'Like smoothed out with people holding it.'

Sher huffed out a little laugh. 'I see why you keep calling it a club. It sounds like it was a club.'

'It looked like a club. Like a caveman club, you know?'

'All right. So then what?'

'Then I kind of backed away more and started up toward Chestnut.'

'The same way this man was headed when you ran into him?'

Anantha bobbed her head. 'But he waited. I think me running into him must have freaked him out somehow. When I got to the corner, I took a quick look back, and he was still standing where I'd left him. He saw me look back and actually raised his hand and kind of waved at me, like "good luck" or something, and then he crossed over and got in his car.'

'He was parked here?'

'Yeah.' As though it had just occurred to her, and perhaps it had, Anantha opened her apartment door all the way. She excused herself around Sher and came all the way into the vestibule, where she stood and pointed across the street. 'That first metered spot on the other side.'

Sher was barely able to conceal her excitement at this gold mine of a witness. 'Anantha. May I call you Anantha?'

The young woman flashed a perfect set of teeth. 'That's my name.'

'Well, I'm Lee.' She kept her voice uninflected. 'Did you happen to notice what kind of car it was?'

'Small, maybe light blue? A sedan, not an SUV kind of thing. If I had to guess, I'd say it was a Honda Civic, which I only know because that's what I drive. But it might have been any small regular car.'

Sher and Brady were having coffee at an outside table in balmy sunlight close to Anantha's place, directly in a line with Mallorca as it abutted Chestnut.

'So,' Sher was saying, 'he parked all the way up here, walked back there, clubbed Rick Jessup to death, then strolled back along the street in broad daylight, carrying the murder weapon, which must have been covered with blood.'

'Unless he washed it at Jessup's place.'

'Maybe that, but still. If you're looking to make a getaway after you kill somebody, why do you park a few blocks away?'

Brady grinned. 'How about if you don't want to get a ticket or get towed, which, if you're planning to commit a murder, you really don't?'

'You're saying it's a parking issue? Again?'

'You laugh, but you wait. You'll see. Parking figures prominently in more crimes than the average person can imagine.'

'So you've said. About a thousand times.'

'Universal truth bears repeating.'

Brady was starting to get famous in the PD for holding the new record – formerly held by his Homicide colleague Darrel Bracco – for the number of parking tickets he'd collected from clueless traffic patrollers. In spite of leaving his business card – which clearly identified him as an inspector with the Homicide Detail – stuck under the wipers, the traffic cops universally would see his city-issued vehicle parked on sidewalks or in driveways near murder scenes and leave citations on his windshield. He had not paid one of these tickets – out of nearly a hundred – in the past couple of years. Nor would he fill out the administrative form that would have excused the transgressions. In theory, with fines and penalties, his car owed close to twelve thousand dollars in parking tickets, and every time he got a new one, it added to his bill and his legend. A sergeant once asked him what he did with the tickets, whether he threw them away. He said he put them under the seat and let the people who cleaned the car throw them away.

'Hey, I'm not kidding,' he said, returning to their suspect. 'I bet this was the closest spot he could find.'

'Crime solving by parking analysis,' Sher said. 'I like it.'

'You'd better,' Brady replied. 'It's the next big thing.'

13

AT TEN O'CLOCK the next morning, Glitsky was trying to figure out what to do with about eight pounds of peanuts roasted in the shell that filled a bag in the middle of his desk. Over the weekend, he and Treya had made one of their regular pilgrimages to Costco, where, as usual, they had spent about triple their average food bill trying to save themselves money on their food bill. Since Glitsky always tried to keep one of his desk drawers at work filled with peanuts, and he knew he had been getting low, he'd purchased a ten-pound bag. Unfortunately, it took up approximately a cubic foot of space, whereas his desk drawer would hold only a fifth of the bag at most, provided, of course, that he threw away all the other stuff that actually belonged in the drawer.

When Wes Farrell came to his open door and breezed in, Glitsky was scowling in perplexity, sitting behind this enormous bag of goobers, leaning back in his chair with his feet up. Farrell stopped in his tracks. 'Nobody asked me,' he said, 'but I'd say the peanut thing you do in here is getting a little out of hand.'

'Costco,' Glitsky said. 'Ten pounds seems like such a good deal when you're there.'

Farrell took it up. 'We bought some frozen chicken breasts last time. Did I say "some"? I think like six dozen. If we ever finish them, I'm never eating chicken again. But not to worry, because we won't ever finish them.' Farrell snapped his fingers, alight with an idea. 'I got it. Maybe you could drop the bag over at Lou's, and he could put 'em in little bowls at the bar. They'll be gone in a week.'

Glitsky shook his head. 'Good thought, but Chui would probably make Kung Pao everything for the next three months, and then where would we be? Kung Pao tofu, Kung Pao octopus, Kung Pao pineapple dumplings. Schwarma. Eggplant. If people found out I was the peanut source, they'd stone me.' Then, realizing the oddity of the district attorney of San Francisco appearing in his office unannounced, Glitsky brought his feet down and straightened in his chair, his face darkening. 'Is everything all right with Treya?'

'Treya? Sure. I mean, fine the last time I saw her, which was like three minutes ago. Oh, as in why am I here?' His expression went serious. 'You mind if I get the door?' He was already getting it, then coming back and opening one of the folding chairs Glitsky kept against the wall across from his desk. When Farrell was seated, he said, 'Something's come up that we need to talk about.'

Glitsky pushed the bag of peanuts off to one side, all business. 'Hit me.'

Farrell's smile faded. 'Sam gave me a call a few minutes ago.' Sam Duncan was Farrell's live-in girlfriend. She was the executive director of the Rape Crisis Counseling Center on Haight Street. 'As you may remember, she is always superconcerned about confidentiality issues, but ignoring all the disclaimers I had to give her and so forth, she had a young woman come to the center on Sunday morning.'

'Raped?'

'That's why they're all there, Abe.'

'Just making sure.'

'All right. Whatever. This one's a date rape, it looks like. She took a blood test, and they'll have the results about what drugs, if any, were involved in a day or so, but that's what Sam thinks. And so does the victim, for that matter.'

'What happened?'

'The woman, who shall – believe me – remain nameless, she'd been broken up with this guy for a couple of months after he knocked her around. She didn't want any part of him anymore.'

'Good for her.'

'Yeah, well, he didn't feel the same way. He wanted to get back together—'

'So he could knock her around again.'

'Probably. But after the first incident when he got rough, this woman's father sought the guy out and beat the shit out of him.'

Glitsky nodded. 'I'm liking this family more and more.'

'What's not to like? The problem is, the guy decided he could get her to see him again by threatening to press charges against the dad.'

'Opening himself up to where she charges him right back.'

'Maybe she didn't think of that. Or maybe she didn't want it to get that far. Anyway, bottom line, he talks her into coming to see him, and they meet up at Perry's on Union, and next thing she knows, she's waking up at his place, it's like one-thirty in the morning, and she knows he's had sex with her. Without her consent. She's been raped. She lets herself out, wanders around for a while before she finds her car where she left it, and gets away.'

Glitsky, the father of a daughter and a stepdaughter, pulled at the skin of his face. 'They do a rape kit on her?'

'Yes, at the clinic. She didn't want to go to the police.'

The scar through Glitsky's lips burned white with frustration. 'She didn't want to go to the police. She didn't want to charge him with assault. Where have I heard all this before?'

Farrell shrugged. 'It is what it is, Abe. Sam may get the woman to change her mind. She says she's trying. Either way, we've got the evidence if the rape victim wants to go forward and prosecute the guy. Which, as it turns out, isn't going to be necessary.'

'And why is that?'

Farrell threw a quick look over at the closed door. His voice took on a note of urgency. 'Sam got quiet reading the paper this morning, as she sometimes does, so I didn't think anything special about it. But it turns out that the young woman told Sam the name of the man who'd raped her, and there he was in the paper.' Farrell met Glitsky's eyes. 'He was murdered, bludgeoned to death, probably on Sunday night.'

Glitsky didn't even need to think about it. 'Rick Jessup,' he said.

'We have to talk to the woman, sir,' Sher said to Farrell. 'She might become our prime suspect. Your wife's got to give us her name.'

Farrell laughed, but not because he thought what she'd said was funny. 'Good luck with that.'

Brady added, 'She's not a lawyer or a doctor or a psychologist, am I right? Where does she get off claiming privilege?'

'She asserts it,' Glitsky said. 'And dares anybody to do anything about it. Can she do that, Wes? Couldn't you, as the DA, tell her she can't?'

'As the DA and not her boyfriend? I think not. Besides, she's got it – privilege, I mean. Evidence Code 1035.4, if you're curious.' Farrell spread his hands, helpless. 'Listen up, gang. I've lived with this woman for many years and haven't had much luck controlling any tiny part of her wonderful if stubborn personality. We could subpoena the center for records, which is a waste of time and would alert everyone to what we're thinking, but there's got to be a better way.'

They were gathered in Farrell's office after lunch. The inspectors had continued canvassing the Marina District in the morning, locating one more witness, Liza Moreno, who had an interaction with the man with the club on Sunday evening. He had been

standing on the corner of Mallorca and Alhambra, the first intersection south of Jessup's flat. Liza had been out jogging and the
man was just standing there, looking lost, so she stopped and
asked if she could help; he'd shaken his head, thanked her, and
moved on. Liza thought that she might be able to work with an
artist and get a composite drawing, and the two inspectors had
spent the rest of the morning working out the logistics. In contrast
to Anantha Douglas, Liza thought the man was at least fifty years
old. She said he stuck in her mind because he was acting weird.
She would definitely recognize him if she saw him again.

Without the rape, Sher and Brady were thrown back to the
statements of their eyewitnesses, and of these, the most promising
was Liza Moreno's. She was almost an hour into her appointment
with the forensic artist in one of the small interview rooms down
the hall when the two inspectors made their appearance. She and
the artist thought they had made real progress.

'This is actually fun,' she said with an enthusiasm almost never
encountered in this kind of setting, with this type of project. 'Gus
here is amazing. I tell him to change one line, and then suddenly
it's like "Wow, that's it! That part's right." I never thought it
would be like this.'

Gus Huang, in his late forties, had been doing the job on a
piecemeal, pay-as-you-go basis for sixteen years. This was probably his thousandth sketch, of which perhaps forty-three had
played some role in solving a crime; contrary to popular belief,
the purpose of an artist's sketch was not typically to identify one
suspect but to eliminate others.

Brady had used Gus's talents at least twenty times, and he'd
never seen him smile, but today he was beaming. 'She sees this
man,' he said. 'She's got him locked in. We're going to get him.'

Gus was sitting next to Liza, sketch pad before him, because
he didn't want her looking at his face while she tried to describe

another face. (He couldn't have said how many times a witness had him sketch his own likeness before he got wise and started sitting out of their line of vision.) They appeared to have settled upon the basic hairline and jawline and perhaps the eyes, the current version of which they were using as a template, with few skin creases or laugh lines.

'The eyes are that young?' Sher asked. 'They look almost like a boy's.'

'We'll come back,' Gus said, waving away the objection. 'Don't worry about eyes. We'll get him, you'll see.' He turned to Liza. 'Now the nose. Close your eyes, please.'

Closing the eyes was one trick, but by far the most successful strategy had taken place when Gus walked Liza through the hour preceding her encounter with the suspect, taking her up to the minute she had come upon him looking lost at the corner.

The witness did as Gus instructed, settling back in the chair, eyes closed. He drew a more or less generic nose in the middle of the face on his smaller sketch pad, then moved it in front of her and said, 'When you are ready.'

She waited a few more seconds, then opened her eyes, squinted down at the pad, and blinked a couple of times. 'Flatter,' she said, 'wider.' Then 'More off center, to my left, just the one side.'

Gus's charcoal flew over the paper. Liza was all focus, almost as if she'd put herself in some kind of trance. 'Okay, stop. Wait.'

The inspectors leaned in to examine the new changes.

'Put a bump in the middle just below the eyes.'

When Gus had done that, she said, 'That is exactly it. Put it up on Sammy.'

'Sammy?' Brady asked.

Liza nodded. 'That's what we're calling the final. That's Sammy's nose.' She turned to Sher. 'And you're right, now the eyes need to bunch up a little more, a few more wrinkles.'

Gus went back to his sketch pad, drew for a minute, took

corrections from Liza, tried again and again until she stopped him, saying they had it for Sammy now, he could go ahead and add it.

'He's turning out to be a good-looking guy,' Sher said. 'Would you have said he was handsome?'

'I didn't think of it that way at the time. He just looked lost.'

'But this guy, Sammy,' Sher continued, 'he's got definitely attractive eyes.'

Liza studied the easel. 'I guess he does. He did.'

'Just the mouth now,' Gus said, 'and we'll have him.' He looked across at Liza. 'If you please?'

She closed her eyes, and he started on the mouth.

Contrary to Dismas Hardy's hopes and predictions, after weeks of wrangling with the courts, at least a few of the Alcoholic Beverage Control cases – including Tony Solaia's – did not appear to be going away. Liam Goodman had kept up his campaign with the press and other news outlets, bolstering his position with a flood of statistics purporting to show that the city had become a safer place since the raids. In what may have been a simple coincidence but remained persuasive, traffic accidents and DUI arrests involving minors were down nearly 35 percent over the past months.

All too familiar with the ways that statistics could be manipulated to prove almost any proposition, Hardy remained skeptical about the raids' true efficacy, though he had to admit that the numbers appeared to back up Goodman's claims.

Those numbers were not Hardy's pressing concern. His immediate problem came, ironically, in the form of another of his defense bar colleagues, Janice Rodriguez, who shared offices with another low-rent lawyer. The two attorneys had also picked up clients from the conflicts pool in the wake of the bust. They were two Ukrainian immigrants – Igor Povaliy and Vadim

Gnatyuk – who, as it turned out, were in the country and working behind the bar at Burning Rome illegally. Knowing that they would be kept in custody before being summarily deported, the two friends had concocted a conspiracy theory that, were it not proving so difficult for Tony, Hardy would have admired for its cynicism and elegance.

According to Messrs. Povaliy and Gnatyuk, Liam Goodman and the ABC were not by any stretch making up their claims of illegal activity in certain bars, as evidenced by the nice little side business in fake IDs and drug sales that they had been running out of Burning Rome. As soon as the seriousness of the charges became clear to them, they decided to kill a couple of birds with one stone – they could stay in the country via a special arrangement known as a work permit, issued to witnesses of certain crimes if they assisted the prosecution by cooperating in a case in which they were involved; and they could also lay the blame on Tony Solaia, another bartender named Rona Ranken, and the bar's owner, Tom Hedtke, who, according to the Ukrainians, were the true conspirators in the manufacture and sale of the phony IDs and the drugs, as well as the sale of liquor to minors.

Today Hardy sat at the large circular table in what they called the solarium on the main floor of his law offices. It was a large circular room, perhaps twenty feet in diameter, most of it – including the entire roof – made of glass. A veritable forest of indoor plants – palms, ficus, Japanese maple – seemed to bloom in perennial profusion, lending to the feng shui of the space a softer aspect than your typical law firm's conference room.

Next to Hardy, Gina Roake was taking some documents out of her briefcase. 'What I don't understand,' she was saying with a bit of heat, 'is why Wes is going along with prosecuting these bartenders at all. The businesses, the owners, okay, maybe, but most of these guys, like your Tony, what were they supposed to do? Double-ID everybody? And by the way, even if they did that, they would have just seen the same fake IDs that the kids showed at the door. On what legal theory can these charges be sustained?'

'Conspiracy,' Hardy replied. 'Everybody – the owners, the bartenders, the guys checking IDs at the door – they all knew the truth about what was going on.'

'That's ridiculous.'

'I agree with you. And for the record, so does Wes. Meanwhile, he's stuck.'

'He's the DA, Diz. He can get himself unstuck. Just say no. Dismiss the charges against the bartenders, if nothing else. Or at least get 'em knocked down from felonies. I mean, really? Felonies? State prison? That's just absurd. Especially when we know that Igor and Vadim are pure flat-out liars trying to save their own sorry asses so they won't be deported.'

Hardy nodded amicably. 'My call is that Wes is letting it play as it lays for a minute, and then he's going to step in.'

'But why let it play at all when it's so wrong on the face of it?'

Hardy, with a tolerant glance at his partner, said, 'You've been practicing law for how long and can still ask that question?'

Roake sighed. 'I know. You're right.'

'One step after another,' Hardy said. 'Eventually, something happens.'

'Sounds like a Russian novel.'

'Pretty close. Maybe Ukrainian.' Hardy sat back in his chair. 'Changing the subject, did you read about the guy from Goodman's office? Rick Jessup?'

Roake nodded. 'Yeah. Awful.'

'It is awful. It's also potentially close to home. Brittany McGuire – Moses's daughter? – went out with him once a couple of months ago.'

Roake closed the folder she was perusing and turned toward her partner. 'Are the police talking to her?'

'Not that I've heard, but I haven't talked to Mose since it happened. I wouldn't be surprised if they get around to it.'

Gina was silent for a moment. 'What's her situation now? Brittany's?'

'You're going to love this. She appears to be hooking up with Tony Solaia.'

Gina cocked her head. 'Really?'

'Really.' Hardy broke a small smile. 'It's a bit of a disappointment, too, you want to know the truth.'

'Why's that?'

A shrug. 'For starters, he's got at least ten years on her.'

'Last time I checked, didn't you have at least ten years on your blushing bride?'

Hardy grinned. 'I knew you'd say that. And you're right, but it seems different with them.'

'That's for starters, and it's ridiculous, so let's discount it. What else?'

'What else is that it strikes me as a little . . . inappropriate. Moses gives him a job to tide him over when he's going through a tough time, and then he starts going out with the guy's daughter?'

'Maybe he didn't mean to. Maybe it's true love.'

'Of course,' Hardy said. 'Romantic soul that I am, I'd never rule that out. But she's my niece, and I worry about her. Tony's charmed and insinuated himself into a pretty sweet situation, and I guess he moved so fast, I'm leery. Especially since I'm the one who basically put everybody together.' Hardy stared out into the middle distance. 'Anyway, I don't know why I got on to Tony. He's not the issue.'

'So what is the issue? Is there one?'

'I hope not. But evidently, that breakup between Brittany and Jessup – if you can call it breaking up after just one date – didn't go too well. Jessup wanted to see her again, and she wasn't going there. After a few days of stalking her, he apparently pushed her or something—'

'What do you mean, stalking her? He physically attacked her?'

'She fell or tripped or was pushed or something. The bottom line is he did something that put her in the hospital. It's a little unclear exactly what it was. Brittany wouldn't say, or even admit that Jessup did anything. But Moses got suspicious and went down and had a few words with Jessup until he verified what had happened.'

'Uh-oh. And how'd that go?'

Hardy nodded grimly. 'You know Moses. About like you'd expect. He told me he gave Jessup a bit of a tune-up and didn't think he would be much of a problem for Brittany anymore.'

Gina grimaced. 'You think the cops will want to talk to him?'

'It would be a miracle if they didn't. I kind of wanted your take on it. I also thought, on general principle, that you ought to know.' He didn't have to draw Gina a map. Moses in jail, where he might mention the massacre while under stress, or possibly get drunk and talkative on jail-made hooch, was a situation they needed to prevent at all costs.

'I appreciate that.' Then, 'You don't really think he had anything to do with this latest? With Jessup's murder?'

Hardy leveled his gaze at her. 'No comment.'

14

ALTHOUGH THE JESSUP homicide was taking up most of their day-to-day time and imagination, Brady and Sher were almost always working on more than one homicide, and today events surrounding the homicide of Daniel Dejesus were demanding their immediate attention.

On the Sunday one week before Rick Jessup's death, Mr Dejesus, a low-level gangbanger from the lower Mission District, got himself shot by an assailant in a passing car as he stood on a street corner either minding his own business or selling drugs.

The accounts varied.

Although it had been broad daylight and the street was well populated with pedestrians, no one had seen anything. But now, a week and two days later, Juan Rios, the owner of Taco Rios – the taqueria in front of which Daniel had spent his last minutes – decided that he needed to talk to the inspectors who'd inter-viewed him a week before.

It seemed that Juan had rushed out after hearing the shots and taken a photograph with his cell phone of the getaway car as it drove away. The picture had been in his phone since he'd taken it, but he had wanted to wait and see if somebody else would come forward with evidence, so it wouldn't have to be him. As it was, Juan wanted assurances of protection for him and his family if he was going to be any kind of witness. In any event, he wanted the violence in his neighborhood to stop, and the police were welcome to the picture of the car to do with as they saw fit, even if Juan wasn't personally involved.

The two inspectors spent a frustrating but possibly important hour with the local restaurateur. They said they understood what he wanted, but people in hell wanted ice water. If he were subpoenaed, he would come to court and testify or, with the deepest sorrow and regret, they would come and put him in jail. They didn't leave with his commitment to testify, or any deal about his protection, though they did have a good shot not only of the red low-rider Chevrolet but of its license plate. With that, even lacking Rios's testimony, Sher and Brady thought they might be able to shake something loose in the case.

After they got back in their car, Sher turned the ignition but did not shift it into gear. She stayed in the parking place, her face expressionless, her eyes half closed.

'Don't let him get you down,' Brady said, 'he's just scared. He'll come around, and even if he doesn't, we—'

Sher held up a hand, stopping him, and turned her head. 'We're morons,' she said.

'No. We had to get what he had, even if—'

'Not that,' she said, cutting him off again. 'Jessup.'

'What about him?'

'Not him. Let's start with her, the rape victim.'

'Who shall remain nameless because—'

'Right. Privilege. But guess what? We know that our victim, Jessup, dated her a while ago, right? And she must have dumped him, since we also know that he was trying to get back with her.'

'Okay. But so what?'

'So how hard could it be?'

Brady thought about it for two seconds, then said, 'Goodman's office. City hall. Where he worked.'

'That's what I'm talking about,' she said, slamming the car into gear, peeling out into the traffic.

The supervisor wasn't in and hadn't been since a half hour after he'd gotten the news about Jessup. In Goodman's absence and with the tragedy, the office had ceased to function. Diane Galen had sent the interns home at lunchtime, and when Sher and Brady knocked on the locked outer door, she greeted them with a weary politeness, then led them into a small and windowless conference room where she apparently had been sitting with a cup of coffee.

They'd gotten through the preliminaries, and Sher had started to give Diane their condolences, when the woman waved her off rather abruptly. 'This is a very difficult and confusing time,' she said, 'and I don't mean for this to sound callous, but I'm afraid that I wouldn't say Rick and I were exactly friends. We didn't see each other outside of work. I think he considered me and the interns somewhat beneath him. He made it very clear that there were the professionals – which included himself and Mr Goodman – and then everyone else was more or less staff. Although in terms of longevity in the office, I am by far the most senior.'

Sher leaned forward, elbows on the table. 'He didn't share many of his personal feelings with members of the staff?'

'No. He did see Mr Goodman outside the office from time to time.'

'In your opinion, would anyone here besides Mr Goodman know anything about Mr Jessup's personal life?'

'I don't think so. Although you could ask the interns when they come back in, which should be tomorrow.'

'Will Mr Goodman be back then, too?'

'I hope so. We haven't been in contact since he left yesterday.'

'So they were close? Mr Jessup and Mr Goodman?'

Diane found something of interest in the grain of the table, and she studied it for a moment or two. 'Perhaps less close than they used to be. You know they came to work here together from Mr Goodman's law practice before he was elected. I don't suppose it's any secret that Mr Goodman is thinking about running for mayor and that Mr Jessup had *planned* to move up with him.'

The inspectors exchanged a glance. This was far removed from what they'd come here to discuss, but they would get to that in due time. They were investigating a murder, and if an unexpected path opened up, it was usually worth exploring. Brady took the ball from his partner and said, 'Did those plans appear to be changing?'

Diane took another minute, then she sighed. 'I don't mean to speak ill of the dead, but Mr Jessup had a pronounced streak of arrogance that, most of the time, in public, he managed to camouflage very well. He was very jealous of his place in Mr Goodman's life. In the past few months, trying to control access to Mr Goodman, he managed to alienate a few large donors to the campaign, notably Jon Lo, and I think Mr Goodman became aware of that, or was made aware of it. Some days there would be a palpable tension in the office. I don't know if Mr Goodman now would be a source for information about Mr Jessup's private life.'

'Well,' Sher said, 'thank you. We'll keep that in mind when we talk to Mr Goodman. Actually, we were hoping you might know the names of any of Mr Jessup's girlfriends, or women he dated, who might have had significance.'

She was shaking her head. 'No, I didn't know who he dated, and I don't have—' Abruptly, she stopped. 'Wait a minute. A woman he dated?'

'Yes. And broke up with, or she with him, a couple of months ago.'

Diane raised her eyes to one of the room's corners, and the

two inspectors let her remember. At last she came back to them. 'A man came by here several weeks ago, asking for Mr Jessup. He told Rick to stop bothering his daughter, and then they both went out to the hallway. Rick never came back in that day. I think he was out a couple of days after that. The rumor among the interns was that the man had hit him out in the hall. Can you give me a minute?'

'As much as you need,' Brady said.

Getting up, Diane left the room with a resolute stride. Brady crossed his fingers and held them up, and Sher nodded in acknowledgment, then sat back in her chair and crossed her arms to wait.

'Okay,' Diane said as she came back through the door, appointment book in hand. 'I've got it. I keep the calendar for both Mr Goodman and Mr Jessup. It's critical to have a record of who's been in to see whom in this business. Even though this man didn't have an appointment, he introduced himself to me, and I put him in the log. He was' – she looked down as she read – 'Moses McGuire, owner of a bar called the Little Shamrock. He said it was about his daughter Brittany.'

Business wasn't exactly booming at the Shamrock. Happy hour wouldn't start for another forty-five minutes; there were only five customers, a middle-aged tourist couple at one of the tables, Dave with his Miller Lite in his usual place up at the front of the bar, and two hipsters in the back room playing darts. Lyle Lovett's 'This Old Porch' played low through the music system.

Back at the well area, Moses McGuire checked the front door one more time, just to be sure no one else was coming in, and then – seeing no one – he free-poured a half inch or so of vodka, a tiny refresher, into his club soda, squeezed in another wedge of lime. He'd barely taken the first sip when another couple appeared through the large plate-glass window that looked out onto Lincoln Way. A moment later, they were standing in front of him.

Not customers, as it turned out.

They laid their badges on the bar in front of him, and the glib McGuire said, 'I don't need your IDs. You guys look twenty-one to me.'

Paul Brady's entirely businesslike smile came and went as he introduced himself and his partner and said they were hoping to talk to Moses McGuire.

'You found him. How can I help you?'

Sher told him what they were investigating and asked if he'd heard about it.

'I have. I read about it this morning.'

'Did you know Mr Jessup?' Brady asked.

'I did. I talked to him a couple of times. I was wondering when you guys would come by. He dated my daughter a few months ago and treated her badly, so I went and found him and told him he should leave her alone.'

Brady again. 'And how did he take that?'

'I think I convinced him that it would be a good idea.'

'Did you strike him?'

McGuire sipped from his glass. 'Do you have a report saying that I did?'

'Is that a yes or a no?' Sher asked.

'It's an entirely separate question,' McGuire said evenly. 'Are you talking to me because I'm a suspect in his murder?'

The question obviously set the two inspectors back for a beat or two as they exchanged glances. Sher said, 'We don't have any suspects yet. We've barely begun to look.'

Brady added, 'That's another way to say everybody's a potential suspect.'

'Do you want to answer our question?' Sher asked. 'Did you strike Mr Jessup?'

McGuire lifted his glass again, took a serious pull. 'Yes, I did. I didn't really hurt him. I just wanted to get his attention.' He wiped away an imaginary speck on the bar with his towel, then looked back up at the inspectors. 'When was he killed?'

Sher got half a nod from Brady, tacit permission. 'Two days ago. Sunday evening sometime.'

'Sunday,' McGuire repeated. 'Sunday's my day off here, as luck would have it. Sunday and Monday.' He hesitated, squinting in apparent concentration as he tried to dredge up the memory. At last it came. 'I was fishing from about four o'clock till dusk out on the beach by the yacht club. The St Francis.'

'We didn't ask,' Brady said.

'No, but I thought it couldn't hurt to get that out of the way.'

Sher asked, 'Any luck? Fishing, I mean?'

'Couple of small ones I threw back.'

'Were you alone?'

McGuire inclined his head a fraction of an inch. 'I was, except for the usual half dozen Asians or so, who would probably remember me, since I was the only Irish guy down there. Now I've got one for you, if you don't mind. If I'm not a suspect in this killing, what did you want to see me about?'

At the end of the bar, Dave brought his empty beer bottle down with a thump. Several years north of seventy, Dave wasn't much of a raconteur, and when the service slowed to the point where the bartender didn't notice he'd gone dry, he'd tap his bottle with increasing intensity as the seconds ticked.

Lyle Lovett had given way to Michael Bublé crooning 'Everything.'

McGuire excused himself, turned and opened the refrigerator, then popped another bottle of beer and took it down to Dave. When he came back, he asked, 'Where were we?'

Brady told him, 'You were asking why did we want to see you. And the answer is we didn't necessarily. The fact is, we wanted to talk to your daughter Brittany, and you were the fastest way to get to her.'

'Why do you want to talk to her?'

Brady came right back at him. 'Why don't you tell us how to reach her, and then she can tell you after we talk?'

'Because you're Homicide inspectors, and if you want to talk to Brittany, it's going to be about Mr Jessup, isn't it? What is it, exactly, that you want to know?'

'Mr McGuire' – Sher stepped in to ramp down the intensity – 'we understand your concerns and your desire to protect your daughter. We can tell you that she is not an active suspect, but she may have information on the case, and we'll need to talk to her to find out if it relates and how. Does that seem so unreasonable?'

'I never said it was unreasonable. I asked why you wanted to talk to her, and now you've told me. Which you could have done from the get-go instead of laying all of this suspect nonsense on me first.'

'Look,' Brady said, 'you assaulted a guy who later got killed. At some point, we were going to follow that up, so while we had you here—'

'Look yourself,' McGuire shot back, 'the guy assaulted my daughter. I delivered a message that I'm pretty sure he got the gist of. Which I thought would be the end of the story. And now you want to talk to Brittany but won't tell me what you think she knows. Damn straight I'm trying to protect her.'

As they were rolling back downtown, Sher said, 'Bottom line, he gave us her number. We ought to be thankful for small favors.'

'Favor my ass.' Brady was hot from the conversation. 'You're telling me that the guy finds out his daughter's been raped and he doesn't do something about it? I wanted to take his picture on my phone and go show him to some of our witnesses.'

'Oh yeah, getting his permission for that? That would have calmed things down.'

'I didn't want to calm things down. I wasn't necessarily going to ask his permission, either. McGuire admits he assaulted our victim. That puts him closer than anybody else.'

'Paul, come on. Maybe there's a connection between hitting a guy and knocking his brains out with a club. Let's remember, we don't even know for sure that Brittany was raped. All we know is she was dating Jessup at one time. It could have been anybody he happened to rape on Saturday. We've got to get to that first if we're going to get anywhere with McGuire.'

'No. First we pull his DL picture and six-pack it to our witnesses.'

'Well, of course.' That was standard procedure, taking McGuire's photograph from his California driver's license, inserting it into a plastic sleeve with five other photographs – a six-pack – and hoping to get a positive identification. 'I just don't want you to get all psyched up.'

'Perish the thought. I think we can at least admit there's a likelihood that the rape and the murder are connected, wouldn't you say?'

'That's what we're going on,' Sher said. 'It'd be a stretch if it were anything else.'

15

WHEN WES FARRELL got home – a small Victorian house across the street from Buena Vista Park in the Haight – his keen perceptive ability sensed something amiss right away. The chair tipped over on its side in his dining room was the first clue, but the full roll of paper towels on the kitchen floor was another good indication.

Sighing, he picked up the offending debris, then took off his suit coat and hung it over the back of the chair. He considered removing his dress shirt and tie, hoping for a little giggle with today's T-shirt – which read MAMMALS SUCK – but if history was any indication, his sense of humor would not assuage Sam when she was embroiled in a holy cause.

As she was today.

He climbed the steep staircase to their bedroom and, when he discovered she wasn't there, continued to the ladder off the hallway that ended in a half doorway out to the roof. Sam, most beautiful when she was fiery, sat facing him in a low director's chair, arms crossed. Behind her, the sun was unmolested by cloud cover all the way out to the horizon, and in the insane perversity that was San Francisco's weather, the temperature hovered near eighty with nary a hint of breeze – a gorgeous evening.

Wes ascended onto the flat deck they'd built, sixty square feet surrounded by little peaks of roof, protecting them from sight and, on most nights, from wind. He offered an apologetic smile and said, 'I just think the kitchen chair looks better the normal way, on its legs. But the paper towels were a good idea. Who knew? Just unroll 'em first, and it saves a ton of time.'

She had her head canted to one side. Her voice, when it came, was barely audible. 'I told you about the connection to Rick Jessup because I thought it might help bring his murderer to justice, but only under the *express condition* that his victim would remain unnamed, as always. Do you remember that?'

'Yes, of course, but—'

'No buts. This is not a new deal. I believe we've had more than a couple of discussions about it over the years. Who do I hear from twenty minutes before it's time to go home but the woman herself, completely distraught – overwrought, Wes, betrayed by us, the very people who promised to protect her!'

'I didn't—'

'*Yes, you did.* How else could they have found her so fast? The police were at her apartment today. Today! Hours after I told you.'

'And I'm supposed to feel bad?'

'How can you not? This is completely wrong. The last few days have been traumatic enough for the poor girl, and now she finds herself in the middle of a murder investigation that she doesn't want any part of. She might even be a suspect, because getting raped is a motive to kill someone, isn't it? Look where she is now. And all because I thought you could keep it to yourself.'

'Which I did. Listen, ask yourself this: how could they get the woman's name from me? This just in, I never had it. As you know. They went looking for Jessup and found a connection. It was good police work, that's all. So what are they supposed to do? Ignore it, ignore her? I don't think so. Maybe she did kill him. We don't know yet.'

'How can you say that? She's the *victim*, Wes.'

'Victims have been known to fight back, even to kill.'

'Spoken like a true prosecutor.'

'Hey! Check it out. That's what I do. Prosecute people.'

'People I'm trying to protect.'

'Not usually, Sam. Usually, I prosecute bad people, people who've done terrible things. Did your victim tell you they're charging her?'

'No.'

'Well, then. Did she admit that Jessup raped her? I mean, to the cops?'

'I don't know.'

'You don't know? All of this angst and accusation, and you don't know?'

'That's not the point.'

'It sure seems like the point to me.'

'No. The point is that what happened to her is confidential unless she chooses to disclose it. She came to us and trusted us, and because I told my boyfriend her rapist's name, trying to do the right thing, the cops are at her home. That is plain wrong. You never should have given them Jessup's name.'

'Let me repeat, neither of us has a clue how the inspectors got to this woman whose name, P.S., I still don't know. Plus, that's exactly what I had to do if he raped somebody on Saturday night—'

'He did.'

'All right, he did. Seeing as he did, somebody might have killed him because of it. If your victim can help us find that person, then we need her, and we've got every right to talk to her to find out. How is that not obvious?'

She sulked down into herself. 'You never would have argued this before you were the DA.'

'You know what, Sam? I don't care. I'm arguing it now because it's right. Your victim wants to keep the shame of the rape – if there is any – to herself? That's her call. But when she comes to you, it's on the record. If you want my real opinion, you and your center should be mandated to report. You hear about a rape – especially a date rape, like this one – you get the guy's name, if the victim knows it, and call the cops. That's the only thing that will put these scumbags in prison: victims who will testify against them. If that's too big a burden, well, excuse me all to hell.'

Sam stared at him for a good twenty seconds, then shook her head. 'I don't know you anymore.' Standing up, she walked by him, got to the ladder, and stopped. 'I really don't.' She started down and pulled the door shut behind her.

Her husband's sobriety had lasted long enough that the bitter, difficult memories of Moses's drunken past had blurred for Susan Weiss. Her brain had edited out most of the brawling fights, the scuffles, the language, the blood. She considered it a miracle, really, that little of that drunken misbehavior had come home to roost. Their apartment had always been his sanctuary, his castle, sometimes his hospital; out in the world was where he'd gotten himself into trouble.

Though it worried her, part of Susan didn't blame Moses – or at least she was reluctant to call him on it – for the occasional drink she knew he'd started to take over the past couple of months. Certainly the events of the last few days could have driven anyone to whatever crutch fueled an escape from harsh reality.

Agonizing over the pain and heartbreak her daughter was enduring after the rape – to say nothing of her own – Susan had drunk a full bottle of chardonnay herself on Sunday night. She had been unable to stop pouring while waiting for Moses to get home from wherever he'd gone, so she empathized somewhat with her husband's struggle.

But now, at one A.M. on Wednesday, he was waking her up with a phone call that was all but unintelligible. She eventually realized that he needed her to come down to the Shamrock and pick him up. He had walked to his shift at the bar earlier in the day, as usual, so he had no car, and taxicabs out in the Avenues were so rare as to be practically nonexistent. 'And the keys? The extras.'

'What about them?'

He managed to get out a few words, slurring heavily. 'Can't find mine, ones I brought down, an' need to lock up.'

Ten minutes later, she pulled up to the open curb directly in front of the bar; a dim light shone in the back. She honked twice and waited. She honked again. No sign of movement inside.

She let out a breath, got out of the car, slammed the door behind her, crossed the sidewalk, and pushed at the Shamrock's door, which was locked. 'Goddammit.' She slapped a flat palm on the door's glass front. 'Moses!'

No reply.

She remembered that she had grabbed the extra keys at home, so she dug in her purse, unlocked the door, and swung it open. Hearing an unexpected sound, she looked down and saw the original keys on the floor.

She called his name, again got no response.

Okay, she was thinking. This is serious. Then she heard a snort, a snore, some guttural noise.

She moved ahead. In the sixty watts of light emanating from the lone Tiffany lamp, she could make out a figure passed out on one of the couches in the living room-style seating area at the back of the room. As she got closer, she saw one arm hanging down, resting on the floor next to a nearly empty bottle.

She whispered to herself, 'Jesus.'

'You really can't wake him up?' Frannie asked.

'No. I've tried some cold bar towels on his face. He's out. I don't know how much he's had, but he's almost completely unresponsive. I wouldn't have called you and Diz if I had any idea what to do.'

'I know. Don't worry about that. You're sure there's no way you can move him?'

'Frannie, he weighs two hundred pounds, and right now all of it is deadweight. I'm a hundred and twenty. I could barely straighten him up.'

'But you've got him straightened up now?'

'In case he threw up. I didn't want him choking on it.'

Next to her, Hardy whispered, 'Is he alive? Is he breathing?'

Frannie nodded, a finger over her mouth, listening.

'I'm thinking I should maybe call an ambulance.'

'That might be a good idea.'

'What's a good idea?' Hardy asked.

'An ambulance,' Frannie said.

That word got Hardy moving. He slapped at his cheeks a couple of times, threw the covers off, and sat up on the side of the bed. 'Can you let me talk to her?'

Frannie handed the phone to him.

'Susan,' he asked, 'does he have a pulse? Is he breathing?'

'Yes. But, Diz, I can't wake him up. I'm afraid he might die. People die from too much alcohol, don't they?'

'Sometimes. You'd better call an ambulance. We'll be right down there.'

'I don't want to ask—'

'Shut up. We're family. You call us when you're in trouble. It's one of the rules. Listen to me. You need to hang up right now and dial 911. If the ambulance gets there before we do, call my cell and tell us where they're taking him, and we'll meet you there. Clear?'

'All right.'

'Okay. Do it now!'

Driving through the night, under the overhung branches in the western end of Golden Gate Park, Hardy was too worried and too angry to trust himself to speak. Next to him as he sped on the deserted streets, Frannie found her own voice. 'Did you know he'd started again?'

'No.'

'Susan said it's been a couple of months now.'

'Nice of her to let us know.'

'Diz, this isn't her fault in any way. This is my brother.'

'If she knew, she might have mentioned it. That's all I'm saying. There's a tiny little bit riding on him staying sober. You realize that, don't you?'

'So it's about that?'

He shot a glance across at her. 'At least a goddamn portion of it is about that.'

'You don't have to yell at me.'

'I'm not yelling. Yelling entails volume, not only the use of mild profanity. If I'm yelling at anything, it's not you. It's the situation.' He reached over, touched her thigh. 'For the record, I'm grateful you're here with me. You'll keep me from killing him, if he hasn't taken care of that on his own.'

'Don't say that. I'm sure he wasn't trying to kill himself. Maybe he just didn't know his tolerance after all this time, or more likely, he forgot it.'

'Right. Maybe.'

'And I couldn't not come with you. He's my brother, after all. You're the one who doesn't need to be here, doesn't have to be doing this.' She put her hand over his. 'You might slow down a little. If we get in an accident, we won't help anybody.'

'We're not going to get in an accident.' But he lifted his accelerator foot slightly. 'Just to be clear, I'm not doing this out of Christian charity. I'm supremely pissed off. I've got an incredibly busy day tomorrow that I'll have to walk through like a zombie, if I don't fall asleep in the courtroom. The only reason I'm in this car is so I can be there when your moron of a brother wakes up, if he does, and make sure he doesn't get to chatting with his doctors or nurses or the fucking janitorial staff and let slip a little detail or two about something that might have been nagging at him for, oh, six years or so.'

'He's not going to do that.'

Hardy chuffed out an empty laugh. 'He sure could, Fran. And the very real fear that he would was why he stopped drinking, you may recall. The topic kept popping up when he'd had a few. He couldn't stop himself, the philosopher in him, it was all so goddamned interesting. So he stopped drinking instead. Thank God.' Hardy slammed a hand down on the steering wheel. 'What an idiot. What's he thinking? That he can handle it? He can't. He's already proved it a hundred times, a thousand times.'

'Diz. It's a disease. He can't help it.'

'I'm not sure I buy that. But he sure as hell can stop himself from taking that first drink, can't he? We've seen him pull that one off. So he can do it, and he's got to keep doing it.'

'Something must have happened.'

'Damn straight something happened. He fell off the goddamn wagon is what happened.'

Arriving at Lincoln Way, Hardy turned left sixteen blocks out from the Shamrock. Though it was dry, the black street glistened under the overheads and stretched out empty before them. He picked up speed again.

'No,' Frannie said, 'I know that. What I mean is that there must have been a specific reason. Otherwise, why now?'

Hardy looked over at her. 'You really want to know what I think? I think something woke up the vigilante in him. It was close enough to what we all did, and equally justified. And suddenly, there wasn't any point trying to deny what he felt he needed to do. He just did it. And he found he needed a drink.'

'You're talking about after that thing with Brittany, the guy who hurt her.'

'He could have gotten arrested for what he did, you realize

that? It's pure good fortune that the kid didn't call the cops. Now that I think about it, I bet you money Mose had a few the night he told us about it. Hey, he got the bad guy. Something to brag about, right? Have a drink, tell a secret, justify what you did, then have another drink and forget you're confessing to one and all that you actually did it. And here's my favorite part.' No ambulance had arrived yet. Hardy parked right behind Susan's car. 'Then go have another drink or five so you can live with what you've done.'

16

At five o'clock, after logging about forty-five minutes of troubled sleep, Hardy gave up and went downstairs to get himself started on caffeine for the day. For his last birthday, Frannie had given him a Jura espresso maker, the kind Lisbeth Salander used in the Stieg Larsson books. Hardy thought it was as good as advertised, and this morning he would need every drop it could give him.

The machine took a minute or so to warm up, and he used the time to feed his tropical fish. His twenty-eight little babies were all swimming around happily, picking up few if any of the negative vibrations that Hardy was certain he was exuding from every pore.

Placing his coffee mug under the dual spigots, he pressed the start button three times (the strongest blend); while the coffee dripped, he walked up through the house and out the front door into the still-dark morning, where the air seemed to promise another unusually pleasant day. The well of his discontent, near the brim to begin with, overflowed as he discovered that today's *Chronicle* had not yet arrived and probably would not appear for close to an hour.

Fucking Moses, he thought.

Back in the kitchen, he boosted himself onto the counter and sipped his coffee, his mind a blank. Gradually, the caffeine gained a foothold, the pounding in his head abated, his breathing slowed. He closed his eyes more to relax for a moment than to surrender to any urge to sleep. When he opened them again, his gaze fell upon the pearl-black cast-iron pan that hung from its marlin hook over the stove. It was one of the very few artifacts he'd kept from his parents' home. After every use, he cleaned it with salt and a soft rag – no soap, no water – and because it was perfectly seasoned, perfect in its function, nothing he cooked in it ever stuck.

He opened the refrigerator, which, since the kids had left home, had degenerated into a culinary wasteland, with little in the way of real edibles. Frannie had taken to shopping after work nearly every day for dinner, buying small portions for the two of them, thereby avoiding most leftovers and waste. Looking now, Hardy saw condiments galore – seven different types of mustard, an equal number of various hot sauces – two bottles of white wine, and about a dozen assorted beers, but the actual food was limited to four eggs, a small block of cheddar cheese, and the remains of Sunday's dinner: corned beef, potatoes, carrots and cabbage in a clear plastic container.

It would have to do.

Taking down the black pan, which weighed nearly five pounds, he put it on the front burner, turned the heat up high, and threw in a quarter stick of butter. He tipped back his mug and finished the coffee. Suddenly ravenous and moving quickly, he dumped all the leftovers onto the cutting board and chopped and mixed until there was one relatively homogenous pile, which he hefted into the pan with the foaming butter.

While the next cup of coffee dripped out of the spigots into the mug, he turned down the heat a little and moved the hash to one side, then broke two eggs into the cleared area. Finally, after grating some cheddar over the whole thing, he covered it with a lid from another pan that fit perfectly, as if by magic.

While it all cooked, he sipped coffee and brought sriracha and Tabasco over to the table in the dining room, where he was going to sit down to a real breakfast and savor every bite and, until he could get some distance and perspective, try not to think about what he'd learned from Susan last night while they were waiting to find out whether Moses was going to die: that Rick Jessup had raped Brittany McGuire on Saturday night.

'So let me get this straight,' Glitsky said. 'You found a woman who dumped Jessup a few months ago, after which he beat her up, and then this woman's father went and assaulted him. We got a soap opera going on here.'

'A little bit,' Brady said.

They were in Glitsky's office, on the folding chairs in front of his desk, first thing in the morning.

'Why do you think Jessup raped this woman and not someone else?'

Sher sat hunched forward. 'We don't know if we think it, Abe. We went and talked to her and—'

'How did you find her?'

'Her father all but left his card at Goodman's office,' Sher said. 'The secretary there had him in the calendar.'

'Okay, nice work. Go on.'

Brady took it up. 'So we went and talked to her yesterday, and she seemed . . . distraught.'

'She was being interviewed by Homicide cops, and an ex-boyfriend had been murdered. You think that might have contributed to her distress?'

The two inspectors shared a glance, after which Sher nodded. 'Of course.'

'You didn't specifically ask about the rape?'

'No, sir,' Brady said. 'I was afraid if I started with that, it might end the conversation. There's a lot she might be able to tell us that doesn't have anything to do with the rape.'

'I'm with you on that. Keep her talking. Maybe she'll get loose enough to tell us everything, and this whole privilege thing goes away.'

'But,' Sher said, 'if she doesn't admit she was raped . . .'

'Then it never happened.'

Brady straightened up and slapped his palms on his thighs. 'I think it was this girl, Abe. Both of us do.'

'You haven't asked her?'

'If she was raped on Saturday night?' Sher asked. 'No. But she did tell us she'd seen him recently.'

'And she said?'

'She went quiet for about an hour,' Brady said. 'Well, a minute that seemed like an hour. And then she said she had a drink with him at Perry's on Saturday. He wanted to get back together, and she went there to try and let him down easy. That's the last time she saw him.'

'No mention of rape?'

Brady shook his head. 'None.'

Glitsky chewed at his cheek. 'What are the odds she killed him?'

'Essentially zero,' Sher said.

'She is not remotely a guy,' Brady said. 'And I like our guy with the club.'

'So maybe the rape the night before had nothing to do with the murder?'

Sher made a face. 'Do you believe that, Abe?'

'No. Not really. But if it was this woman you talked to yesterday, and she won't acknowledge it, I think we're stuck.'

Brady sat back, frustration all over him. 'I realize I'm a Neanderthal, but I really don't understand why they won't acknowledge it. I mean, they're the victims. They're not going to get in trouble, saying what happened to them.'

'They might,' Sher replied, 'if their rapist decides to shut them up before they testify.'

'Or,' Glitsky added, 'if their rapist turns up murdered. Then they've got a motive to have killed him.'

'While we're at it,' Sher said, 'it gives somebody else a motive. Like her boyfriend, for example, or her father, who already went down and beat up on Jessup after he assaulted the daughter the first time. But that all goes away – the motive, I mean – if the rape is never acknowledged.'

'You're saying you think it's the father?' Glitsky asked.

'I don't know if I'd go that far. But if it is, it would give her a reason to deny the rape.'

Brady said, 'Then why'd she go to the center in the first place?'

Sher shrugged. 'Maybe that was her first reaction, all freaked out, not knowing what to do, and remember, that was before Jessup was killed . . . But then she finds out he's dead, and it's a brand-new ball game.'

'Still,' Glitsky said, 'let's not forget that we don't have the rape. Period. So all this is pure conjecture. What's the father look like?'

Brady, who'd started bobbing his head in agreement about halfway through Sher's hypotheticals, said, 'Not to get all excited about things, but he pretty much fits the description of our guy with the club.'

Glitsky narrowed his eyes. 'You're kidding me.'

'Not really,' Brady said. 'Not even a little.'

'What's this guy's name?' Glitsky asked.

'McGuire,' Sher replied. 'Moses McGuire. He runs a bar out in the Avenues.'

Glitsky didn't even trust himself to talk to Treya.

After Sher and Brady left his office, he gave it five minutes and then, his stomach churning, moseyed out toward the general area of the rest-room and kept on going, first to the world's slowest elevator, then down to the lobby and out the Hall of Justice's back door, past the morgue and the jail and into the parking lot.

Fifteen minutes later, going on instinct alone because rational thought felt too dangerous, he drove almost all the way back to his duplex, but after getting to Third Avenue on Geary, he realized where he'd been heading and turned right and drove the short block up to Clement. Here, a small duplex building, typical in this part of town, sat a couple of doorways down from the corner. At this time of the morning, parking turned out to be no problem, a sign of if not actual divine intervention then at least some kind of cosmic approbation.

It didn't escape Glitsky's notice that the relationship between his eighty-five-year-old father, Nat, and his wife, Sadie, was a direct consequence of the events that had led to the Dockside Massacre. Six years before, the thugs killed by Glitsky, Hardy, Moses, Gina, and John Holiday at Pier 70 had robbed Sam Silverman's pawnshop, shooting him to death, leaving Sadie widowed. That a loving second marriage for both had bloomed from this barren soil was a blessing neither had anticipated and both treasured.

Abe touched the mezuzah on their doorpost, then pressed the bell.

'Abraham.' Nat's iceberg-blue eyes – which Glitsky had inherited – sparkled at the sight of his son in the doorway.

'Nathaniel.'

The old man stepped forward and reached up with both hands, then brought his son's face down for a kiss. 'It is so good to see you.'

'You, too, Pops. Sadie okay?'

'Still a wonder of the world. Are you staying more than a minute? Come on up and find out.'

Nat and Sadie had a nice-sized, east-facing outdoor patio off the kitchen at the back of their flat, which, because of the weather, they could enjoy only about thirty days out of the year. Today was one of those days. They had a large Cinzano umbrella open and tilted for some shade, and the three of them sat at the mesh-metal picnic table, sipping tea in dainty cups. They fell into discussing plans for Passover, coming up in two days, which they'd be celebrating at Abe's place.

Treya and Sadie had already worked out most of those logistics, and at last Nat said, 'I'm sure it will be a seder to end all seders. Moses himself may never have had such a seder. But I'm not sure that's what brought Abraham over here this morning.' He leveled a piercing look at his son.

Abe put down his cup. 'I can't believe you just brought up Moses.'

'I should bring up somebody else? Passover, the Exodus, Moses. They all go together.'

'No, it's not— Never mind that. It's just a problem I'm having. The guy's name is Moses.'

'What's the problem?'

Abe laid out the basics, omitting his involvement – or anyone else's – in the Dockside Massacre. 'The point is, I know this guy pretty well. We've done things together. He's Dismas Hardy's brother-in-law, and though he's not my favorite person, he's not a bad guy. And now, with no proof at all, I'm ninety percent certain that he's committed this homicide. So for personal reasons, I don't want him to be arrested.'

'Do you think he was justified?' Sadie asked. 'After all, if the man he killed raped his daughter . . .'

'You may want to,' Abe said, 'but you can't just go murdering people who hurt your children.'

Sadie clucked and sighed. 'I understand wanting to, though.'

'Everybody understands it,' Abe said. 'But it's against the law.'

'If that's so clear,' Nat asked, 'what's your problem?'

'I've got a few of them, Pops. First is, I'm more or less sworn to uphold the law. If I don't do that, what have I been thinking all these years? More immediately, there are my inspectors.'

'What about them?'

Abe paused, twirling his teacup. 'It might seem straightforward enough. But this is very hard.'

'We've got time, Abraham. Take all you need.'

Abe let out another breath. 'I find myself wanting them to go slow on the pursuit of this rape. If the victim – that's Moses's daughter – doesn't admit it, then it never officially happened. Needless to say, once they really pick up the scent and see it as a motive for the homicide, my inspectors will be pushing her hard to admit it. Talk to her friends, go to her work, pull her phone records, the whole shebang. On the other hand, if I tell them to back off . . .' He stopped, sighed again. 'If my role is to tell them not to do *their* job – which is identifying this killer – then what am I doing in *my* job?'

'Could you just,' his father asked, 'what is the word – recuse yourself from this one case?'

'And not say why? Not give a reason?'

'If he's your friend . . .'

Abe was shaking his head. 'Then I'd really be saying, "I know who you're looking for, but I can't tell you." I don't think that would fly on gilded wings, Pops.'

'No. Probably not.'

'Besides, if I back off this case because he's my friend, whoever takes over will have to lean over the other way and arrest McGuire, just to prove he's being impartial and not doing me a favor.'

'Would it be so bad to let Moses get to trial?' Nat asked.

Abe scratched at the table. Moses going to trial could in itself become a minefield. He could imagine any number of scenarios where a stressed-out or exhausted Moses might slip and say something incriminating about the massacre to a fellow inmate, an appointed attorney. He didn't think it likely, but there was a remote possibility that Moses might be tempted to trade his terrible secret – their terrible secret – for leniency, some kind of a plea deal. Glitsky couldn't mention any of this to his father. Instead, he said, 'One thing, it might cost me a best friend.'

'You don't think Dismas would understand? If you were just doing your job? You've been on opposite sides other times and pulled through.'

'Maybe, but this feels different. This is Frannie's only brother.'

Sadie joined in. 'But you don't know for sure that it was Moses's daughter who was raped. Didn't you say that?'

'Right.'

'And even if she was, that doesn't mean Moses is the killer. I'm not trying to give you an excuse to do something you're uncomfortable with,' she said, 'but as long as you don't know for sure that this rape occurred, then the real answer – the true answer, if anybody asks you – is "I don't know." You're not withholding a fact you know to be true.'

Nat produced a dry chuckle. 'Note the tortured Talmudic rationalization,' he said. 'Where, supposedly, I am the scriptural scholar in this family.'

Sadie smiled at her husband. 'You're around it enough, it rubs off. But Abe, what about that?'

'It's fine as far as it goes, Sadie. There's also the point that if we got anything by abusing or even compromising a privileged communication, it would be inadmissible anyway. So I can tell myself I'm actually helping the case, if they can find a way to make it.'

'I hear a "but",' Nat said.

'That's the problem, Pops,' Glitsky said. 'I hear a whole chorus of 'em.'

Glitsky found a parking place on Tenth Avenue, around the corner from the Little Shamrock. As was the case when he'd dropped in on his father and Sadie, he wasn't clear in his own head what had brought him here.

Whatever it was, it was to no avail, since the front door was locked, the interior dark.

Glitsky's lips went tight in frustration. On the window, the hours of operation were listed as noon to two A.M. He checked his watch – eleven-twenty – and reasoned that somebody should be coming around to open the place any minute now.

With his hands in his pockets and one foot propped against

the wall, he watched the traffic in the glaring sunlight while he checked his watch five times in the space of three minutes.

Ninth Avenue near Irving Street, just south of the Shamrock, held its own nicely amid the heady bazaar of available foodstuffs that you'd find in the Mission or on Clement Street. Following some vestigial memory of smell and taste – before Glitsky stopped drinking, before children, when they were young cops together, he and Hardy sometimes hung out at the Shamrock, went around the corner for food, and returned to the bar for darts and philosophy and nightcaps – Glitsky found himself strolling, an activity not in his usual repertoire, and enjoying himself in the unaccustomed warmth, the air redolent with exotic spices and great smells: Italian, Thai, Middle Eastern, American diners and delis, juiceries, a brew pub, and a coffee shop.

And then there it was, almost exactly as he'd remembered it, the Russian bakery that sold piroshki – the savory, meat-filled, doughnut-like pastry that he hadn't tasted in probably two decades. The woman behind the counter, who hadn't mastered English in her own twenty-plus years of service, was nevertheless sweet and cooperative and understood enough of Glitsky's pointing that he wound up with what he wanted: two of them and a bottle of sparkling water.

He sat, the lone customer, on one of the three stools in front of an eating counter in the tiny front window. Gradually, the yawning emptiness of uncertainty in his gut gave way to the satisfaction of the peasant comfort food, and he found the urgency of Moses McGuire had receded to a bearable level.

It was a simple equation. None of the privileged information from the Rape Crisis Counseling Center could be used in court. Therefore, the only responsible action, from Glitsky's perspective, was to tell his inspectors to follow the evidence but evaluate the case on what they could prove. Which was what he was doing.

The letter of the law.

PART
THREE

17

At a few minutes past noon, an exhausted Dismas Hardy stood on the front steps of the Hall of Justice, clogged as they often were with the dregs of humanity, talking to his sister-in-law on his cell phone. 'How is he?' he asked.

'I'm afraid he's going to live.'

'You don't mean that.'

'More than you'd think. Do you realize what this is doing to Brittany?'

'What "what" is doing to Brittany?'

'Dismas, she feels like she killed this boy.'

'Don't say that. I mean it, Susan, don't say it out loud, even to me. Or anybody else. Brittany had nothing to do with that.'

'She thinks she did, if Moses in fact—'

'Susan. Stop! Really. We're not talking about that. You remember what I told you last night. It's off-limits, period. And we do know what Moses did. You told me he said he'd gone fishing, so he went fishing.'

'Brittany doesn't believe that. And I'm not sure I do, either. You know the last time he went fishing before Sunday? Got to be a couple of years, at least.'

'That's the way fishing is. You go a year, two years off, then you go out again. Especially if something's happened to your little girl and you need to cool off and think about things.'

'Do you believe that's what he did?'

'I'm going to believe him, yes,' Hardy lied. 'Brittany's got to try to believe him, too.'

'I don't see how she's going to get to that. After what Moses did to him when he hurt her last time. Now she wishes she'd never told us.'

'As I recall, she didn't tell you about that, either, did she?'

'No.'

'So how many times does he get to hurt her before she tells somebody and he gets stopped?'

'She didn't think her father would kill him.'

'You don't think he deserved it?'

'I don't know what he deserved. I can't think about him being killed. It's too confusing.'

'It is? You're not relieved that he can't hurt your daughter anymore? She's not okay with that?' Hardy drew a breath and lowered his voice. 'Susan, listen to me. This guy was a plague upon the earth. And now he's gone. For you or Brittany to feel bad about that is a waste of your time and energy. What you've got to remember now is that this is a strategic issue. Brittany must not tell anybody else – and I mean anybody – about what happened to her on Saturday night. If she needs to talk about it, she can go back down to the center, see a psychologist, whatever it takes, so long as it's privileged.'

'You're protecting her father.'

'Well, yes.'

'That sounds like you believe he did it.'

'No, I said it's strategic. In case he did, we don't want to supply the DA with a reason.'

In a different voice, Susan said, 'Dismas, how am I going to keep living with him?'

'Do you love him?'

'Of course.' Then, 'I don't know.'

'Yes, you do. Whatever he did, I'm sure he thought he was justified.'

'Justified like before? I mean the other thing.'

'A little bit, yes.'

'And that's what matters? That you feel justified? That's enough?'

'No. Obviously not. The last time, we were out of options. We were going to be killed if we didn't do something. This time, maybe, just maybe, Moses read this guy as a threat to Brittany's life. He'd already beaten her and raped her. Moses didn't want to find out what would happen next.'

'What if he gets mad at me one day? Or one of the girls? What if all of a sudden I think he's dangerous to us?'

'Do you think that now?'

'I don't know. When he's drinking, maybe. Which seems to have picked up right where it ended.'

'Yes, well, I agree that the drinking has to stop.'

'Even if it does,' Susan said.

'What then?'

He heard her sigh. 'I just don't know.'

'Where are you now?'

'Back home. Both of us. He's sleeping. The bar's locked up.'

'Don't worry about the bar,' Hardy said.

'I won't. There's a lot more to worry about than the damn bar.'

Brittany opened her eyes.

Sunshine outdoors, the window open a crack, the breeze, without any nip, fluffing the bright yellow curtains in her bedroom. What day was it?

Her head rested on a man's chest, which was covered by a lightweight green sweater. In her sleep, she'd thrown an arm over him.

'She moves,' his voice whispered.

Leaving her head where it was, she closed her eyes again, aware that she was wearing all of her clothes from the day before. Or was it two days?

'How long was I sleeping?'

'I don't know. Three hours, maybe. Four.'

'Was my head on you the whole time?'

'Yeah. It's been hell.'

'Thank you.'

'You're welcome. But I could use the bathroom.'

She took in a deep breath, reluctant to move her head, to move anything, to wake up officially and have to face it all again. 'Can I leave my head here another minute?'

'Okay.' She felt a gentle hand brush the hair away from her forehead. 'Long as you want.'

'It's a nice day,' she said, then closed her eyes.

Brittany lived in a second-floor one-bedroom apartment in a six-unit building on Oak Street near Divisadero.

When she came back into her bedroom after the shower, wrapped in a towel, he had gotten off the bed and closed the door behind him, leaving her some privacy.

Now in the living room, he was on the couch, leafing through a copy of *Popular Mechanics*. She had changed into cargo pants and an orange tank top. She'd combed her wet hair and wore no makeup. 'Hey,' she said.

He put down the magazine. 'Hey yourself.'

'Thank you.'

'For what?'

'The space.'

He shrugged. 'I just wanted to make sure you were okay.'

'I'm not.'

'Right. I know.'

'I'm not ready for anything yet.'

'Of course not. I wouldn't expect you to be.'

She walked over to the kitchen table and pulled out a chair. 'I feel like I've taken advantage of you. Especially Saturday. But I didn't know where else to go. I thought my dad would be tending—'

'No sweat. It was me. I'm glad I could be there, take you to your mom and dad, where you needed to be.'

'My point is, I didn't mean to get you involved. I should have just stayed on at Mom and Dad's. But I couldn't be there anymore. And then asking you to stay here, and sleeping around the clock . . .'

'Yeah,' he said. 'It's been agony, being here. Making sure you're okay.' Tony looked at her for a moment, then stood up and took the chair next to her. He put a finger under her chin and lifted her face. 'Hey.'

A tear broke from her left eye. A bitter little laugh escaped. 'Here I go again,' she said. 'Little Miss Drama Queen.' She shook her head, wiped the tear. 'I just can't seem to help it. I'm so sorry.'

'What you've been through the last four days, some people never get over it.'

'I don't know. The way I feel right now, I hate the way I am.'

'And how is that?'

'Irresponsible. Stupid. If I hadn't started it all by flirting with him.'

'So now it's your fault that he raped you?'

'Maybe I led him on somehow. I didn't want to meet him at Perry's. I should have listened to myself, but I didn't, because that's not what I do, is it? I don't know what I was trying to accomplish.'

'You were trying to be a good person, to be fair to him, to protect your dad.'

'If I hadn't done that, he'd still be alive.'

'You don't know that. You don't know why he died. If it had anything to do with what he did to you.'

'Of course it did. If I hadn't gone to Perry's—'

He placed his index finger on her lips. 'Brittany. Get this into your head. No part of this was your fault. You were the victim, not Rick Jessup. He did what he did, and whatever happened to him, he's the one who made it happen. Whether it was because of you or something else altogether.'

'No,' she said. 'It was me. It was my dad. I saw his face when I told him. I never should have told him. Or anybody else.'

'And then what? Then it's your secret forever, and it eats away at you and ruins your life because you haven't done the right thing, which is report what he did. And then maybe Rick Jessup does it again. Hell, he *does* do it again, just like he'd probably done it before. His being gone is a good thing, Brittany.'

'Not if he's gone because of my dad.'

'You don't know that. For all you know, it might have been me. I knew what he did. I could have gone over and taken care of him. Or how about all the other women he probably did this to? Or their fathers. Or their brothers.'

'Except you were bartending when it happened.'

'No, I wasn't. Sunday was Lynne's day. I was home alone, no alibi.' She pushed him away. 'Let's not do this. It's not funny.'

'I'm not being funny. I'm telling you there are other possibilities.'

'Then how do you explain my dad last night? Almost drinking himself to death?'

'You think he was trying to kill himself out of remorse over killing Jessup?'

'He could have been.'

'Coulda, shoulda, woulda, Brittany. He could also have been having a hard time coping with your situation, for example, and lost track of how much he drank. He hadn't been drunk in how long? Maybe he miscalculated or didn't see it coming till it whacked him upside the head.'

'I don't know,' she said. 'It all seems connected.'

'It might be, I'll concede that. But it doesn't have to be.'

Supervisor Liam Goodman, back at his desk at city hall, knew nothing about any rape. Nevertheless, Diane had told him about the Homicide inspectors' visit, and their discovery, based on the hard evidence of Diane's calendar, that a man named Moses McGuire – whom he'd never heard of – had come to the office to talk to Rick about Brittany McGuire.

To complain about how Rick had treated her.

Goodman remembered, again with the help of Diane's calendar, that Rick had taken the following two days off from work. When he returned, he had the remains of a black eye and swelling in his cheek. His nose looked as though it had taken something of a beating. The excuse had been feeble – an elbow in a pickup basketball game – Goodman had seen no reason to follow up on it.

Now he had a good one.

Rick Jessup had had his own life, one that had been getting increasingly out of control on a lot of levels over the past several months, but Goodman had been thinking that the best thing was to stay out of the investigation unless and until it began to touch upon him or his political relationships.

His three interns were standing in front of him, and Goodman was giving them something of a pep talk. 'No one,' he was saying, 'appreciated Rick more than I did. And I don't see how we're going to function as an office without everything he did on a daily basis. But the only thing we can do to honor his memory is go on in the job, try to serve the needs of our constituents, be sensitive and caring and honest, the way Rick was.

'I hope the couple of days we've been shut down have allowed all of us to come to some sort of closure, although of course it will take a lot longer before we're back to normal. I understand that, and if you feel like you need more time to come to grips with this senseless and terrible tragedy, just clear your time with Diane and take as much as you need. Of course, we'll be closed again tomorrow morning for the funeral. While we're on that, if you have an idea that you're leaning toward needing more time, maybe you could let me know for planning purposes?

'Nobody? Thank you. You're as fine and loyal a staff as anyone could hope for. If you change your mind, though, please, there is no problem. I may take an hour here and there myself. This is not an easy thing to get through, and no one knows it more than me.'

Goodman met each of their eyes in turn – Joseph, Rochelle, Logan. Though he didn't think any of them had been particularly close to Rick, they all appeared moved by Goodman's sincerity, if not by Rick's misfortune. Rochelle's eyes were shining with unspent tears. The other two nodded with sober expressions.

'Before I let you go today, I also want to tell you, if you haven't already heard, that a couple of Homicide inspectors investigating Rick's murder came by the other day.' With an understanding smile, he held up a hand at the silent chorus of concerned looks. 'Don't worry. To my knowledge, and it is accurate, none of us is under any kind of suspicion. The police were just doing their job. But they did make a discovery here that they evidently thought was important, and they asked if we might enlarge upon it in some way.

'Apparently, about two months ago . . .'

He briefly laid out the scenario as Diane had explained it to him. 'The problem is,' he concluded, 'that we know this McGuire fellow came here and went out in the hall with Rick to discuss something about McGuire's daughter, but we don't know what happened out there. If it helps jog any of your memories, Rick took a couple of days off following that incident, and he returned looking like he'd been in a fight. The point is that the police need to know if McGuire attacked Rick in a violent rage. If we can verify that he did, the police will want to ask him some hard questions. Yes, Rochelle? No need to raise your hand.'

'Do they think he killed Rick?'

'It's possible,' Goodman said, 'that if he beat Rick once, he found a reason to do it again. Or take care of what he'd left unfinished. I think that's what they're going on. But as far as I know, they don't have any real proof.'

After a small silence, Joseph spoke up. 'It's probably not proof, since I didn't actually see them fighting, but the guy just went off on him.'

'You're saying McGuire hit Rick?'

'I don't know why Rick would lie about it.'

'He told you?'

'Absolutely.'

'Do we know why?'

'Rick had gone out with the daughter, and evidently, she was a crazy person. When he broke up with her, she made up all these stories for her father about how bad he'd treated her, and McGuire came down here and attacked him without any warning.'

'And Rick didn't report it to the police?'

Joseph shrugged. 'He didn't want to get the girl in trouble. Obviously, the family was pretty dysfunctional. Rick figured this was a onetime thing, probably worth it if the girl would leave him alone. So he decided he could handle it; he'd just ignore it.'

'Yes.' Sorrow dripped from Goodman's voice. 'That sounds like Rick, doesn't it? Able to handle things. I hope that decision didn't help get him killed.'

Twenty minutes later, with the ammunition he needed, Goodman was on the telephone with San Francisco's chief of police, Vi Lapeer. 'Yes, ma'am,' he was saying in a patient tone, 'but all

I've been hearing, all anybody's been hearing, for the past few days is that the investigation is proceeding. The investigation is ongoing. Now, the last thing I want to do is add to your many concerns, but frankly, I'm getting a little frustrated with the refrain. I'd like to hear that the investigation is progressing, not just proceeding or going along. This fine young man has been dead for three days, and I haven't heard a shred of information about any leads, any possible suspects. And we all know the statistic that after two days, if a murder isn't solved, there's a great chance it never will be. We can't let that happen in this case.'

'I appreciate your frustration, sir,' Lapeer said, 'but we've got two experienced Homicide inspectors working full-time and then some on this. It's my understanding that they are pursuing some eyewitnesses, and—'

'All that's fine, but it doesn't appear to be taking them any place fast.'

'Fast isn't the primary goal, sir. Getting it right is the goal.'

'Meanwhile, evidence gets cold, maybe the murderer leaves town, people forget what they saw.'

'Yes, but—'

'Excuse me, Chief, but it seems that when they've got what appears to be a substantial lead in the case, they should be using all of their efforts to pursue it. Wouldn't you agree?'

'Of course, but I haven't heard of any such lead. You're saying that you know of one?'

'I believe I do, yes. As you may know, your two inspectors came by my office a couple of days ago. They identified a man who came here, irate over what he thought was Mr Jessup's treatment of his daughter. The two men went into the hallway, and I just learned from my staff that this man assaulted Mr Jessup, injuring him badly enough that he had to take a couple of days off work.'

'When was this?'

'A couple of months ago. I can get the exact date, if you need it.'

After a moment, the chief said, 'A couple of months is a relatively long time for this to be automatically, as it were, connected to the murder. You say the inspectors discovered this man when they talked to your people?'

'Yes. His name is Moses McGuire. I don't know if they had the information that he brutally attacked Mr Jessup. This was a violent, crazy man who hated Rick.'

'Yes, but if the inspectors got his name, I'm certain they would have interviewed him. Or are planning to soon.'

'They need to know about the beating. That's a whole different animal than if he stopped by to say hello. Even if it was two months ago.'

'Yes, I understand that. Would you like to talk to the inspectors again, or would you like me to bring it to their attention?'

Goodman took a breath, dialing back the urgency. 'God knows, Chief, I'm not telling you how to do your job. Or your inspectors. It could be I'm letting my frustration get the better of me. It's been a tremendously difficult time, as you might imagine. Everybody loved Rick, and nobody seems to be doing anything to find his killer.'

'Yes,' Lapeer said. 'I know it can seem like that.' A pause. 'I'll tell you what. Why don't I put in a call to Homicide, convey your information, and see how far they've pursued the angle? If there's anything worth reporting, I'll get right back to you. Or not. Either way.'

'I just thought it was too important not to mention it.'

'Those are good instincts. I'll follow up and get back to you. Moses McGuire?'

'That's the name. Thank you, Chief.'

'Anytime.'

18

As CHIEF OF police, Vi Lapeer attended a host of mostly ceremonial functions. She took a lot of breakfasts and lunches and dinners and gave a lot of speeches. She went out to neighborhood meetings and talked about problems in the community and how the police could more effectively interface. She talked to business leaders about security issues, to homeless advocates about drugs and other problems on the streets, to the other brass within the police department about union issues, relations with other law enforcement agencies, budgets. She reached out to politicians of all stripes, kept up with the press, met with victims' groups, child safety groups, youth guidance groups. She had regular meetings on everything from the Muni bus system and cable cars to graffiti abatement, dog policy in the city's parks, hate crimes, and elder abuse.

What she almost never did, especially alone, was drop in on her rank-and-file officers and inspectors as they went about their daily work.

That was why Glitsky was significantly taken aback when, at the end of the day, sensing a shadow in his doorway, he looked up from a forensic report and saw her standing there, a solidly built, no-nonsense African-American woman in full-dress uniform. Bringing his feet down off the corner of his desk, Glitsky closed the binder and was immediately on his feet. 'Can I help you, Chief?'

She stepped inside the door. 'At ease, Lieutenant. I just thought

I'd drop by and see if you could spare a few minutes of your time.'

'Of course, ma'am. Whatever you need.'

Although a vast chasm in chain of command yawned between them, Lapeer and Glitsky had forged something of a bond in the first weeks of her tenure as chief, just arrived from her assistant chief job in Philadelphia a little over two years before. She had stood up for him in front of the mayor in a complicated no-warrant arrest Glitsky had felt obligated to make on the son of one of the city's most powerful political families. In turn, he'd proved her ally against that same mayor – the current one, Leland Crawford – when, in the wake of her not doing his bidding in another matter, he'd polled the police heads in a ham-fisted effort to get a no-confidence vote against her.

'You don't mind?' She checked behind her, pulled the door closed, turned back to him, and sighed. 'I just got off the phone with Liam Goodman.'

Glitsky nodded. 'He's impatient about the Jessup thing.'

'He is. And you know how he loves to talk to the press.'

'So he called you.'

'And if he doesn't get action from me, you know who gets the next call.' She pulled a chair up to Glitsky's desk and sat down. 'Where the buck stops and all that. I figured I'd see if there's anything new that I can tell him in the name of progress. Meanwhile, he gave me some information he hoped your inspectors would find useful.'

'Rather than call them directly at the numbers on the cards they left at his office?'

'That wouldn't have sufficiently underscored his importance, now, would it? Or what he had to say. I might not hear that he's personally interested.'

'No, I suppose not.' Glitsky shook his head in disgust. 'What a clown.'

Lapeer broke the hint of a smile. 'Yes, but he's our clown for the moment, not the mayor's, which I predict will be his next stop if we don't pat his hand. And for the record, what he gave me might have some relevance, even though it sounds like old news.' She glanced up at the whiteboard with all of Homicide's active cases. 'Brady and Sher?'

'That's the team.'

'Have they checked in with you recently?'

'Yesterday.'

'You mind if we see where they are today? Are they out in the detail?'

'I'll find out.' Glitsky picked up his phone, punched some numbers. 'Paul, Abe. If you and Lee have a minute, I've got the chief in here, and she'd like a word. That's right, yes. Chief. Yes. Of police.' He hung up. 'They'll be right in.'

'Yes, we know who Moses McGuire is,' Brady said. 'We've already talked to him. He's in a six-pack we're showing our eyewitnesses today.' Since the chief remained standing, neither he nor Sher saw fit to avail themselves of folding chairs. They stood at one corner of Glitsky's desk, hands clasped behind their backs.

'They gave us his name at Goodman's office,' Sher added. 'Jessup dated his daughter a few months ago.'

The chief was nodding, paying attention. 'That's what Supervisor Goodman told me. I had a discussion with him a little while ago, and he seemed to think you didn't have all the information you needed.'

'You mean that McGuire hit Jessup?' Brady asked.

The chief tilted her head to one side. 'So you did hear about that?'

Glitsky, blindsided anew with McGuire's name, leaned back in his chair, rested both his hands on his stomach, and tried to be subtle as he clawed at it.

While the discussion continued.

'Yes, ma'am,' Sher said. 'We asked him directly, and he didn't make any bones about it. Jessup evidently hurt his daughter Brittany – pushed her, knocked her down, something like that – and McGuire came downtown to, as he put it, get Jessup's attention and get him to stop harassing her.'

Lapeer considered that. 'The supervisor's version is that Jessup dumped her and she went wacko on him, filling her father's head with lies.'

The two inspectors shared a glance.

The chief didn't miss it. 'Not true?'

Brady took it. 'We don't think so. We think he manhandled her.'

'Why do you think that? Why her word over his?'

'First,' Sher answered, 'we never got his.'

'And second?'

Sher threw a mildly desperate, questioning look at Glitsky, then at her partner. She drew a breath, checked Glitsky again, came up with something that would probably fly for the moment. 'Second, the admin in Goodman's office didn't paint too flattering a picture of Jessup.'

'In any event,' Lapeer said, 'Goodman characterized McGuire's visit as a brutal beating that kept Jessup out of work for at least a couple of days.'

'Maybe,' Brady said. 'But McGuire reminded us that Jessup didn't file any report. You'd think if it had been that bad, he might have. Except then it might have come out that he'd pushed around McGuire's daughter.'

Lapeer nodded again. 'So you've looked at McGuire, but you're not considering him a suspect?'

'We haven't ruled him out,' Sher said, 'but . . .'

Lapeer finished her sentence. 'But it's been a couple of months since this alleged beating, and why would he just jump up on

Sunday night and decide to go and finish things with Jessup? That's what I told Goodman, and that's what I'll tell him again. It doesn't make much sense, even if McGuire's a hothead. He's already made his point to Jessup. He doesn't need to go kill him.' She put it out to the three of them. 'The bottom line, I guess, is there's no reason to focus on McGuire over anybody else. That's what you're all saying, right?'

After a moment, Brady cleared his throat. Sher studied the tile on the office floor. Glitsky moved his right hand from his stomach to his desk and drummed his fingers a couple of times, quickly.

The chief eyed them each in turn. 'Or maybe not right,' she said. 'What are you not saying?'

Clearing his throat again, Brady came out with it. 'Brittany went and had a drink at Perry's with Jessup last Saturday night.'

Lapeer's back went straight. 'The night before he was killed?'

Sher nodded. 'He couldn't seem to get the message. He wanted to see her again or else he was going to file charges against her dad for the beating. She decided to go down and see if she could talk him out of it.'

'You're saying they had a date Saturday night?'

'Yes, ma'am. Although I don't know if I'd call it a date.'

On the street below, someone's car alarm went off. No one in Glitsky's office said a word while it ticked off uncounted time.

Finally, the noise stopped, and the chief found her voice. 'That strikes me as a moderately important fact. Is there some reason you were stonewalling me on it?'

Sher dared a response. 'We said we hadn't ruled anybody out, ma'am. Including McGuire.'

'True, but this is exactly the kind of thing I could bring to Supervisor Goodman to get him off my back. Tell him that we are making progress and are maybe close to making an arrest.'

'That may not be true, ma'am,' Brady said. 'We're very light on evidence. We need to work with some of our eyewitnesses and see what we can come up with before we go back to McGuire. If we're led in that direction.'

'Have you talked to the girl? Brittany?'

'Yes.'

'What does she say? How did the date go? Did Jessup mistreat her again? Did McGuire have a new reason to confront Jessup? Maybe kill him? Come on, people. It sounds like progress to me. It'll sound that way to Mr Goodman. We don't have to name McGuire, but at least we can say we've got some real leads and we're looking at some persons of interest, how's that?'

Sher once again looked at Glitsky. 'Sir?'

Pulling himself up to the desk, he clasped his hands. 'Here's the deal, Vi,' he said. 'We got a tip through the DA's office that a woman was raped on Saturday night. That woman may or may not have been Brittany McGuire. Brittany has not admitted it, and the information is privileged. We may never know. In any event, the victim of the rape identified her assailant as Rick Jessup.'

'So Brittany went home and told her dad—' Lapeer began.

'We don't know it was Brittany,' Glitsky said.

'We know she went out with Jessup that night?'

Brady nodded. 'Yes, ma'am.'

'Well, then.' Lapeer wiped a hand across her forehead. 'Jesus Christ, I'm not going to believe we're talking about coincidence here. It's too long a stretch, and without that, it sounds to me like you've got yourselves a prime suspect.'

'Except,' Sher said, 'we can't use the rape, because we can't prove it happened.'

'So go show his picture to your eyewitnesses. Bring a witness in and pick him out of a lineup. Get this man off the street, and I mean yesterday. Do any of you have any doubt that he's got at least motive and history?'

No one answered, because the answer would have been 'So what?' and that would have been insubordinate. They all knew – even the chief – that motive and history played little real role in convicting criminals. What mattered in a courtroom was direct evidence, preferably someone who saw a crime being committed. Here, though it would be nice to have a witness positively identify the suspect near the scene, even that would not be evidence of a crime, since none of the witnesses had seen whoever it was doing anything but walking down the street.

They had nothing yet. On what evidence were they supposed to act?

Nevertheless, the chief wasn't here to split hairs. Her visage was stern and unyielding, and looking at her, Glitsky felt a thrum of foreboding – perhaps their subtle alliance had taken an irre-coverable body blow. It didn't help that she was standing, looking down at him, arms crossed over her chest. 'I'm serious as a heart attack here, all of you,' she concluded. 'I don't want excuses. Find a way and git 'er done.'

'In spite of the chief's good intentions,' Glitsky said, 'I would caution you against arresting Mr McGuire until we've got something in the way of physical evidence tying him to the crime. Even if your eyewitnesses are on board. Not that I don't agree that, as far as motive goes, he looks pretty good for it. But motive is highly overrated.'

'Maybe not so much,' Sher said.

'No?' Glitsky came forward. 'My personal theory is that every human being who has reached the age of reason has already provided a motive for at least half a dozen people to kill him. Or her. Even as we speak, I can probably think of ten or fifteen people who'd be happier if I were dead.'

Brady grunted. 'There's an optimistic worldview.'

Glitsky shrugged. 'Just a comment on motive.'

In spite of the banter, the mood after Lapeer's departure stayed strained. Sher had lowered herself into a chair. Brady sagged against one of the filing cabinets. He said, 'I don't know, Abe. I thought she was pretty clear that we ought to turn up the heat. If McGuire's the guy, we need to find a way. Talk to his family. Check his alibi—'

'He's got an alibi?'

Sher raised her head. 'Volunteered it first thing. He went fishing. Alone.'

'He knew somebody from Homicide would want to talk to him,' Brady added. 'He told us that. He was ready. It was all thought out.'

'I'm thinking if we get an ID,' Sher said, 'and it's him – the guy with the club, I mean – we bring him downtown.'

'Still,' Glitsky said, 'I'm not hearing any evidence.'

Brady stepped in. 'At that time we get a warrant.'

'Good luck with that,' Glitsky said, although he knew Brady was right.

'Why not?'

'Where's your probable cause? You think some judge is going to sign off without one tiny piece of actual evidence?' Glitsky didn't know why he was continuing in this vein. He knew that an eyewitness ID, along with the motive evidence, would probably be enough for a judge to sign off on a warrant. Somehow, he realized he wanted to slow his inspectors down, buy a little more time. But for what? For whom? He couldn't have said.

'It could happen,' Brady persisted. 'With enough details. If he's got a blue car or our witnesses pick him out of a lineup.'

'That's still just the guy walking down the street.'

'Okay, so in a pinch, we mention the rape,' Sher said.

Glitsky shook his head. 'The rape's a nonstarter, guys. It might not be Brittany, and even if it was, we can't prove it.'

'Same old song,' Brady said.

'I hear you,' Abe said, 'but that's what's playing right now.'

After a short silence, Sher looked up again. 'So what do you suggest, Abe? Clearly, the chief wants him brought in.'

And with good reason, Glitsky thought. His inspectors were calling him on his untenable objections. But let them believe he was playing devil's advocate. Let Brady and Sher think he was being hypothetical, trying to keep them from procedural error. 'Clearly,' he said. 'But there's no point bringing him in if we're just going to have to let him go, now, is there? So my suggestion – not too groundbreaking, I know – is find something that'll speak to a jury. Otherwise, you're wasting everybody's time, including your own. That's just reality.'

'So what about the chief?' Brady asked.

'What about her?'

Sher said, 'She's not going to be happy unless we come up with something pretty soon.'

'She's making this bed,' Glitsky said. 'She can lie in it.'

On a tip from his wife, Glitsky caught up with Farrell in the reporters' room on the third floor. It was nearly twenty minutes after five, all the trial departments had closed for the day, and Farrell was alone with a can of Dr Pepper in the small room with its big pitted table, surrounded by vending machines that dispensed nearly every form of snack and nonalcoholic drink imaginable. The wrappers from two PayDay bars bore silent testimony to Farrell's last few minutes.

Glitsky closed the door and slid in across the table from him. 'Treya said she thought I'd find you here.'

'It was supposed to be a secret. I was going for a minute without interruption.'

'She knew you'd want to make an exception for me. She made me promise not to tell anybody else. What happened to you?'

'What do you mean?'

'You look in the mirror recently? Your eyes?'

'Oh, them?' Farrell didn't laugh, though his shoulders rose and fell once. 'It's the next new thing. I call it the Beagle. Anybody can do it. Just don't sleep.' He scrunched his eyes closed, then opened them. 'Sam's moving out. I think this time she means it. You know what it's like being basically a left-wing kind of guy and your girlfriend dumps you because you're too conservative? She thinks I've sold out to the prosecution side.'

'I don't see how that breaks right or left. What? She wants bad guys to go free?'

'Most of the time, yeah. I think so. They need to be understood, you know, more than punished.'

'Again,' Glitsky said, 'not mutually exclusive.'

'Don't tell Sam.' He closed his eyes again. 'She thinks I betrayed her on this Jessup thing.'

'How'd you do that? He was dead when you found out about him, wasn't he?'

'Deader than hell, but that's not the point.'

'What is?'

'I should have somehow known that giving his name up would eventually expose her victim. But this just in, Abe, I don't even know her victim. *Shit.* Excuse me.'

Glitsky was famous for deploring the use of profanity, but this time he waved it off. 'You want Sam to go? To leave?'

'Not at all. I love the damn woman, pain in the ass though she is.'

'I've got an argument for you, if you want to use it, maybe change her mind.'

'I'm listening.'

'She's mad at herself.'

'She is? Why?'

'Because she's got it backward. She's the one who betrayed the privilege, not you. And she knows it. That's why she's so angry. As soon as she said the name Jessup out loud to you, you had no choice. If his name let you bring us in to help find his killer, you had to use it. She's the one who let it out. And once she did that, it was public.'

Farrell lifted his soda can, took a sip. 'That might be worth saying.'

'For what it's worth, it's true.'

'If that's really what's bothering her. Sometimes I think it's just me.'

'If it's that, I can't help you. But if it's a fight over this one thing . . .'

'It's an idea, anyway, Abe. I appreciate it. It's something.' Farrell picked up one of the wrappers expectantly, went to the second one. Same result. He forced a tired smile. 'But if memory serves, you came down here to talk to me. And probably not about Sam.'

'Probably not,' Glitsky said, 'although it's about Jessup.' He took a breath. 'Chief Lapeer came by my office just now.'

'In person?'

'Very much so. She'd been talking to Liam Goodman, who had some information about somebody who'd beaten up Mr Jessup a couple of months ago because Jessup had beaten up his daughter. You want to take a stab who that was?'

'You mean the guy who beat up Jessup? You're saying I know him?'

Glitsky nodded, dropped the familiar name.

Farrell's jaw went slack. 'You're shitting me.' The DA leaned back, his gaze off in the distance. 'Wow,' he whispered. 'Fuck. Is he a suspect? In Jessup's murder?'

'Vi wants him to be, in the worst way.'

'Why?'

'Because he's close at hand. It gets Goodman off her case before he goes running to the mayor. I'm coming to you because after the chief's pep talk to my people, there will be pressure to move ahead, and I thought you'd want to be in the loop.'

Farrell met Glitsky's eyes. 'McGuire? What do you think?'

'It's possible. Brittany saw Jessup not just two months ago but last week. They had a date the night before he got killed.'

'The night before?'

Glitsky nodded. 'Saturday. Although when our guys went to see her yesterday, she wouldn't admit anything about the rape, so we don't know for sure that she was the victim, but if she was and she told McGuire about it . . .'

'Holy shit,' Farrell said. 'Yes, we do know she was the victim. We do now.'

'What do you . . . ?'

'My fight with Sam. The real, actual rape victim – the one who had named Jessup as her assailant – called Sam yesterday, in hysterics that the cops had just come to visit, asking her about Saturday night. Now you're telling me that your team went out and interviewed Brittany yesterday, which more or less brings it full circle and identifies her as our victim, doesn't it?'

The two men went silent.

'Jesus Christ,' Farrell whispered. 'You know what else? This is Sam, too.'

'What is Sam, too?'

'She told me about the call she got from Brittany, without which . . .'

'. . . we'd never know it was Brittany who got raped. And now we do.'

'Fuck,' Farrell said. 'Fuck fuck fuck.'

19

From time to time, to keep his hand in as a bartender, which he didn't really need to do, Dismas Hardy worked behind the bar that he co-owned.

Wednesday was usually date night, when Hardy and Frannie would leave the kids with a babysitter (when the kids were still home) or (now) go out alone and explore the restaurant subculture of San Francisco, one of the greatest food towns in the world. Often these excursions would begin with a drink at the Little Shamrock, some bons mots with Moses, a reaffirmation of the family connection.

But on this Wednesday night, there was no sign of Frannie, and of course none of Moses, still in bed nursing his monster of a hangover. Even though Frannie hadn't gotten up as early as her husband this morning, she had basically pulled an all-nighter herself before getting dressed and off to work at seven a.m. The hour and a half of sleep she'd managed hadn't been remotely restorative, and tonight, date night or no, she was crashing early at home.

Hardy, in some ways worse off in terms of fatigue, nevertheless felt a responsibility to his bar and – gallingly – even to his stupid eccentric genius of a brother-in-law who was the source of so much heartache and trouble.

What the hell had Moses done?

Hardy wasn't going to work a full shift. Although nobody in the family, least of all Rebecca, was thrilled that Tony Solaia appeared to be hooking up with Brittany, Hardy had called him somewhat reluctantly, and Tony would be arriving shortly to take the late shift and close the place up. But Hardy wanted to open up and work awhile for reasons that were obscure even to him.

After his usual Sunday and Monday off, Moses had been at the bar last night, getting himself blasted nearly to death in the process, and the state of the place reflected his condition. When Hardy came in at four-thirty today, he'd locked the door before getting to work. The sinks were messes of skimming soap and cold water, dirty glasses sat on many of the tables, the back bar was in total disarray, the condiment trays – lemon peel, lime, cherries, cocktail onions, celery – obviously neglected. Moses had left the refrigerator open behind the bar, and needless to say, no one had noticed while negotiating him into the ambulance. The cream for the Irish coffees had gone sour. Hardy would have to send Tony out for supplies first thing.

Even more disturbingly, up near the beer and stout spigots, somebody had damaged the 108-year-old bar. It looked and felt to Hardy, as he rubbed his hand over the ancient wood, as though this had been an act of conscious vandalism – someone had smashed something heavy and solid into it, and it was now uneven, chipped, splintered at the edge. When could this have happened that Moses or one of the other bartenders wouldn't have seen it? How could Hardy not have heard a word about it? He couldn't imagine.

Maybe Tony would know.

Reaching under the bar for a towel, he automatically felt that something was different, although what it was didn't register until he'd taken out a clean dry towel and tucked it into his belt. Suddenly he stopped dead still, a sense memory – or rather, the lack of it – tickling at the corners of his consciousness.

He leaned over and looked into the dark space above the stack of towels, where, for the whole time Hardy had worked here – well over thirty years – the shillelagh had hung from its leather thong down over the towels, within easy grabbing distance for when things got out of hand.

The shillelagh was gone.

'I'm pretty sure it was here Saturday night,' Tony said. 'That's the last I worked. I think I would have noticed if it was gone.'

They had a dozen or more customers now, and Hardy had moved around to the front of the bar. He was sitting on a stool directly in front of the damaged area. It was still light outside, although a quick glance at the bending cypresses across the street in the park announced the return of normalcy in terms of weather.

It wouldn't do to betray the degree of his concern regarding the latest intelligence from Tony – if the shillelagh had been here Saturday night, then its removal for another use on Sunday became so plausible as to be probable – so Hardy kept his tone even as he leaned back on the stool and indicated the cratered wood. 'So what happened here?' he asked. 'You know?'

Tony was drying glasses, standing behind the beer taps. 'Moses said one of the customers went a little apeshit and started smashing his glass on the bar.'

'More than once, it looks like.'

'At least.'

'Except,' Hardy went on, 'wouldn't the glass have broken?'

Tony nodded at the logic. 'You'd think. Maybe it was one of the Guinness pint glasses. They're pretty solid.'

Hardy ran his hand over the pitted surface. 'More solid than this wood?'

The question brought Tony up short. 'Maybe not. There was some glass on the floor the next day, but I didn't notice how thick it was, whether it was one of the pints. It could have broken after a few hits. It's a damn shame, in any event. The bar was just about perfect. Before, I mean.'

'I'm surprised Moses didn't kill the guy. Take out the shillelagh, break it over his head. I know he would have wanted to.'

'Maybe he did. Maybe that's where the shillelagh's gone.'

'But you said it was here Saturday.'

'I don't know. Maybe. I thought it was, but only because I figured I would have missed it.'

Hardy took a moment, sipped at his club soda. 'Moses mention who it was? So we can keep an eye out for the guy. Eighty-six him before he gets in again.'

'No. Not to me. How is he, by the way?'

'Mose? Hungover, I'd imagine. The idiot.'

Tony turned his head both ways, then leaned in toward Hardy, lowered his voice conspiratorially. 'You know what happened, don't you?'

'I know about last night. Susan called us at home, and Frannie and I came down here in time for the ambulance. Good time had by all.'

'Not just last night.' Tony leaned in again and said, 'I mean with Brittany.'

Hardy drew in a breath. So Tony knew, too, which was disconcerting news. He turned the glass around in a full circle, then looked up. 'We're not going to mention anything about Brittany,' he said. 'I may or may not know what you're talking about, but whatever it is, it would be better if it never, ever came up again. In any context. Under any circumstances. How about that?'

Tony, stunned by the intensity, retreated a half step. 'I was just—'

Hardy held up a hand. 'Doesn't matter. Let it go. Right now. I mean it.'

'He's still pretty much in agony,' Susan said.

'Good,' Hardy said. 'I want him to hurt. I want him in severe pain.'

'That's if you can even wake him up.'

'I bet I can.'

They were in the McGuire living room, a much less ordered space, albeit marginally larger, than the Hardys' counterpart. Two large, soft, bulky upholstered couches squatted on the hardwood on either side of a brown twelve-by-fourteen-foot industrial-carpet remnant. Since the apartment didn't have a separate family room, this area functioned as one, with a large television mounted on one wall and an old upright piano against the facing one. Susan had filled one sagging bookcase with about twenty years of *National Geographic,* another one of old oak with paperbacks, a third with CDs, DVDs, and videocassettes from an earlier era. An IKEA computer desk with an older Apple occupied one corner. Every flat surface in the room – the top of the piano, the coffee table, various nooks in the shelves – and nearly every square inch of wall space held a frame with a family picture.

When the Hardys came here for dinner or a party, they most often congregated in the kitchen or on the roof, both of which felt down-home and comfortable, but today Dismas found the living room particularly claustrophobic, even run-down. Of course, Susan had just spent the previous night in the hospital with her husband, and tidying up probably had not made the first cut on her to-do list. Still, he found the clutter and lack of decorative style emblematic of the family's problems, and more than a little depressing.

'I just came from talking to Tony at the bar,' he said, 'in case it seems that I'm a little teensy bit wound up about things. He knows about Brittany.'

'Well, of course he does. He was closing up when she came by, right after it happened. He brought her back here to us and then took her home on Monday.'

'So? They're an item? I mean officially.'

'I don't know about that, Diz. After what she's been through,

I don't think she's much in the market. And probably won't be for a while. You said you were just with Tony. Did you ask him?'

Hardy shook his head. 'I didn't want to appear to be prying.'

'Why would you care?'

'No reason, really, except that I think the Beck had a little bit of a crush on him. Not that she won't survive.'

'I don't know if Brittany knows that.'

'Maybe not,' Hardy said. 'Anyway, I'd hate to see the two of them have a falling-out about some guy.'

'I know they won't. If Brittany knew anything about how the Beck feels, I'm sure she'd back off. In fact, I'll tell her the next time we talk.' She sighed. 'It is so hard to be a single straight woman in this town. It's no wonder – you find one eligible guy, the pickin's are all his. But I really don't like it if he's playing one against the other.'

'Yeah, well, I'm the one who brought him around. How do you think I feel? Answer: a little like I've been played.'

'I don't know about that. He seems like a truly nice person to me.'

'Every con man does.'

'Do you think he's that?'

'I don't know. I'm not comfortable with him knowing about Brittany and what happened to her. Again, strategically.'

'You keep saying that.'

'I keep thinking that way, that's why. And that's why I've got to talk to Moses right now, pain or no pain.' Hardy paused. 'We're going to get him through this, Susan. We've just got to stay disciplined.'

Susan shifted her weight, folded her arms, took a beat. 'But, Diz. We just don't kill people. No matter what they've done. I mean, okay, if it's true self-defense, sure, you can defend yourself. Otherwise . . .' She took a breath. 'This is why we have the law, isn't it? Or the next thing we know, this young man's brother or father or sister decides it was Moses, and they come after him. Or all of us.'

'Right. I know. That's the theory. I even mostly believe it. The law's a good thing. But if that's not our question anymore, then we need to be prepared for . . . contingencies.'

'I hate this.'

Hardy nodded. 'It's not my favorite, either.'

'And you know, ever since I mentioned it to you, it keeps coming back to me. I don't know if I can stay with him.'

'I think you can. I hope you can.'

She shook her head. 'I honestly don't know.'

'Well,' Hardy said, 'that's between you and him, but it would break my heart. And Frannie's.'

'And mine,' Susan said, her eyes going glassy. 'But I've got to be honest. It might happen.'

Hardy stood at the foot of the bed and took a swat at Moses's foot. 'Hey.'

No response.

He did it again. Harder, letting his own anger simmer, putting a little more English on the swing. 'Mose. Wake up.'

Movement under the covers, followed by a low moan, cut off midway. Moses opened his eyes, sighed, closed them again. His face had a pronounced pallor under a second-day stubble. Red-rimmed eyes lay sunk in their sockets. Cracked, dry lips removed any sign of life from his mouth. He managed a syllable. 'What?'

'That's what I want to know,' Hardy said. 'What in Christ's name were you thinking?'

Moses closed his eyes again. 'I guess I stopped there for a while. Thinking.'

'I guess you did.'

'Susan said you and Frannie came down and helped.'

'What else were we going to do?'

'Still.'

Hardy could go on berating his brother-in-law for an hour. The experience might even be cathartic, but somehow he couldn't find the heart for it. So he tamped down his instinct and said, 'I'm going to assume that this is the first day of your new commitment to sobriety. You think you'll be able to handle that?'

'I hope so.'

'It's not a question of hoping, Mose. You're either going to do it or you're not. You get to decide.'

Moses met Hardy's eyes. 'I don't know exactly what happened.'

'I don't, either,' Hardy said, 'and I don't care.' Coming up around the side of the bed, without any forethought, he cuffed McGuire in the back of the head. 'You realize that you could lose Susan over this. You could lose everything.'

Moses put his hands to his head as he moaned through another pained breath. 'You here to bust my chops? Go for it.'

'Partway, at least, yeah. I'm pretty disgusted, if you really want to know. But that's not the main reason I'm here.'

'You want me to guess?'

'No. I don't want you to guess. What I need you to do is retain me, and I mean now.'

'What am I retaining you for?'

'My expert representation. I'm going to be your lawyer.'

That brought a weak pulse of humor. 'No way could I afford you. You've told me that a hundred times. Besides, I don't need a lawyer.'

'Yeah, you do.'

Taking on a wounded look, Moses asked, 'Why is that?'

Hardy fixed him with a hard glare. 'Let's not play this game. And don't worry about what I charge. We'll work something out. Maybe I'll wind up owning the bar, who knows? I'm now your lawyer. Anything we say to each other is a privileged communication. I'll have Phyllis draw up some formal papers in the next day or so, but in the meanwhile, we've got an agreement, correct? You hear me?'

Moses closed his eyes in resignation for another few seconds, then opened them and lifted his right hand off the mattress.

Hardy took it, gave it a formal shake. 'If the police happen to drop by and want to talk to you about anything at all, your answer is that you'd love to cooperate, but you can't talk to them outside of the presence of your lawyer. Do not say anything else. That's "not anything," as in "nothing." I gather you've already told them that you were fishing on Sunday night, is that right?'

'I was fishing.'

'Okay. Even that, don't repeat it. Don't go into any detail. Leave it as it lies. They need to prove you weren't. We don't have to prove you were. Remember that.'

'I won't say anything. Except to you. I can talk to you, can't I?'

'Yeah. But you might want to remember that there's a lot I don't need to know.'

A silence settled, until Moses said, 'Except, you know, I didn't—'

Hardy put a hand out, stopping him. 'Not now, Mose. Maybe not ever. The important thing is, I'm your lawyer, and let's hope you're not going to need me.'

Moses hesitated. 'You know, really, I don't think I am.'

'That's good to hear, but I'm not so optimistic.'

'You're not? You ought to be. Glitsky pretends not, but I believe he actually likes me, as far as he likes anybody.'

'That's really special, Mose, but he's the head of Homicide. It's not like he gets to choose. His inspectors will go where the facts lead them. Do you honestly think he'd back off if the evidence seems to point in your direction?'

'What evidence? For what crime? I haven't heard about any evidence.'

'No?' Hardy saw a good moment for a curveball. 'Where's the shillelagh?'

McGuire's eyes sharpened right up. 'What shillelagh? The Shamrock's?'

'You know any others?'

'It's not under the bar? If it's not under the bar, I don't know where it is. Are you kidding me? It's gone?'

'You didn't notice it was missing yesterday?'

'I can't say I was paying close attention.'

Hardy searched McGuire's face for signs of duplicity and saw none.

'Diz, listen. They're not going to come for me. I tuned the kid up a few months ago, sure, but that doesn't put me anywhere near him on Sunday night.'

'Well, let's hope nothing else does.'

'How could it,' McGuire asked, 'if I wasn't there?'

20

GLITSKY SAT ON the development he'd broken with Wes Farrell – that the rape victim was undoubtedly Brittany McGuire – until he got to work the next morning. When he walked into the Homicide Detail's main room at seven forty-five, Brady and Sher were already there, hunched over something on Lee's desk, eating doughnuts, drinking coffee.

For reasons that might have had to do with the quality physical time he'd gotten with Treya after they put the kids to bed last night, Glitsky was in rare joviality, and he gave it a short run. 'I don't want to tell you what an embarrassing cliché you guys are at this moment,' he said. 'Coffee and doughnuts? What are you thinking? This is San Francisco. It ought to be quiche and tea, don't you think? Maybe a croissant.'

'No,' Sher replied. 'Doughnuts are okay now. They're selling them at the Ferry Building.' This was the city's gourmet mecca. 'Which means they're automatically hip.'

'Maybe for normal people,' Glitsky said. 'But cops? Doughnuts? Really?'

'They're awesome,' Brady said. 'You can have one if you move fast.'

'Can't,' Glitsky said, putting his hand to his heart. 'Ticker.'

'One won't kill you,' Sher said.

'My doctor says it might.' Then, striking like a snake, he grabbed a fat glazed one and took a bite. Chewing happily, he added, 'On the other hand, the signature you want on your death certificate is your cardiologist's.' He pointed to the surface of Sher's desk. 'What's that you're studying so intently?'

'That's Sammy,' Brady said. 'Gus Huang's take on the guy with the club.'

Sher cast a glance at the artist's rendering, then came back up to Glitsky. 'Except we're thinking of changing his name to Moses.' She lifted the sketch and revealed under it the six-pack of photographs they'd put together. 'McGuire. He's top middle. The resemblance is pretty damn close, wouldn't you say?'

'Gus is good at his job.' Glitsky had another bite, chewed thoughtfully. 'What'd your eyewitnesses say?'

Brady clucked in frustration. 'We couldn't reach any of them yesterday, but one of them got back to us this morning. It's our first stop. By then, hopefully, we'll connect with one or both of the others.'

'For the record,' Sher said, 'we're betting the farm it's McGuire.'

'Funny you should mention,' Glitsky said, and launched into a quick rundown of the talk he'd had with Farrell. 'So after you two left Brittany yesterday,' he concluded, 'she called Mr Farrell's girlfriend, which pretty much identifies her as the rape victim, doesn't it?'

'Which also gives her dad his motive,' Brady said.

Glitsky nodded. 'No flies on you.'

'Plus,' Brady added, and put a finger on the six-pack, 'this.'

Any discussion about McGuire put Glitsky in a tenuous position. It was already far past the time when he should have admitted to his inspectors that he and Moses knew each other. As the once delicious doughnut curdled into a noxious ball in his stomach, he realized that every second he continued to withhold the information would make the omission that much more difficult to explain.

He cleared his throat. 'Now that we've gotten to this point

with Brittany's identity and McGuire's possible motive, I ought to tell you that I was hoping we wouldn't.' He hesitated, let out a breath, met their eyes in turn, and continued. 'The fact is, I know McGuire. I can't say we're close, but it's going to come out, and I don't want it blowing up among us. If he's our suspect, then that's what he is, and that's how we treat him.'

Sher sat back in her chair, threw a look up at her partner, came back to Glitsky. 'You know him? How do you know him?'

'You know Dismas Hardy the lawyer? He's an old pal. McGuire is his wife's brother. We've been to some of the same parties.'

'So you're saying you want to treat him—' Brady began.

Glitsky cut him off. 'Like a murder suspect. If he's our guy, bring him in.'

Hardy didn't get home from the McGuires' until nearly eleven, didn't get to sleep until midnight. When he opened his eyes and saw 9:38 on the digital by his bedside, incredulous, he double-checked with his watch. Frannie, God bless her, had let him sleep in. A glance out the window verified what he'd surmised driving home – the weather was going to be nasty for a while. On the spur of the moment, without much conscious thought, he realized that he wouldn't be making it down to the Dolphin Club for a little early-morning dip today.

The thought occurred that the whole Dolphin Club thing hadn't been his brightest idea ever. It wasn't any easier or more pleasant than it had been at the start. His wet suit was a constant if minor hassle. And face it, he thought, no sane person would call those temperatures swimmable.

Eyes closed, he turned on his side for another second or two of shuteye. Then he became aware of what dimly sounded like a conversation between two women floating up through the house. How could that be? Frannie would be at work by now, and otherwise, there was only him.

Throwing off his covers, he sat up, grabbed the rarely used bathrobe from his closet, and all but tiptoed downstairs, the sounds becoming more recognizable as he descended.

Rebecca was sitting at the dining room table with his wife, wearing a Hastings law school hoodie. When she saw her father appear in the doorway, her tear-streaked face broke into a heart-breaking smile that faded as soon as it had begun to appear. 'Hi, Daddy.'

Hardy crossed around behind Frannie, his hand possessively crossing his wife's shoulders, then went to a knee next to his daughter, putting his arm around her. She leaned in to him, and her shoulders shook once, twice, a third time. He held her until she grew more settled, then pulled far enough away to kiss her on the cheek, rub away her tears.

'I'm sorry,' she said. 'I don't mean to be a baby.'

'It's okay,' Hardy said. 'It doesn't matter. What's happened?'

'Nothing. It's really nothing.'

Jerry Paiz didn't call himself a barber. Since he'd moved downtown about a block from Hardy's office and founded Jerry's Style Lounge, he'd called himself a stylist, and judging from the plethora of women who kept most of the twelve chairs full, he was a good one. To Hardy, who'd known Jerry for fifteen years, ever since he was an unashamed and half as expensive barber at a no-apologies barbershop (Jerry's!) on Clement Street, he remained and probably always would remain a barber.

Now Hardy, the only male customer, sat at styling station number one, feeling a little foolish, as he always did here, while Jerry hovered and ministered to his never-changing haircut as they continued their conversation.

'You've got to stop moving your head while you're talking, Diz,' Jerry chided him. 'I'm doing precision work here.'

'I can't help it. I keep thinking about what I could have done differently.'

'Like what?'

'Like not introduced the guy to anybody I know.'

'That's not you. You're a friendly person. Especially for a lawyer. If I didn't know you were one, I'd never believe it.'

'Thanks, I think. But now it turns out that this guy is breaking my daughter's heart and, not only that, hitting on my niece.'

'Ouch. Cousins?'

'Yeah.'

'Guy's a player.'

'Yeah, but I'd like to see him playing someplace else. Except now it's too late. He's already in the mix.'

Jerry put a hand on the top of Hardy's skull. 'Hold still.'

'I know.' Hardy's neck suddenly tensed.

'You think of something else?'

'I'd nod, but you'd get mad at me.'

'So. What?'

Hardy considered. One of the great things about Jerry – maybe about barbers in general – was that he had no reference to anything else in Hardy's life. They'd known each other for a long time, had told each other countless jokes, anecdotes, stories, had shared pictures of kids, but essentially, they were strangers. When Hardy bounced something off Jerry, he always got back an absolutely honest response, uncluttered by pretense, bullshit, expectations, repercussions. He got Jerry and his human reaction, which was what Hardy thought he could use a dose of, possibly why he'd decided to get a haircut today.

'Evidently, he's one of these guys who bares his soul to women early on. Tells them a deep dark secret only they can know, a sacred trust, and since it's a secret, they can't tell anybody else.

Creates a bond, don't you know. Plus, makes him mysterious and special.'

'But your daughter told you.'

'Only after he moved along to her cousin. Because Rebecca was worried about her.'

'Not to worry. He's probably told her, too.'

'You think so?'

Jerry shrugged. 'If that's his shtick. So. You gonna tell me what it is? I love a good secret.'

'You'll love this one.' Hardy checked his face in the mirror. It remained neutral, showing none of the roiling concern that he felt. Good. He'd lay it out to Jerry as an entertaining factoid, a little anecdote to fill the time. He wasn't completely sure how he felt about it yet, and thinking out loud here was as good a way to break it down as he could imagine. 'So the Beck asked him why he wasn't hooked up with anybody else. She couldn't believe somebody so cool wasn't swarmed with women.'

'Somebody shot his nuts off, like in that Hemingway book.'

'Nope. That's not it. My guess is his nuts are in fine working order. He tells her he's only been here in the city a few months. He's been finding work, keeping busy. He hasn't had time for romantic entanglements.'

'Until her.'

'Apparently. So the Beck asks the obvious next question: where's he from? Why'd he come here? He hems and haws and then, you know, he can't lie to her, but he really shouldn't tell her. It could be dangerous. Thinking about it, he realizes the real truth – that being with him at all could be dangerous. He really shouldn't get involved with anybody. But they get along so well . . .'

'Setting the hook.'

'Right. So now she's got to know. It couldn't be that dangerous. Whatever it is, she can help him. They can fight it together.'

'I give up.'

'I don't blame you. It turns out he's a federally protected witness. His name's not his real name. He's one of the government's main witnesses in this huge human trafficking case out of New York. Cops on the payroll, as many as forty defendants, millions and millions of dollars at stake. And the Beck's guy, he's the whistle-blower. Anybody finds out who he is, and where he is, and he's a dead man.'

'Jesus Christ. You're saying he's a crook?'

'He says not. He says he was a Vice cop in Manhattan. Never mind that like ninety percent of protected witnesses are ex-Mob guys who cut deals with the feds so they'll get their own cases dropped – their own murders, their own extortions – that doesn't paint our boy in too heroic a light, does it?'

'You think this is true?'

'At least part of it. I think I believe he's an ex-cop. The rest of it, I could believe it. Actually, I think I do believe it.'

Jerry had stopped trimming Hardy's hair and now went back to it. 'That's some serious shit, Diz. If I were you, I'd be glad the Beck's out of it.'

'I know. I am. Except for the heartache part.'

'What about the cousin?'

'Yeah, I hear you,' Hardy said. 'There are some issues there, too.'

Anantha Douglas told Brady and Sher that, judging from the photograph in the six-pack, she was 'a hundred percent' certain that Moses McGuire had been the man with the club whom she'd run into on the sidewalk in front of her apartment. With that information, along with the previous assault, Brady thought they had enough information to run back downtown, get a warrant, and make an arrest.

Sher wasn't in perfect agreement. 'Look,' she said as they were waiting for their sandwiches at Lucca's deli on Chestnut, 'all I'm saying is we get one of our other witnesses to make an ID, we're in a lot stronger position, evidence-wise. If we go down and throw the cuffs on him now, we've got to Mirandize him, and once we do that, we're done talking. You know I'm right. And this is a guy, you'll remember, who likes to talk.'

'So what do you want to do?'

'I say we go visit him again. We're halfway out there anyhow. We tell him we know about the rape. Things are different. We know how he must feel about his daughter. We get him talking. Do a little good cop/bad cop – I'd be the good one, naturally – and see if he doesn't give the whole thing up. It might be our last chance before he gets himself lawyered up. If that doesn't work out, then we follow up, get a warrant, yada-yada. Meanwhile, we have an opportunity. Why pass it up?'

A half hour later, three parking spots west of the Little Shamrock's front door, Brady and Sher sat in their car and waited until Moses McGuire had unlocked the door to the bar and let himself in. With a perfectly timed mutual nod, they exited their own vehicle. As they came abreast of McGuire's robin's-egg-blue Honda Civic, they slowed and exchanged a meaningful glance. In another ten seconds, they were inside the bar.

From somewhere in the gloom, out of sight, a voice called out, 'Sorry. We're not open yet. Come back in a half hour.'

Brady gave their names with their ranks and waited. Nearly a full minute later, he was about to call out again when Sher put a hand on his arm, stopping him, and McGuire appeared in the short hallway that led to the dart room.

To Sher, he seemed somewhat diminished from the last time they'd spoken to him. He wore a simple maroon cotton long-sleeve shirt that was at least a size too large for him. His hair was uncombed. He carried a single bar towel in both hands, wringing it in an unconscious way. His face looked hollowed out.

This comported perfectly with Sher's expectations. McGuire would, of course, be devastated by the rape of his daughter. It would have started, or continued, to take a toll. He shouldn't have been and obviously wasn't expecting another visit from Homicide inspectors, as he'd been last time, and so he hadn't thought to steel himself.

'Mr McGuire,' she began, 'how are you holding up this morning?'

'Running on fumes,' he said. 'It's been a long couple of days.'

'I can imagine,' Sher said in her most sympathetic tone. Then continued, 'We know what happened to Brittany on Saturday night. We know she met with Rick Jessup at Perry's on Union. This was the day before he was killed.'

'The day before you said you were fishing,' Brady said with an edge of belligerence. 'How many did you say you caught?'

'Paul.' Sher put a restraining hand on her partner's arm, came back to her suspect. 'The point is, sir, that your daughter's . . . situation would have given you a very good reason to go look up Mr Jessup the next day, the same way you'd done a few months ago. Did you get an opportunity to do that?'

McGuire said nothing.

Sher pressed. 'We know what happened. We just don't know why. Did he insult Brittany, maybe threaten her? Maybe he attacked you and it was self-defense. Right now it looks like cold-blooded murder, but I don't think that's what it was. I don't think you're that kind of guy. If you're not, you'll have to be the one to tell us.'

'You're saying that now I'm a suspect in Jessup's killing.'

'Wouldn't that make some sense,' Sher asked gently, 'given what we know?'

'What do you think you know?'

'We do know, sir. About the rape. We found out by accident, to tell you the truth. But we know it is the truth. And you knew it, too, didn't you? You knew it by Sunday morning.'

'I'd like to cooperate with you,' McGuire said, 'but I'm afraid I'm under my lawyer's instructions not to say anything else.'

'You've got a lawyer already?' Brady asked.

'Yes, sir. Dismas Hardy, my brother-in-law.'

'Why'd you get a lawyer?'

'No comment. Should I call him now?'

'That's not necessary,' Sher said, 'although you have the absolute right to do that if you want. But you're not under arrest. You don't have to talk to us at all. You can kick us out right now. Unless you'd like to say something.'

'I don't have anything to say.'

'You don't want to deny killing Jessup?' Brady asked. Even getting a simple denial would be useful if it kept McGuire talking.

'No comment.'

'Come on,' Brady went on. 'Just say you didn't kill him. You can't say that?'

'I'm not saying anything.'

'Mr McGuire,' Sher said in dulcet tones, 'it's not like we don't understand how you feel, how you must have felt. I think most people would sympathize with their daughter having just been raped. Whoever killed him, it sounds to me like Mr Jessup got what he deserved. Wouldn't you say that's true?'

'No comment. Am I under arrest?'

'No.'

'But I am a suspect, is that right?'

Brady jumped in again. 'More than a suspect, McGuire. You're our prime suspect. And you know why? Because we've got eyewitnesses who saw you by Jessup's place. Because you've got all the motive in the world. Because from another witness, we've got a sketch that looks just like you.'

'Look,' Sher said, 'once we come back with handcuffs, it's going to be too late. I really would like to get your side of the story now. So I can describe you as cooperative and forthcoming and not as bad a guy as the evidence makes you look.'

'If you got so much, why don't you arrest me?'

'We want to give you a chance to say something in your defense,' Sher said. 'And look, you've already told us you were out fishing that evening. If you want to elaborate on that, we'd love to hear it. But if, as we both know, you were in Jessup's apartment, then what we really want to know is what happened.'

'I'm sorry,' McGuire repeated. 'I have no comment. And a bar to open in the next few minutes. So if you're done, I am, too.'

'I don't want to say this,' Brady began after a lengthy silence, Sher driving on Oak toward downtown alongside the Panhandle of Golden Gate Park, 'but did you get the impression that he'd been tipped?'

Sher was chewing her bottom lip, her face drawn down. 'I didn't expect he'd be lawyered up so soon, that's true.'

'Dismas Hardy,' Brady said. 'Glitsky's pal.'

'I knew the name rang a bell.'

They drove a few more blocks without a word.

Sher sighed. 'Okay, Paul. What do you want to do?'

'Maybe we should pull over and talk about it.'

'I've done some experiments,' she said. 'I can think while I'm driving.'

'All right.' After another moment, 'What do you think we should do?'

'That's not necessarily the same as what we want to do.'

'Right. I hear you.' Brady scratched his face. 'You think Glitsky called Hardy?'

'Not to mention how long it took Abe to admit he knew McGuire. And what did he tell McGuire while we're dicking around with sketch artists and six-packs? Or what did he tell Hardy, for that matter?'

'Yeah.' Brady sighed. 'This is fucked up.'

'Tell me about it.'

'I just did.' Brady blew out in frustration. 'I hate going outside the chain of command. It never works out right.'

'Lapeer came to us, remember. We didn't start it.'

'It was Glitsky's office. He was there. He was part of it.'

'Did he say anything about knowing McGuire then? While she was there?'

'You know he didn't.'

'Why didn't he?'

'Hoping we wouldn't get enough to charge him. He almost said as much after Lapeer left.'

'Jesus Christ,' Sher said. 'As if the job isn't hard enough. How long do you think he was going to let it go on? Dicking around with us?'

'Maybe he really was being careful. Keeping us on the right track.'

'Like we need that?' Sher asked, her anger palpable. 'Like he's ever done that before? This purely sucks. The one who's out of line here isn't us. You know what I mean?'

'I'm just sayin', maybe his reasons—'

'Screw his reasons. He's warning our witnesses that we're coming, for Christ's sake. I know what you're saying. But am I right or not? Abe's playing for the other team. Are we going to split hairs?'

Brady looked across at his partner, wagged his head back and forth in disgust. 'I guess not.'

21

AT THE FRANCISCA, the city's oldest women's social club, the chief of police had finished her lunchtime speech on bullying and youth violence and her outreach program to combat same in the city's public elementary schools. She was about to sit down for dessert with the other women when her driver and administrative aide, Sergeant Dermot Moriarty, came up and whispered in her ear. A minute later, she opened the door to a small but well-appointed conference room down the hall, where Homicide inspectors Brady and Sher were standing behind a mahogany table, slightly backlit from the windows that looked out over Sutter Street.

The door closed, and the chief looked from one inspector to the other. 'Brady,' she said, pointing at Paul then moving her finger, 'and . . . I'm sorry.'

'Sher, ma'am. Lee Sher.'

'I'm sorry,' Lapeer repeated. 'I won't forget again. Dermot said it was important, though the fact that you've sought me out down here would have clued me in. What can I do for you?'

'An issue's come up,' Brady began, 'around Moses McGuire, the suspect in the Jessup case.'

'I'm assuming that you've brought this up with Lieutenant Glitsky? And he's sent you down to brief me?'

'Not so much that, Chief,' Sher replied. 'The problem, more or less, is Glitsky.'

'In what way?'

Sher's explanation didn't take long. As she was finishing up, Lapeer's expression clouded, and she squinted at the corner of the ceiling. Her hands gripped the back of the chair she stood behind. In the gathering silence, she drew in a breath, then let it out. 'Your assumption is that the lieutenant notified McGuire's lawyer, who then advised his client not to talk to you. Meaning that Glitsky is not only friends with McGuire but the connection is McGuire's lawyer, who is also a friend of the lieutenant?'

'Yes, ma'am,' Brady said. 'His name is Dismas Hardy.'

After a beat, Lapeer's countenance darkened. 'You're joking,' she said.

'No, ma'am. Do you know him?'

'I know somebody who used to be his law partner. Currently, he's employed as the district attorney.'

'Farrell?' Sher asked. 'You're saying Hardy and Wes Farrell . . . ?'

'Partners,' she said. 'Not long ago, the firm was Freeman Farrell Hardy and Roake. And if I'm not mistaken, doesn't the lieutenant's wife – isn't she Farrell's secretary?' The weight of these connections seemed to settle on the chief's shoulders. She pulled out the chair she'd been leaning on and lowered herself into it with another deep sigh. 'No wonder,' she said, 'the wheels of justice aren't turning so smoothly in this case. They're all gummed up with conflicts. Lord, Lord, Lord.' She ran her hands back through her hair. 'So where are you now? With the investigation? How solid a suspect is McGuire?'

'We like him,' Brady said. 'We thought about bringing him downtown this morning after we got a decent ID.'

'You got an ID?'

'Six-pack,' Brady said. 'A hundred percent.'

'Plus a motive?' Lapeer said. 'Sounds like you've got plenty to me.'

'We'll need search warrants while we're at it,' Sher added,

'although we might be a little light on evidence. Especially if we know that Farrell's not inclined to charge—'

Lapeer put a palm up. 'Hold on. We're talking about the murder of a respected city employee, chief of staff to one of our most popular and visible supervisors. How am I supposed to go back to Mr Goodman, knowing what I know, and explain why we haven't arrested Mr McGuire yet? Either of you want to tell me that?'

'We could—' Brady began.

Again Lapeer cut him off. 'No. No, no, no. Here's what's going to happen, starting right now. Both of you, as of this minute, are reporting to me and me alone on this case. You are not to go to the DA, and you're particularly not to go to Lieutenant Glitsky. Does either of you know who's the duty judge this week?'

The duty judge, who signed off on search and arrest warrants, was a rotating position among the superior court judges, although any judge was empowered to sign any warrant.

'Thomasino, I think,' Sher said.

Lapeer shook her head, dismissed him with a wave of her hand. 'No good. Defense bias. How about Braun? Is she at trial now? You could catch her at a recess. She's kind of famous for her animosity toward Mr Hardy. Remember that guy who got killed in her courtroom? She blames Hardy for that. She's going to be our warrants judge on this case. I want McGuire in jail by close of business today.'

'Excuse me, Chief,' Sher said, 'but if we do that, we're going around everybody. Our boss, the DA. If we get a Ramey warrant and Farrell winds up not charging the case, cites lack of evidence, then what?'

Lapeer shook her head. 'We're not going to worry about that. I am telling you, do not go to the district attorney first with this case.'

'But—' Brady began.

Lapeer stopped him. 'If Farrell refuses to file on what we've got now, we can't turn around and go to a judge for a warrant. No judge in the world would authorize an arrest knowing there wasn't going to be a prosecution.'

Sher said, 'So we're making it Farrell's problem.'

'Right. Better we go with a Ramey.' Typically, inspectors filed a report and sent it to the DA, who decided whether he could convict the suspect on what they'd given him. If he thought so, he filed a complaint and asked for an arrest warrant. In some cases, police could go directly to a judge and get a warrant themselves, which made for a legal arrest, but it deferred the DA's decision on whether to file charges. 'We put probable cause in our affidavit,' she continued. 'The judge agrees and signs it. We make our arrest. And we get our search warrants at the same time. Maybe we get lucky, and the case gets better.'

'If it doesn't?' Brady asked.

'If it doesn't, after that, if Farrell publicly wants to disagree with us and the judge and say there's not enough to go forward, then he can let McGuire off right in front of God and everybody. As far as I'm concerned, we've got enough. What happens next is not our issue. Which is why DAs hate Ramey so much. But it gets us – you guys – what you need in cases like this one. I believe I've mentioned that I want to see McGuire in handcuffs by tonight. Let's see if we can make that happen, why don't we?'

Sergeant Moriarty was driving the chief out to a meeting with the Outer Sunset Graffiti Abatement program, which was a long way from the Francisca Club, geographically and psychologically, so there was plenty of time to talk, although Moriarty wasn't sure how to subtly slide into the topic. The chief was reading something in the backseat, and in the rearview mirror, he saw her lower the pages, close her eyes, and sigh.

'Everything all right?'

'Fine.' She hesitated. 'I'm wondering if this is serious enough to take to Internal Affairs, or have our guys make the Ramey arrest and let it go.' Moriarty wasn't going to correct his boss about the name of the unit that investigated police misconduct. Internal Affairs nearly everywhere else, in San Francisco – ever politically correct – it was called the Administrative Investigation Division. She went on, 'I don't know if I see any real collusion here, much less a conspiracy. It's a small town, after all. People are going to know each other, right? You think Glitsky got McGuire lawyered up?'

'Like one of 'em said, it's hard to avoid that conclusion, isn't it? You want to hear a rumor?'

She met his eyes in the rearview. 'Always.'

'Maybe you've already got wind of it. The Dockside Massacre? Down at Pier Seventy? Five or six years ago?'

Lord, she thought, had she heard of it. After the *Courier* column a few months before, when Sheila Marrenas had aired the department's dirty laundry from the past twenty years, it had been another issue that made her vulnerable to attack from the mayor. Even though she'd had nothing to do with any of the notorious unsolved murders – indeed, she hadn't been on the job for any of them – she supposedly could have started investigations on any of the so-called skull cases. Somehow her failure to embark on any of those quixotic journeys, using staff and resources she did not have, meant that she wasn't as serious as she could be about solving crimes. If the Dockside Massacre even tangentially intersected with Moses McGuire, she wanted to know all about it right now and move on anyone involved with all due haste.

Even if that person was one of her department heads.

Lapeer cocked her head to one side. Her eyes flitted away from Moriarty's to the southeast corner of the city falling off behind them as they climbed Market Street up to Twin Peaks. If Dermot Moriarty had any information at all, even if it was the rankest rumor, she wanted to hear it. 'Remind me about this so-called massacre,' she said.

'I'm probably off on the timing,' Moriarty said. 'Barry Gerson was running Homicide.'

'I don't know him.'

'No. You wouldn't. Before your time. He got himself killed trying to arrest a murder suspect named John Holiday, who got killed the same day, along with I think either three or four other private security guys. Patrol Specials, actually. Essentially cops, as you know. Although what they were doing there, God only knows.'

'Maybe Gerson needed their help with the arrest.'

'Patrol Specials, not regular cops? Not in this lifetime. But it doesn't look like anybody will ever know.'

'Wait a minute. You're saying – what? – five or six cops were shot dead in one day at one place? This was at Pier Seventy?'

'Right. Don't forget, one suspect shot, too. They didn't call it a massacre for nothing. Smack in the middle of the afternoon. Also, they found about a hundred shell casings lying around, twenty or thirty bullet holes in the structures out there, not to mention the carnage to the victims. It was a balls-out firefight.'

'Not an execution?'

'No, ma'am. Bodies all over the place where they fell.'

'Who were the killers?'

'That's the thing. Eventually, the whole episode got laid off on the Russian mafia, something to do with stolen diamonds, blood diamonds, I don't know. It got too complicated to follow; finally it all went away.'

'Six homicides just went away? How'd that happen?'

Moriarty shrugged, checked the rearview, slowed for a light. 'The shooters went back to Russia, maybe by diplomatic flight.'

He paused. 'You see why there were rumors. It was all a little squirrelly.'

'I get it.'

'Here's the kicker. You want to guess who was the lawyer for the murder suspect, John Holiday?'

'Farrell.'

'Close but no cigar, which leaves . . . ?'

'Dismas Hardy.'

'See? This is why you're the chief.' They started moving again.

'Yeah, well, it took me two guesses,' Lapeer said. 'What does it mean, though, that Hardy was his attorney?'

'Nothing, maybe, by itself. But with a few other facts, things get more interesting. Like – you'll get this on the first try – who got promoted into Gerson's job?'

In the rearview, Lapeer took her chin in her hand, squeezed her lower lip.

'Glitsky,' Moriarty went on, 'had been in Homicide before he got shot, and took a year or so to recover. When he came back to work, they brought him in to supervise Payroll, which – he made no secret – he didn't find very challenging.'

The chief made a dismissive noise. 'Dermot, please. Glitsky didn't kill Gerson to get his old job back. That I flatly don't believe.'

'I'm just telling you what people were saying.'

'Okay, but that's ridiculous. What people?'

'Mostly other cops. Most of whom are gone.'

'Gone where?'

'Retired, reassigned, quit. Gone. But Glitsky taking over Homicide? Maybe that's why the investigation into all these murders kind of ran out of steam.'

After a beat to consider the possibly relevant point, she asked, 'And where does Farrell fit into the scenario?'

'Nowhere. But you know Hardy's other partners? Farrell's partners, for that matter? David Freeman and Gina Roake?'

'What about them?'

'Freeman got mugged a couple of days before Pier Seventy. He died in the hospital on the same day as the shoot-out.' Moriarty paused for effect. 'Roake and he were engaged.'

At this, Lapeer allowed herself a small chuckle. 'Okay, Dermot, this is really getting into the realm of fantasy.'

'Maybe, but you might as well hear all of it. There's one other player. Fought alongside Hardy in Vietnam, both of them experts with weapons. And P.S., Hardy saved his life over there and then came back home, bought in to his bar, and married his sister.'

'McGuire.'

Moriarty nodded into the mirror. 'McGuire. Oh, and one last thing.'

'I'm listening.'

'Of course there was an investigation at the time. You could look it up. There'd be files on it, all the details. Glitsky was ruled out because he had an airtight alibi. You want to guess what it was?'

'I don't believe my imagination is up to it.'

'He was with Gina Roake at David Freeman's apartment all afternoon, picking out a suit for Freeman's funeral. You'll notice how nicely this dovetails into Roake's alibi. How 'bout them apples?'

After Sher and Brady left, Moses pondered his situation while he set up the back bar, loaded up the condiment bins, peeled the lemons, whipped the cream for the Irish coffee, rolled in a new keg of Bass. Somewhere around one o'clock, he made the decision that a little hair of the dog wouldn't kill him.

He'd monitor the alcohol intake more carefully this time, that's all.

By four o'clock, when Sher and Brady showed up again, he'd had three carefully measured shots – well, double shots – of vodka. Scotch was really his drink, but if he drank Scotch, Susan would smell it on him.

Vodka, maybe not so much.

So it was only Moses and Dave and two couples on the couches under the Tiffany lamps in the back when the front door opened and the two inspectors trooped in with a sense of urgency they hadn't displayed before.

He greeted them with weary tolerance. 'You guys, you guys. Don't you ever take a break?'

Neither of them was in the mood for casual repartee. Brady got up to the bar in a couple of steps, Sher staying back by the door. Her arms were crossed over her chest, but one hand was tucked inside her jacket, no doubt on her service weapon. Looking over at her, next to the front windows, Moses saw a couple of black-and-white patrol cars on the street outside.

'Mr McGuire,' Brady said, 'I'd like to ask you to come around the bar, please.'

Moses, still trying to brazen things out, flashed some teeth and said, 'It would be easier to pour you a drink from back here. What are you having?'

'I'm asking you again, and for the last time, to come around the bar.'

Brady's tone alerted Dave, seated where he always was at the front of the bar by the window, who raised his head and tried to focus on Brady. 'How's he going to get you a drink from out in front of the bar?' he asked.

Sher, wound tightly, took a quick couple of steps over to Dave's side and flipped her badge in front of him. 'Drink up, pal. San Francisco police. This bar's closing right now.'

Dave gave her an uncertain glance. 'Bullshit,' he said. 'It's the middle of the day.'

Brady patted his hand firmly on the bar. 'McGuire. Now.'

Unloading a heavy breath, Moses wiped his hands on his bar towel. 'All right, all right, I'm coming.'

Dave didn't like this much and took the opportunity to pop his beer bottle down on the bar. 'Mose, what is this bullshit? Give 'em what for. Whack 'em one with the shillelagh.'

Moses had already pulled up the hinged part of the bar on his way out from behind it. He stopped, turning abruptly. 'Shut up, Dave. Just shut up.'

'What shillelagh?' Sher asked.

'He's got a big ol' shillelagh hanging down under the bar. Been there forever. That's what.'

One of the mid-twenties men in the back was on his feet. 'Is there a problem up here?'

Brady held up the wallet with his badge, slapped the bar again, raised his voice, moving back toward where the young man and Moses stood in close proximity. 'Everybody, listen up. We are San Francisco police on official business. Please, everybody stay where you are.' He advanced on the younger man. 'Except you! Back up! More! Now sit down!' Brady didn't want the well-meaning but stupid interloper anywhere near McGuire, where, in a heartbeat, he might find himself held hostage by his friendly local bartender.

Brady never got all the way past McGuire; he didn't want to show the man any part of his back. Suddenly, the plan had gotten unscripted, out of hand. Brady knew they had backup units parked all along the street, hand-picked teams planning to search the premises – along with McGuire's car and his apartment – and he almost yelled at Sher to open the door and call in the troops.

Then McGuire took a small step toward him, holding up both hands. 'Easy, easy, easy,' he said. He looked over and down at his customers. 'Nothing to worry about. No problem.' Back to Brady. 'Here I am, as ordered. What can I do for you?'

'Moses McGuire,' Brady said, holding up a piece of paper, letting out a sigh of relief. 'I have here a warrant for your arrest for the murder of Richard Jessup. You have the right to remain silent. If you give up that right, anything you do say can and will . . .'

McGuire wouldn't shut up, and using their secret sign language, Brady and Sher decided they wouldn't try to make him.

'I don't see why you need these handcuffs,' he was saying. 'They're too goddamn small. They feel like shit. Come on, you guys, I wasn't going anywhere. I came around from inside the bar on my own. Here I am, all cooperation, and the back of this car is locked up anyway. I couldn't go anywhere if I wanted to. And you could pull over right here and take off the cuffs. Come on. Brady? Inspector Sher? Come on! Shit.'

After they had him locked in the backseat of their car on Lincoln Way with one of the patrolmen keeping an eye on him, they told the customers in the back of the Shamrock that they had to leave. They would be closing down the bar while officers executed a search warrant.

Sher went over to Dave, whom she'd told to shut up and finish his beer and wait for her. She got his full name, address, and phone number, since he would be a witness about the shillelagh, which by the way was nowhere to be found. Dave wasn't too happy about this development, but Sher thought it was more that he would have to find another local bar to drink away the day.

Moses was going on in the backseat: 'Do you really think you've got anything at all on me? Where's the murder weapon? I didn't kill that little son of a bitch, although he needed killing, and I'm glad he's dead.'

And: 'I'm having a hard time believing that Glitsky let you get away with this. We've been buds for twenty years. There's no way he's going to let me get anywhere near a trial, trust me. I've got nothing to worry about. You're both wasting all this time when you could be out looking for somebody to convict.'

And: 'Either of you have kids? No? What do you think you'd do if you had a daughter and found out some little punk had first beat her and then raped her? You think you'd sit around wringing your hands? C'mon, you guys are cops. You'd go and handle things, wouldn't you? Tell me you wouldn't. Because sometimes the law doesn't get it right. A little prison time for some fucking loser is nothing next to the time my girl's going to take to get over what he did to her. You think that's fair? You think that's right?'

Downtown, while Brady walked McGuire into the Hall of Justice and upstairs to begin processing his arrest, Sher pulled the tape recorder out from under the backseat, checked to see that it had picked up everything McGuire said on the ride downtown, then double-checked that neither she nor Brady had said so much as one word to prompt him. Satisfied, she brought the tape to the transcripts pool office to be typed up for inclusion into the case record.

22

BECAUSE FOURTEEN YEARS ago Sam Duncan and Wes Farrell had met and hooked up – although that wasn't the term used in those days – at the Little Shamrock, Wes took it as a promising sign that she had asked to meet him there after work. On the other hand, the fact that it was a public place allowed the interpretation that she wanted to avoid a scene, which would surely ensue if she broke up with him. Indeed, such an event had come to pass at least once, even twice if one counted Sam's abrupt departure over another argument whose subject was lost in the mists of time – something about Wes's incorrigible lack of sensitivity, no doubt.

Since that's what the arguments were always about.

Sam had been staying at her mother's place since their rooftop discussion about Brittany McGuire had broken down so disastrously, and the thought that he would at least get to see her again and argue his position – bolstered by Glitsky's comments that Sam should be mad at herself – gave him a modicum of hope, mitigated slightly by her saying that she didn't want to talk on the phone. 'Some things,' she had told him, 'need to be done in person.'

At just short of six o'clock, Farrell came around the corner into the teeth of the gale at Ninth Avenue and, seeing the line of patrol cars parked at the curb on Lincoln, stopped as though getting his bearings.

What the hell?

Only then did he realize – so focused had he been on his

girlfriend issue – that the long-familiar hangout was the work-place of the suspect in a murder investigation. And where, judging from the police presence, something major had tran-spired recently. His first thought was that Moses had killed himself, and sad to say, his first instinct was a wash of relief.

The door was locked, but he could see movement inside, and he knocked. Then knocked again, tried the door again, rattling it. Inside, a figure in uniform appeared and said through the glass of the door, 'This establishment is closed until further notice. Police investigation.'

Farrell reached for his back pocket, knocked again on the window, and held up his wallet with its entirely bogus badge – after his election, he'd bought the badge at a police equipment store in Daly City; district attorneys aren't cops and are not entitled to pretend they are, but the badge tended to work wonders with people who couldn't read an official ID and knew generally what a badge meant. For most associate DAs, the badge's primary function was to be flashed at traffic cops to get out of speeding tickets and DUI arrests.

Sure enough, the uniformed cop stepped closer, got a good look at the badge, and proceeded to unlock the door. 'Sorry, sir,' he said, 'we've had customers coming by all day. How can I help you?'

'Wes Farrell,' he said, getting to the point. 'The district attorney. Who's running the show here?'

The cop straightened up, decided he ought to salute, then said, 'Yes, sir. Sorry, sir. Just a minute,' and disappeared into the bowels of the bar. Farrell took the opportunity to glance around and realized that he'd arrived in the midst of a fairly rigorous search. All the bottles from the shelves behind the bar were on the bar. So were most of the glasses. The pillows from the couches and upholstered chairs in the back had been removed and piled against the wall. Farrell crossed over to look behind the bar and saw that everything had been cleaned out – the refrigerators were open and empty, likewise the cash register. Someone had piled the bar towels on the counter. Most startling, the sixty or eighty photographs on the 'Wall of Shame' corkboard – from women baring their breasts to men posing with yards of ale or whatever else they'd consumed – had been removed.

To Farrell, this struck deep, and not only because he had made the wall after breaking the record of five Long Island iced teas on what had been a memorable night that he couldn't remember. His record six held, although he shared it with two other guys and one woman. Paul McCartney once stopped in for a pint of Bass and played somebody's random right-handed guitar, by common consent, perfectly.

Farrell looked over at the sound of footsteps as another uniform came out of the hallway to the dart room. 'Mr Farrell,' he said before he'd gotten close, 'Sergeant Dankers. What brings you out here?'

'I was going to ask you the same thing, Sergeant. I gather you're searching this place. I presume you've got a warrant and affidavit.'

The implied rebuke brought confusion to the man's face. 'Well, yes, sir. Of course. This is on the Jessup homicide. A couple of inspectors arrested the suspect here, and we came in right after. Two, three hours ago.'

'What are you looking for?'

'Pretty much the usual. Clothing, shoes, weapons or objects that could be used as weapons, obvious signs of blood or other fluids, receipts, photographs, computer records if any.'

'They arrested a suspect?'

'Yes, sir. The bartender. The owner, I think. Moses McGuire.'

'Yes. He's the owner. But I don't understand. Was he fleeing? Did he try to break away when they were questioning him? Did he put up a fight?'

'I don't think so, sir. I was outside waiting, and they went in, served the warrant, then came out with him in cuffs like five minutes later.'

'They had a warrant? An arrest warrant?'

'As far as I know. Yes, sir.'

'That's interesting.'

'Sir?'

'I say it's interesting because it's my office that issues warrants. I've been following this case very closely, and I would have imagined I'd be told, since I specifically asked to be, if they'd gotten enough to make an arrest.'

Dankers shifted from one foot to the other. He reached over and picked up a folded document sitting on one of the tables. 'Would you like to inspect my search warrant, sir? It looks like legitimately signed paper to me.'

'Who was the judge?'

Dankers unfolded the paper, glanced down. 'Braun.'

That brought a deep frown. 'She's not this week's magistrate. Why did she sign off on this?'

Dankers shrugged, mystified. 'I don't know, sir. Are you saying we should call off the search? We're almost done as it is.'

'No. You finish up. I'm sure there's a reasonable explanation. I'm just somewhat confused as to why I wasn't informed. But that isn't your problem. Are you also searching McGuire's home?'

'I'd assume somebody is. My team drew the bar.'

Farrell took a last long look around the room. It seemed to him that the team had done a thorough and relatively respectful legal search. Dankers clearly had no ax to grind; he was simply doing his job. Farrell saw no point in drawing more attention to his reservations. Obviously, they'd found evidence that Moses had killed Rick Jessup, although the reality of actual arrest struck Farrell as surreal. More disturbingly, he had been in his office until after five. The arrest warrant must have been signed (by Braun!) no later than two. What Homicide DA had authorized it? How had he not been told? Could it have been an oversight? That was hard to imagine, given his admitted level of interest. Had Glitsky somehow gone around him? If so, why?

None of this was Dankers's concern. Farrell came back to the present, tried to muster a positive tone, a half smile. 'Well, Sergeant, you and your men carry on. Sorry to have bothered you. I've obviously just fallen out of the loop a little bit. I'm sure all will be explained in good time.' He extended his hand. 'Thanks again.'

'Thank you, sir. And if I may?'

Half-turned toward the door, Farrell stopped. 'Yes.'

'I'm impressed to see someone in your position out walking the walk. It's not something that happens every day.'

'I'm taking that as a vote of confidence. When you win your election by ninety votes – and that's after your opponent dies the week before – you've got to take every one you can get.'

Sam sat across from Wes at a small two-top in the Pacific Café, great seafood on the way out to the beach on Geary, the backup rendezvous she'd suggested when he'd told her the Shamrock was closed. She had placed her hand over his on the table top, a good sign, he thought. A couple of sips into their first glasses of wine, Sam cleared her throat. 'Thank you for saying you'd come out and see me.'

'Not just saying it. Walking the walk.'

A tolerant smile. 'That, too.' Though it was the kind of response that she tended to underappreciate, she kept her hand over his. 'I've been thinking a lot about . . . this last thing. Me telling you about Rick Jessup, dropping his name by mistake, and your guys coming out to see Brittany, and what that meant, and now it's led to poor Moses getting arrested. All because I wanted to share what I do with you.'

'You were right. Maybe I shouldn't—'

She squeezed his hand, stopping him. 'No,' she said. 'Listen. This was my fault. Not yours. You did your duty. I'm the one who ought to be able to keep secrets, especially secrets like these. And I've been treating them like cheap gossip, where I'll only tell my three best girlfriends or, in my case, my one best guy friend. But it's not gossip. It's really and truly privileged stuff. I am privileged to hear it at all, to have somebody trust me with it, and to treat it as any less is plain irresponsible. If I can't keep those secrets – and I mean every single time – I don't deserve to do what I do.'

She lifted her hand to wipe a tear from her eye. Then returned it immediately. 'There are actually two reasons I wanted to see you tonight. The first is to apologize—'

'Sam, you don't—'

'Shh. I do. I am always so sure of myself, so always in the right, so stubborn and ready to pick a fight on some political or moral issue. A fight pretty much to the death, while I'm at it. But now these last couple of days, hanging with my mom, seeing how she likes living alone – which is to say not at all – I started thinking about why I do that all the time. Especially to you. Time after time, you take it and we get back together and don't talk about it until the next one because I know you don't want to get me going again, get me all upset, mostly over a radical interpretation of some fine abstraction.'

Farrell broke a true smile. 'Radical interpretation of some fine abstraction. There's a nice turn of phrase.'

'Yes, but it's not a good way to live.' She took a sip of her wine and drew a breath. 'Anyway, that's the first reason I wanted to see you. To apologize and not just for this time. For all the times.'

'Okay,' he said. 'And thank you. Accepted but unnecessary. I love you. I love our life together. We're good. We just fight sometimes.'

'No. I just pick fights sometimes. And then I give you no choice; you have to wade in.'

'Yeah, but I'm a lawyer. We live to argue.'

'Let's not now, though, okay?'

He nodded, sat back a bit in his chair. 'Okay.'

'I don't want to be that person anymore. I don't want to fight about every little thing. We can have different opinions, I don't have to tell you my privileged secrets. We can be together and support each other. How would that be?'

'If I said "weird," would you hit me?'

'No,' she said. 'I would support your right to say "weird."'

'In that case,' Farrell said, 'I think it would be good. Very good.' He put his other hand over hers and let out his own breath. 'I was thinking you were leaving. I didn't know what I was going to do.'

'I'm not leaving, if you still want us.'

'I don't want anything else.'

'Okay, then. Here's the second reason I needed to talk to you, and why we needed to do it in person.'

Dismas and Frannie Hardy lived on Thirty-fourth Avenue, down near its intersection with Clement Street. The farther intersection was at Geary, and that corner was the home of the Pacific Café. Though there was often a line to get into the tiny place, tonight the drizzly cold monsoon was keeping the crowd close to a manageable level. When Hardy opened the door for his wife, he found himself looking at Wes Farrell, who said to Sam just loudly enough to be heard: 'Here he is now. I'll tell you later.' With a big phony smile, shaking hands, bussing Frannie on the cheek, 'Hi, Diz. Frannie. Small world. You've got to have the halibut. Incredible.'

'Always,' Frannie said.

'But first,' Farrell began, stopped, spoke to Sam. 'Should we tell them?'

'I believe we should.'

'What?' Hardy looked at Sam, over to Wes. 'You're pregnant,' he said to Wes.

'Good guess, but that's not it,' Sam said, 'for either of us.'

'There's a relief,' Frannie said, 'although if it were Wes, you guys could get rich.'

Farrell ran with it. 'We're already rich in spirit, but pregnant is close, in the sense that pregnant people are sometimes married.'

'But rarely male,' Frannie countered. 'In fact, never, I think.'

'Except seahorses,' Hardy said. 'Pregnant males. You could look it up.'

'Darn,' Farrell said. 'I was thinking that could be us. The next phase, I mean. After the marriage.'

'I'm picking up a theme.'

'Dismas Hardy, thematic wizard.'

'Married? Really?' Frannie beamed at them. 'After all this time. That's great, but what happened?'

Farrell took Sam's hand again. 'She asked me five minutes ago. I caved immediately.'

'Caved,' Sam said. 'There's a sweet way to put it.'

'Bowed to formidable pressure,' Farrell explained. 'Caved.' He patted her hand. 'Happily.'

Hardy spun around for the waiter. 'We should order some champagne.'

'We should,' Farrell said, but then a shadow crossed his face. 'Wait . . . not to put a damper on things, but I'm guessing, you both being down here for a nice date, that maybe you haven't heard about Moses.'

'Damper' was hardly the word. Frannie turned a shade lighter and reached a hand out to steady herself on Hardy's arm. 'What about Moses?'

'I just came from the Shamrock. They had a warrant and were tossing the place. They said they picked up Moses on the Jessup thing a couple of hours ago.'

'They arrested him? Who did?'

'Homicide, I presume. Although I called, and my office didn't sign off on the warrant. I don't know what happened.'

Hardy looked like he was trying to place an unfamiliar flavor. 'They couldn't have arrested him. I mean, that's impossible. Abe would at least have given me a heads-up, had me deliver him downtown. Or he would have called me first thing.'

'You're his lawyer?'

Hardy nodded. 'Couple of days now. I can't believe he wouldn't have—'

On his hip, his cell phone rang with Warren Zevon's 'I'll Sleep When I'm Dead.' Hardy glanced at the screen. 'Here he is now.'

Frannie squeezed his arm. 'Diz, you've got to—'

'I know,' he said, and punched to pick up. 'Mose, where are you?'

Moses was in jail. In the end, Farrell's charging decision was unfortunately simple. The crime lab found Jessup's blood on a pair of hiking boots in McGuire's apartment, in his car, and on his jacket.

Now Dismas Hardy paced the semicircular glass-block wall along one side of the relatively spacious attorneys' visiting room at the county jail. He'd been here dozens if not hundreds of times, and in spite of its size and modernity, the place never failed to depress him with its vague smell of disinfectant, its ice-cold fluorescent lighting. In the middle of the room were its only furnishings – a metal desk with a pitted green surface and three folding chairs.

Hardy stopped pacing and looked at his watch. Eight-fifteen. He'd gotten to the jail exactly half an hour ago. In near-record time of only five minutes, the front desk had verified his business and admitted him to wait until Moses got delivered. It was common practice to keep defense attorneys waiting, just as the jail guards rarely took with any sense of urgency an order to produce an inmate. They'd get to it as soon as they could, but there usually was another errand or two to run first. Or a mandated break. Or another prisoner to deliver. Or a bathroom stop.

Everyone inside the jail lived with the reality that things happened when they did, at their own speed. What was five minutes, or even twenty-five? What else were these people doing?

Once, several years ago, after an hour or so cooling his heels in this very room, Hardy had grown impatient enough to go out to the admitting desk and politely inquire as to the status of his client. Were they, perchance, having trouble locating him within the jail? Was there anything Hardy could do to speed up the process? Was there some other problem? Forty minutes after that inquiry, the admitting sergeant knocked on the visiting room door and informed Hardy that there'd been an administrative error and, unfortunately, his client was on his way to County General Hospital with a group of inmates scheduled for psychiatric evaluation. The client shouldn't have been put on that bus, but it was too late to do anything about it now, so Hardy should come back the following day, when his client would probably be back in his cell.

Hardy had learned his lesson. You waited as long as it took.

His stomach growled at him. Moses's phone call at the Pacific Café had brought to an end the dinner portion of the night, before it began, and portended a lengthy next portion.

Finally, he stopped pacing and sat down on one of the chairs. Several minutes after that, the knock sounded, the door opened, and Moses came in wearing an orange jumpsuit. This was always a depressing moment, especially when the client was a friend who'd never been in jail garb. Hardy's heart went out to his brother-in-law as the guard gave Hardy an all's-well nod, then left and closed the door behind him.

'I've got to be honest,' Hardy said. 'I'm getting a little tired of your shit. When did they pick you up?'

'Four. Somewhere around there.'

'Did it occur to you to ask them to let you call me then?'

'No, and they didn't offer. They just packed me up, put handcuffs on me, and threw me in the back of their car. By the time anybody was listening to me wanting my phone call, it was kind of moot.' Moses came closer, pulled around a chair, and straddled it backward. 'Meanwhile, look at this, my skin's all scraped off. Those things are cruel and unusual punishment all by themselves.'

Hardy wasn't looking at McGuire's wrists. He was staring at his face. 'Have you been drinking?'

'What?'

'It's not a trick question. And you just answered it.'

'Hair of the dog, that's all. A few drops.'

Hardy lowered his head, rubbed his eyes with the thumb and index finger of his right hand. After he stopped, he looked across at his brother-in-law. 'Mose,' he said wearily. 'We're all pissed off at what happened to Brittany. Nobody's crying over Jessup being dead. But you being dead or drunk isn't going to help her get over it. It's only going to make it worse because she'll think it's her fault. You're a smart guy. You're telling me you don't see that?'

'No, you're right.'

'I know I'm right. The question is, what are you going to do? What are you even trying to do? If you're not going to suck it up and deal with this like a grown-up, maybe we need to get you a lawyer who wants to live with the aggravation, which there will be plenty of even if you're at your best. So answer me, what the hell is going on with you? Is this it? Are you just giving up? Is your life over?'

McGuire stared at the wall behind Hardy's head. He

swallowed, his Adam's apple bobbing a couple of times. 'I can't seem to find a place to put it, Diz. I mean, what he did to her. I start thinking about it, and before I know what's happening, there's this, this rage . . . it's just overwhelming. I can't get a handle on it, so I've got to black it out, I mean obliterate myself. And we know what works for that.'

'Yeah, except it doesn't.'

'I know.'

'Really, Mose. It doesn't.'

'I know.'

'But you keep pushing it? And please don't tell me you can't help yourself. That's not you.'

McGuire hung his head, barely whispered, 'That's what it feels like this time. Like it's all too much to handle.'

'Spare me,' Hardy said, his own outrage kicking in a bit. 'Grow the fuck up. This didn't happen to you. It happened to Brittany. You've still got Susan and both of your girls, and you're trading them in for a bottle. Is that what you want, who you're going to be? Because if it is, I'm done and out of here before we even start.'

Hardy surprised himself by standing up, heading for the door, knocking for the guard.

'What are you doing?' McGuire was up, too, standing back by the desk.

'I'm letting you make some decisions. Or really, only one. I'll see you tomorrow morning. I assume you're getting arraigned.'

'I don't know.'

'I'll find out, and they'll tell you and bring you down, so we ought to meet up sometime.'

'Until then, what?'

'Same drill,' Hardy said. 'Keep your mouth shut.'

23

MASSAGING THE SKIN over his heart, Abe Glitsky stared down through the plantation shutters that covered his living room's picture window. Though it was not yet nine o'clock, darkness had come on rapidly with the approaching storm, and already the west-facing window thrummed with the lashing rain. In the back of the flat, he was vaguely aware of Treya's bedtime rituals with the kids, who had stayed up later than usual because the family was preparing for tomorrow's seder, a good reason to amend the nighttime schedule if ever there was one.

Five minutes ago, Abe had been in with them all, the furthest cry from a hard-ass lieutenant of Homicide as could be imagined. With his second family, Glitsky was in many ways a different human being than he'd been on the first go-round, with his cancer-stricken wife and his three boys, now all grown up. When he married Treya, she'd brought a lovely teenage daughter, Raney, with her. In short order, they'd had Rachel and Zachary. For some reason – Glitsky attributed it to the two girls when he thought about it at all – he had discovered a spark of, if not true goofiness, than at least levity, that he loved sharing with his children.

He made faces, told jokes, worked the occasional pun, waxed sarcastic. He found that he loved slapstick – tonight at dinner they'd had one of those everybody-spills-milk moments. Zach's went first, and when Treya reached to catch it, she knocked over her own glass, pretty much into the lap of Rachel, who jumped up and – yes – knocked over her own glass. Glitsky, facing an imminent meltdown, remained calm, looked around the table at the stricken faces, and said, 'Let's not have a meltdown. Let's have a milkdown.' He picked up his glass and slowly poured it on the table. Crisis averted, and probably a story for the kids for the rest of their lives, one that their older half brothers would never believe. Rachel and Zach were already reliving the moment, laughing, loving the idea of a milkdown as Glitsky was helping to tuck them in.

Then the landline rang on the kitchen wall, and since he remained the kind of guy who always answered the phone, he excused himself with a final quick tickle of his son and went in and picked up.

Whereupon he got the news from his best friend that his two inspectors had arrested Moses McGuire, and what did he know about that?

As he watched the rain, it was as though he felt the darkness trying to get inside his house and to invade his soul. In a bad mood, Dismas Hardy nevertheless had been his usual confident self, assuring Abe that Moses posed no real risk. At least in terms of what they'd all been through in the past.

Glitsky knew Hardy as well as he knew anybody, and understood that he was capable of self-deception sometimes. He did not want to see the bad in people, whereas Glitsky, outside of his home, tended to see it more than anything else.

How could Brady and Sher have made an arrest without telling him? And wouldn't Farrell have told him or at least tried? Potentially even more worrisome, neither of his two inspectors had called to bring him up-to-date on this rather huge development in a case.

Had McGuire, in his cups, already said something to his inspectors, not about Jessup but about what had happened six years ago?

He was so deep in his thoughts that he wasn't aware of Treya coming up behind him until she put her hand on his shoulder. He nearly levitated with the surprise.

'Whoa! Are you okay?'

'I just didn't hear you coming up.' He reached his hand back and touched hers. 'They arrested McGuire and didn't tell me anything. Did you get any word of that at Farrell's office?'

'No. How could they do that?'

'A few ways, none of them normal. I can't believe I haven't heard from either of my people.'

'Maybe he resisted. Maybe they got hurt.'

He shook his head. 'Diz would have told me.'

'What's he got to do with it?'

'Guess.'

'I think I can, now that you mention it. What are you going to do?'

'I don't know. I'd say call Paul or Lee, except I'm thinking they already should have called me. But they haven't, and what's that about?'

'It had to be something unusual. Maybe Moses was trying to get out of town or something.'

'All the more reason to tell me, wouldn't you think?'

'You'll worry it until you know. Call one of them, at least get the story.'

'You think?'

'I do.'

Once his dinner plans got ruined, Hardy had thought he'd stay down talking to his brother-in-law until well into the night, getting his version of things, formulating a defense plan. But after his temper had sabotaged that idea and ridden him out of the jail's visiting room on a wave of frustration and disgust, he found himself sitting in his car across the street from the Hall of Justice, rain pouring down, trying to decide upon an outlet, almost any outlet, for his rage.

Calling Glitsky hadn't helped, since – astoundingly – he seemed to know nothing about the arrest. It wasn't the kind of thing he would kid about. This meant that he hadn't kept the news from Hardy in some misguided attempt to intimidate Mose by letting him rot in jail overnight. Which was about the only thing Hardy thought it could have been, if Glitsky had been involved. That left him nothing to berate his friend with. Besides which, Abe was clearly worried enough for both of them – it would serve no purpose to add to that concern by spouting some self-righteous horseshit about due process in the service of alleviating Hardy's own fury.

Who else, he wondered, could he spew some of this venom at? To bring all this negative energy home to Frannie would be thoughtless and unfair.

He punched in another number. 'Where are you?'

'In my home, such as it is, reading. Why? You need me to pull a shift? I could be there in fifteen.'

'No. The bar's closed down. Moses got himself arrested today.'

'Shit. Really?'

'Really. I just saw him in jail. You feel like a drink?'

San Francisco is a bar town. You've got your fancy Burning Rome-type hip places and your neighborhood haunts such as the Shamrock. You've got biker bars and gay bars, restaurant bars, sports bars, pop-up bars, and hotel bars. Then there are the old-timey traditional bars, the nightclubs, the theme bars. A bar for every time and place, every mood and every person. If you live in the city's Tenderloin District, you can find any number of bars that are more or less invisible even as you walk right in front of them. If they had a name once, the paint has faded or the neon has blown out. You push at the door, surprised that it gives. You walk inside, and if the smell doesn't drive you right back out, you're in a small dark room with no more than a dozen tables, maybe the same number of stools at the bar, behind which is one middle-aged or older bartender. Male or female, it really doesn't matter. A small television drones in the far corner, up by the ceiling.

Tonight three people sat at the bar at the corner closest to Tony's apartment. The Giants game was on, but Hardy and Tony took two adjacent stools at the end away from the television. The bartender threw a couple of napkins down on the bar in front of them. 'Gentlemen,' he said. 'Wet enough for you?'

'Just about,' Hardy said. 'You got Beck's?'

'Heineken, Bud, Miller Lite.'

'Heineken.'

'Double Crown Royal,' Tony said. 'Rocks.'

Hardy had been husbanding his anger since he left Moses. During his call to Glitsky. On the short drive out to Tony's, on the walk from Tony's dive here with the rain in his face, the two of them catching up on the news, such as it was, about Moses. Now Hardy took a careful slow sip of his beer and waited for the bartender to revert to the neutral corner at the other end.

'You think he did it?' Tony asked.

Hardy put down his glass. 'I don't know. I don't want to know. That way I can believe anything I want and defend him in good faith.'

'What if you knew he did it?'

'I'd still defend him. My heart wouldn't be in it as much, that's all. Do you think he did it?'

'I haven't really thought about it.'

'Really?' Hardy gave him a sideways glance. 'I'd have thought once he got arrested, you'd assume he did it.' He paused. 'That's the usual cop take, isn't it?'

Tony twirled his glass on the bar, glanced at the television, brought his drink up to his lips. 'Rebecca tell you?'

'As much as she knew. What I'd like to know is why you didn't tell me way back when, once I became your attorney. What was I, some kind of mark for you? Or was the Beck just a better audience?'

'I don't blame you for being pissed off.'

'There's a relief. I certainly wouldn't want you mad at me. What's your real name?'

'Tony.'

'You're playing wise with me? I don't recommend it. I'm not really in such a good place right now.'

'Spataro. Tony Spataro.'

'Where are you from?'

'Manhattan.'

'And you were a cop?'

'Vice. Everything I told Rebecca was true, you know.'

'Leaving aside the little niggling identity issue of who you actually are.'

Tony shrugged. 'What am I gonna do? I'm in witness protection. They find out where I am, they come and get me.'

'Who's they?'

'I can't tell you that. Bad people.'

'But you're not one of them? You weren't with them and then sold them out for immunity? 'Cause that's mostly how it works, you know.'

'Not in this case.' Tony tipped his glass up, finishing, then signaled the bartender for another round. When that was poured, he went back to the slow twirl. 'You're pissed at me because of Rebecca.'

'Why, yes, as a matter of fact, since you put it like that. I bring you into my house as a guest, and you hit on my daughter and then dump her for her cousin. How do you think that makes a father feel?'

'I'm not with Brittany yet.'

'Yet.' Hardy could barely get the syllable out through his teeth. 'I like that.'

'Is that why you wanted to see me tonight? Kick my ass?'

'Mostly. Yeah. I'm feeling a little abused lately and wanted to take it out on somebody who deserved it.'

'What do you want me to do?'

'Let me ask you one. What are you going to do after they call you back to testify or whatever it is you're doing? Are you coming back to San Francisco and staying here? This is your new life? Or when your bad guys back there are in jail, you go back to your old life as a Manhattan cop?'

'I don't know. I haven't thought it out that far. My marshal tells me if I go back, the program can't be responsible for me anymore. But I've got family, cousins, friends, a whole life back there, and I haven't been able to contact any of them, let 'em know I'm even alive. I don't know how long this will go on, and it sucks, believe me.'

'My heart's breaking for you. But you know what really sucks, Tony? Leading these girls on. Making them think you'll be here when you're planning on going back. Making them think you're somebody they can count on.'

'I don't know if I'm going back. I don't know what I'm going to do.'

'Well, then why don't you figure that out before you get other people involved in your drama and your bullshit. And other people's daughters.'

'I never planned to stop seeing Rebecca. It just—'

Hardy held up a hand, his face a slab of dark marble. 'Don't go there, Tony, I know what it just was.' He took a pull at his beer, made a face, pushed the bottle out to the lip at the edge of the bar. He stood up. 'I'll be passing your case off to one of my associates. Whoever it is will call you.'

At 10:42, he picked up the kitchen telephone on the first ring. 'This is Glitsky.'

'Lieutenant.' Vi Lapeer's voice was firm, commanding. 'I'm sorry to be getting back to you so late, but your call said to try at any time. I was going to let this wait until tomorrow, but I gather you've already spoken to some of your people regarding the Ramey warrant we served on Moses McGuire this afternoon.'

'That's right. Paul Brady said you'd ordered him and Lee to report directly to you on this case. I don't understand why you thought that was necessary.'

'I would have thought that was obvious. You are friends with Mr McGuire.'

'I know him, yes. I would not say we are close friends. I had instructed my inspectors to treat him exactly like any other suspect.'

'In fact,' the chief said, 'when they went to interview him, he was evidently aware that he was under suspicion and had already retained a lawyer.'

'The lawyer is his brother-in-law, ma'am.'

'And your good friend, is he not?'

'I did not contact him regarding this on any level. I didn't know he was representing McGuire and don't know when he began. Do you?'

'Of course not. Nevertheless, in a case with substantial visibility such as this one, we sometimes have to go to some lengths to avoid the appearance of impropriety or conflict of interest.'

'I understand that. But in this case—'

'Lieutenant.' Her repetition of his rank struck him as ominous. As recently as this morning, he had rarely been anything but

Abe. She went on. 'I really don't feel that now is the appropriate time to air this matter completely. In the past several hours, I have heard several allegations – unsubstantiated, to be sure, but bothersome nonetheless – regarding your relationships with Mr Hardy, Mr Farrell, and some other members of their law firm, which, I must say in a police officer, are at best unusual. I was hoping that tomorrow you and I could set aside a little time to discuss these matters privately and determine to what extent you will still have my confidence as a department head. Am I making myself clear?'

'Yes, ma'am.'

'Let's make it in my office at noon. Oh, no, wait. Tomorrow is Good Friday. Why don't we make it three, and we'll see where we are then? Would that suit your schedule?'

'Yes, ma'am.'

'Three o'clock, then. Good night, Lieutenant.'

'Good night, ma'am. See you tomorrow.'

PART
FOUR

24

If Hardy could have had his way, the trial of Moses McGuire would not have begun in the same calendar year as his arrest, and maybe not until another year or more after that. If you were a defense attorney, your best friend was delay, during which time witnesses could forget or change testimony or even die. Evidence could get lost. Arresting officers could quit and/or move away or mix up the current case with any number of similar others.

Given enough time, the prosecution pool might turn over, and you could wind up facing an inexperienced and easily intimidated relative newcomer instead of someone like the assistant DA who had been assigned this case, none other than Paul 'The Big Ugly' Stier, a very good prosecutor who also seemed to bear Hardy personal animus. All these were powerful incentives for delay and more delay, though by far the main reason to put off the trial as long as possible was that it ended in a verdict. Until the jury came back with a decision saying otherwise, the person on trial was, legally and technically, innocent.

Innocent until proven guilty.

These four words were not window dressing, not mere legal jargon. They provided an enormous tactical and psychological advantage. Because while a defendant was still innocent, the burden of proof fell on the prosecution. The defense never had to prove anything. And if you were a defense attorney, you wanted to deal from that position, where your client got the benefit of every doubt every time, where only one person on a jury had to remain unconvinced of your client's guilt and you got the verdict you wanted. The longer you could keep the jury's foreman from saying the word 'guilty,' the better job you had done for your client.

For the defendant awaiting a murder trial, there were some equally compelling incentives to have it end as soon as possible, particularly if you didn't want to cut a deal and had high hopes for an acquittal; even more so in the unlikely event that you hadn't committed the crime and were therefore that rarest of creatures, the innocent man, falsely accused. The first of these incentives was that, since bail tended not to be an option in murder cases (McGuire's was set at $10 million, which he had no chance of making), every minute that the trial was delayed was another minute that you were in custody, which was a depressing, debilitating, psychologically destructive experience even in the best of jails, which San Francisco's was not.

Second, when a trial was on the fast track, the prosecution often found itself at a severe strategic disadvantage. With time at a premium, the People may not find the time to prep witnesses adequately. Expert witnesses might be unavailable on short notice. Critically, there might not have been time to find all the possible physical evidence, or for the various laboratories to come in with their findings. The prosecutor would like, and could undoubtedly use, more time to perfect a theory of the case and a game plan for how to present it effectively to the jury.

On this fog-bound and chilly morning of Monday, July 9, as Dismas Hardy unpacked his enormous lawyer's briefcase at the defense table in Department 24 of the Hall of Justice, Judge Carol Gomez presiding, he didn't care about any of the reasons McGuire had wanted to keep the trial on track. He'd heard them all before and had an argument against every one of them.

For all the good it did him.

Moses had told him on his second visit, day two after the

arrest, that he wasn't going to be spending any greater portion of his sunset years than he absolutely had to in jail. He told Hardy to get him his Px, or preliminary hearing, on the first day it was available, which by law had to be within ten court days of his arrest.

Hardy had argued for all the usual reasons. The Px had a probable-cause standard of proof, much lower than a trial's proof beyond a reasonable doubt. And the probable cause was based upon two things: is there reason to believe that a crime was committed and that the defendant committed it? Beyond that, in a Px, a single judge made the decision, not a jury of McGuire's peers; and in a Px, hearsay was admissible, further stacking the deck against the defendant.

If Hardy were going to try to fight the good fight at the Px, he needed months of preparation, wily strategies arrived at after lengthy discussions and briefs from his associates, alternative theories of the crime, expert witnesses, the whole arsenal available to a defense attorney. In the event, he got ten court days to prepare, and Moses was held to answer and bound over for trial. The preliminary hearing had been such a complete no-brainer, given the evidence from the searches at the Shamrock and the McGuire home – to say nothing of the Homicide inspectors' hearsay about the eyewitness testimonies – that Hardy had barely a word to say in his client's defense.

Two weeks after that, Moses had pleaded not guilty at the arraignment, then refused to waive time, meaning that the trial had to begin within sixty days.

And now here they were, with the rest of a man's life at stake. Absurd.

Today might be the first formal day of the trial, but it would be a good little while before the actual shooting began: the statements, evidence, witnesses, and arguments. First they had to do their motions and pick a jury. In this case, Hardy believed, jury selection – always significant and always a crap shoot – would assume an almost mythic importance, far more than in any other trial in which he'd been involved, since the case hadn't gotten the opportunity to fade from incessant media coverage. If one accepted the dominant theory about Brittany's rape being the inciting incident – and everyone did – it was the kind of crime that gathered onto itself all the frenzy that sexual politics usually brought to public discourse: women's rights groups of all stripes had flocked to condemn Jessup and the 'culture' of date rape; the *Chronicle* had run a four-part series on date rape, its prevalence, its aftereffects, the drugs affiliated with it.

This had led to a backlash by people who felt the newspaper had given too specific instructions to young men on doping up their victims. Others picked up on the reality that Brittany already had a relationship with Jessup, and that the so-called date rape was probably not exactly that; either she had 'asked for it' or was crying rape to punish him for breaking up with her. Naturally, talk radio called her a slut and worse, and Brittany's picture appeared on CNN and cable news, which led to several more invitations for screen tests, all of which, to Hardy's knowledge, she had turned down. What she couldn't avoid was becoming somewhat of a reluctant media darling, her picture showing up in all the tabloids.

McGuire himself became the subject of intense debate. What should a father do if he finds out his daughter has been raped? Is he justified in going after the perpetrator? Can he be forgiven if he does? Why do so many victims of rape fail to report it? And if the daughter doesn't report it, how then can the rapist be brought to justice? Despite firm stonewalling on any of these issues and Hardy's constant reiteration that, rape or no rape, his client had pleaded not guilty to Jessup's murder and must be presumed innocent, McGuire got his own local magazine cover, *Mother Jones*, accompanied by an unflattering piece about the scourge of vigilante justice.

Tick, Hardy thought when he'd read that. *Tock.*

All of which meant that jury selection, to say nothing of bigger issues about McGuire's life – what kind of guy would allow himself to become a vigilante? Had there been a history of anything like that in his life? – was shaping up to be a nightmare. It was going to be very difficult, if not impossible, to find a San Francisco citizen who would make the cut – who was unaware of the basic facts of the case, who would not be prejudiced one way or the other, who would be able to be fair.

That, although bad enough, was the least of his worries.

Hardy had considered asking for a change of venue. Though a judge almost certainly would have granted such a motion, Hardy was more concerned with finding at least one or two jurors whose not-guilty votes could thwart ten other jurors who wanted to convict. He knew that his chances of finding such jurors were far greater in the politically active, opinionated, strong-willed, anti-authoritarian, counterculture folks who made up the traditional San Francisco jury pool.

Gina Roake walked up from her seat in the gallery and turned to look at the buzzing, murmuring chamber, with standing room only around the side walls and in the back. 'How big is your pool?'

'Two hundred a time for disqualification for publicity and hardship, three panels a day for three days,' Hardy said. 'We want to get a hundred people who can be here for regular voir dire.'

'It might take a month.'

'I told that to the judge. Stier even agreed with me. Gomez figures a week.'

Gina gave him a tight smile. 'It's nice when things start off on such a positive note. And where's our client?'

'They forgot him.' He held up a hand. 'True story. He ought to be down any minute.'

'In time to do a perp walk in chains from behind the bench?' Gina asked. 'They shouldn't have brought the pool in here yet.'

'You think I should tell Gomez to get them out of here so Mose can walk in like a free man? Set us back another half hour or so?'

'It's a murder,' Gina said. 'Does anybody seriously think the jurors don't know he's in jail?'

'Actually,' Hardy said, 'no chains, no kidding. The appellate court would call me incompetent for letting it happen.'

'If it's incompetent and Moses gets convicted and some appellate court wants to let him out for that, God bless it. Meanwhile, he'll at least be dressed out, right?'

'Right.' Meaning Moses wouldn't be in front of the jury pool wearing the jail's orange jumpsuit; he would be sporting his nice slacks and ironed shirt and coat and tie. The handcuffs and shackles would be removed in the hallway before he came in.

Hardy realized that they were into it already. The tiniest details. From here on out, even before the judge entered the courtroom, everything counted. 'I'll go talk to the bailiff and make sure I walk in with him,' he said. Pushing back the chair, Hardy stood up.

To his left, closer to the jury box – which was now filled with twelve prospective jurors and six alternates – Paul Stier sat with one of his acolytes at the prosecution table, ostentatiously going over the computer sheet with names of people in the jury pool, as though by themselves they could tell him anything.

Hardy, his game face on, stopped without apparent premeditation at Stier's elbow. 'Excuse me, Paul,' he said, offering his hand. 'Before we get going, I just thought I'd say good morning.'

It was another small but calculated move on Hardy's part, demonstrating to anyone among the prospective jurors that the defense side and the prosecution side were cordial professionals, that Hardy's identification with the defendant should not make them think any less of him and, by extension, his law partner Amy Wu, who would be sitting second chair at the defense table.

Stier straightened up, shook Hardy's hand, introduced his associate as Lars Gunderson, a young man pushing the envelope of acceptable courtroom dishevelment with almost shoulder-length red hair and a luxuriant mustache. More handshaking.

Up by the bench, Hardy explained his situation to the bailiff, who nodded and led him back to the interior corridor that ran behind all the courtrooms. Just as he turned to look down toward the elevator leading to the jail, Judge Gomez exited her chambers in her robes and came walking down toward him.

She was a slight woman, even bulked up by her robes. Hardy had checked her out when she'd drawn this trial. He would have preferred a man or at least a parent because of the nature of the crime, and she was neither. Appointed by Jerry Brown, she was relatively new to the bench, forty-six years old, Georgetown Law, single. She wore her dark hair down to her shoulders, and with her glasses off, her face was close to beautiful, especially when she wasn't frowning, which unfortunately was her default expression when she was in thought.

As she came closer, she obviously took a moment to place Hardy, standing by the back of her courtroom. As the recognition clicked in, she stopped and did not offer a handshake but said, 'Mr Hardy. Graciously escorting me to court?'

'Unfortunately, waiting for my client. They seem to have misplaced him.'

Apparently amused, the judge shook her head. 'The biggest case I've ever tried, and they forget to bring down the defendant. I'm sure that says something, but I don't know what it is.'

'I'll have to make sure he's dressed out, Your Honor. I won't object to him coming in with the jurors already in the courtroom, provided he's uncuffed and I can walk in with him. It may be a few minutes, if you'd prefer to wait back here.'

A wry smile. 'I don't suppose you'd like to go in now and we start without him?'

'If it were just me, I would. Honest. But it's his trial, Your Honor. He's supposed to be there. Face his accusers and all that.'

'Yes,' she said. 'Of course.' Her brow furrowed, she sighed, and she aged ten years. 'I'll be in my chambers,' she said. 'Would you please have the bailiff come get me when you're ready?'

'Certainly, Your Honor.'

As she turned, the thought occurred to him that he'd scored a minor victory. He wasn't going to attach too much importance to it, but something small and human had just passed between them.

He'd take it.

Critical though it was, jury selection had its mind-numbing moments.

The first jury dismissals were for publicity and hardship, instances in which a juror's lengthy time on the panel would badly disrupt that person's life. Into this category fell single parents without adequate child care, some people who owned their own businesses, those working for companies that did not pay for jury duty, folks with certain illnesses or medical conditions, and other similar situations. Dismissal for publicity didn't include everybody who had heard about the case; virtually everybody had heard about the case. Those dismissed were people who had formed fixed opinions, based on what they'd read or heard, and couldn't give the defendant a fair trial. The final hardship was that the trial wasn't going to take just a few days and would be more time than a great many people could spare.

Amy Wu had a Chinese mother and a black father. She had been with Freeman Hardy & Roake since the firm's founding and had become a partner a year ago. At thirty-three, she was a skilled and experienced criminal attorney. She was also easy to look at, and Hardy thought she spruced up the defense table nicely.

Now Wu, Roake, and Hardy were at a table along the back wall across the street at Lou the Greek's. Today's Special was a bowl of lamb meatballs, eggplant, kalamata olives, and Chinese noodles, all heavily seasoned with Mae Ploy sauce. Surprisingly delicious.

Hardy, using chopsticks, lifted an olive. 'Conflicts.' He didn't have to go into detail; both of these women were attorneys and knew the questions: Are you related to anybody in law enforcement? Have you ever been the victim of a crime? Convicted of a crime? Arrested? Is there anything that would prevent you from being able to render a fair and impartial verdict in this case?

Each juror who passed hardship had filled out a twenty-three-page questionnaire. Hardy and Wu had read and scored all of them, and now they were trying to get their heads around 120 people, twelve of whom would become their jurors, four of whom would be alternates.

'I'd say good-bye to the rest of this week, at least,' Hardy went on. 'I'm praying we get to start the actual evidence by Friday afternoon, but I'm not betting on it. You don't have to stay through all this, you know, Gina. I'm not going to need you until we get to witnesses.'

Another result, and arguably a good one, of the trial's fore-shortened schedule was that Gina, taking pity on Hardy's work-load, had offered to sit in the back of the courtroom and help out as needed. An experienced trial lawyer, Roake would bring another perspective and a sharp legal mind to the defense table. It went without saying that for reasons of her own, she wanted to be close to McGuire, to keep him somewhat in check if she could, to be a buffer between Mose and Diz when the two alpha males decided they had to mix it up, which had happened in trial strategy talks more than once.

'Mose looked good,' Amy offered. 'Well rested, personable.'

Hardy said, 'Yeah, but I had to poke him about four times to wake him up. We've got to keep him from looking bored to death. Or falling asleep.'

'That's a tall order for anyone in there.'

'Agreed. But the man is looking at the rest of his life in jail. It wouldn't be so bad if he seemed like the kind of person that would bother just a little bit. You know, like other humans.'

Gina put her chopsticks down next to her bowl. She lowered her voice. 'He doesn't think he's looking at the rest of his life in jail, Diz – even if the jury convicts him, which he thinks won't happen, because people believe he's justified.'

'They're going to change their minds when they see the autopsy photos.'

'Maybe not. Especially if we get any fathers of daughters on the jury.'

Hardy's shoulders lifted and fell, a laugh of sorts. 'Yes, and good luck with that. You think Stier would ever let that happen?'

'Probably not, I agree. But let's keep good thoughts. All we need is one.'

25

Hardy remembered the Big Ugly very well. The man was a formidable opponent. In their first trial, Stier was probably ahead on points when Hardy had an eleventh-hour revelation that blew the case wide open, exposing the real killer, who was not Hardy's client. Without that truly fortuitous discovery, Hardy would have been licked, and his innocent client would probably still be in jail.

That was when Stier was relatively new to the DA's office. Now he had several years under his belt, several big victories, was on his way to becoming a star. He'd lobbied Farrell hard for this assignment, and Wes, still bristling from the unproved and untrue implication that he'd colluded with Glitsky and Hardy to protect McGuire, had taken the opportunity to let the legal and police community know that he was exercising the full might of his office in going after McGuire and naming Stier the prosecutor.

So great was Stier's reputation and confident demeanor that, when jury selection was complete, Hardy was left with a nagging unease that he had somehow screwed up. Badly. Against all of what Hardy considered common sense – and Amy agreed with him – Stier had allowed not one father of a daughter onto the panel. He had allowed five.

Hardy's initial reaction that he'd outfoxed the fox gave way to a gut-wrenching certainty that he'd missed something substantial. Stier had put an unorthodox strategy in play right at the beginning, and Hardy had no idea what it was, which was deeply disconcerting. All that effort to get a jury he and Amy were reasonably comfortable with, he thought, and now he felt that if he were to do it over again, he'd be wise to do it differently.

Exactly how, he didn't know.

Every working lawyer knew that the thing you wanted to avoid at trial, at all costs, was surprise. And Hardy felt absolutely bushwhacked at the outset.

Now, however, on Friday morning, he had to put all of those very real concerns and worries out of his mind. The courtroom gallery was again filled to capacity, but no longer with a jury pool. The hard blond wooden chairs contained a horde of local and national reporters and members of the DA's office, including Wes Farrell, who, when he came in, had pointedly refrained from greeting either of his former law partners, Roake or Hardy, and sat on the prosecution side. Just behind Hardy, Moses's wife, Susan, sat frozen-faced in the first row, perhaps missing her daughter Brittany who, as a potentail witness, was not allowed in the courtroom. Directly across from Susan, equally grim, sat a woman whom he'd come to learn was Jessup's mother. Conspicuously not present was Abe Glitsky. Hardy couldn't afford to think about him right now. That was a whole different subject.

Moses sat between him and Amy. He'd looked good all week in the suits Susan had brought down for him, had avoided going to sleep in the courtroom, and seemed almost carefree as he waited for the show to begin. He radiated the supernal calm of a man with many options before him.

And then – it always seemed sudden – everyone in the court-room rose as Judge Gomez entered and took her seat at the raised bench. The lawyers introduced themselves to the court for the record, and the waiting was well and truly over. Stier had gotten up and was standing in front of the jury, facing them. He had a distinctive, athletic stance, with his arms slightly out in front of him, as though ready to field a ball.

'Ladies and gentlemen of the jury. Good morning.

'I want to thank you for your patience in sitting through jury selection. In a few minutes, I'll be calling the witnesses whose testimony will prove the charges against this defendant. But to start, I wanted to take a few minutes of your time to give you an outline or preview of what the evidence will show. Hopefully, you will find it useful in understanding why we're asking certain questions and in helping you organize the information the witnesses will be giving you.

'This is really a very simple case. The defendant took a club – a shillelagh, actually, a distinctive Irish weapon that sat for years under the counter in the bar that he owned – and he beat a man, Rick Jessup, to death with it. He broke his arm. He fractured his skull. He hit him so hard and so often that the victim is almost unrecognizable in the autopsy photos, which, unfortunately, you will need to look at as the medical examiner explains to you the savagery and viciousness of the attack. He hit him so hard that he left an imprint of the club on Rick Jessup's head.

'After the attack, the defendant threw the club away. The fact that it went missing right after the murder is itself significant evidence that it was the weapon involved. Even more significant is testimony you will hear from an expert who will tell you that a photograph of this defendant, taken in his own bar, shows him with the club, and that it is the same club used to kill Rick Jessup.

'I'm not going to take the time now to tell you everything that every witness will say. If I did that, my opening statement would be as long as the trial. I do want to let you know that witnesses will tell you they are certain – absolutely certain – that they saw the defendant with that club in his hands, walking down the street from Mr Jessup's apartment just about the time he was murdered. Even more compelling, the crime lab found Mr Jessup's blood in his car, on his jacket, and on a pair of the defendant's shoes in a closet in his home.'

Hardy struggled to keep all emotion out of his face. Amy gently and slowly put a hand on McGuire's arm. This moment was unavoidable, and it was a truly bad one if Hardy was going to argue that Moses hadn't committed the murder, which would be the defense position. The discovery of the blood would have sealed the arrest even if there had been no other evidence.

Stier went on, 'Why would the defendant do something like this? Why would anybody do something like this? Simple revenge.'

Stier continued, outlining Brittany's relationship with Jessup, her alleged assault, McGuire's first attack on Jessup, and finally, the accusation of rape that had sent Brittany's father into a homicidal rage.

It was clear. It was clean. It was compelling.

Hardy hated every word of it.

Stier continued to roll along. 'Ladies and gentlemen. Vigilante justice is not justice. This defendant took the life of another human being under circumstances that the law defines as murder. When you've heard this evidence and the instructions that the court will give you as to how to evaluate it, that is the verdict I will ask for and the verdict your oaths will compel you to return. Thank you.'

Hardy often let fate decide his actions. He thought it kept him flexible, better able to roll with the punches, on top of his game.

Driving west on Lake, he decided that if a parking spot presented itself anywhere within reasonable walking distance to Glitsky's, he would stop and check in. It had been nearly a month, a long time for them.

A space appeared at the very corner.

A minute later, he had walked down half of the dead-end block and up the twelve steps to Glitsky's front door. He rang the bell, waited, rang again. This couldn't be right, he was thinking. The parking place was too perfect. Glitsky had to be home. What else would he be doing? Although, to be fair, maybe Hardy should have called. But where was the spontaneity in that?

A long sigh later, he was halfway down the stairs when he heard the door open behind him. He stopped and turned, saw his friend barefoot in jeans and a plain white T-shirt with maybe a three-day growth of gray stubble. Hardy didn't remember the last time he'd seen Glitsky in blue jeans and was sure he'd never seen him in a T-shirt. Or unshaved. 'I'm looking for an Abe Glitsky. Old, feeble, often in the way.'

Glitsky nodded. 'I'll see if he's in.'

'All in all, I'd say it went okay,' Hardy said. He was drinking iced tea, sitting on the couch in his friend's living room, while Glitsky, just awakened from a nap, had lowered himself down and sat Indian-style on the floor. The lieutenant – the ex-lieutenant, technically – was at a low ebb, and to keep both of their spirits up, Hardy was regaling his pal with the highlights of his opening statement, such as they were. 'Ugly had left out a few little details that seemed to resonate, so I hammered them pretty hard. Like when Mose beat the shit out of Jessup the first time.'

'That was one of the *good* moments?'

'In the sense that it provides an alternative answer to what is otherwise unanswerable. Blood on the shoes. Blood on the jacket. Blood in the car. Deal breakers, if we don't have the earlier fight.'

'Which, if I'm not mistaken, nobody witnessed.'

'Picky, picky. At least it gives them something else to think about.'

'If I were on the jury, I'd think about how Moses is a hothead who goes and beats people up.'

'He got it all out of his system.'

'Real good,' Glitsky said. 'Not. They ever find the shillelagh?'

'No. But they've got some witness who's analyzed the picture – you know, from the Wall of Shame at the Shamrock. There's Mose brandishing the damn thing, big as life, terrific detail, and this witness is going to say that the trauma pattern on Jessup's head is pretty much a dead match. Then I'm going to eat his lunch.'

'What's your argument?'

'He didn't do it. Plain and simple. And that means somebody else did.'

'You got any idea who?'

'Several. Liam Goodman, Jon Lo, a random hit man. We haven't had a lot of time, but Mr Jessup wasn't everything he's been painted as. He was involved in quite a bit of squirrelly stuff, and some of that might have proved embarrassing to people with money or power or both.'

'Liam Goodman the supervisor?'

Hardy made an extravagant gesture of possibility.

'Do you believe any of this?'

'Some days, some of it. Almost never all of it at once. We're a work in progress at the moment, and here we are in the thick of it. I need more of everything – theories, distractions, exculpatory evidence. Everything.' Hardy drank some tea. 'So how's retirement suiting you? I ask 'cause I'm thinking about it myself.'

'Not really?'

'No, not really. That was by way of jest.'

Glitsky thought for a moment. 'It's somewhat overrated. You'd hate it.'

'You?'

'Pretty much. Time and then more time. Kids at school all day, Treya at her job. I've never been much of a TV guy.'

'Books,' Hardy said. 'They can take up a lot of time. You're a voracious reader, are you not?'

'To a point. More than, say, three hours every day, it gets a little old. And if you say "golf" next, this interview will be over. I'm good,' Glitsky said. 'I'll figure it out.'

'I had a reason to ask you about this retirement of yours. Get you out and about a little, which it looks like you could use.'

Glitsky leaned back against his reading chair. 'I'm listening.'

'How would you feel about being a witness? In this case. For me.'

Glitsky's mouth dropped open an inch in surprise. 'As if I'm not already in low enough esteem among my former colleagues.'

'They haven't treated you very well, have they? What do you owe them?'

'Nothing, but still . . . What would you want me to say?'

Hardy shrugged. 'Just talk a bit about how you thought the investigation got pushed through so fast because it was so high-profile, because Goodman was pushing Lapeer for action and she caved to the pressure and went outside of due process. As soon as they got the rape motive, they made up their mind that it was Moses and stopped looking for anybody else.'

'Diz. Who cares what I think about any of this? Why is the judge going to let me say any of it?'

'Because I want to argue that there was pressure on the inspectors to arrest Moses, and they put undue pressure on witnesses, deliberately or no, to tailor testimony and make the IDs. This whole case is tainted by the politics.'

'They had three IDs and blood work, Diz. What do you want?'

'I want the jury to think that the cops – specifically Lapeer – didn't look at anybody else. Some other dude did it, Abe, and the cops let him get away in their haste to round up the most obvious suspect.'

'And so it was.' Glitsky scratched at his stubble, grew pensive. 'But I bring any of that up, and it leads . . . you know where it leads.'

'Sure. Our friendship, such as it is, and the blatant collusion among all of us. Which is so much crap. It simply never happened, as you and I well know.'

'Right, but the appearance—'

'Never mind that. It's totally bogus.' After a pause, Hardy went on. 'Look, Abe, this is also an opportunity for you to face all those rumors head-on, put them all behind you for good. Here you are, forced out of the job you loved and were good at.'

'Not good enough, evidently.'

'Bullshit. On top of that, the way it happened, your reputation took a pretty good hit as well.'

'Tell me about it.'

'That's what I'm doing. So you get up on the stand, under oath, and you say the chief overreacted. If they go there, you swear you never called me to tell me how close they were to arresting Moses. The truth, by the way. Oh, and here's another little something. The Ramey warrant that cut you out of the decision? It also went around Wes and his office. That is, the very office now prosecuting the case.'

'Blood, DNA, eyewitnesses,' Glitsky said.

Hardy, impatient now, shook him off. 'All explainable. Plausibly explainable. And two out of three discovered after the arrest. The point is that it puts Stier in the absolutely impossible position of defending his office and his boss for their vigorous prosecution while the record shows that Lapeer believed Farrell was colluding with both of us enough that she couldn't trust him to be in on Mose's arrest.' Hardy broke a grin. 'I might even call Wes. The DA testifying for the defense! Isn't that fucking great?

Pardon my French. I could go down in legal history. Make Wes swear to the same thing as you. The alleged collusion never happened. We all know each other, sure, but we're professionals. We've all been on the opposite sides of cases before. Welcome to the big city. I really like this. Hell, I *love* this.'

'You're delusional.'

'I'm not. If nothing else, it gets the truth about you out there. You won't have to spend the rest of your pathetic life hiding out here in your living room, avoiding your former colleagues, to say nothing of the other blandishments of city life.'

'That's not—'

Hardy held up a restraining hand. 'Please. Find a mirror. Look at yourself. You tell me.'

An uncomfortable silence gathered.

Glitsky made a brief pass at *the glare,* but it didn't take. In any event, Hardy had seen it too often to be cowed. Seconds ticked on. Glitsky took a breath. 'When Lapeer called me in, she alluded to the other thing, too.'

'What about it?'

'Everything about it. The rumor.'

'So what? It's a rumor. Spread mostly by people who got passed over for promotion because you were better at your job than they were at theirs. This just in – rumors get spread by jealous people who don't like you. Absent evidence, rational people consider the source and discount the rumors.' Hardy sat back, sipped his tea. 'Abe, it's been almost seven years. If there were any evidence – and I mean the smallest scintilla of evidence – don't you think something would have happened by now? You know what? There is no evidence. There is never going to be any evidence. Moses got rid of all of it in the deep blue sea, and only he knows exactly where.

'So what do we need to do? We need to get Moses off on this thing so he doesn't get drunk on pruno in jail and start talking about things he should leave alone. Meanwhile, your testimony discredits Lapeer, weakens Stier and the whole prosecution side, restores your reputation, and gives the jury a passel of other theories they'll need to consider.'

'I'd hate to go up against you in court,' Glitsky said. 'You can wear a guy out.'

'I love that part. It's why God put me here.'

'What was she thinking?' Glitsky asked.

A few minutes later, Hardy came back in after a pit stop and, as Glitsky was rinsing their glasses in the kitchen sink, started in again without preamble. 'There's one other thing.'

'There always is.'

'This is more in the line of a personal favor.'

'The other one wasn't? Testifying for the defense? Do you have any idea—?'

Hardy waved him off. 'We've gone over that. Your testifying restores the order of the universe. Hence, it's universal. This other thing is a mere bagatelle.'

Glitsky threw his eyes to the ceiling. 'Lord spare us.' Then, back across to Hardy, 'What?'

'There's another sideline player. Nothing to do with this case that I know of. You met him at my house once. You might remember. Tony Solaia.'

'Sure. He's a player in this how, if he's not in the case?'

'If I knew, I wouldn't need the favor. You remember how you thought he seemed like a cop, how he talked, carried himself? It turns out you were right. He supposedly worked Vice in Manhattan.'

'That's hard-core cop. And now he's a bartender? That's not the traditional career arc. How'd it happen? Did he burn out?'

'Apparently, he's a protected witness. Big federal case. Human trafficking, sexual slavery. Huge money.'

'How did you find out?'

Hardy made a face. 'He told the Beck in a moment of sensitivity and confidence just before he dumped her for her cousin Brittany.'

Glitsky was drying his hands with a dish towel. He stopped, cocked his head, mute.

Hardy went on. 'He's taken over Mose's shifts at the Shamrock these past months. He and Brittany are at least going steady, maybe a lot more. I don't know if you know, but she's my goddaughter as well as my niece, and I feel a little responsible for her. Hell, a lot responsible for her, although maybe I shouldn't. She's a grown-up, after all. But after all she's gone through and is still going through with this trial . . .' Hardy sighed. 'At least I don't want her to get caught up with some guy who may not be what he says he is.'

'You think that?'

'I don't know. I was going to check him out when all this first came up, but the trial went into overdrive, and here I am, nowhere.'

'What about Wyatt Hunt? Isn't this why you have a PI on standby? Didn't you put him on it?'

Hardy nodded. 'He tried under both names. Tony's real name, or maybe not, is Tony Spataro, though that appears to be an alias, too. There's no record of him – cop, foot soldier with the Mob, nothing. The case, if there is a case, is sealed back east until they're ready to move. It's not in any of Wyatt's databases, and as I say, the whole environment is federal, and you know how they're always bending over backward to be helpful, especially to defense attorneys, especially the marshals.'

'What do you think I can do if Hunt can't get anywhere?'

'I thought you'd never ask. You, as a law enforcement person, have had professional dealings with the FBI, have you not? More than a few.'

'Yep. Bill Schuyler.'

'I thought you might ask him what he could find out.'

Abe folded the dish towel and carefully draped it over its rack. 'Bill and I are not what I'd call intimate, Diz. He's not going to give up a witness because I ask him. They invest a lot of money in these people and take pride in never having lost one. The marshal might not even tell Bill. Probably wouldn't.'

'I love that can-do attitude. It's kind of inspiring.'

'I'm just telling you it probably won't happen.'

'Not unless you figure out some way it will.'

26

FIRST THING THE next morning, Saturday, Hardy was breakfasting at home and got a phone call.

'Mr Hardy. Winston Paley here. I'm sorry to bother you on the weekend, but something's come up that might be a bit of a problem, and I thought we might need to discuss it right away.'

Paley, a psychologist who specialized in the reliability of eyewitness testimony – a crucial element of this trial – was a professional expert witness who was charging Hardy thirty-five hundred dollars for each day of his testimony, whether or not that testimony took all day, or parts of two or three days, or indeed, whether he was used at all. If he was in the courtroom, he got paid. If he flew up to San Francisco and wasn't used, he got paid. If he cleared his schedule and did not need to fly up, he got paid. He was a big, charming man, loud and florid, and a brilliant marketer, salesman, and – by reputation – witness. Hardy had never used him, but they'd taken a half day of prep together (two thousand dollars, not including Hardy's flight to L.A. and back), and Paley had impressed him.

Hardy's gut twisted as he put down his coffee cup. 'Whatever it may be,' he said, 'I'm sure we can work it out. What's the problem?'

Paley said, 'I had it calendared that you would be calling me starting Monday of next week, nine days from now.'

'Right.' Hardy didn't have to look it up. 'That's what I've got.'

'Yes, well' – the good doctor cleared his throat – 'the fact is that I've been invited to be the keynote speaker at an international seminar being held in Zurich all of that week. I was their second choice, but unfortunately, the colleague who was originally scheduled has suffered a stroke and will not be able to attend. I don't want to be coy with you, Mr Hardy, but the honorarium I'm being offered is seventy-five thousand dollars, and I don't see how in good conscience I can afford to turn them down.'

Hardy had no problem seeing how Dr Paley could in good conscience turn them down. In good conscience, he had already committed to Hardy, they had a signed contract, backed up by the money that had already changed hands. That was how. And he was sorely tempted to say as much. But before he could force a word out through his shock and dismay, the man was going on, addressing that very issue. 'I'll be happy to refund you for the moneys you've paid me to date. I truly regret this turn of events, but this is an opportunity that I can't pass up. I don't suppose there's any way you can get a continuance?'

'Unlikely,' Hardy said. 'In fact, not a prayer in hell with a jury sworn. We gave opening statements yesterday. We're already under sail.' Even on the weekend, Hardy was in trial mode, which came with a heightened sense of awareness to unimagined possibilities, and his next words fell from his lips without a moment of conscious forethought. 'What are you doing this Monday? Day after tomorrow?'

A pause. 'I believe I have some patients.'

'Could they be rescheduled?'

'Yes, I believe they could. Nothing's life-threatening.'

'Would you be willing to do that if I could get permission to have you testify on Monday?'

'Certainly. That's an elegant solution. Can you get the court to go along?'

'I'm not worried about the court. I'm worried about the DA. But I don't see why it would matter. The jury's going to hear your testimony one way or another. Basically, it's background information. Why would they object to letting it in first?'

'I don't really know. It hasn't come up in my experience.'

'Well, give me a few hours. I'll get back to you.'

When Hardy hung up, Frannie came in and poured some fresh coffee into his cup, then pulled out a chair and sat. 'That sounded ominous.'

'That was Paley, my eyewitness expert. He got a better gig in Zurich and decided to take it.'

'In Zurich?'

'Don't ask.'

'Can he do that? Don't you need him?'

'I think I do need him. I'm certainly paying him as if I need him. I could probably get the judge to issue an order compelling him to appear, but what good would that do me? The whole idea is he's supposed to be on our side, and if we take away his big paycheck – which is not the one we're giving him – he's going to be resentful, if not actually hostile.'

'So what are you going to do?'

'Try to get Stier to let him in on Monday. If he doesn't object, the judge will probably let it go.'

'So you're going to be on the phone a while?'

'Why? Do you need something?'

'No. Well, yes. It can wait. If you need to make your calls.'

'Just one,' Hardy said. 'Stier.'

'What about the judge?'

Hardy shook his head. 'Ex parte. Can't do it.' In any criminal case, all discussion with the judge had to have both attorneys present. 'That's not happening until Monday morning.'

'Won't that be too late? If the judge says no and your guy is already up here?'

'Then Paley won't testify and I lose thirty-five hundred bucks, plus hotel plus airfare plus car rental, but who's counting?'

'All that, and Moses won't get his expert, either.'

'True. In which case, I'll probably ask for a mistrial.'

'And start over? And Moses stays in jail while all that goes on again?'

Hardy sat back, leveled his gaze at his wife. He put his hand over hers and squeezed it gently, spoke in his mildest tone. 'He'd better get used to being in jail, Frannie. Expert witness or not. I'm doing my damnedest to keep him out, but he's got himself in a pretty deep hole, you must admit.'

Frannie sighed, looked around the dining area, came back to her husband. 'You always say you don't want to hear the actual truth, that it doesn't matter. But it does.'

'Agreed. The truth matters.'

'Well.' She paused. 'He didn't do it, you know.'

Still gently, Hardy pulled his hand away from hers. Crossing his arms, he said, 'We're talking about killing Rick Jessup?'

She nodded. 'He didn't.'

'He's never mentioned that to me.'

'You keep telling him you don't want to know. You stop him if he starts to say. You say it doesn't matter, that you just argue the evidence.'

'All true. I don't want to fit his lying into my motivation to get him off.'

'What if it isn't a lie?'

'What makes you think it wouldn't be?'

She hesitated for a long moment. 'He told Susan. Just yesterday. After the opening statements. She went to see him, and he told her he didn't realize how bad it looked for him until he heard Stier lay it all out.'

'He should have. I've told him a hundred times.'

'I don't know. Maybe it didn't hit home before. But yesterday it finally did. So she flat-out asked him how he could have done it, put the family in that much jeopardy, risked their marriage. She

282

told him that even if you got him off, she wasn't sure she could be with him when he got out. And he just told her.'

'That he didn't do it? Didn't kill Jessup?'

'Right.'

Hardy hung his head.

Frannie said, 'You don't believe it.'

Hardy looked at her. 'What's changed?'

'You don't believe him?'

'I haven't even heard him say it, Fran, so it's not a question of believing him.'

'Maybe you should ask him.'

'I will. Now. I will. Absolutely. But you must admit the possibility that he told Susan what she wanted to hear so she wouldn't give up on them staying together.'

'You're saying he lied to her?'

Hardy was silent.

'He wouldn't have done that,' she went on. 'That's not who he is.'

'What, do you think—?' Hardy stopped, scratched at the table, raised his eyes to Frannie's. 'What happened to the shillelagh?'

Reached at his daughter's soccer game, Stier had a little trouble hearing Hardy on his cell phone but picked up the gist in the end. 'You want me to let you poison the jury with your expert witness telling them the many ways that my eyewitnesses' testimony is flawed, so they're primed to disbelieve everything those eyewitnesses say before I even call them? Why is it that I would agree to that?'

'Couple of reasons.' Hardy, the voice of, plowed on. 'First, if I don't get Paley, I'm asking for a mistrial. That's not a threat. That's a statement of fact. Half my defense is attacking the value of your eyewitness testimony. If I can't do that, I've got to punt. Then we're another sixty days out, starting from scratch. Neither of us wants that.'

'Why would I mind it?'

'Your eyewitnesses are that much further from the event. We get a whole new jury you might not like half as much. My private eye finds an alternate suspect. Somebody gets run over by a bus. Who knows?'

'In your dreams,' Stier said.

Conceding the point, Hardy kept up his press. 'All right, how's this? If Paley testifies for me up-front, he's that much further from the jury deliberating. They'll have heard your eyewitnesses, with basically no rebuttal. They'll remember the testimony, not the ways it might be flawed.' Hardy did not really believe that, but he thought it made a good argument. 'The main thing is that I don't believe it's going to help or harm either of our cases. Paley's testimony is going to come in someday, now or later, and how they take it is going to be part of the jury instructions when we're done.'

After a lengthy pause – Hardy heard the wind blowing, the other parents cheering – Stier spoke. 'Tell you what, Mr Hardy, I'll give this some thought and have an answer for you Monday morning. How's that sound?'

'It doesn't sound like a "no." Thanks for considering it.'

As soon as he rang off with Stier, Hardy punched up Dr Paley's number and left an unequivocal message that the DA had agreed to the Monday testimony and Paley should cancel his patients and plan on being in San Francisco for the start of the court day.

As Hardy put down his phone, he realized that this was nothing if not an out-and-out lie. Which reminded him that he needed to go downtown and have a talk with his client.

Inside the glass-block curvature of the attorney visiting room, Hardy paced against the long wall, over to the admitting door, back to the far end.

Moses sat at the table in his jumpsuit. 'I don't try to tell you how to run your business,' he was saying. 'You say you don't want to know, I take you at your word. Call me a literalist. If I say I didn't do it, you think I'm lying. If I say I did, then you're defending a guilty man, and why do you want to do that?'

'Actually, I'm good with defending you if you're guilty. Somebody did what Jessup did to the Beck, I might have done the same thing. I understand it.'

'Susan wasn't understanding it so well. All this time, she's thinking I went and killed this guy and—'

'You let her go on believing that? What was that about? You could have told her right off and saved her a load of grief.'

'You're assuming she would have believed me.' Moses pushed at the bridge of his oft-broken nose. 'I was pissed off, to tell you the truth. Everybody's so ready to believe it was me. Even Susan. Even Brittany. You. Okay, if that's who they really think I am, I'll be that person for a while. See how they like living with that.'

'And it would have killed you to set any of us straight?'

'Fuck that guilt trip. I'm thinking it wouldn't be so ridiculous if my wife and daughter and, oh yeah, my best friend, simply believe in me. Believe I'm not the kind of guy who goes and beats a kid to death, even if he did deserve it. Did it ever occur to you that I might feel a tiny bit abandoned by the people who know me best? Do you think it might tend to piss me off?'

Now Hardy stopped. 'You've got a history, Mose.'

A dull light flared in McGuire's eyes. His voice came out in a low rasp. 'You've got the same one, Diz. How about that? Did that slip your mind in all the excitement?'

'It's not the same.'

McGuire threw up his hands in emotion. 'Goddamn right it's not the same. That's my point. That time we had an overt warning that they were going to murder our children. They'd already killed Sam Silverman and David Freeman. That was an ongoing vendetta, and they had us against a wall with no other options. Five of us were in agreement on what we had to do. No choice. Life or death. That was not the situation with Jessup. But everybody jumped on the old Moses bandwagon, didn't they? Meanwhile, do you see anybody believing that you, for example, are capable of cold-blooded murder? Why me and not you? Not anybody else?'

'Yeah, well guess what? You remember what Ugly said yesterday: blood, DNA, eyewitnesses? You must admit, they add up.'

McGuire sighed. 'That's why I finally told Susan.'

'The truth?'

'That's right. The hard-to-believe, honest-to-God truth.'

'Everything before wasn't?'

'I never said anything about it, either way. Those were your instructions, if memory serves, and they suited me fine. If people were going to believe what they believed, I wasn't going to help everybody out. To hell with 'em. The evidence remained the same. You were going to get me off either way, right?'

Hardy, hands in pockets, leaned against the admitting door. He stood planted across the room, at least halfway because if he went closer, he didn't trust himself not to take a swing at his client. He stared off, trying to get a handle on his temper, cursing his Irish genes. Cursing McGuire's. The whole situation.

'So,' he said at last, 'you want to tell me what happened? You're trying to tell me you really did go fishing?'

'No. I didn't go fishing.'

'Your alibi is a lie?'

'So sue me. I knew what the cops were thinking the first time they came by. I knew Jessup had been killed. I had to think of something. Nobody's going to come along and disprove it, so who gives a shit?'

'The jury might, if I decide to tell them the truth, except for "oh yeah, the alibi."'

Not amused, Moses chuckled nevertheless. 'You're not going to do that. Nobody believes I went fishing anyway.'

'What did you do?'

'I drove down there.'

'Why?'

'I don't know. Maybe kill him, definitely hurt him. It wasn't all thought out.'

'And you brought the shillelagh?'

'Of course. Last time I'd hit him, my hand was sore for a week.'

'You got there and . . .'

'Knocked on his door, no answer, so tried the knob, and it was open. He was lying on the floor just inside, blood pooled out under him.'

'So what'd you do then?'

'I'm not sure, to tell you the truth. Stood there a minute, thinking, Shit. Maybe I prodded the body a time or two with the shillelagh.'

'Maybe? A time or two?'

'Maybe more than that. I don't really remember. He was dead, which meant I was in trouble just being there. I might have whacked him another time out of frustration. Then I had to get out of there.'

'How about the eyewitnesses?'

McGuire shook his head. 'I don't remember any of them. I just wanted to get to my car and be gone.'

'And you didn't tell Susan?'

'I didn't *do* anything. There was nothing to tell her.'

'How about the bare fact? Jessup being dead.'

'We were all going to find that out soon enough, weren't we? If I could avoid it, I didn't want Susan thinking I was any part of it. I was trying to save her some anguish. She had enough going on, dealing with poor Brittany. It was a rough day or two. I told her I went fishing to clear my head.'

'And the shillelagh?'

Moses's shoulders settled. 'I shouldn't have taken that. I loved that old thing. It's someplace out at the bottom of Stow Lake.'

Hardy came across the room, sat at the table with Moses. He spoke in a conversational tone. 'You're asking me to believe that somebody else altogether came to Jessup's place before you did?'

'I don't know when anybody came, Diz. He was dead when I got there.'

'Why?'

'I thought that was your job.'

'Something totally unrelated to Brittany?'

'I don't know. I'll keep saying I don't know as long as I don't know. All I do know is that I didn't kill him. You can believe me or not, I don't care. But it's the truth.'

'Really, this time, huh?'

Moses met his gaze. 'Yep.'

'Well, thanks for sharing,' Hardy said. 'I'll keep it in mind.'

Absolutely unconvinced, although believing with all his heart that Moses had at last come up with the explanation – weak and in many ways indefensible as it was – that his client was going to live with from now on, Hardy stood up, walked across to the admitting door, and knocked to call the bailiff.

By mid-June, the conspiracy racketeering charges against Tony Solaia, his fellow bartender Rona Ranken, and their boss, Tom Hedtke, had fallen apart. Their Ukrainian accusers, Igor Povaliy and Vadim Gnatyuk, hoping to parlay their testimony into a couple of special work permits, had woven a web of fraudulent detail that they weren't able to keep up with. The cases against the Burning Rome defendants were settled with light fines. Povaliy and Gnatyuk were deported back to the Ukraine. Burning Rome reopened, although its prime-time mixologist had moved on to the full-time position at the Little Shamrock once held by its owner, Moses McGuire.

It wouldn't be fair to say that Tony changed the entire ethic of the place – after all, the Shamrock was a tiny and unassuming Irish dart bar that had been at its current location since 1893 – but on the weekends, the crowds picked up dramatically, while the average age of the clientele dropped by about ten years. Tony was pouring drinks whose names McGuire wouldn't have known if he'd been there to see them. New ingredients – infusions of herbs, fruits, homemade bitters, and digestifs – lined the bottom shelf behind the bar. Wheat beer appeared on tap for the first time. They went from the old jukebox to a downloadable stream of music controlled from behind the bar and ten decibels louder.

Stuck in his jail cell, McGuire saw no reason to stay involved. Whatever happened to him with this trial, Moses was in his sixties. Maybe it was time for him to pass along the day-to-day bar duties to someone with more energy and even, dare he think it, more charisma. There was no arguing with the bottom line, and gross sales at the bar in Tony's first six weeks were up 22 percent.

What recession?

They still had the back dart room, wide with low ceilings, and it was packed to the seams. Brittany was back there now, ten-thirty on Saturday night, playing darts on a team with her mother – by no means a regular before McGuire's arrest – against a team of her cousin and Rebecca's new boyfriend, Ben Feinstein. With the encroachments of unwanted celebrity, Brittany had retreated to her family – making amends with the Beck and Ben, then matchmaking and watching things between them start to develop nicely, albeit slowly. Susan was riding the rush, believing her husband innocent for the first time. She'd called Brittany to share the news, see if they might celebrate in some way, and the bar was where they'd all wound up.

Susan had just retrieved her darts and was turning around when she was blinded by a flashbulb in the hall leading back to the main bar; at the same time, a woman screamed out in the front, and a tremendous crash seemed to shake the whole building.

The room they were in contained four dartboards and comfortably held about twenty people, about half the number trying to push into the narrow opening to the hall.

'Brittany!' a male voice called out as another flash exploded. 'Brittany McGuire!' Another flash.

Susan reached for her daughter, got hold of her arm, then yelled, 'Ben, grab the Beck! Back this way.'

Someone had started turning the lights on and off, but Susan didn't need them. Although the mob was pushing in the opposite direction – toward the hallway that led to the main bar – she held on to Brittany and kept moving steadily toward the door at the back, always locked while the bar was open, that led outside to a covered, fenced-in storage area where they kept kegs and cases of beer, snacks, liquor.

Susan had her master set of keys and got the door open. Another eight or ten customers followed them outside as Susan switched on the floodlight.

'What's going on?'

'Is everybody all right?'

'What happened up front?'

More screams, the sounds of panic, too many bodies in too small a space. And somewhere, off in the night, the sound of sirens.

27

THE FIGHT EVIDENTLY started with one of the drunk photographers hassling a cluster of attractive women for pictures. The eventual recipe for the mêlée included lots of inebriated young adults, an overcrowded, overheated, overloud bar, and several chivalrous testosterone-laden boyfriends. No one seemed to remember who threw the first punch, and things got out of hand in a hurry. The cops came and helped restore order and sent a bunch of people home.

'That guy is the kiss of death,' Hardy said.

In bright warm sunlight the next morning, he stood on the sidewalk in front of the Shamrock, hands on hips, staring with disbelief at the plywood where the front window used to be. The Beck had called the Hardys at nine-thirty and given them the short version. Hardy, as the unjailed partner in the Shamrock, felt they ought to go over and check out the damage, the makeshift repair.

'He works at Burning Rome,' Hardy went on, 'the ABC busts the place. He works here, they have a riot and break the damn window. And that's a hard window. I've thrown people up against that window and it didn't break.'

'Well, it did last night. But it wasn't Tony,' Frannie said. 'The Beck said it was the photographers.'

'Now you're going to bat for him.'

'Just correcting the record.'

'Okay. But who's the lawyer here?'

She took his hand. 'You are. Seen enough?'

He stepped forward, knocked at the plywood a couple of times. It seemed to be holding. 'If he's trying to open at noon, he'll be here soon enough, and I don't think I want to see him. I've had enough drama for one weekend.'

She started leading him back to their car. 'I'm just afraid this is going to start another round.'

'Of what?'

'"Of what," he asks. You'd think they'd just leave her alone.'

'Actually, no, I wouldn't think so. Beautiful rape victim. Father on trial for killing her assailant. Now provoking a range war among the paparazzi. Who even knew there were paparazzi here? Or that many of them?'

'Well, there are going to be more now. And she hasn't even testified yet. Imagine if they found out she was dating a protected witness? It would be a free-for-all. She'd have to go into hiding.'

'To say nothing of Tony, whose cover would be blown. That might not be such a bad thing. At least for Brittany, maybe for all concerned.' Hardy shook his head. 'You know what I don't understand?'

'Quantum physics?'

'Besides that. And don't say string theory.'

'You don't understand string theory?'

'Not so much. But what I really don't understand is the frenzy. I mean, Brittany's a pretty girl, okay, but a hundred thousand dollars' worth of pretty?'

'That's naked. In *Playboy*.'

'They think all normal pretty young women want to be in *Playboy*?'

'A lot of them do.'

'Am I a prude because I'm glad Brittany doesn't?'

'You're not a prude, period. It's not about that, anyway. It's about privacy. All that's happened to her, did she ask for any of it? She's going along with her life, and suddenly, everybody wants to take her picture, all her ex-boyfriends want to talk about how promiscuous she is, what a slut she was in college. Next thing you know, somebody's going to turn up with a sex tape.'

'Please, God, no. For Susan's sake, at least, not to mention Mose's.'

A shrug. 'Beck said she couldn't rule it out.'

'Could Brittany have been that dumb?'

Frannie shot him an arch look. 'Have you checked out Facebook lately?'

'Not exactly my thing. Is she on that?'

'Everybody's on that, Diz. Everybody's stalking everybody else. Hopefully, Brittany's posts aren't too extreme. Probably not, or they would have come out already, but there's no sense of anybody's private business. And not just there. Why wouldn't you want to be naked in *Playboy* for money if you're already naked on the Web for free?'

'How about if you just don't want to be naked in public?'

Frannie smiled, stopped, and kissed his cheek. 'You are such a sweet little Victorian,' she said.

After the riot, Susan and Brittany stayed at the bar to help clean up. They found the plywood – used many years before on the same front window, so a perfect fit – in the back storage area. When they finished, they went home to Susan's together.

So this morning, Susan had let her daughter sleep in. Now, closing in on noon, Brittany sat at the kitchen table in running shorts and a Cal T-shirt. Susan had opened the windows to let in the warm breeze, and Brittany was finishing a cheese quesadilla. 'The only thing,' Susan was saying, 'is if your father didn't, who did? I want to believe him. I don't think he'd lie to me. But if he really thought I was going to leave him . . .'

'Did you say you were going to?'

'Not in so many words. Maybe I gave him that impression. If he could do that in cold blood, I thought I might leave. I didn't know. But if he didn't . . .'

'Yesterday you absolutely believed it.'

'I know. But sometimes you can want something so badly that you make yourself believe it. I've thought a little more about it since then. How reasonable is it that somebody else was there at almost exactly the same time for the same reason?'

Brittany swallowed, lifted her coffee mug. 'The same-time part is a little hard to believe,' she said, 'but not impossible. Exactly what time he died is a real window. But why for the same reason? There could have been any number of reasons.'

'You mean reasons not having to do with you?'

Brittany nodded.

Susan said, 'Wouldn't that be wonderful. But how?'

'How could any of those reasons come up when we were all thinking it was Daddy, no matter what? When he told you it wasn't, well if that were true, it changed everything, didn't it? Do you want to know what Tony thinks?'

Susan sat back. 'Sure.'

'Well, you know the bogus charge he's had hanging over his head forever that they finally dropped? Needless to say, he got familiar with how the whole thing came about, the sting and everything. His lawyers, including Uncle Diz, were all over it from the beginning, but there was nothing they could do.'

'You mean about the sting?'

'Right. The sting was legal, as far as it went.'

Susan's brow furrowed. 'We're still talking about your father?'

'Wait. You'll see. The point is that the sting was pretty much the brainchild of guess who? Liam Goodman. Who was . . .'

Susan leaned forward, all interest, elbows on the table. 'Rick Jessup's boss.'

'Correct. And you know why Mr Goodman wanted the sting

to happen? To take the heat off one of his donors, maybe his main donor, Jon Lo, who is in the Korean massage parlor business, also known as sex slavery. The city was cracking down on him until it got knocked sideways by the whole underage-drinking issue.'

'Okay, but I don't see how—'

'I'm getting there. Really. Anyway' – she took a breath – 'Tony was a policeman in New York before he came out here. With the Vice team, and one of the things he dealt with was human trafficking and sexual slavery.'

'We're getting a long way from your father.'

'Not really. It turns out that when these people have an enemy they need to get rid of, they fly somebody in from China or Korea or wherever. They land in Montreal, drive across the border, catch a flight down to New York, rent a car, drive to the address they've been given, kill whoever it is they've been contracted for, drive back to the airport, and catch the next plane out of New York back to Asia, sometimes by way of Vancouver.'

'This happens a lot?'

'Whenever it needs to. Often enough that Tony knows about it.'

'Did they ever catch any of these people?'

'Never in the act. Once in a while, the feds will burn down a whole gang, like the Flying Dragons and the New York Ghost Shadows.'

'How do you know these names?'

'Tony. That's how they found out the way it worked. And you know the really interesting thing about this, at least as far as Daddy is concerned?'

'What's that?'

'These men who fly in from Asia? They can't bring guns or knives on the airplanes, right? So they tend to use other things. Their hands. Rope.' She paused. 'Blunt objects.'

'And so Tony's theory is . . . ?'

'It's not exactly a theory. He doesn't know any details. Maybe none of it relates. But here in the city, we've got Jon Lo into sexual slavery, connected to Liam Goodman and Rick Jessup. Maybe Rick did something to get on Lo's wrong side. We know what kind of person Rick was. Maybe the timing was just really unlucky for Daddy.'

Susan pushed herself back from the table. She crossed her arms over her chest, let out a breath. 'Do you think there could be something to that?'

'I don't know, Mom. But if Daddy didn't kill him, somebody else did, and this is at least an alternative.'

'Have you mentioned it to Uncle Diz?'

Brittany let out a brittle laugh. 'Mom, I barely finished telling you. And there isn't much to tell him, is there? There's no proof.'

'He doesn't need proof,' Susan said. 'The DA needs proof. All Uncle Diz needs, all your father needs, is doubt.'

It took two days for Hardy's advice to sink in.

On Sunday, Glitsky looked in the mirror.

Now on this beautiful afternoon, clean-shaven, Glitsky sat on the landing that overlooked his small backyard while his wife buzzed his head. Hardy might have his own professional barber, but Treya worked just fine for Abe. Zach and Rachel and a couple of the neighbor kids had some kind of intrigue going around the play structure below. For the briefest of moments, and for the first time in about three months, he considered that all was right with the world.

'So you're going to do it?' she asked him.

'I'm leaning in that direction, but I wanted to clear it with you, see how Wes would take it.'

'Wes will not be thrilled, but in that flinty heart of yours, you already know that. You also know you don't have to clear things with me.'

'Okay, get your opinion, then.'

'Should you testify for the defense?'

'That's the question.'

'How much trouble could you get in?'

Glitsky's lips went up a fraction of an inch. 'More than being fired, you mean?'

'You weren't fired. Lapeer was going to demote you, so you retired.'

'Semantics.'

'Not really. Not exactly. If you'd been fired, they wouldn't be throwing you a retirement dinner next month.'

'Those things are pretty sarcastic.'

'Just because they say sarcastic things about you doesn't mean the event is ironic. You don't get roasted if they don't want to honor you. And your service.'

'Nice of you to say so, but it's pretty pro forma. You put in your thirty-plus years, they got to do something.'

Treya switched off the clippers. 'I'm not going to argue about whether you are held in high esteem by the great majority of your colleagues. You got caught in some political cross fire between Lapeer and Goodman and didn't feel you could fight back because of Moses and your connection to him. But that does not negate your whole career, and it doesn't say one damn negative thing about your character, which is unimpeachable. Can you get that through your skull?'

Glitsky breathed in and out for a moment. 'Are you mad at me?'

'Almost. I think if you have the chance, you ought to take the stand and say what really happened. They rushed to judgment. You didn't go running to Diz. You didn't alert Moses to anything. You never talked to either of them. Give them your phone records. You wanted to follow protocol, that's all. The chief saw an opportunity to make some political hay, and your inspectors probably could have built a better case if they'd taken a few more days. If they're more interested in politics than in getting it straight, why should the jury believe them? All that's true, right? It's true and it helps Moses, which is also in your best interest, isn't it?'

'Except I've built a life around not letting murderers get off.'

'He's not a murderer until he's proven guilty.'

'Not really, Trey. He's a murderer right after he murders somebody.'

'Maybe he didn't.'

'Please. That's not in any real dispute.' He reached back and patted her hand, resting on his shoulder. 'Even if it's somehow in my best interest for him to get off, and I'm not denying that, it goes against the grain to testify against my people.'

'Vi Lapeer is not your people. She's a politician.'

'And Brady? And Sher?'

'You're not saying one bad word against them. And you know our little semantic difference about whether you were fired or you retired?'

'Vaguely. It rings a bell.'

'Just have Diz ask you about that, straight out. "Mr Glitsky, did you in fact resign after this egregious display of obstructionism and political cronyism by the chief of police?" And your answer, of course, is yes, which is the literal truth. You were not fired. You quit after a distinguished career. Who'd have the high ground then?'

After a minute, Glitsky nodded thoughtfully. 'I'd prefer it, I think,' he said, 'if he addressed me as "Lieutenant".'

28

Monday morning, 9:18. Twelve minutes until court convened.

Stier had given his okay, Hardy had sold it in a low-key way to his new friend the judge, and now Winston Paley, in a brown corduroy suit, a yellow shirt, and a purple and red tie a few inches too wide, sat in the front seat of the packed-to-the-rafters courtroom on Hardy's side.

The doctor seemed to be in high spirits – and why not, Hardy thought, looking at a minimum of one and possibly two thirty-five-hundred-dollar days – and he was clearly taken with Gina Roake, who had come down from her gallery seat and perched on the bar rail, making small talk with him. This inadvertently, or maybe not, showed off her zaftig profile to best advantage.

Suddenly, Stier and his associate rose as a unit from their table and crossed over to the defense side, which broke up Roake and Paley's rhythm enough for Stier to lean in to the expert witness and extend his hand. 'Dr Paley, Paul Stier for the prosecution. I just wanted to say hello and welcome you to San Francisco.'

Paley beamed, shook the prosecutor's hand.

'And this,' Stier went on, stepping back, 'is my associate, Lars Gunderson. He had occasion to study some of your testimony during a mock trial in law school at McGeorge and remembers it to this day. He's a big fan. Says you're one of his heroes.'

At this, Paley came up out of his chair and warmly greeted the young man, shaking his hand. 'That's extremely flattering.

Thank you.' Then, to all, 'It's so gratifying when one's work takes on a life of its own.'

'If you don't mind' – Stier had his cell phone out, holding it up – 'a quick picture, the two of you? Mr Hardy, no objection?'

Hardy didn't know what to make of the obsequious display, but there was nothing objectionable on the face of it – court wasn't in session; Paley was a defense witness – and Stier had been nothing if not gracious in chambers this morning. 'Sure. Go ahead.'

'I'm afraid,' Stier was going on after taking the shot and checking that it had come out, 'that Lars is going to miss most of your testimony today – he's got a hearing in another courtroom on another matter – but when I told him you were going to be here, he wanted to come by and shake your hand.'

'Nice to have met you, Doctor,' Gunderson said. He nodded to Hardy and Wu, then opened the gate at the bar rail and excused himself back through the crowded gallery.

Stier made a polite small bow and retreated to his table.

'It's nice to see adversaries who get along so well,' Paley said.

To which Amy Wu replied, 'Oh, yes. Every day's a lovefest up here.'

After the judge was seated and court was called to order, she wasted no time getting down to it. 'Counsel have agreed, and I am going to allow the defense to put on a witness out of order at this time. Mr Hardy?'

'Thank you, Your Honor. Defense calls Dr Winston Paley.'

Paley moved with the confidence and comfort of a man who'd done this kind of thing hundreds of times. Nodding amiably, seemingly to one and all, he made his way through the courtroom's bullpen and up to the witness chair, where he turned and held up his right hand, ready to be sworn.

Hardy knew the testimony would be lengthy. The doctor's credentials alone would take the better part of an hour. If Paley didn't have such a disarming personality, Hardy would have feared that he'd bore the jury to death. But he had no such concerns. With his raconteur's touch, Paley was going to elucidate his educational and professional journey almost like high adventure, and perhaps, in a way, it had been. The man's lifetime of achievement could hardly fail to impress.

'Doctor, can you tell the jury your current occupation or profession.'

'Certainly. I am a psychologist working as a consultant in the general field of health care. My specific work is as what's called a forensic psychologist.'

'What is that, precisely?'

'I bring a certain background or specialty into a legal process like this one.'

'Would you please tell the jury about your academic background?'

Paley began to lay it all out. After obtaining his bachelor's degree in psychology with honors from UCLA, he went on to both medical school and graduate school in psychology at USC. While in school, he joined the faculty at UCLA, where he received a public health fellowship. At the same time, he was teaching courses, doing research, and pursuing his Ph.D. in psychology.

Slacker, Hardy thought. In a mostly passive role – even though he was in theory questioning the witness – Hardy had to resist the urge to wax wise. 'And what did you do next, Doctor?' he asked.

Paley went on, 'I was fortunate to be offered several faculty positions, I believe about ten, and eventually decided to work at Harvard, where they had offered me positions in three departments.'

At this, a small trickle of laughter rippled through the

courtroom. Paley took it in good humor, shrugged with a 'what can you do?' expression, and went on. 'While at Harvard, I received grants to work with the Department of Defense, the Advanced Research Projects Agency, the U.S. Navy and Marines, and several other government agencies. After that, I went to Texas and a tenured faculty position at the University of Houston; I stayed for five years before returning to California, where I took another tenured position at USC and began working part-time as a psychologist for the Los Angeles Police Department. During that time, I started working in what I do now. That is, as a forensic psychologist.'

Hardy interrupted the flow every few minutes to break things up, although he needn't have worried. Even with all the detail, Paley wasn't losing any of his audience, and it was information that Hardy felt the jury needed. Paley's credibility would have to be unassailable for Hardy to undercut Stier's eyewitnesses.

It went on and on. Retired from teaching to form and become president of a medical group of a hundred and fifty thousand patients in Southern California. That group got bought by another, which, naturally, Paley became head of. First court appearance in the seventies. He began to be called as an expert witness who specialized in eyewitness perception and identification.

Again his credentials were impressive, and again Hardy felt that the jury needed to hear all of them: a large briefcase full of publications, presentations at national and international (Zurich!) congresses on the issue, legal seminars in front of bar associations, over three hundred appearances in superior courts in California and twelve other states, in federal court, in the U.S. Virgin Islands. Paley had addressed the California state bar on eyewitness identification; he'd prepared a judge's school video on the topic; he'd formulated continuing education courses on how people see and recognize each other; the accuracy of these identifications; discrepancies between actual data and people's opinions of what they thought they saw.

Paley went on to explain that this had been a rich field of research for over eighty years in the U.S. and even longer in Europe. There was a huge body of evidence in the fields of identification, perception, and memory. Hundreds of doctoral dissertations. In all, Paley's opinion was that his field was as close to a hard science as could be found in psychology.

As the clock ticked toward the lunch break, Hardy took his cue. 'Your Honor,' he said, 'at this time the defense offers Dr Winston Paley as an expert in the field of eyewitness identification and perception.'

Gomez nodded, turned to the prosecution table. 'Voir dire, Mr Stier?'

'I'll wait for cross, Judge.'

'I'll allow Dr Paley to testify as an expert in the field. But I think first we're going to take a break for lunch.' She wielded her gavel for the first time that morning, tapping once. 'Court is adjourned until one-thirty.'

Hardy was a bit torn as to whether he should take Winston Paley or Susan Weiss to lunch, but Gina saved the day by volunteering to take their expert witness to Le Central, while he could take his sister-in-law anywhere but Lou's.

The phonetic syllable must have been in the air, since they wound up at Lulu's, a few blocks from the courtroom. Open and airy, especially with the nice weather and after the windowless claustrophobia of Department 24, the restaurant was a perfect choice.

Even if Susan hadn't been among the only family he had in the world, Hardy would have liked her. As it was, she had been one of his favorite people over the past twenty years. Soft-spoken, honest to a fault, prodigiously gifted in music, and sensitive to human reverberations far beyond those of which Hardy was even aware, she was the last person he would have picked to be the mate to his fiery, difficult, stubborn, alcoholic brother-in-law.

Hardy held her chair, seated her, and sat across from her. At sixty or so, Susan retained more than a soupçon of the beauty that she'd passed down to her oldest daughter. Perhaps she could no longer stop traffic, but Hardy found that if he sat across from her one-on-one, he could lose himself for seconds at a time.

'So?' Shaking out his napkin. 'You look like you finally got a little rest.'

She forced a smile. 'After the all-nighter Saturday, if I hadn't slept last night, I would have died. I was in bed at eight and got eleven hours.'

'In one night?'

'I know. A miracle.'

'I can't even imagine. You look a little relieved.'

'You find out your husband is not a killer after all, it helps.'

Hardy took in a breath, let that pass. 'How's Brittany?'

'Sick of all this. Sick of being pretty.'

'Good luck with that.'

'It's funny.' Susan broke off a bite of bread, dipped it in a shallow dish of olive oil. 'Her big joke used to be that she didn't want to waste the pretty. Last night she told me she was swearing off makeup.'

'It might help a little, but I wouldn't get my hopes up. Is she still seeing Tony?'

She nodded. 'Taking it slow, I believe, in a welcome change of pace.'

The waitress came, filled their water glasses, took their orders. Hardy came back to it. 'I've got a few issues with Tony.'

'Brittany mentioned that. Did you know he used to be a policeman?'

'That's what he says.'

'You don't believe him?'

'I don't know what I believe. Except I don't like him playing our girls one off the other. I don't like the aura of mystery he cultivates. I think he's got some real secrets, and that worries me. He's told me some things that have turned out not to be true.'

'Like what?'

'His name, for example. A meaningful detail, you'd think.'

Susan closed her eyes and sighed. 'You know all you have to do to make a young girl fall in love? Tell her she can't see somebody.'

'I hear you,' Hardy said.

'But, you know,' Susan went on, 'leaving that aside for a minute, Tony did tell Brittany something that I thought you might want to know. About this case. It might even be important. Especially now that we know Moses didn't do it.'

Hardy gave her a smile that he hoped did not come across as insincere. He listened while she ran down Brittany's theory of the Asian hit man. Somewhere in the middle of it, much to his surprise, he found himself warming to the idea, if not as a fact, then as an element of strategy. When Susan had finished, he asked, 'Does Brittany know anything specific about Jessup's relationship with Lo? Did they have some kind of falling-out?'

'Nobody seems to know. The reason we're having this discussion is that Brittany thought you might be able to find out.'

'Tony didn't have any ideas?'

She shook her head. 'Not other than Jon Lo being involved in sex slavery on the one hand and Liam Goodman on the other. This is evidently the way some of the sex traders take care of their problems.' She touched his hand. 'Diz?'

'I'm thinking,' he said. 'If there's one thing this case has been sorely missing, it's an alternative theory.'

'It might not even be a theory. Diz, this could be what actually happened.'

Leaving aside all that pesky evidence that implicated her husband and no one else, Hardy thought. Just then the waitress appeared; he motioned for a refill of his water, waited for her to pour. 'So,' he asked Susan, 'what do you think about the good Dr Paley?'

No sooner had court reconvened than Hardy decided he had a defensible reason and it was high time to put Stier off his feed – always a plus – by requesting a sidebar. His idea, born at lunch, followed by a call from Glitsky, would give Stier something to think about while his assistant was gone for the day and while Hardy's expert witness continued to set the stage for the upcoming confrontations with Stier's eyewitnesses.

Now the two attorneys were standing by the judge's bench and Stier was shaking his head in apparent disbelief at Hardy's disdain for the rules. 'Your Honor,' he said, 'counsel is supposed to have supplied me with his witness list thirty days before the trial. Adding new witnesses is highly irregular and objectionable.'

'Your Honor,' Hardy countered before Gomez could reply, 'speaking of irregular and objectionable, because of the speed at which the police investigation led to my client's arrest and hearing, I have been scrambling to catch up to various evidentiary issues that I couldn't have known about thirty days ago.'

'And yet you're the one who refused to waive time to hurry up this trial.'

'Exactly wrong, Mr Stier. *My client* declined to waive time because it was his absolute right to go to trial within sixty days of arraignment and because he did not want to rot in jail for a crime he didn't commit.'

'So you're saying you just found out about these witnesses?'

'Two of them over lunch, as a matter of fact. And the other – whom I haven't mentioned yet – over the weekend.'

'You haven't mentioned—?'

'I've been trying to—'

'And what are they going to testify about?'

The judge leaned down over the bench. 'That's enough of this bickering. Counsel will direct remarks only to the court, not to opposing counsel. Mr Stier?'

'Your Honor.' He spread his arms. 'Now he's telling us he's got yet another witness. What? Will he be allowed to introduce witnesses whenever the mood strikes him?'

'He'll be allowed to include witnesses when the court allows him, counsel. And not until.'

Poker-faced, Hardy was loving this exchange. In his zeal, Stier had managed to anger the judge by appearing to undercut her authority.

'Of course, Your Honor,' Stier said. 'No disrespect intended. Maybe defense counsel could give us the name of his third intended witness, then perhaps mention some of the evidentiary issues they'll be addressing.'

With every word, Ugly was digging himself in deeper.

'Thank you, Mr Stier,' said Gomez with a cold smile. 'I was hoping to ask Mr Hardy some of those very same questions before ruling on his motion.' Her smile thawing a few degrees, she turned slightly. 'Mr Hardy, please so inform the court.'

'Thank you, Your Honor. Besides Supervisor Liam Goodman and his political donor Jon Lo, I may call Lieutenant Abraham Glitsky, the former chief of Homicide.'

In a skilled attorney's hands, the flexible and ambiguous witness list could become a powerful weapon, and Hardy was using it as such today. Its great advantage was that people named on the list did not have to appear at trial. Of course, they could at any time be called. What made it beautiful was that opposing counsel had to be prepared for either eventuality. Not only could that tremendously increase opposing counsel's workload, it could also introduce any number of spurious arguments, far-fetched theories, and rock-solid evidence, while providing no clue as to which might be which.

'Oh, for the love of . . .' Stier threw up his hands again. 'Your Honor, if it please the court!'

This time Gomez snapped. 'Enough with the histrionics, Mr Stier. This is a court of law, not an acting class. Further displays like this will not end well for you. Consider yourself warned.'

Stier hung his head. 'Apologies, Your Honor. But Lieutenant Glitsky?'

'Mr Hardy?'

Matter-of-fact, Hardy began. 'Your Honor, in some ways, this entire case hinges on Lieutenant Glitsky's role in its earlier handling. Because of a perceived conflict of interest that San Francisco's chief of police, Vi Lapeer, painted as a conspiracy between Glitsky, the defendant, me, my partner Ms Roake, and even Wes Farrell, she first obtained a Ramey warrant to arrest the defendant before the evidence warranted prosecution; then she expressed a lack of confidence in the lieutenant's handling of his inspectors that led to his retirement. Glitsky's rebuttal of Chief Lapeer's accusations and actions will highlight the political machinations and the resulting defective evidence that was the proximate cause of the defendant's arrest.'

Stier wasn't going to let it all go without a comment. 'Which has absolutely nothing to do, Your Honor, with the evidence we're relying upon to convict this defendant. It has nothing to do with the blood in the defendant's car. It has nothing to do with the blood on the defendant's shoes or his jacket. It has nothing to do with the conveniently missing shillelagh that happens to be the murder weapon. And I'd love to hear that it has nothing to do with the facts that the defendant beat up Rick Jessup in city hall and, later, that Jessup raped his daughter. This is an absolute red herring.'

Unperturbed, Hardy sailed on. 'As to Mr Goodman and Mr Lo, I am not sure of their testimony at this time. Mr Jessup worked for Mr Goodman; Mr Lo is one of his major donors; and obviously, there are unexplored relationships that I believe may be relevant to this case, particularly the defendant's alleged motive. I intend to have my private investigator talk to these witnesses and explore the relationships, and then, if they so warrant, I intend to call them. In this context, it is not impossible that I may ask the court to add both Wes Farrell and Vi Lapeer to the witness list.'

'Mr Stier?'

'Seriously, Your Honor? Seriously? Mr Hardy doesn't even try to articulate a connection, however tenuous, between Mr Lo, Mr Goodman, and this case. It is, to coin a phrase, the mother of all smokescreens, and the court shouldn't tolerate it.' The prosecutor's face glowed a dull red. 'With respect, Your Honor, these three witnesses are intended to confuse and mislead the jury. They have no place at this trial.'

'Thank you, counsel.' She turned to Hardy. 'Counsel,' she said, 'I'm going to allow you to add these names, but that's all I'm saying right now, and I'll tell you what: before any one of them gets on the witness stand, I'm going to want to hear a much more focused recitation of relevant testimony that they can give. Because, frankly, what you've told me so far is unconvincing, and if I had to decide now, I might just sustain Mr Stier's objections. Consider yourself on notice.'

Buoyed by his success, Hardy cautioned himself against complacency or overconfidence. After Dr Paley was settled again in the witness chair, Hardy took an extra moment apparently studying his notes at the defense table. All business, he sipped from his water glass, looked neither at Wu nor Stier nor to the gallery, and finally stood to face his witness. 'Dr Paley,' he began, 'would you mind starting out by giving the jury the definition, as it were, of eyewitness identification and perception?'

'Certainly.' Paley had lost none of his energy or enthusiasm over lunch. 'Let me say to begin with that, obvious as it may be, you can't identify someone unless you first observe him. Once you've done that, then eyewitness identification is the ability to pick out the very same person you saw – that is, observed – before.'

'You say "the very same person," Doctor. Are you trying to distinguish that very same person from some other person?'

'Excellent question, Mr Hardy. Excellent.' As well it should be, Hardy thought; they'd rehearsed it enough, to the tune of about a thousand dollars. 'What I am trying to distinguish is what that so-called very same person is not. He is not, for example, somebody whom you assume to be the person; nor is he someone who you think other people may think is the person. He's not somebody who somebody else told you was the person, or who the police believe was the person, or who a photograph suggests is the person. All of the above are not eyewitness identification.'

'And why not, Doctor?'

'Because they all have to do with assumptions and inferences. And eyewitness ID is the demonstrated ability, based on the memory of what you've observed, to pick out the very same person you saw before.'

'Is that difficult?'

'It can be, yes.'

'Are there specific conditions under which it can be more difficult?'

'Absolutely.'

'Such as?'

'Well, if it's dark or far away, or if there's a lot of other stuff going on or too many people around. And if I might just add something . . .'

310

'Go ahead.'

'The other thing is that we've all got opinions about how eyewitness identification works, but the fact is that when we compare how we think it works and how it actually works, we're often way off. It doesn't happen the way lots of folks think it does. Studies over the past decades have proved that we don't do it nearly as well as we think we do.'

For the next twenty minutes, under Hardy's careful questioning, the doctor homed in on this point – we are not video cameras; we are severely influenced by other observations as well as by what else is going on at the time of the observation. And not only are the original observations often impacted by surrounding events; our fragile memories become mixed up during the act of recovery, and the observation degrades because of the other information in our memory – assumptions and things we know from other sources, many of which we never saw.

Again, the information could have been sleep-inducing, but Paley managed to drop a few bombs that shook up not just the jury but the entire courtroom.

'You know, everybody uses confidence as a measure of how accurate we are, but in hundreds of studies – some of them right here in this briefcase, if you'd like to see them – there is no relationship at all. You can be one hundred percent certain of what you saw, would swear to it, and still be one hundred percent wrong.'

And: 'No matter how detailed, vivid, and strong your memories are, they can be completely erroneous.'

Particularly: 'If there are weapons involved. People who are holding weapons are seen to be much bigger. A young man who is five feet eight and holding a gun could easily, and has often, been described as six feet two.'

And: 'Our certainty increases every time we repeat ourselves. We more readily commit to saying what we've said before, rather than what we have seen. And this isn't about people lying. People honestly tell you what they think they remember, and they are just wrong. Eyewitness IDs work in such a way that people can tell you exactly what they saw with confidence and in great detail and be totally mistaken.'

After the afternoon break, Hardy asked, 'Doctor, do you cite studies about people who have been convicted of a crime and later found innocent because of something like DNA evidence – in other words, where there was no longer any doubt that they were innocent; they were convicted mostly on eyewitness evidence – what percent of those erroneous convictions were based on erroneous eyewitness IDs?'

'Ninety percent.'

At this statistic, Gomez had to gavel the courtroom into silence.

'Let's go the other way,' Hardy said. 'Do you have any studies where the actual bad guy was shown to the victim and the victim let that person go?'

'Yes.'

'How many studies?'

'Again, hundreds.'

'Doctor, does it matter who asks a witness for his or her ID? For example, if a policeman asks, would that be different than, say, a teacher in an academic study?'

'Oh, definitely. Most people overwhelmingly believe that the police wouldn't waste your time showing you an innocent person. In fact' – Paley again went on without any prodding – 'many studies show that eyewitnesses can be influenced merely by a policeman knowing the expected, or right, answer. That's why a policeman who shows photographs should not know which is the suspect in a case. Eyewitnesses pick up cues that they're not even aware of. Plus, if you pick someone out in an identification procedure and then see a similar face in another procedure, you're going to pick out the first face again because it has more familiarity than any of the others.'

'It sounds to me, Doctor,' Hardy said, 'that in spite of our belief to the contrary, eyewitness identification is not particularly accurate. Is that true?'

Paley had no doubt. 'It is the least reliable form of identification.'

'And in-court identification? That is, where an eyewitness points to a defendant sitting in a courtroom? What is the degree of reliability in that scenario?'

'There is no reliability at all. By that time, the witness knows what is expected. He knows the defendant is the man in court sitting next to his lawyer and that he is supposed to identify him. He feels enormous pressure to make the ID whether or not he is certain in his own mind that it is correct.'

Hardy stole a glance at the courtroom's clock. They had only a few minutes until the evening adjournment. 'Doctor,' he asked, 'is there anything else you think is important about eyewitness identification that you would like to tell the court?'

Paley glanced at the jury box and decided to reward them with a small joke. 'I've got at least another day's worth, if you've got the time.'

Hardy let a small ripple of chuckles flow across the courtroom. 'Let's just stick to the important stuff,' he said.

'Well,' Paley replied, 'there are two points that are unquestionably important. The first is called the cross-racial effect.' The picture of confidence, he looked over at the jury, out to the gallery. 'Although it sounds like a slur of some kind, it is not. It's not an insult, either. It's not even a racist statement. What it relates to is that if someone looks different, we tend to label them. We get details of their faces less thoroughly and are less accurate picking them out later.'

'Is this always true, Doctor?'

'Yes. Even if you've had a lot of experience with the different look. There was a great study in South Africa where the white people had a difficult time picking out individual black people, even though blacks are the majority culture in South Africa. Anyway, there's one, the cross-racial effect. It's real and it happens.

'The second thing I'd guess is important is that sometimes we've seen a face but don't know where – maybe the clerk in our grocery store – and that person is among the pool of potential suspects whom an eyewitness will be asked to identify. Almost always, the grocery clerk will get picked out as the suspect by an eyewitness. This is known as the innocent-bystander effect. It works on the basis of unconscious transference.'

'Doctor, like everything else you've told us today, that sounds fascinating. But the judge has asked us to be aware of the clock. We're getting toward the end of the day, and as you know, we have prepared a video for the jury's benefit. Your Honor, if it please the court, we'll need a few minutes to set up.'

Hardy didn't normally like to use audiovisuals in the courtroom. They were rarely conducive to the introduction of evidence; they were subject to all kinds of editing that cast doubt on whatever point they were trying to prove; there were always foundational issues – where the tape or CD had been stored, for how long, and by whom in an unbroken chain; and in the dark courtroom in the late afternoon, even the best of them had been known to put jurors to sleep.

But Paley had so blown Hardy's mind with the three-minute video they were about to show that he couldn't resist. They had to play it in its entirety so that Stier and Gomez could both approve it. Stier had vehemently objected, but Hardy had won the argument and thought it would be one of the high points of the defense. To Hardy it was brand-new, though both Stier and Gomez had apparently heard of it on YouTube. Neither had seen it before Hardy brought it into the judge's chambers. So some of the jury might have seen it or heard of it as well. Nevertheless, Hardy was playing for one vote to acquit, one person to convince, and if even one juror had the same reaction he'd had, he thought it was worth the effort.

Now Paley was on the stand, and the television they'd set up was facing the jurors. Before they darkened the courtroom, Hardy laid his foundation. 'Doctor, what is this exhibit designed to demonstrate?'

Paley: 'Subjects are asked to count how many times the players wearing white pass the ball.'

Hardy hit play.

Six young women were lined up in casual athletic clothing, three wearing black jerseys, three wearing white ones. Each team had one ball, and the girls started to bounce or throw it to their team members. After about twenty-five seconds, the screen went black, and Hardy said, 'Doctor, what is the correct answer?'

Paley replied, 'The correct answer is sixteen passes, but you asked earlier what the purpose of the demonstration was. This film is designed to demonstrate that subjects asked to concentrate on one thing often overlook highly salient information.'

'How does it do that, Doctor?'

'It does that because most people say they did not see the gorilla in the film.'

An audible gasp resounded in the courtroom, followed by a light chorus of nervous laughter.

Hardy said, 'Doctor. Are you kidding about the gorilla?'

'No, Mr Hardy, I am not. This is not a joke. This is a widely circulated video found not only in psychology classes but on such popular media as YouTube. We have been talking all day about eyewitness testimony and about observation, and you've all just had a demonstration on the reliability of your own eyewitness testimony, especially when the mind is concentrating on something else, such as the presence of a weapon or how many times the girls wearing white passed the ball.

'Now,' Paley continued, 'let's replay the tape and take another look at what you've just seen. Knowing about the gorilla this time, see if you also notice that the curtain in the background changed color or that one of the black-shirt-team girls left the game at about the same time that the gorilla came on.'

Hardy pressed the play button again, Paley testifying that about 50 percent of people viewing the video for the first time did not notice the gorilla. As the game progressed the second time around and the gorilla came on at the same place, a great deal more laughter broke out in the courtroom – no doubt, Hardy thought, people seeing the damn thing for the first time.

When the video ended again, Paley said, 'When you're looking for a gorilla, you often miss other unexpected events.'

'So, Doctor, if people were focusing on a weapon, such as a club, do your studies indicate that they would be unreliable in processing and recollecting other observations – for example, the facial features of the person holding such a club?'

'Absolutely,' Paley said. 'Studies show that an ID under those conditions would not be reliable.'

'Thank you, Doctor.' Hardy looked up at the bench. 'Your Honor, this concludes my direct.'

29

FARRELL HAD WANTED to sit in on the opening statements, and last week he had done so, but he wasn't interested in listening to Paley elucidate the many ways that an eyewitness was a worthless redundancy as far as identification was concerned. Farrell had hired Dr Paley more than once in his earlier defense practice, and he had no doubt that, if anything, the tireless and enthusiastic expert witness would have upped his game.

Fortunately, the familiarity gave him an opportunity: if you know what your opponent will say, you should be able to turn that to an advantage. And Farrell, after the end run around his position orchestrated by Lapeer, needed to make a strong prosecutorial showing in this case. It wasn't so much that he wanted to see Moses McGuire convicted – after all, he had known and liked the bartender for over twenty years. But Farrell's ability to function in his job and, not incidentally, to get himself reelected, would depend on his ability to retain the loyalty and confidence of his troops, both of which had suffered a tremendous hit after the Ramey warrant.

Now, a little after five o'clock, a strangely unfamiliar Lars Gunderson sat on the couch across from him as they ticked off the points that Stier would use tomorrow in his cross-examination of Dr Paley. Farrell had suggested that Gunderson pull the transcripts of several other trials in which Paley had testified. Taken together, those transcripts were a road map pointing the way to lines of questioning that would help to negate or severely deflate the claims that the jury had heard.

But first, Farrell had to know. 'Lars, is it me, or are you sporting some kind of a different look?'

The young prosecutor broke a smile. 'I cut my hair and shaved off my mustache. Paul wanted a different approach for the jury.'

'Ahh, there it is. Never let it be said that I'm not observant.'

'No, sir. Never entered my mind.'

'I had a ponytail for a couple of years early in my career. Did you know that?'

'I didn't.'

'It was meant to be a statement. I decided I wasn't going to cut my hair until something – almost anything – made sense.'

'How'd that go?'

'As I said, a couple of years went by.'

'Was there one thing that finally happened?'

'You mean made sense? Not really. My hair would be all the way down to my ass if I'd stuck to my guns. But you've got to remember, I was a defense guy in those days, so my clients tended to identify with me more than with the suits who were trying to put 'em in jail.'

Gunderson took a beat. 'If I could ask, how are you doing with this McGuire thing?'

'Me knowing him and all?'

'Yeah.'

'He did the crime, he does the time.'

'Really? Just like that?'

Farrell sat with the question, then got up from the couch, picked up a Nerf basketball, and shot it at the basket over by the law books. He missed by a couple of feet. 'The corollary is that if he didn't do the crime, he walks. Personally, I hope he walks. I hope he didn't kill that kid. But if he did . . .' He shrugged. 'It's not as personal as people made it seem.'

'You mean Lapeer?'

Another shrug. 'She had her priorities. She could have come

to me and sold her pitch. But she never gave me any pitch, which is where she went wrong.'

'So you think she was wrong?'

'I just said that, didn't I?'

'So McGuire's innocent?'

'Not at all. I hope he's innocent. I think he's guilty as sin. Although, vigilante at heart that I am, I kind of understand where he was coming from. Tell no one.'

'Right. Of course.'

'So? We good? Back to Dr Paley? Ream him a new one?'

Gunderson nodded. 'Back at him.'

At approximately the same time, Dismas Hardy was in his office, talking on the phone with his investigator, Wyatt Hunt. 'At this point,' he was saying, 'it's open season on both Lo and Goodman. We know absolutely nothing about either of them in terms of Jessup, other than he worked for one of them.'

'What am I looking for, specifically?'

'Some kind of leverage he might have had.'

'Is it my imagination, or do I keep coming back to the word "specific"?'

'I know. I apologize for that, but I need to find another plausible reason for somebody to want Jessup dead.'

'You realize that would be a pretty big reason, right? I mean, we're talking a motive for making somebody dead, which is not so easy to keep hidden. As of now, there's no sign of whatever it might be.'

'Right.'

'Or evidence.'

'We don't have to prove anything, Wyatt. It just has to be marginally plausible.'

'And you think a city supervisor looks like promising hunting grounds? Don't get me wrong, I'd love the work, because work

319

is always good, but Goodman is more or less a pillar of the community, is he not? And isn't it pretty well established that the rape was the motive? Mose's motive, I mean.'

'If we believe it was him, yes. But we don't want the jury going away to deliberate without a couple of other theories rattling around.'

Hunt didn't say anything for a moment. Then he asked, 'And who is Lo, again?'

'He owns a bunch of Korean massage parlors.'

'And kills people, too? Kind of as a sideline?'

Hardy chuckled. 'You do make it sound slightly absurd.'

Hunt said, 'Not my intention. I'm just trying to save you a little money by barking up some possibly more productive trees.'

'I'll take any and all suggestions.'

'All right. Like, what about the rest of Jessup's personal life?'

'What about it?'

'I don't know. Maybe he stole one of his friend's girlfriends. Maybe he sold dope on the side and stiffed his supplier. Maybe he had a jealous gay lover. Maybe he ran over some crazy lady's cat. The dude was a rapist. He had roofies, right? So there probably were other victims. What about if one of them killed him? Did he have any family?'

'He's got a mother and a sister ten years older. Apparently he wasn't close to either, although they were sad to see him killed and all.' Hardy heard a heavy breath over the line. 'Am I getting desperate?' he asked.

'Sounds a little like it to me.'

'Can you give me twenty hours?'

'I'll give you all the time you want. But I feel like I'm wasting your money, and I hate that.'

'If that feeling gets too bad, you don't have to take the money.'

320

'Good one, Diz.'

'I know,' Hardy said. 'I'm a laugh riot.'

Susan stood outside the bathroom door adjacent to her daughter's bedroom and knocked softly. 'Brittany, are you all right?'

'I'm fine.'

'You've been in there for a half hour.'

'I know. I'm fine.'

'I don't want to bother you, but I'm starting to worry.'

'You don't need to.'

'Are you coming out to eat? I brought home some Chinese.'

'In another minute.'

'Okay. I'll be at the table.'

With a heavy heart, Susan walked back to the kitchen. She put down a place mat on either side of the Formica table. On each one she set chopsticks, a cloth napkin, a plate, and a wineglass. She took a half-filled box of white wine out of the refrigerator and put it in the middle of the table. Finally, lifting the individual packages out of the paper bag on the counter, she arranged them, still closed, on the table within easy reach. Shrimp lo mein. Potstickers. Barbecued ribs. General Tso's chicken. Steamed rice.

Stepping back, she surveyed the table and sighed. Soy sauce, she thought, and turned to grab the bottle from the pantry shelf.

Brittany was standing in front of her in the doorway to the kitchen, wearing a borrowed pair of her father's pajamas. She had been crying; her eyes were swollen and bleary with tears, her beautiful face was flushed, almost bruised-looking, without any sign of makeup. 'I so hate myself,' she said.

A guttural noise escaped from somewhere inside her as Susan walked up to her daughter and wrapped her arms around her.

Brittany, stiff and resistant, held on for a couple of seconds, then broke down and began to sob.

Glitsky sat in the passenger seat of Bill Schuyler's car in front of his home. The fog was in and dusk well advanced. The FBI agent, about ten years Glitsky's junior, was never a terribly relaxed man, and here in these close quarters, he fairly hummed with tension. Glitsky had invited him upstairs, but Schuyler clearly didn't want whatever this was about to take up much time. He didn't want to meet the family. He didn't want anything to be personal.

'I don't even know why we're having this meeting,' he said. 'I told you I don't have any pull with the marshals. It's a different jurisdiction.'

'I understand that.'

'Obviously not.'

'Are we going to argue about this or get down to it?'

Some of the fight went out of Schuyler. 'You're lucky to be out of the business,' he said. 'I'm cranky because I'm in the middle of something else. It's making everybody crazy. One crisis after another.'

'I remember it well. And I wasn't even federal.'

'From all I hear, you got screwed.'

Glitsky coughed out a laugh. 'Well, thanks. I'm looking on it as a blessing. Doing something else with my life.'

'And yet here you are, very much in the life, calling me.'

'Doing a favor for a friend. And before you tell me for the fifth time that you can't help me, let me tell you that my friend and I, we've got no interest in disclosing the identity of the witness. We just want to know what he's in for.'

'How do you even know to ask?'

'He bragged to his girlfriend, then dumped her.'

'What a unique story. And you think what he told her might not have been the whole truth?'

'We don't know. He painted himself, no surprise, as something of a hero. Saw some bad guys doing bad things and decided he had to step up and testify against them.'

'Out of the blue? With no coercion? No trades for a lesser plea? He just came forward?'

'Apparently.'

'Well, I can tell you from my own experience that if that's true, it's one of the very few times. Usually, if somebody gets close enough to be a useful witness, they're part of it, and not way down at the bottom, either. They get turned because we've got something to threaten them with, and then we disappear them.'

'I know that. It's why we're skeptical of this guy's story. His first name is probably Tony, last name maybe starts with an S.'

'Soprano?'

'Good guess, but maybe something else. Probably out of the New York area, maybe Jersey. The big clue is we know he's here, working as a bartender. One of your marshals will have him.'

'And you don't want his name?'

'We just want to know what he did. If he was a soldier or what. Particularly if he's ever killed anybody.'

Schuyler looked across at him. 'So all talk of retirement aside, you're still in the homicide business? You're saying this is a murder case?'

'I don't recall using precisely those words. But I'd say they're within the realm of the possible.'

With a curt nod, Schuyler said, 'I'll see what I can do.'

Hardy didn't get home from the office until a quarter to eight.

When he wasn't at trial, he and Frannie were relatively democratic in their division of household chores. During trials, though, Frannie made it a point to try to keep potential sources of stress out of his life, and she took over most of the domestic duties.

She got up early with him, made him a good breakfast, checked to see that his suits had been pressed, his shirts were back from the cleaners, his ties didn't have stains, his shoes were shined. He made it a point to be home by eight, and when he showed up, she fixed him a cocktail – tonight an ice-cold dry martini of Hendrick's gin with a slice of cucumber – while she had one glass of chardonnay.

For the next twenty minutes, while dinner simmered or baked or waited for Frannie's return to the kitchen, they sat together on comfortable chairs, usually in their living room, and talked but did not mention anything about the trial. This was a hard-and-fast rule, arrived at early in their marriage when Hardy would get so engrossed in his work that he was unable to discuss anything except a trial for weeks at a time. Then he would stay up late, reading over his binders, after which he would usually suffer from insomnia. More often than not, his immune system would revolt and he'd get sick. Frannie finally convinced him that his trial habits were not only unhealthy for his mind and body, they detracted from his performance in the courtroom. Twenty minutes of nontrial conversation was never going to lose him a trial, and it might help him win one.

Tonight they had more than enough to fill up their talk time. Their son, Vincent, in Barcelona the summer before his senior year, had Skyped Frannie during the day, catching them up on his latest adventures – he had lost his backpack for an hour the previous night; it turned out he'd left it at a tapas bar, but miraculously, the owners had picked it up and stored it in the back room. This morning, he had climbed the curving tower of the Sagrada Familia, Gaudí's ornate and monstrous cathedral. He thought he might be addicted to paella.

That day, they'd received the invitation to Wes and Sam's wedding, which would be held in early September at Buena Vista Park, across the street from their house. Frannie had called Sam and learned that there would be only sixty guests, surprising in an aspiring politician.

Hardy's secretary/receptionist, Phyllis, had called in sick this morning, and he opined as to how many days in a row she'd have to miss before he would be justified in letting her go. After her forty years with the firm – in truth, since before it was a firm – it seemed cruel of him to demand perfect attendance. But if she missed three days in a row, then surely a case could be made.

The Beck, meanwhile, had invited Ben Feinstein to a picnic thrown by the firm where she was interning this summer. More developments to come.

Oh, and Abe and Treya were taking a real vacation for the first time perhaps ever, in late August, and asked if the Hardys had ever been to Santa Catalina island, and would they like to go along?

Dinner was Caesar salad, which Frannie made from scratch with Romaine lettuce, a raw egg and an entire tin of anchovies, garlic and Worcestershire sauce, Dijon mustard and the juice of a Meyer lemon, all emulsified with Parmesan cheese and extra-virgin olive oil. Frannie left out the croutons but added three jumbo prawns each, and they ate every speck.

By now the trial was no longer off-limits, and they replayed everything, beginning with the gorilla video, then proceeding from Dr Paley's exhaustive testimony to Susan's hit man idea, to Glitsky's decision to become a defense witness if Hardy needed him, to Wyatt Hunt's objections to the wild goose chase of an investigation.

At nine-thirty, they were in bed.

At ten, he kissed her one last time, again told her he loved her, reached over, and turned out the bedside light.

30

PAUL STIER CAME out of his corner the next morning like a boxer who'd taken a bad hit in the previous round and wanted to prove he was still in the fight. Gone was the friendly avuncularity he'd shown to Winston Paley when he introduced himself and Gunderson. Similarly absent was the petulant and overmatched debater from the sidebar with Hardy yesterday.

Exuding confidence, Stier could barely wait to get out of his chair – indeed, from the corner of his eye, Hardy noted that Stier stood up twice as the judge first welcomed the jurors back for another day and then recalled Paley to the stand. For a man who hadn't objected once the day before, he came out at the bell with an enthusiasm that Hardy found a bit unnerving. What the hell was he so excited about?

Stier's opening line of cross-examination hammered Paley on his reference sources. It was well and good that the doctor had all the credentials in the world, and admittedly interesting that, in his opinion, buttressed by dozens if not hundreds of studies, eyewitness testimony was essentially useless. But could he cite specific studies that would lend credibility to his overall testimony?

For example: 'Dr Paley. You've testified that a short man with a weapon will be identified as over six feet tall. Does this happen every time?'

'No. I don't think so.'

'You don't think so. You're not sure?'

'It happens a majority of the time.'

'Do you have an exact percentage?'

'I'd say about ninety-five.'

'And the other five percent, do they get the size of the person with the weapon correct? Or perhaps someone who is five-eight, they say is five feet?'

'No. That doesn't happen.'

'Never?'

'I've never heard of it happening. The differences – and now we're only talking about the five percent – tend to be off by an inch or two.'

'Can you give us the study that corroborates this?'

'Not specifically. But James McDowell conducted several studies—'

'Who?'

'James McDowell, one of the first expert witnesses in California on this topic. He was a well-recognized and respected forensic psychologist.'

'Doctor, I notice you said "was." Is Mr McDowell deceased?'

'Yes.'

'When did he die?'

'I'm not sure. Six or seven years ago.'

'And – I hope I'm getting this right – you say he wrote the primary study about the issue of people with weapons being identified as larger than they actually are?'

'Yes.'

'Again, the name of that study?'

'I'm afraid I don't have it at my fingertips.'

'How about a publication that one of these seven-year-old studies appeared in?'

Hardy, if only to break up the attack, stood at his table. 'Objection, Your Honor. Argumentative and badgering.'

With what Hardy saw as a look of mild disappointment, Gomez shook her head. 'I think neither,' she said. 'Overruled.'

Stier didn't even seem to take a breath. He reminded the doctor of his last question. 'A publication where any of these studies appeared?'

The doctor, straining to maintain his air of affability, motioned down in front of the witness stand. 'I'm sure some of the publications and studies are in my briefcase.'

'But you don't remember any specific names or publications?'

'Not at this time, no.'

This was a slight loss for Hardy. Paley's value hinged on his credibility as a scientist who had the right answers. Stier was making it sound as though he might be making the stuff up, and therefore, by extension, it wasn't even true.

The next exchange didn't improve matters. 'Doctor, you said yesterday that you have appeared as an expert witness over a hundred times?'

'Yes. Well over a hundred. Perhaps two or three hundred.'

'Three hundred times?'

'Approximately.'

'Out of those three hundred court appearances, how many times have you testified for the prosecution?'

'They haven't asked me.'

'They haven't asked you?' Stier, low-key, nevertheless managed to convey his astonishment to the jury. 'They have never asked you?'

'No.'

'So you have never testified for the prosecution?'

Hardy stood. 'Objection. Asked and answered. Badgering.'

Again, Gomez overruled him. 'Not exactly. Doctor?'

'No. I've never testified for the prosecution.'

Stier, perhaps getting ahead of himself in his enthusiasm, did not want to appear to be badgering the witness, who remained, after all, sympathetic. Tearing a page from Hardy's own playbook, he cleared his throat and walked back to his table for a sip of water. Returning to his place in front of the jury box, he continued, 'Doctor, you have described yourself as a forensic psychologist. Would you characterize your profession as expert witness?'

'Yes.'

'Appearances like this make up at least part of your income, is that right?'

'Yes.'

'What percentage, would you say?'

Hardy pushed his chair back, got all the way to his feet. 'Your Honor, immaterial. Irrelevant.'

Stier wasn't the only one getting caught up in the moment. Hardy gave himself a mental kick in the pants almost before the words were out. He was objecting far too often to stuff he knew would be overruled, therefore alienating Gomez, and now he had given Stier an opportunity to make a speaking rebuttal.

'Your Honor,' said Stier, rising to the opportunity, 'the fact that this man makes a living testifying for the defense gives him an obvious motive to color his testimony. He's a gun for hire.'

Gomez: 'Enough. Both of you. Mr Hardy, the question is clearly proper. The objection is overruled. Mr Stier, we can live without the editorializing. Confine yourself to proper legal argument.'

Paley threw an apologetic glance at Hardy. An experienced witness, he knew he was being skewered, but there was nothing he could do. Stier had done his homework. 'Lately,' Paley said, 'this type of work has comprised a large percentage of my income. Maybe eighty percent.'

Having won that skirmish, Stier elected not to risk another objection by asking exactly how much Paley was getting paid. He was flying along and had made the point: Paley's testimony was for sale and far from objective. Ugly, living up to his nickname, moved along to the meat of the matter. 'Doctor, have you ever received a request to testify where you've looked over the eyewitness testimony and said you'd prefer not to testify because the ID or IDs looked good to you?'

'Yes, I've done that.'

'And what did you do in preparation for this case?'

'I saw police reports, read the eyewitness testimony, looked at some transcripts.'

'And did you read about the identification testimonies of Anantha Douglas, Liza Moreno, Susan Antaramian, and Fred Dyer?'

'I did.'

'And which of these identification testimonies was the strongest?'

'I didn't think any of them were particularly strong.'

Although he'd known that this answer was coming, Stier pretended that it surprised him. 'None of them? Well, then, can you differentiate between the testimonies of these four witnesses?'

'Well, obviously, they are from four different people who had different interactions with the person they hoped to identify.'

'So each one of them got it wrong in his or her own way?'

'In fact, counsel, each of the witnesses got it wrong in part for the same reason. It appears they were improperly influenced by the police. To that extent, each of them got it wrong for the same reason.'

Stier straightened up, clearly stung by the body blow. But he came right back. 'But just to be clear, Doctor, four separate witnesses picked the same wrong person?'

'I'm not here to say whether any given witness is right or wrong. I'm saying the IDs were not strong. Each for different reasons. I'm not going to comment on which were stronger, because none of them were strong.'

'They didn't see who they said they saw?'

'Their testimonies did not establish that.'

'Doctor, let me ask you this. Is there any hypothetical identi-fication anyone could make, ever, that you would accept in a court of law? Could a son incorrectly identify his own mother? A husband his wife? A father and—'

'Your Honor,' Hardy said. 'This is badgering, pure and simple.'

Before Gomez could rule, Stier said, 'I'll withdraw the ques-tion, Your Honor.'

'Court will take this opportunity for a recess,' Gomez said. 'Let's all meet back here at eleven o'clock.'

On his way to use the restroom, Paley, looking genuinely contrite, stopped by the defense table. 'The bare fact remains,' he said, 'that none of the eyewitness testimony is very good. What was I supposed to say?'

'You did fine,' Hardy said. 'It's all going to come down to the specifics anyway. Why Anantha was wrong. Why, separately, Fred Dyer was wrong. Liza Moreno. Susan Antaramian. We'll take them individually when they come up and prove what you've just said is true. Don't you worry about it.'

Paley still didn't like the way it had gone, and Hardy didn't blame him in the least. 'I should have the names of those studies and the citations at my fingertips. If you want to redirect, I'll spend this break and find the articles.'

'That might be worthwhile,' Hardy said. 'Let's see what he pulls out next and take it from there.'

'I'll throw in a couple of footnotes; that always impresses.'

Hardy, wishing Paley had come into the courtroom with that mind-set and a little more attention to detail, gave him a confident grin. 'We're not killing them, but after yesterday we're still winning,' he said. 'Just stay friendly and comfortable up there. Don't let him rattle you. It's all about credibility, and you've got more of that than Stier on his best day. As long as you stay loose, we're golden.' Hardy thought he'd lighten things up with a little humor. 'Now go do what you've got to do. We don't want you squirming up there on the stand.'

Having established that Paley was a hired hand citing unsubstantiated claims about the basic facts of eyewitness testimony, Stier could have dismissed the witness, feeling that he'd done an adequate job of discrediting him. Hardy certainly thought he'd done enough damage, but this time, as Stier returned to his expert witness, he was the same boxer who'd knocked his opponent down in the second round and now planned to finish him off.

Hardy had no idea what he had up his sleeve.

'Dr Paley,' Stier began. 'Yesterday morning, I introduced myself to you right here in this courtroom. Did I not?'

'Yes, you did.' Paley, heeding Hardy's advice, added, 'And very graciously, I might add.'

'Thank you.' Stier backed away and half turned, gesturing toward the People's table. 'And do you recall that at that time you also met my assistant, Lars Gunderson?'

'Yes.'

'The gentleman seated at the table right in front of you?'

'Yes.'

'That's the man you met yesterday with me just inside the bar rail?'

'Yes.'

'You're certain it's him?'

Paley took an uncomfortable ten seconds or so, scowling briefly, then regaining his amiability. 'Yes, that's him.'

'With what degree of certainty, Doctor, can you say that Mr Gunderson is the same Mr Gunderson you met yesterday?'

Paley, too experienced in cross-examination to believe that this was all in good fun, paused again, glanced at the jury and then at Hardy, who raised his eyebrows ambiguously. Paley was in this one all alone. 'I'm certain it's him. Ninety-nine to a hundred percent.'

'Ninety-nine percent. That's very certain. So you had a chance to observe him at close range in good light, and you're ninety-nine percent convinced that Lars is the man you met yesterday.'

'Actually' – Paley rose to the bait – 'I'm a hundred percent certain. Unless he's got an identical twin.'

'No. He has no twin.'

Paley never took his eyes off Gunderson. 'Then that's the man.'

'Splendid, Dr Paley. Now, you have testified that the witnesses in this case are not reliable because of, among other things, discrepancies in their descriptions of the clothing that the man was wearing and because, in some cases, they couldn't describe the clothing at all. Is that correct?'

'Yes, it is.'

'Do you remember what Mr Gunderson was wearing yesterday when you observed and met him?'

A longish pause. 'No. I assume some kind of business attire. I didn't specifically notice it. It seemed to fit in here at the courtroom.'

'Was he wearing a tie?'

'I think so, yes.'

'Might it have been a bow tie?'

A beat. 'Maybe.'

'Would you care to guess at the color?'

'It would only be a guess.'

'What about eyeglasses?'

Paley flicked another glance at Gunderson. 'I don't remember.'

By now Hardy knew it was futile, but he had to try something to slow Ugly down. He stood and objected.

'Grounds, Mr Hardy?'

'Undue consumption of time, Your Honor. Mr Stier has made his point.'

Gomez nodded, thoughtful. 'Mr Stier,' she said, 'have you made your point?'

'Not remotely, Your Honor. I'm just getting started.'

Gomez smiled sweetly. 'I thought that might be the case. Once again, Mr Hardy, overruled.'

Hardy didn't know what he'd done to fall so far, so fast. It crossed his mind that Gomez might be one of those judges who hated objections and the lawyers who raised them. Surely Stier had risen in her favor only since yesterday, when he hadn't objected to a word of Hardy's direct with Paley. While, since this morning, Hardy had been picking on the tiniest of tidbits, slowing down the process, interfering with the flow, objecting and objecting and objecting and getting overruled just about every time. And now here he was again, on the wrong end of a ruling.

Stier reined himself in. His enthusiasm, not to say glee, was palpable. 'Dr Paley,' he said, 'is there anything else about Mr Gunderson that you particularly recall from your direct observation of him that has helped you reach the conclusion that your identification of him is one hundred percent, or at worst ninety-nine percent, correct?'

Paley stared for a few more baleful seconds at Gunderson. 'No.'

'And you are still certain that is the Lars Gunderson you met yesterday?'

This had been asked and answered a couple of times, but Hardy bit his tongue.

Paley said, 'Yes.'

Drawing a cleansing breath, Stier walked up to the evidence table in the courtroom and turned over a movie poster–sized color photograph. 'Your Honor,' he said, 'I'd like this photograph marked as People's Exhibit One and would ask the witness if he can identify the people in it.'

It was the picture Stier had taken on his cell phone the day before, the hirsute, mustache'd, bow tie-wearing Lars Gunderson shaking hands with the expert witness.

Hardy wanted to hide his face in his hands. How could he have been so stupid as to think Stier's picture-taking had been innocent? No. It had been a tactic, and a brilliant one. And they were paying for his stupidity now.

Paley's voice, his equanimity destroyed, was nearly unrecognizable as he identified himself and Lars Gunderson.

'Let's see, Doctor. You are one hundred percent certain that Lars Gunderson is the very same man you met yesterday, and yet when you met him yesterday, he had long hair and a mustache. He was wearing a red bow tie and a pink shirt, and eyeglasses, not his usual contact lenses. In spite of all the details that you either did not observe or did not recognize, the bottom line is that you did make the proper and correct identification of someone with whom you had only a one- or two-minute interaction. Isn't that correct?'

Paley nodded, but Stier, going for blood, demanded that he speak out loud. At last the doctor said, 'Yes.'

'Now, Doctor, I am a district attorney and officer of the court asking you these questions, am I not?'

'Yes.'

'When you testified earlier that you had seen Mr Gunderson yesterday, was your ID influenced in any way by the fact that I was the one asking you the questions?'

'No.'

'How about making the ID in court? Would you have hesitated to say he was not the man if that were the case just because you were in a courtroom?'

'No.'

'In fact, some people, asked to make an identification, may be uninfluenced by the apparent authority asking for the ID or by the fact that the ID is to be made in the courtroom, isn't that true?'

'Yes, but—'

Stier cut him off. 'Thank you, Doctor. I have nothing further.'

As Paley walked back through the gallery, Moses leaned over and poked Hardy in the arm. 'What are we paying this guy?' he asked.

Hardy gave him the deadeye. 'You don't want to know.'

31

From where he stood in the impressive lobby of Jon Lo's fifteenth-floor northeast-corner office in Embarcadero One, Hardy's investigator, Wyatt Hunt, could see four of the bridges – the Golden Gate, the Richmond, the Bay, and the San Mateo – that spanned San Francisco Bay. Down below, Fisherman's Wharf and the Ferry Building bustled with tourists. A little farther to the right, he could make out the Audiffred Building, home to Boulevard Restaurant and, on the second floor, to his own offices. Traffic on the bay testified to a maritime economy that was at last showing signs of life: three container ships on the water between the Golden Gate and the Bay Bridge; the Sausalito ferry plying the waters out by Alcatraz; three or four dozen private sailboats tacking and hauling in the ever-present breeze and fitful sunshine. Just this morning, Hunt had been out on the bay himself, in his wet suit, windsurfing under the Golden Gate.

Now he wore pressed khakis and a light blue dress shirt under a navy blue blazer. Hunt was a little above average height, strong and angular, and carried himself with an easy grace. Jon Lo's secretary, a lovely Asian woman, barely came to his shoulders when she appeared right behind him and said, 'Mr Hunt, Mr Lo will see you now.'

She led him over to the door and opened it.

Lo sat behind an immense teak desk, the surface of which held nothing but an iMac. The rest of the furnishings were equally spare – a couple of filing cabinets, a fax/printer on a small table, a built-in counter with a sink under mostly empty book-shelves, three industrial chairs, some random, generic, poorly framed Asian landscapes on the walls. Whatever Lo did for a living, Hunt thought, did not involve a lot of paperwork.

Lo came around his desk and greeted Hunt cordially, offered him a seat, and returned to his own chair behind the desk. 'So,' he said, 'you're investigating some matters to do with the murder of Rick Jessup. I'll be happy to help all I can, but I have to say at the outset that I barely knew him, although we were acquainted.'

After Hardy put him to work, Hunt had done some research into the bust of the Golden Dream massage parlor and the ensuing events. Essentially, Hardy had asked him to go fishing, and this pool appeared to be the only one where he was likely to get any kind of bite. 'I thought maybe we could start there, with how exactly you were acquainted.'

Lo appeared to consider the question. 'Well, he was the chief of staff to my friend Liam Goodman. I don't remember where we first met, but he was active in most of Liam's work, particularly fund-raising, so we were at a few events together. That's pretty much all of my involvement with him.'

'How about your staff?'

Lo smiled politely. 'You've met Li-Su, my secretary. I don't believe she ever met Mr Jessup.'

'I meant the staff in some of your massage parlors. I understand you have bodyguards in some of these locations for the girls' protection.'

The smile chilled a degree or two. 'I'm sorry, Mr Hunt. I'm afraid I'm not clear about why you're asking me these questions. There is no question as to who killed Mr Jessup, is there?'

'There is some, yes. I am working for the defendant.'

'I take it, then, that you are trying to identify another suspect?'

'That would be the jackpot, yes. We're looking a little more deeply into Mr Jessup's personal life, hoping we can find some areas of conflict, someplace he might have made an enemy.'

'Among my staff? How would he have met any of them?'

'I thought between Mr Goodman and yourself, staff to staff.'

A mirthless chortle. 'There is no point of contact. I barely knew Mr Jessup and doubt that any of my employees knew him at all. Besides which, your defendant had a very good reason, I recall.'

'True. Jessup raped his daughter.'

'If that's true, who could blame the man? I'm afraid I still don't understand why you decided you needed to speak to me.'

Hunt, recalling that these were almost precisely the words he'd used to tell Hardy that this assignment was ridiculous, bobbed his head, suitably chagrined. 'I can't really give you too good a reason myself. I thought you might have heard about something, some rumor . . .'

'If that had been the case, I certainly would have gone to the police.'

'Yes, of course.' Hunt got to his feet. 'I'm sorry to have taken your time.'

'Really. Not so much of it. Leave your card, and if I think of anything, I'll get back to you.'

Feeling like an idiot, Hunt rode the elevator down to the lobby. He'd check in with Hardy and make another pitch for not continuing down this path. He'd decided not to charge for the hours he'd put in. It was senseless. And he hated taking a job where he couldn't get results. A few too many of those, and you stopped getting calls for work. He should have gone with his gut and turned down the job outright. There was nothing there, because McGuire killed Jessup, and for an excellent reason.

Out on the sidewalk, Hunt called his office and learned that Supervisor Goodman had gotten back to him while he'd been out and could see him if Hunt showed up at his office in city hall by noon sharp. Hanging up, cursing himself for a fool, Hunt wrestled with his conscience for the better part of a minute, then hailed a passing cab.

Sometimes, Hunt realized, you just had to put yourself out there. You didn't necessarily need a plan. You just had to stay in the game.

When he got to Goodman's office, the supervisor had been called out to an unexpected meeting with the mayor down the hall and should be back within a half hour. He had specifically told Diane that she should ask Mr Hunt to wait – if it was anything about Rick, he wanted to do all he could to help.

So Hunt found himself sitting across from the secretary's desk while she worked on the computer and answered the occasional phone call. After perhaps ten minutes, she stopped typing and asked if she could get him anything, and he said he wouldn't mind a cup of coffee. When she returned, she'd brought one for herself as well. 'You're here about Rick?' she asked as she handed him the mug.

'That's the idea,' Hunt said. 'The man was a little enigmatic, to say the least, and we're trying to get a handle on him.'

'Why would you need that after he's dead?'

'It might help us understand why he died.'

She sipped her coffee. 'So you're, what, with the defense team?'

Hunt gave her a self-deprecating smile. 'Coming off the bench, so to speak.'

'But don't we know why he died? He raped that girl, and her father—'

'There's some question about that.'

'What? The rape?'

'The murder. The rape. The whole thing.'

'Really?'

Hunt leveled his gaze at her. 'Does that surprise you?'

'I didn't realize there was a question about the rape. From everything I've read, I thought that was established.'

Something about her tone struck Hunt, and he came forward on his chair. 'Diane. It's Diane, isn't it?'

'Yes.'

'What did you think was established?'

The question stopped her. 'Well, you know, the rape, the motive, all of that.'

'So it didn't surprise you when you heard that your chief of staff had raped someone? That's something you thought he might be capable of?'

She sat back in her ergonomic chair, aware that something had shifted. She threw an almost furtive look at Hunt, then half turned to check the offices behind and beside her. Putting her mug down on the desk, she lowered her voice. 'He was a very arrogant man. I think he hated women. You had to be a little careful around him. He'd gone out with her a couple of months before, you know.'

'Yes, we knew that.'

'Not a nice man. I shouldn't speak ill of the dead, but really. The office is so much better now. Or at least nontoxic, which is about the best you can hope for with most politicians.'

'He made it toxic? How'd he do that?'

'You haven't heard that? Nobody's talked about how he was?'

Hunt shook his head. 'He's the victim, Diane. He's dead. Lots of people don't even believe he raped the woman. As you say, people aren't going to say bad things about him. What would be the point? He's already been punished enough, right? And it doesn't matter about the actual fact of the rape, at least legally. What matters is whether our client thought the rape happened. The concentration was never really on Jessup, because who he was and how he was didn't matter.'

She emitted a quiet snort. 'It sure mattered here.'

Hunt leaned in closer. 'Diane, you just asked me if I'd heard something. Was there something specific that poisoned the atmosphere in this office?'

Clearly nervous, she glanced around again. 'Do you know about Jon Lo?'

Hunt kept his expression neutral. 'Vaguely,' he said. 'He's one of your big donors, I believe.'

'That's right. He's also . . .' She laid it out for him. Lo coming to Goodman and then the supervisor's brutal examination of all the male interns, everyone's eventual certainty that the guilty party had been Jessup, although no proof had ever materialized. The point was that Jessup had threatened the job of every male in the office. Everybody hated him, and he in turn felt threatened by every one of them. Always arrogant, he became capricious and hot-tempered. Even Goodman seemed to have come around to believing that Jessup had stiffed and beaten Lo's girls – in any event, he had put out feelers for people to interview for Jessup's job. Diane had booked the first of the appointments.

'How can it be,' Hunt asked, 'that no one's talked about this?'

Diane looked hurt. 'Why would we? As you just said, why would it matter? Rick was dead. We were all glad to have him behind us. You can't imagine.'

The door from the hallway opened, Diane stopped talking, and the next moment, Hunt was shaking the hand of Liam Goodman. 'I see Diane the gem has been taking good care of you. I'm sorry to have kept you, but when the mayor calls . . .'

The conversation with Goodman started out the same way as the Lo interview, with the decided advantage that Jessup had a substantial history with Goodman. It was within the realm of logic to suppose that the supervisor had more information about his chief of staff's personal life. Goodman did not separate himself with his desk but sat catercorner to Hunt, relaxed yet somber about the pain he was enduring associated with the loss of his second in command.

After listening to Goodman's first few pro forma comments about how good and loyal and competent a person Jessup had been, Hunt decided to cut to the chase. 'So he was this great guy. I gather that means you don't think he raped the girl? You think she accused him but it never happened?'

As he'd hoped, the question stopped Goodman cold. His shoulders rose and fell, rose and fell. 'It was a horrible charge,' he said. 'And it got him killed.'

'You don't think he did it?'

'I don't think we'll ever know. How can we know?'

'We can look at his behavior,' Hunt suggested. 'See if there's any kind of a precedent.'

Goodman's eyes ticked over at Hunt. 'I don't know what that would be. He had no criminal record of any kind. Certainly nothing suggesting rape.'

Hunt sat back, put an ankle on his knee, spoke the absolute truth in an almost apologetic tone. 'Before I came to see you this morning, sir,' he said, 'I went up to Jon Lo's office and had a little talk with him.'

The wheels turned for a second or two. Goodman's shoulders settled, and he turned to face Hunt square on. 'I don't know what happened to him.' Goodman pulled at the skin around his mouth, exuding sadness. 'After we won the election and I made him chief of staff, I think it must have gone to his head. When it looked like we might be going further, after a few moves we made panned out, he must have come to believe that nothing could touch him. No matter what he did. So he started taking advantage of his position.'

'Why didn't you fire him?'

'At first I had no proof. Besides, we had a long history, and I thought he'd come around. I liked him as a guy, at least in the early days, and I was hoping we could get back there.'

'You eventually got proof?'

Goodman nodded. 'Jon brought Rick's picture around, and six of the girls identified him.'

'Six?'

'Six we know about.' A deflated shrug. 'There may have been as many as twenty, twenty-five, maybe more. There's no way to know. To all appearances, he was out of control.'

'And still you didn't let him go.'

'I'm a politician, Mr Hunt. I wanted to have a replacement in the wings so there was no hint of instability in the campaign. Did you meet Brad, by the way? He should be back from lunch any time.'

'I'll catch him next time, if there is one.'

The uncomfortable stuff over with, the supervisor perked up a bit. 'But – the bad news for you – is I don't see how any of this is going to make a difference to your client. The fact remains that Rick raped the poor woman and her father killed him for it. I mean, Rick's history changes none of that.'

'No. That's true.' Hunt got to his feet. 'I appreciate your time.'

Hunt was getting out of the cab when he spotted his quarry probably coming back from lunch, all alone, crossing at the closest corner. Waiting until they were nearly abreast, Hunt stepped out in front of him. 'Mr Lo,' he said, extending his hand, 'Wyatt Hunt. We met in your office this morning.'

Lo stopped, squinting in the sunlight. He extended his hand and broke into an easy smile. 'Have you been hanging out here on the sidewalk in front of my building all this time?'

'Not exactly. I was down talking to Liam Goodman. I wondered if you could spare me a few more minutes?'

The smile vanished entirely. Lo ostentatiously consulted his watch, his face etched in regret. 'I'm afraid I've got a couple of meetings I'm already late for. Maybe we could set up an appointment in a couple of days, and I'll be happy to give you all the time you need.'

Not on your life, Hunt was thinking. No way was he giving

Lo the opportunity to call Goodman and find out what they'd talked about so they could prepare a cohesive response. And no way would he give up the chance to press Lo for the real reason that Goodman hadn't fired Jessup as soon as he'd learned of the perfidy. Hunt had both the hammer and the element of surprise, and he wasn't going to risk losing either. 'I'm only talking a couple of minutes, sir,' he said. 'I could ride up the elevator with you, and we'd be done.'

Lo flashed a grin, looked at his building, came back to Hunt, and nodded. 'If you're sure we can make it fast.'

'Lightning,' Hunt said.

Neither man started walking.

Hunt said, 'When we talked this morning, you told me you had met Rick Jessup at a couple of fund-raisers but had no other connection with him. You also said that, to your knowledge, Mr Jessup had no contact with any members of your staff. Knowing I've just come from speaking to Mr Goodman, would you like to amend those statements in any way?'

'What did Liam tell you?'

'About Jessup and your girls.' Hunt paused for effect, then continued, 'Which, of course, gives you a reason to have wanted Jessup out of the way, and one of your bodyguards to actually get that done.'

'That's absurd. Did Liam make that accusation? Because he had as much reason as anyone to want Jessup dead. More than most. Did he mention that Rick was blackmailing him to keep his job? Did he tell you about his Army Business?'

Hunt loved it when knaves fell out. Lo had barely heard what Goodman had revealed to Hunt, certainly nothing resembling an accusation of any wrongdoing on his part, and he was already striking back with accusations of his own.

'I don't believe I've heard about anything called the Army Business.'

345

'Elaborate, lucrative, smart, and illegal.'

'Well, that sounds fascinating,' Hunt said, 'but I don't want to keep you from your appointments.'

Lo narrowed his eyes. 'Don't play games with me, Hunt. I may look like a sweetheart, but you'll find I'm a very serious man indeed.'

Something inside Hunt shuddered at the calm words and the certainty with which they were uttered. 'Maybe we want to go up to your office,' he said.

The new front window at the Little Shamrock had been installed that morning, Tony Solaia – who was the de facto manager – helping to supervise. At 1:20 P.M., U.S. Marshal Frank Ladoux knocked on the front door, and Tony came out from where he'd been hunkered down – invisible from the street – on the back love seat and let him in.

'Can I get you a beer?' Tony asked, leading him into the shadows at the end of the bar while he went around behind the spigots. 'Anything?'

Ladoux shook his head. 'Too early.'

Ladoux was chewing a toothpick. He put a cowboy boot on the low rung of a stool. He was wearing black denim slacks and an REI jacket that didn't hide the bulge of his gun underneath. Hooking his elbows casually on the back of his stool, he offered Tony a tired smile. 'Thanks for seeing me. I thought it was time for a little face-to-face meetup.'

'As long as you weren't followed.'

'Not likely. Somebody's been asking around about you, and you know that's not how we like to do it.'

'Shit.'

Frank nodded. 'I thought you'd say that. Although you've been playing it so close to the line, I don't know what else you'd expect.'

'None of that, none of this, has been my fault.'

'I'm not saying it is. I'm just saying look at what's happened in these last months. First you're busted at Rome, then out of all those bar busts, you get one of the squirrelly cases with those fucking Russians—'

'Ukrainians.'

'Whatever. Still, you're almost in the paper. Meanwhile, you move to this bar, where your boss is going on trial for murder, and you're on the witness list for the prosecution. Oh yeah, and you start hanging out with Miss America, and next thing you know, there's paparazzi in here fighting to get her picture. And maybe yours with her. I mean, what the fuck, you know? You call this laying low?'

'I like her.'

'Yeah, well, who wouldn't like her?'

Tony looked at him. 'So what'd you want me to do, Frank? Relocate again?'

'It's been known to happen. Better than getting yourself killed.' Frank moved the toothpick to the other side of his mouth. 'You know why we marshals have that hundred-percent safety record we're so proud of, never losing one of our protected people?'

'You're world-class bodyguards?'

'That, too. The other reason is because if somebody blows his cover enough on his own, we bust them out of the program.'

Tony shook his head and gave his minder a cold smile. 'Don't bullshit me, Frank. You're not busting me out of any program. You need me to testify. If I don't, two hundred lawyers just wasted three years. You're not going to let that happen.'

'It's not my decision. And I'm not down here today because I've been missing our special times together. Important though you are, you are not invaluable. The word is that you're scheduled to testify in this trial you're mixed up in, maybe as early as tomorrow.'

Tony waved that off. 'They're not going to call me. I've got nothing to say. Who's following this, anyway?'

'My superiors. Let's just go with that. These public appearances of yours are matters of some interest to them, and they're concerned that your value as a witness might be compromised.'

'How?'

'If you give perjured testimony, for example, which is a felony. As you know, one of the rules is that if you commit a new felony while you're in the program, then you are out of the program. And let me remind you that one of the fairly predictable consequences of losing your protected-witness status is that you're identified by your enemies, usually sooner rather than later, and you wind up with a bullet in your brain.'

'Well, that's—'

Frank held up a hand, stopping him with a grin that looked friendly and completely nonthreatening. 'Please. I just want to add that perjury is a difficult felony for us to deal with, because it calls into question your basic integrity as a witness, which is where your value lies. If you'll lie under oath in one trial, what's to stop you from lying under oath in another?'

'What makes you think I'm going to lie?'

Frank shifted the toothpick around. 'Let's recall,' he said, 'when you first came to me with the information that you'd talked to Mr Stier and he wanted you to be a witness in the case. Because of concerns about your identity coming out if you testified in a high-profile trial, you told me about that meeting, and I asked what he wanted you to testify about. Does this more or less ring a bell?'

'Sure.'

'Good. Then you'll remember telling me that you'd just spent a couple of days with Brittany and she had confessed to you that she'd told her father about the rape right after you dropped her off at their place in the middle of the night.'

'Right.'

'She actually thought that her father had killed Jessup.'

'Right. She did.'

'And now you and she are an item?'

Tony acknowledged the fact with a shrug. 'Okay?'

'Okay, so it doesn't take a genius to figure out what's going on here. Stier's going to ask Brittany if she told her father, and she's going to say no, because if she says yes, he goes to the slammer, and she's not going to let that happen. So then he's going to call you, and you're going to say no, because although that would be perjury, she's your girlfriend, and if you said yes, that'd be the end of that.' Frank propped his elbows on the back of the bar stool. 'You see the dilemma this poses for me?'

Tony thought for a second or two. 'You could just let it go,' he said. 'Nobody else has to know.'

This brought a faint smile. 'There are so many ways that's impossible that I almost don't know where to begin. Start with if Brittany told anybody else that she told you or any variation thereof. Or somehow it comes out that I knew the truth but had a deal with you not to tell, which would effectively end my career. No, the simple fact is that you've got to tell the truth, because if you don't, I will be forced to go to Mr Stier and tell him about your perjured testimony, which will result in you going to jail under your real name because you would no longer be in the program. How long do you think you'd last in jail, Tony, before they found you?'

32

AFTER LUNCH, HARDY spent the better part of ninety minutes on redirect with his expert witness. In a somewhat tedious and soporific display, Paley flawlessly recited chapter and verse of every specific source that he'd quoted in his earlier testimony and, in this way, perhaps to some degree, reestablished his credibility. Included in that effort was Hardy's attempt to spin Paley's identification of Lars Gunderson to buttress the defense argument that eyewitness identification, even for a man as well trained and experienced as Dr Paley, was a tenuous business at best.

Yes, Paley had correctly identified Mr Gunderson in spite of getting wrong most of the details about how he looked, but that only went to show that eyewitness identification was unreliable, period. That was always Paley's point. Not reassured that the jury was buying it, Hardy could only hope that Paley had planted a seed that would bloom when the eyewitnesses testified.

In the end, he was glad to hear the last of Paley's testimony, although it meant that the main event was about to begin.

Brittany McGuire's testimony would be central to the prosecution's case. That put her in the untenable position of supplying the motive evidence that might send her father to prison. When Stier had named her early on as a prosecution witness, she had resisted at every step. There was no way that she was going to testify to anything that would put her father in jeopardy. Taking Hardy's advice, Brittany had hired her own attorney, Tracy Edwards, to make her case to the judge.

There had been a hellacious hearing in chambers before the jury was sworn, with Edwards doing all in her power to persuade the judge that Brittany shouldn't have to testify: Brittany's attorney's first move at that hearing was to assert the rape victim's privilege; her client would refuse to testify about the sexual assault or anything to do with it. If someone had been charged with raping Brittany, she could have refused to testify, and there was damn little Stier could do about it. The legislature had passed a statute. The case law was clear. That would have been the end of it.

But Stier, no slouch, had countered that he wasn't going to ask about the rape. Not about what happened to her, not about who did it, not about whether she'd ever been sexually assaulted in her life. He was simply going to ask whether she told her father that Rick Jessup had raped her and about McGuire's reaction to that news.

It had been the low point in the pretrial motions for Hardy (and Edwards) when Gomez sided with Stier. Brittany would have to take the stand and answer questions about what she had told her father and his reaction to it. Through Edwards, Brittany advised the court that she'd never told her father anything about the alleged rape, therefore arguing that her testimony was irrelevant.

Gomez hadn't bought it. 'Mr Stier has evidence that arguably demonstrates the opposite, Ms McGuire. You're going to testify under oath. I can only advise you, as I am sure your attorney has already advised you, that there are serious consequences for not telling the truth. I'll say no more than that.'

After the judge's decision, Hardy realized that Brittany wouldn't have any choice – unless she decided to deliberately perjure herself, she would have to admit what she'd told her father and when. By now, even after Tracy Edwards had lost her argument, Hardy had spent several hours with Brittany, counseling her, arguing that perjury was never a good idea.

Especially in this case, where Brittany's decision to lie, if she kept on in her intransigence, would accomplish nothing. As a matter of actual fact, Stier was going to present several witnesses, including Tony Solaia, who would contradict her testimony. That would leave little to no doubt in any juror's mind that McGuire knew about the rape – from Brittany's own admission – by early Sunday morning. There was no point in keeping to her mendacious story.

In spite of his arguments, Hardy knew he hadn't made much, if any, headway. Brittany understood what he was saying, but there was no way she was going to supply the jury with the motive for her father to have killed her rapist. Let her friends and acquaintances contradict her. She didn't care. She'd go to jail for perjury if need be, but she wasn't going to betray her father.

And now, suddenly – with Hardy not sure what she would do, still feeling he needed more time to convince her that he was right, that in this case, it wasn't a betrayal to tell the truth, that she should not lie – it was upon them.

Stier had used his own witness list as a blunt instrument, including in it the names of almost anyone with whom Brittany had any kind of relationship, although somehow Rebecca (possibly because she was Hardy's daughter) had not made the cut. Among these friends and acquaintances, Stier had found several people to contradict Brittany's testimony and thereby help confirm Moses's motive.

Now it was no longer conjecture. Stier called Brittany as his first witness. So he would lead off with motive, which Hardy thought was the obvious strategy, which did not make it a bad one. Without it, the case against Moses made no sense.

Hardy turned in his chair to look as the bailiff escorted her in from where she'd been waiting out in the hallway. For an instant, he almost didn't recognize her. Beside him, Moses grabbed his arm and whispered, 'Mother of God.' He heard Amy Wu release an involuntary and pained moan that seemed to echo throughout the courtroom.

Brittany had hacked off every inch of her long, beautiful hair.

No lipstick, no makeup of any kind. She wore brown men's brogues, a pair of brown slacks, a pale yellow pullover, and a white shawl over her shoulders.

In spite of Stier's success at the pretrial hearing, Hardy knew that the prosecutor would have to tread carefully. Brittany was a hostile prosecution witness. She was testifying against her own father, a terrible and uncomfortable situation. Although it was perhaps irrelevant, Hardy was fairly sure that Stier believed she was also a victim of rape; most if not all of the jury would come to believe that, too. They would feel sympathy for her. Stier probably was not immune to the feeling himself; at least he would try to convey that so as not to seem an unfeeling bastard to the jury.

There was also the simple fact that Brittany was going to perjure herself. On top of conveying his sympathy for and understanding of Brittany's plight, Ugly would have to lead the jury to that obvious and unavoidable conclusion, in spite of the words that came out of his witness's mouth.

Finally, Hardy knew that Stier must be shaken by Brittany's appearance, as they all were.

After taking the oath and getting settled into the witness stand, Brittany shot a brave look across the courtroom to her father, tried a buck-me-up smile that found little traction, then settled back in the seat. In contrast to the way he'd bounded enthusiastically out of his corner to take on Dr Paley, Stier rose from his table and, in slow, measured strides, made his way in front of the witness stand.

'Ms McGuire, good afternoon.' In the opening moments, as

he needed to be, Stier was deference itself. He had Brittany introduce herself to the jury, state her relationship to Moses, admit her reluctance to testifying. Setting up an easy, almost conversational rhythm, letting her get to some kind of comfort level.

And finally beginning to explore the meat of things. 'Did you know the victim in this case, Rick Jessup?'

This was a delicate point, and Hardy, Gina, and Amy had debated it at great length. On one hand, Hardy felt that there was a good chance Gomez would stick to the letter of her ruling: Stier would be permitted to ask only if Brittany had told her father about the rape and his reaction to it. They could probably get the judge to keep out everything else about the relationship between Brittany and Jessup as irrelevant or covered by the rape victim privilege. On the other hand, that might leave the jury with the impression that there had never been any rape, that the murder was the result of some crazy woman and her violent father, and that poor Rick Jessup – the handsome up-and-coming politician – had been the innocent victim of these lunatics.

In the end, once they knew Stier was going to get his motive in front of the jury, they decided it was much better that the jury knew the rape really happened. It was all coming in.

'Yes, I knew Rick Jessup.'

'How did you know him?'

'We went out one time. It didn't work out, and we stopped seeing each other.'

'And when was that?'

'I'm not positive of the exact day. Early in February, I think.'

'When you say you stopped seeing each other, do you mean you stopped dating?'

'Yes.'

'But did you see Mr Jessup again? Back in February?'

'Yes.'

'And what were the circumstances of that meeting?'

'He came in to where I worked, at Peet's coffee shop. He said he wanted to see me again, and I told him I wasn't interested.'

'Did you have an argument?'

'Not really, no. It was a disagreement, and I went into the back room, and my manager asked him to leave.'

Hardy caught his niece's – his goddaughter's – eye and gave her a small nod, telling her she was doing fine. She was coming across to the jury as honest, well spoken, and sympathetic.

'After this meeting at Peet's, still back in February, did you see Mr Jessup yet again?'

'Yes. He met me another day after work in a shortcut alley while I was walking to the bus stop for home.'

'Did you have an argument at that time?'

'Yes. I told him I didn't want to see him. I wanted him to leave me alone.'

'And what happened then?'

'I tried to walk past him, to go by, but he grabbed me.'

'He put his hands on you?'

'Yes. He shook me and pushed me up against a building. And then my face had started to bleed, so he was immediately all apologetic. I was scared, and I tried to get by him again, but he grabbed me a second time and threw me down on the ground.'

Hardy patted Mose's arm and cast a surreptitious glance at Amy. Brittany testifying about her earlier dealings with Jessup was something he had convinced her to introduce in her witness interviews with Stier. Though not necessarily relevant to the night of the rape, it was powerful stuff, casting Jessup in the worst possible light. In spite of that, Hardy had a hunch that Stier would want it in because it led to Moses beating Jessup, which illustrated his temper and inclinations. More important, from Hardy's perspective – and perhaps not perfectly appreciated by Stier – was that this was demonstrably a time when Brittany did not go running to her father after she'd been hurt, a point Hardy hoped to exploit during his cross-examination.

Stier, pursuing his own agenda, continued, 'Were you badly injured?'

'I went to the emergency room, but I was mostly shaken up, with scrapes and bruises.'

'Did you tell your father Mr Jessup had assaulted you?'

'No, I did not.'

'Never?'

'Never.'

This was Stier having it both ways. He was going to argue that Brittany had told her father about the rape, and it was a motive for the homicide. Even if the jury didn't buy that, he had this other incident where Brittany had not named Jessup but McGuire somehow found out about it and beat up the young man for it. It was possible that even if Brittany had not mentioned the rape, McGuire could have discovered it the same way he'd discovered the beating. Once again, Stier would have his motive.

Ostensibly feeling Brittany's pain, Stier paused, walked over to his table, pretended to read from his legal pad, then went back to his place in front of her. 'This was not the last you heard from Mr Jessup, was it?'

'No.'

'When was that?'

'End of March.'

'How did he contact you?'

'He texted me and said he was going to file charges against my father for assault unless I met him again.'

Feigning surprise at this development, Stier took in the jury, then came back to the witness. 'How did you respond to this text message?'

'I agreed to meet him at Perry's that Saturday night.'

'Why, in spite of your history and his violence toward you, did you agree to meet him?'

'I wanted to know what he was talking about and, if I could, talk him out of harassing my family.'

'Are you saying you did not believe that your father assaulted him?'

'I didn't know. It was the first time I'd heard about it. Rick was politically connected. I thought he could make trouble for us. My dad owns a bar, the Little Shamrock, and Rick worked for Supervisor Goodman, who'd been busting bars all over town over the past couple of months. That's why I agreed to talk to him.'

'Ms McGuire. Would it surprise you to hear that your father has admitted to assaulting Mr Jessup in the wake of his beating of you?'

'I've heard that by now, yes. I didn't know about it when I met Mr Jessup at Perry's.'

'You're saying you didn't know that your father had assaulted Mr Jessup?'

'No, sir. I mean, yes, sir, that's what I'm saying.'

Stier knew this was going to be her testimony, but he needed to have the jury hear it and decide if the answer sounded remotely plausible. After hesitating as though thinking of the right question to pose, Stier went on, 'Ms McGuire. Let's back up a little bit. When you were in the emergency room after you were assaulted by Mr Jessup, did you contact anyone?'

'Yes. I called my mom to please come and get me.'

'Did you tell her what had happened to you?'

'No.'

'Why not?'

'I didn't want to get Rick in trouble. I didn't think it was going to happen again. He'd just lost his temper, so I was going to let it go.'

'Where did your mother take you from the hospital?'

'To her apartment. I mean, hers and Dad's.'

'And did you see your father there?'

'Yes.'

'Did you tell him what happened?'

'No. I told him the same thing I'd told my mom. That I'd slipped and fallen down, running to catch the bus.'

'Did your father believe you?'

'Apparently not.'

This brought a titter of laughter to the otherwise rapt and tense courtroom. Stier let it subside, then continued. 'All right, then. So you met Mr Jessup at Perry's on Union Street?' Walking her through the horrible events of that night, Stier treaded lightly but got her to the point where she woke up in Jessup's bed, knowing she'd been raped. 'What did you do then?'

'Rick was sleeping, so I grabbed my clothes and got out of there, out of his apartment. I found my car where I'd left it up by Union and then drove to the Shamrock.'

'Why did you go there?'

'My first reaction was to go to my father. I thought he'd be bartending, but he wasn't.'

'You wanted to see your father?'

'Yes.'

'To tell him what had happened?'

'I don't know if I was going to tell him or not. I just wanted to be home safe, you know? I couldn't believe what had happened to me.' She wiped her eyes.

'But your father wasn't there?'

'No. Another friend of mine, Tony Solaia, was bartending. By this time, I was a wreck. It was closing time, and I told him what had happened, and he drove me to my mom and dad's.'

'You told Tony that you had been raped?'

'Yes.'

'And Tony, did he accompany you to your parents' home?'

'Yes. My mom came to the door, and he left me with her.'

'What about your father? Was he there?'

'He was asleep. It was about two in the morning.'

'So you did not see your father?'

'No.'

'Did you tell your mother that you had been raped?'

'No.'

'Why not? If you had already told Tony?'

'I don't know. I just thought . . . I didn't want to upset her.'

The tears were glistening on Brittany's cheeks. Stier looked from her, over to the jury, up to the judge. 'Your Honor,' he said, 'I've got a lot more questions for this witness, but if opposing counsel doesn't object, perhaps we could take a short break to allow Ms McGuire to compose herself?'

Gina Roake was the first one up, coming forward with a stash of Kleenex. Brittany had her elbows on the front of the witness box, her hands to her forehead. Stier had evidently surprised her with his offer to recess, and whether in gratitude or the simple release of tension, she was shaking with emotion.

Gina put her arms around her. 'Hey hey hey. It's all right. You're doing fine.'

Brittany took a Kleenex and wiped her face. 'I'm such a baby. I'm sorry.'

'Don't worry about it. Really. This happens all the time.' Gina leaned in and kissed the top of her head. 'Nice 'do, by the way. Quite the statement.'

Brittany managed a note of laughter through the tears. 'I'm just so sick of it all.'

At the defense table, they spoke in whispers.

Moses said, 'I'm going to go up there and hug her.'

'Move away from this table, and the bailiff will kill you,' Hardy said.

'She's breaking my heart.'

'Mine, too. But she's doing fine. She's tough.'

'I don't want her to be tough. She's gone through enough, don't you think?'

'More than enough, but it's a long way from over, here. Ugly's just making points, being a good guy for the jury, giving her this little break. He comes back, it's going to get serious in a hurry. You watch.'

Moses looked across the room at his daughter, with Gina's arm still around her, the two women talking, head to head. 'I never wanted her to have to do this,' he said. 'Or any of us, for that matter.'

Hardy started to say that it was a little late for that sentiment, that Moses should have thought things through a little more clearly back when it would have made a difference and he could have saved everybody all this grief. But in the end, he bit his tongue. What the hell was a lecture going to accomplish?

All of them were committed to their positions. There was nothing else any of them could do.

'Ms McGuire.' Stier's voice had taken on a slight edge, as though his patience was wearing thin. In fact, he was well into the second hour of Brittany's testimony, having taken her from her arrival at Susan and Moses's – where she told Susan only that she'd drunk too much and wanted to walk back and get her car near the Shamrock in the morning – to her visit to the Rape Crisis Counseling Center at seven-fifteen A.M. Now, according to her testimony, she was back at her parents' place at about ten-thirty that Sunday morning, and they were having breakfast in the kitchen. Stier had clearly decided it was time to turn up the heat. 'Do you mean to tell the jury that when you came back to the house that morning, your father did not ask where you'd been and what had happened the night before?'

'That's right.'

'Was it a common occurrence for you to stay over at your parents?'

'Not very, but it happens.'

'And on that morning, having just returned from reporting your rape at the hands of Mr Jessup, you mentioned nothing about it to either of your parents?'

'That's right.'

'You did not?'

'No.'

'To be precise, I'd like you to tell the jury specifically. Did you tell your father that the victim had put a date rape drug in your drink at Perry's?'

Amy Wu was up as though shot from a cannon. 'Your Honor, objection! The witness has already answered this question.'

'Overruled.'

Stier: 'Ms McGuire?'

Brittany: 'No, I didn't.'

'Did you tell him that you woke up in Mr Jessup's apartment and knew that you had been raped?'

'Objection!'

'Overruled.'

'No.'

'Did you tell your father that the victim had sexually assaulted you?'

At this point, Hardy himself could take it no more. 'Your Honor, if the court please . . .' He was aware of the frisson of energy flowing through the audience behind him, but he didn't care.

Gomez, slamming her gavel, glared first at him, then over his head at the gallery. 'The court will not please, Mr Hardy. Counsel will approach the bench.'

Hardy and Wu got to their feet and came around either side of their table. Stier fell in beside them in front of the podium. Gomez leaned down so they could hear her fierce whisper. 'I'm not going to tolerate this tag-team approach. As to any given witness, either you, Ms Wu, or you, Mr Hardy, will address your objections to the court, but I will not allow both of you—'

'Your Honor,' Hardy said, 'meaning no disrespect—'

Gomez held up her index finger, cutting him off. 'I'd advise you to exercise great care in what you say next, Mr Hardy. It's my experience that lawyers who start off with "meaning no disrespect" often follow it up with statements that can get pretty offensive. If that happens here, there will be immediate and serious consequences. Have I made myself clear?'

Swallowing his bile, Hardy said, 'Yes, Your Honor. But Mr Stier is clearly badgering this witness, who is a victim. She's already said that she didn't tell her father she'd been raped.'

'He is having her clarify her position so the jury knows exactly what she did or did not do. I made it clear that I would permit him to ask her what she told her father. You made it clear, as did Ms McGuire's attorney, that she was prepared to testify about the entire incident. Now, all of you, let's get the show back on the road.'

Hardy and Wu returned to their table. No sooner were they back in their seats than Stier had the court recorder reread his previous question. 'Did you tell your father that the victim had sexually assaulted you?'

Brittany, tight-lipped, shook her head. 'No.'

Stier went on. 'Did you tell your father that you felt violated and hated the victim, after which your father became angry?'

'No.'

'In fact, wasn't his reaction to your situation so violent that you feared he would do something drastic?'

'No! That's why I couldn't tell him. I had just learned the night before about Rick's version of what happened between him and my dad after Rick assaulted me in February. I didn't know if I believed him; Rick was such a liar. But I didn't want there to be any more trouble. So when I was driving over to my parents' place with Tony, I thought about that and knew I couldn't tell him even if I wanted to. I was afraid to.'

'You didn't tell him?'

Braving the elements, Amy pushed back her chair and stood up. 'Objection, Your Honor. Asked and answered several times over.'

Gomez finally seemed to agree that Stier had gone on long enough in this vein; she sustained this one.

Getting a bit histrionic, Stier blew out heavily in apparent frustration. But he hadn't gotten to the point he'd been driving for, and now he came to it. 'Ms McGuire, did you ever tell anybody that you had a conversation with your father during which you told him all of these details – the drug in your drink, the rape itself, your fear and hatred of the victim?'

Wu cast a look around Moses at Hardy. Should she object again? Hardy gave his head a small shake. Though he hated it, this wasn't the same question, not at all, that Stier had been asking in one form or another.

Brittany also got the difference. She looked to the judge, then turned back to Stier. 'The question is whether I told anybody that I had told my dad any of this stuff?'

'Yes.'

'Why would I do that if I hadn't done it?'

'Your Honor,' Stier responded, 'would you direct the witness to answer the question?'

Gomez leaned over and did just that.

Brittany paused. Finally, the one perjured word: 'No.'

'You never told anybody that you'd told your father about the rape sometime during that first day when you were at his apartment, is that correct?'

'Yes.'

Stier looked at her for a long moment, both stern and disappointed. 'No further questions,' he said, and turned on his heel. 'Mr Hardy. Your witness.'

Gomez tapped her gavel. 'If there is no objection,' she said, 'we've all just sat through a long day of testimony, and tomorrow looks like it's going to be the same. We've only got about fifteen minutes before we'd be adjourning anyway. Mr Hardy, if you don't mind postponing your cross-examination of Ms McGuire until tomorrow morning, I propose we call it a day.'

'That's fine with me, Your Honor.'

'Mr Stier? Good. See you all tomorrow morning, nine-thirty sharp.' She gaveled again, and court was adjourned.

33

'TWENTY-FIVE WOMEN?' GINA Roake stopped pulling papers from her briefcase and looked across the expansive circular table at their investigator. 'Really? You've got to be kidding me.'

It was five-thirty on the day of Brittany McGuire's testimony. Wyatt Hunt had stretched his lanky frame out in a chair in the solarium at the law offices of Freeman Hardy & Roake. 'That's what Goodman said. Although he only had absolute proof from the six who identified him.'

'Six who identified who?' Dismas Hardy, coming in from his office across the lobby. 'And all of those identifications, by the way, are probably no good. Ask Dr Paley. That'll be ten thousand dollars, please.'

Hunt looked over at Gina. 'What's he talking about?'

'Sometimes it's hard to tell.' She turned to her partner. 'Jon Lo's massage parlors.'

'What about them?'

'Wyatt here was telling me that Rick Jessup was a regular customer in any number of Lo's places and thought his job description had a clause that said he didn't have to pay. Oh, and sometimes he'd smack a girl around.'

Hardy looked at Hunt. 'Sometimes?'

'Maybe most of the time. It sounds like he's a profoundly disturbed dude.'

'Was,' Hardy said. 'Thank God. And I think we already knew that. But you got this at Goodman's?'

Hunt nodded. 'And lest they tell you otherwise, Lo and Goodman both knew about it for some time. Goodman was shopping for a new chief of staff even as Mr Jessup was getting himself killed. It's entirely possible that Lo didn't think Goodman was moving fast enough or being punitive enough.'

'You got all this today?' Hardy pulled out a seat and sat.

'With all due modesty,' Hunt said, 'I homered in every at bat.'

'There's more?' Gina asked.

'Just a little bit. Do you know what Mr Goodman did before he became a supervisor?'

'I know he was a lawyer,' Roake said.

'True, but not the same kind of philanthropic do-gooder lawyers as the present company.' He launched into a description of the Army Business. 'In any case,' he concluded, 'this would have been a clean way to put would-be surrogate mothers together with rich couples, and everybody's happy. It could have been completely legal, except where's the fun in that?

'Goodman came up with the wrinkle to hit on servicewomen who were back in the States after getting pregnant and coming back to deliver their babies. Soon, too soon, after the birth, they'd be up for another hitch in a war zone overseas, and this will shock you, but many didn't want to go back. So Goodman paid them twenty grand out of his hundred-grand fee for brokering the deal, and meanwhile, all their medical expenses were paid by the government; plus, they remained on salary.'

Roake clucked derisively. 'What a sleazeball.'

'But wait,' Hunt said. 'That's not the good part, at least for our purposes. The good part is Jessup.'

'Let me guess,' Hardy said. 'Jessup helped find and identify the women.'

'Right so far. With a three-grand bonus for every one.' Silence built around the table. Hunt said, 'Here's a hint. Why didn't Goodman fire him as soon as he found out about Lo's girls?'

Hardy's eyes, drawn and tired most of the day, threw a spark. 'He couldn't. Jessup would go public with what they'd done.'

'You think he was blackmailing him?' Gina asked. 'Overtly, even?'

'Not impossible,' Hunt replied. 'At least enough so that Goodman hadn't figured out a way to fire him.'

'How'd you get all this, Wyatt?'

Hunt grinned. 'That was probably the best part.'

Only belatedly had Hardy realized that putting Wyatt and Gina in the same room might have been awkward. In spite of a relatively significant age difference – fifteen or sixteen years – the two had gone out for a couple of years. So when Hardy got back to the solarium after letting Hunt out, he addressed the issue head-on. 'I hope you were okay with that? When I told Wyatt to come up, I didn't think—'

Gina waved off the apology. 'I'm a big girl, Diz. He's a good guy. We're cool.'

'You are cool,' he said. 'Both of you. I love working with adults.' He sighed. 'Especially after watching Brittany all afternoon. The poor girl is so confused. Did you ask why she cut her hair?'

'She didn't want to be pretty anymore. She thinks that's what got her in all this trouble.'

'She's not all wrong.'

'It's not the pretty,' Gina said. 'It's how you handle it. She'll figure it out someday.'

'Spoken by one who knows.'

Gina gave him a look, then broke a wide smile. 'Although sincere flattery,' she said, 'always has its place.' With that, she opened her briefcase on the table in front of her. 'Now, do you want to help Amy prep her cross of Brittany or talk about this new stuff?'

Hardy pondered. 'I like the idea that we have two new guys in play and two new motives.'

'You really think we do? If you bring up either one, you're essentially going SODDIT with both Goodman and Lo.' SODDIT, an acronym for 'some other dude did it,' was a common defense tactic. 'I'm thinking it sounds good in theory, but it's a bit of a stretch if we're asking the jury to believe even for a minute that one of these guys had Jessup killed, even if they both had a reason to. In Goodman's case especially . . . I mean, a city supervisor. You're stirring up a big hornets' nest. You can expect to get yourself stung. Not to mention that as we sit here now, we can't prove any piece of any parcel of any morsel of it.'

'I'm not worried about that. Let's remember, Dan White was a supervisor, so we've got precedent.'

'Dan White was a wackjob.' That may have been true, but White did shoot Mayor George Moscone and Supervisor Harvey Milk dead in their city hall offices in 1978. 'Precedent doesn't put Goodman in our victim's house that Sunday.'

'Maybe he hired it done.'

Roake drew her eyebrows together. 'Well, one way or the other, you'd better find out what he was doing that day if you're going to bring that up. It would be embarrassing if he was, say, in Hawaii or up at Tahoe.'

'All right, but what about Lo? He's evidently got a whole staff of enforcers and bodyguards. They keep his women in line; maybe they keep his enemies in line, too. Or the people who beat up on his people.'

Gina sat still for a minute. 'Don't get me wrong. This is interesting stuff, and we need to get it in front of the jury to give them something else to think about. But if we're going down that road, we ought to decide which choice is better, so we're not just pointing at people Jessup knew more or less at random, since he was evidently a prick to everybody. And, again, it wouldn't hurt to have at least a shred of evidence to back up whatever we're going to propose.'

'You don't think it's worth it to show what a son of a bitch Jessup was?'

Roake shrugged. 'There isn't anyone on the jury who doesn't already believe he's a rapist. How much do you want them to hate him?'

'With all their hearts. But I get your point. He can't get more dead than he already is. More's the pity.' Another thought struck him. 'Hey, maybe it was one of Lo's girls. One of the ones he beat up.'

'Diz, whoa. Maybe it was Bigfoot. You're getting carried away. When in reality, guess what?'

'What?'

'Maybe it was Moses.'

For reasons too karmic to explain, at least two of Hardy's favorite lifetime moments had occurred at the front door of Abe Glitsky's duplex.

One time Glitsky had opened the door holding his daughter, Rachel, at his shoulder. She had already puked down the diaper on his shoulder, and one of her pink booties had found its way to his ear, where it hung for at least thirty seconds before Abe became aware of it and ripped it off. Hardy's visual of it could still make him laugh out loud.

The other time, when Hardy was many years younger and in the immature phase that had probably lasted far too long, he and Abe had been coming back from wherever they'd been, and it had been pouring rain.

Glitsky had thrown Hardy his keys – probably because in those days Hardy tended to take stairs two at a time – and Hardy had gotten to the door and let himself in, and then (proof that Satan was continually at work in the world) that darn devil had made him close the door and lock it in time for Glitsky's arrival.

'Diz, you crazy person, what are you doing? Open the door.'

'Say "please."'

'I'm not going to say "please." Just open the door.'

'Come on, Abe. Just say "please."'

Through the peephole, he watched Glitsky stoically bear the burden, rain pelting down on his head, fat drops running down the lines of his face. After thirty or more seconds, Glitsky sighed and gave in. 'All right,' he said at last through gritted teeth, 'please.'

'Fuck you.' A jovial Hardy couldn't say it fast enough. 'Say "pretty please."'

Over the years, Glitsky had tried to get him back in myriad ways any number of times, but try as he might to appear ferocious and unyielding, at base he didn't have the streak of utter cruelty that Hardy kept in a special place close to his heart. Nevertheless, every visit to Glitsky's door contained the tiniest germ of the possibility for adventure, revenge, and retribution.

Tonight Hardy's stop wasn't going to depend on fate. Glitsky had texted him that he'd be home by six, and about an hour after that, Hardy walked up the twelve steps that led to the landing and rang the doorbell.

No one answered.

Hardy rang again, heard the chime inside. Nothing.

He knocked, then put his ear to the door. Nobody home.

Swearing at the wasted precious time, especially when he was at trial, he turned and started down the steps. Abe didn't usually propose a time and then not show up. Hardy hoped he was okay. The kids. Treya. Life with young children was endlessly uncertain. Whatever it was, he thought, Abe would have to tell him about it on the phone, or maybe they could meet somewhere in the morning. In fact . . .

Stopping at the bottom of the stairs, he got out his cell and was locating Abe's number when the door opened above him and Rachel and Zachary called down at him: 'Uncle Diz, Uncle Diz!'

'Hey, guys.' Wondering where they'd been hiding out, or maybe they'd just been in the backyard, he waved and started up the stairs, got to the landing, and saw the door was closed, so he knocked. 'Guys!'

Behind the door, he heard both of them cry out in unison, 'Say "please."' And howl with laughter.

Now those jokester kids frolicked in the backyard while Hardy and Abe sat on the stairs and watched them. 'No, really,' Hardy was saying. 'That was great. I enjoyed it. Especially since I'm in trial and have nothing important to do with my time.'

'Your time.' Glitsky puffed out a chortle. 'Maybe a minute and a half.'

'If I were Winston Paley,' Hardy replied, 'that would cost you almost ten bucks.'

'Who's Winston Paley?'

Hardy told him, then went on a bit about Brittany and her testimony.

'So it's not going well?' Glitsky asked when he'd finished.

'I didn't say that.'

'No? I read between the lines.'

'Actually,' Hardy said, 'we may have had a little bit of a breakthrough. Wyatt Hunt found a couple of guys – you know them, Goodman and Lo – who hated Jessup and may have wanted to do him harm.'

'Did they have opportunity?'

'We're working on that. Did you guys ever talk to them about this?'

'Us guys?'

'You. The police. Homicide.'

'You forget I was removed about that time.'

'I didn't forget. I forget nothing. I thought it might have been before they got around to you.'

'Well. No.'

'Just thought I'd ask.' Hardy chanced a quick perusal of his friend. Clean-shaven, casually but nicely dressed, cop shoes on and laced up. In all, a significant improvement in a very short time. 'But you had something for me, unless that was part of the setup for that laugh riot of a joke your kids played at the door.'

'No. That was separate.' Glitsky took a beat. 'I heard back from Bill Schuyler.'

'This is turning out to be a fruitful day,' Hardy said. 'What'd he know?'

'He knows your guy. Or rather, he knows the marshal who handles your guy.'

'Does he know his real name?'

'That was not happening. He's sticking with Tony.'

'Tony's okay,' Hardy said. 'What'd he do?'

'He is evidently a cop, which we suspected. The other thing he did, though' – Glitsky drew a breath – 'was kill people for money.'

Tony sat with a Sierra Nevada pale ale on the couch in Brittany's tiny living room. She sat across from him, curled up in pajamas, a towel wrapped turban-style around her head, a glass of white wine beading onto the glass-topped coffee table. A reggae playlist pumped softly out of an invisible speaker. 'I let myself off early,' he said. 'I booked Lynne for my shifts for the rest of the week. She was happy for the work.'

'Where are you going?'

'I'm not sure I'm going anywhere. But they want me in court tomorrow, and I don't know how long that will go. I thought

I'd give myself some time. Also, I wanted to see how it went with you today. I missed you down at the bar.'

'I can't go there for a while. After the riot the other night . . .'

'No. I hear you. Of course. I didn't expect you. You mind if I'm here?'

'Not at all. You mind if I'm not feeling particularly sexy?'

'No.'

'You wouldn't be, either, if you saw my head.'

He grinned at her. 'I bet I would. But we don't have to test the theory. I actually like the turban look. But that's not what I'm here for.'

'Pretty obviously.'

'If it's meant to be, it'll be,' he said.

'So what *are* you here for?'

He paused, met her solemn gaze. 'You, I suppose. Just you.'

'You probably think I've been stringing you along.'

'I probably think you got raped, is what I probably think. Anybody who doesn't get that doesn't deserve you.'

'Okay, but almost four months?'

He leaned back into the cushions. 'Hey, if you're trying to talk yourself into something, you won't hear me complain. But I'm good. I'm a grown-up. I can handle waiting around for something that's supremely worth it.'

'It might not be.'

'I'm willing to chance it.' He sipped at his beer. 'So how'd it go today?'

'Pretty rough. Reliving it, I suppose. My uncle tried to ease things up a little, but he didn't have much luck.'

'He's a good guy,' Tony said. 'Even if he isn't much of a fan of mine lately.'

'Oh, I'm sure he is. He's just working. He gets preoccupied.'

'Maybe.' He paused. 'It's like he doesn't trust me.'

'Why wouldn't he trust you?'

'Well, the Beck, for one. That was pretty shitty of me, though it never went anywhere. I just hadn't met you yet.'

'You don't have to apologize. I get it. I'm as guilty of that as you are. I think she's over the whole thing, anyway. Ben's great for her.'

'Still,' he said. 'Her dad.'

'Yeah.' She sighed. 'Maybe I'm feeling a little sexy after all.'

Tony didn't have any clothes on. The covers were messed all around him. He lay back on Brittany's bed, hands behind his head. 'Did I say supremely worth it?'

She was curled up next to him, her head against his chest. 'Yes, it was.' Bob Marley started singing 'Stir It Up.' 'This is going to sound weird,' she said, 'but I'm glad we waited.'

'Not weird at all. This was the time. I love this song.'

'Me, too.'

'Three chords, five words. Go figure.'

'I know.' She boosted herself onto an elbow. 'You really don't mind my hair?'

'This just in,' he said, 'you don't have any hair. And I love it. If you did have hair, I'd love that, too. If you had a thick pelt of fur . . .'

She laughed and put her hand over his mouth. 'Okay, okay, I get it.' She lowered herself back down to his chest. 'So they subpoenaed you for tomorrow?'

'Yeah.'

'That must mean they're going to ask if I told you.'

'I know. I figured that out.'

She stayed silent for a long moment. 'Do we want to talk about this?'

'I think so.'

'What are you going to say?'

He breathed in and out a couple of times. 'You know I've told

374

you I used to be a cop? I have to be honest. It's not going to feel natural to me to lie under oath.'

She went dead still beside him.

'I wanted to ask you to think about something,' he said.

'What?'

'About whether your dad really did this.'

'I've thought about that a thousand times.'

'And?'

'I guess he did. I can't think of any other explanation.'

'What do you think the jury's going to say?'

'I don't know. My uncle says you can never predict.'

'If you had to guess?'

'If I were on the jury, I think I'd say he was guilty.'

'And why'd he do it?'

'We know that.'

'Do you think the jury's going to know it?'

'I don't see how they couldn't.'

'Regardless of what you said today?'

'Pretty much, yeah.'

'Or what I might have to say tomorrow?'

She breathed against him. 'I see where you're going.'

He chose his words carefully. 'You saying it is betraying your father. If I say you told me you'd told him, it's once removed. Plus, it's hearsay. In the end, it's not going to make any difference to the verdict. Unless you think it will.'

'I don't know.'

'Nobody knows, Brittany. I won't say it if you don't want me to. I don't want to be the person responsible for sending your father to jail. But you know I already talked to the police. If I change my story, they're going to play that tape, and then they'll know that I lied, and it's more likely that they'll think you lied. It gets worse and worse. I think there's a good chance your father's going to jail anyway, but I can't have what I say come between you and me. Especially not after tonight. I would lie if you asked me to. I would do anything you asked me to.'

'I don't know,' she said. 'I just don't know.'

'Maybe we could sleep on it,' he said. 'Talk about it again in the morning.'

After a second's hesitation, in a small voice, she said, 'Maybe we could do that.'

34

If Brittany thought that violently chopping off her hair would make her less interesting to photojournalists and television news crews, she was mistaken. Local and national media vans blocked two lanes of Bryant Street, and reporters and camerapeople were waiting three-deep on the front steps of the Hall of Justice, clogging the inner lobby. The day before, when it wasn't clear to the media that she'd be there, much less be the first witness, the crush had failed to materialize. She'd entered the building with her shawl on to no fanfare, accompanied only by her mother, and no one had paid her any particular attention.

This morning, she and Tony had driven down together on his motorcycle and, after stopping by his apartment so he could change, parked two blocks away and walked up. Now they stood on the corner across the street. Seeing the mob, Tony said, 'I'm afraid this is about you.'

She let out a sigh. 'God, it gets old.' She was wearing an outfit similar to the one from the day before – men's shoes, brown slacks, a bulky black leather jacket. Instead of the white shawl, she wore a Giants hat, which she pulled down low. 'There's a back way in,' she said. 'You want to try that?'

'I'm with you,' Tony said.

They crossed Bryant at the corner of Seventh Street, half a block from the doors to the Hall, for all the world at that distance looking like a couple of guys minding their own business on their way to wherever they were going. Picking up their pace, they entered the employee and staff parking lot behind the building, then came around the monstrosity of the jail and onto the walkway leading past the jail's entrance and the medical examiner's office. No one was walking in front of them, though there was a small knot of humanity lined up at the rear entrance, a simple glass door with a manned desk and metal detector just inside.

Tony put his arm around her, leaned in to her ear. 'This was a good idea.'

She leaned in to him. He kissed the side of her head.

And then, suddenly, it wasn't such a good idea. With Tony's arm around her, they no longer looked like a couple of guys strolling along, passing the time of day. Now they looked like what they were, a couple, and several of the people lounging by the back door were ready for them, turning and snapping away with their cameras. Tony held out a hand to them. 'Leave her alone! Come on! Show a little class. Let her by, let us in.' He pulled her closer to him, hiding her face with his hand, getting them to the door and inside, where the cop waved them through the metal detector and they made a run for the stairway.

Hardy did the cross on Brittany himself, pleading that Amy had to attend to another witness. Stier threw up his arms in disgust, and Gomez, with bad grace, allowed that at this point, she'd permit almost anything that would keep the trial moving.

'Ms McGuire,' Hardy said, 'you and I know each other well, do we not?'

'We do.'

'Would you please tell the jury our relationship?'

Hardy wanted her to smile. She'd been mostly in tragic mode yesterday, and though that might elicit sympathy with some members of the jury, her hacked off hair, masculine clothing, and generally defensive tone had made her seem, even in ultra-tolerant

San Francisco, somewhat of an edgy figure, not quite a 'normal' young woman. Hardy wanted to humanize her, get the jury, if possible, to like her a little more.

She didn't disappoint, flashing an embarrassed, somewhat apologetic smile first to him, then to the jury. 'He is my uncle,' she said, then added a little bonus: 'My favorite uncle.'

Never mind that he was her only uncle – a recurring joke in the family – the comment played well. Several of the jurors smiled in return, and Hardy gave the moment its due before turning back to her.

'Brittany,' he began, 'would you mind telling us how old you are?'

'Twenty-three.'

'Do you live in your parents' home with them?'

'No.'

'For how long have you not lived with them?'

'I think about five years. Since I went away to college.'

'Did you graduate?'

'Yes.'

'Do you still live alone?'

'Yes. I have an apartment in the city.'

Stier pushed up from his chair. 'Objection, Your Honor. Relevance?'

The judge cocked her head. 'Mr Hardy?'

'It's basic background on the witness, Your Honor, and I'm trying to demonstrate Ms McGuire's independence from her parents.'

'All right. I'll allow it. Objection overruled.'

The questions in this vein went on for a few more minutes. Do you pay your own bills at your apartment? Electricity? Gas? Do you own a car? Did you pay for it yourself? Do you pay for your own gas? How about car insurance? Health insurance? Are you employed? Do your parents help you financially in any way?

Having established Brittany's physical independence from her parents, Hardy moved on. 'Going back to your testimony yesterday, you said that Mr Jessup pushed you up against a building, cutting and bruising your face, and he then threw you down with enough force that you felt you should go to the emergency room to check out the damage. Is that right?'

'Yes.'

Hardy crossed back to his table and picked up some pages. 'Now, Brittany, I have here a copy of the record of your admission that day to St Francis Hospital.' He passed the paper over to her. 'Is this your signature at the bottom of this form?'

'Yes.'

Hardy had the document entered into evidence, then came back to his witness. 'Would you please read what they have listed here, and which you have signed off on, as the reason for your injuries that day?'

Brittany hardly needed to look at the paper, since they'd been through all this in preparation. '"Patient slipped and fell headlong while running to catch a bus. Multiple bruises and contusions to the head, hands, and legs."'

'In other words, Brittany, you did not give the ER doctors the true reason for your injuries, is that right?'

'Yes, that's right.'

'How did you get home from the hospital?'

'I called my mom – I mostly take the bus to work – and she picked me up.'

'And what did you tell her about your injuries?'

'The same thing I told the doctors. That I fell.'

'Why didn't you tell her the truth?'

Brittany let out a long breath. 'I didn't want to get anybody in trouble.'

'You mean you didn't want to get Rick Jessup in trouble?'

'Right.'

'Why not?'

'I don't know. I didn't think he was a bad guy. I didn't think he did it on purpose. He just got mad. It wasn't like he beat me with his fists or anything. I didn't think it would happen again.'

'All right. And where did your mother take you from the hospital?'

'To her and Dad's place.'

'And did you see your father there?'

'Yes. Later that day.'

'And did you tell him the same story you had told the doctors and your mother?'

'Yes.'

'For the same reasons?'

'Yes.'

'Brittany, did you ever subsequently tell your father that Mr Jessup had hurt you?'

'No.'

'Never?'

'No. I mean, not while Rick was alive. Of course, he's heard about it now.'

'Of course. Thank you.'

Hardy half turned toward the jury, not playing to them, since that would bring on the wrath of Gomez, but subtly conveying to them his satisfaction with Brittany's answers. She was coming across as an independent, friendly young woman whose first instinct in adversity was not to run to her parents but the opposite – to deal with it herself, to shelter them from the knowledge that she'd been hurt.

He turned back to the table where Moses sat to give the message another minute to sink in. After a sip of water, he returned to his place in front of the witness box, softening his tone of voice.

'Brittany, after you woke up at Mr Jessup's house, realizing that he had raped you, on the day before he was killed, you drove to the Little Shamrock. Why did you do that?'

'I don't really know. I was afraid and pretty freaked out. I wanted to cry on somebody's shoulder, tell somebody what had happened.'

'By "somebody," do you mean your father?'

'Yes. I thought he'd be working there.'

'And was he?'

'No. There was another bartender that night. Tony Solaia.'

'And did you tell Mr Solaia what had happened to you?'

'Yes. I had to tell somebody.'

'Then what happened?'

'Tony closed up right away and then took me to my parents' place.'

'Why did he do that?'

'Because I told him I wanted to go there.'

'And what time did you arrive at your parents' place?'

'Two-ish, something like that.'

'Did you have to wake them up to let you in?'

'My mom woke up.'

'Not your father?'

'No.'

'Did you tell your mother what had happened to you?'

Brittany's eyes went from Hardy to the jury. 'No.'

'But here you were, obviously upset, in the middle of the night, asking to come in. Didn't she ask you what had happened?'

'Yes.'

'Did you tell her the truth?'

'No.'

'What did you say?'

'Just that I'd had too much to drink and wanted to be within walking distance of the Shamrock to get my car the next day.'

'In other words, you told Tony Solaia but did not tell your mother, is that right?'

'Yes.'

'Why did you do that?'

'I don't know. Telling Tony, that got it out of me. As I was telling him, I realized I didn't want to tell anybody else. I needed to process it a little, figure out what I needed to do, all the implications. I made him promise not to tell anybody, either.'

'What did you do then?'

'I hardly slept at all. Sometime early the next morning, I got up and went down to the Rape Crisis Counseling Center on Haight and reported the rape.'

'All by yourself?'

'Yes. It's not far from my parents', a couple of blocks.'

'What happened then?'

'They kept me there a few hours and took a statement from me, did some tests and blood work, then let me go.'

'And where did you go from there?'

'I walked back to my mom and dad's, and they made me breakfast, and after that, I went to my car and drove home to my apartment.'

'And did you tell your father about the rape that day?'

'No. I didn't see my father for the next couple of days.'

'So to be clear, you never told either your mother or your father about the rape?'

'No. I thought it would break their hearts, and I didn't want to do that. So I never told them.'

Hardy paused, letting the simple humanity of her answer resonate with the jury. Then he bowed and said, 'Thank you, Brittany. No further questions.'

During the break immediately following Brittany's testimony, Hardy allowed himself a moment of hope. Moses and Gina, up from the seat in the gallery, although keeping any sense of celebration low-key, were no less enthusiastic. The two parallel stories – the pushing incident and the rape – though vastly different in scale, nevertheless had a symmetry that was compelling. Brittany wasn't going to get her parents involved in solving her problems, no matter how big they were. That just wasn't her style.

'I'm almost thinking they're not going to get motive,' Gina said. 'In which case things get shaky for them pretty fast, wouldn't you say?'

'No motive and I walk,' McGuire whispered.

'Knock on wood,' Hardy replied. Strategically, he thought he'd done a good job, though knowing it was all in the service of a lie took away some of his euphoric visceral kick. The fact remained that he knew Brittany, in contradiction to her sworn testimony, had told Moses about the rape that Sunday morning, and further, that Moses had gone down to Jessup's with the shillelagh that evening, intending to beat him, perhaps to death.

By lunchtime, all that confidence was but a pale memory.

Stier's first witness after the morning recess had been Tony Solaia. As befitted a former policeman, he exuded a calm certainty as he recounted his relationship with Brittany. Yes, she had come by the Shamrock after the rape and told him about it. Over the next few days, he'd gone by her apartment several times to make sure she was okay, and on one of those occasions, she had told him unequivocally that on Sunday morning when she got back from the Rape Crisis Counseling Center, she had told her father what had happened to her. She had described his reaction as 'furious.'

Now Hardy, Gina, and Moses were sharing a deli lunch Susan had brought in, in the prisoners' holding tank, a jail cell built into the hallway outside the back door of Department 24. Moses, in high dudgeon at the turn of events, was going on, 'This is the thanks I get for being the guy's savior these last couple of months? He's busted out of his job and I give him a new one, and he

384

turns around and sticks it to me? Meanwhile hooking up with my daughter?'

'You know what I'd do?' Hardy asked, all seriousness.

'What?'

'I'd kill him. No, really. Beat him on the head with a shillelagh.'

'You're such a funny guy,' McGuire said. 'I'm cracking up over here.'

'I'm working on my stand-up act if this whole law thing doesn't work out, which it's starting to look like. Not on this case, anyway.'

Gina looked up with a frown. 'Guys. Come on.' Then: 'But no cross on Tony, Diz? None at all. I admit I was a little surprised.'

'I reserved the right to recall him, and I will if you can tell me something you think I ought to ask him. You didn't believe him?'

'No. I believed him.'

'So what am I supposed to get him with?'

McGuire shook his head. 'Why, though? That's what I don't understand. Why'd he screw me like this?'

'If you stay in jail,' Hardy deadpanned, 'you can't kill him for hanging out with Brittany.'

'Jesus,' Gina said. 'You guys.'

Hardy drank some of his soda. 'Somebody was going to let it out. It just turned out Tony was first up.' Hardy, with no love lost for Tony Solaia, and even with the new information about his past and present, nevertheless wanted his client to understand that this wasn't an error his attorneys had made. 'You saw Stier's witness list, Mose – including everybody Brittany has talked to in the past three months, folks from work, the Shamrock, yoga class – and you've seen their statements. Guess what?' He lowered his voice. 'She told you, Mose. She told a bunch of her friends that she told you. It was going to come out.'

'Yeah, well, we've got to get some traction someplace. I don't need to tell you.'

'We're working on it,' Hardy said. 'We're working on it.'

It turned out – and the afternoon session proved – that Hardy was right about the truth coming out. To a generation for whom it was routine to appear in all kinds of compromising positions, in various social media outlets, the idea of a secret that was really a secret – in the sense that it was inviolable and you didn't tell anybody – was not exactly in common currency. The afternoon in the courtroom was an object lesson in that reality.

Besides Tony and the Beck (which was why, Hardy realized, his daughter hadn't been on Stier's witness list – Ugly didn't need her), three other friends of Brittany knew, and all of them testified, that she had told them not only about informing her father but when.

Sunday, at her parents', before she'd gone back to her apartment.

If nothing else, by the time they adjourned for the day, Stier had locked up motive. Whether or not anyone on the jury believed that the defendant had murdered Rick Jessup, Hardy felt they must already be unanimous in believing that he had a reason to.

35

Date night tended to be a casualty of Hardy's trial schedule, but today he had called Frannie after his lunch with McGuire and Gina and asked if she would meet up with him tonight. He told her he needed to see her as his counselor and adviser and, not incidentally, as the sister of his client.

Frannie took a cab from the house, and they met at seven o'clock at the Elite Cafe on Fillmore, one of their favorite places, with great gumbo and a curtained booth – similar to the private booths at Sam's – that Hardy had reserved before court reconvened after lunch. He caught her surprised and somewhat disapproving look when he placed his order for a Cajun martini. After the waiter had gone, he said, 'You make these for me at home all the time.'

'They make them stronger here.'

'They just taste stronger because of the pepper.'

'I think it might be the alcohol.'

'Sometimes a man needs more alcohol.'

'So they say. But most of the time you don't, especially when you're at trial. Is tomorrow an off day?'

Hardy chuckled at the idea. 'No, though probably it won't be too bad. If I'm guessing, tomorrow is either more of Brittany's unreliable friends, which Stier doesn't really need, or he goes to eyewitnesses, who will basically cross-examine themselves, I hope. Especially after the good Dr Paley. The bottom line is that nobody saw your brother doing anything but walking down the street.'

'Don't forget the shillelagh.'

'I never would. But still, a guy with a club. So what?'

'Not exactly a fishing pole.'

Hardy shrugged. 'None of that puts him in Jessup's place.'

The waiter returned, pushing back the curtain of the booth, delivering their drinks. When he'd closed it again, Frannie lifted her chardonnay and said, 'If you're not concerned about the eyewitnesses, why do you need the stronger drink?'

Hardy sipped his martini, paused. 'They nailed down motive today. Brittany's friends were lining up to say that she had told them all about telling her dad, how pissed off he was, almost incoherent with rage. So angry that he scared her and Susan.'

'They said that?'

'And so much more.'

Frannie put her glass down, untouched. Hardy saw a tremor in her hand. 'You're saying they're going to find him guilty.'

'I never say that until the last gavel falls. With juries, we know, anything can happen. But I have to say that after today, it gets way trickier. He knows it, too.' Hardy hesitated. 'I thought maybe you could talk to him.'

'About?'

Hardy let out a breath. 'The usual. That he's got to watch himself, never let his guard down, especially if he's surprised and gets mad. He's sick of hearing that message from me, but you might remind him how important his silence on the other matter is not only to me and him and Gina and Abe but also you, his favorite sister.'

'He already knows that, Dismas. He really does.'

'Okay. But I think you'll agree that when his emotions get involved, he might do something stupid and forget.'

'And you think I could influence him?' Sitting back, Frannie met her husband's eyes, looked away, then came back. 'What do you think I could say that would make any difference?'

'Well, that's the other thing.'

'What?'

Hardy turned the stem of his martini glass. 'As we know, his story now, lately, is that he didn't kill Jessup. And if that's true, he shouldn't do time for it. There's no argument to that.'

'But . . . ?'

'But if he did do it . . . ?'

'But he didn't.'

Hardy stared at her. 'If he did do it,' he went on, 'and the jury convicts him, you might be able to make him see that this is his solitary burden, that he brought it on himself. It's got nothing to do with the dockside thing, but because he's who he is, he'll be tempted to talk about it, bring up the moral similarities. Except in this case, Jessup, Moses knew when he did it that he might get punished, probably would get punished. Hell, Jessup might have fought him off and killed him. He took the risk alone, and this is the consequence for him alone. It's harsh, and he doesn't want to hear it, but there it is.' He spread his hands. 'You know him, Fran. He's a philosopher. And at least that's an argument.'

'And you want me to make it?'

'More than that, Fran,' he said. 'I think you're the only one who can.'

The heavy stuff wasn't over yet. Hardy was moving fried oysters around on his plate, his appetite having deserted him before the gumbo even arrived. 'Brittany,' he was saying, 'is who I'm really worried about. Especially if it's true.'

'You think Abe's FBI guy lied to him?'

'No. At least not on purpose. Which doesn't mean he didn't get lied to and pass along the bad information. These U.S. Marshals have been known to misdirect inquiries, get people off their trail. Unlike, apparently, the majority of Americans under thirty, they take their secrets pretty seriously.'

'If it's true, we have to tell Brittany.'

'That's what I've been wrestling with, Fran. What good is that going to do? Maybe, probably, she already knows. They've been going out for three months. He told the Beck about himself after about three minutes.'

'Leaving out the good part, though.'

'That he's a professional killer? That part?'

'What if she doesn't know?' Frannie asked.

'Then how would knowing about it help her?'

'Well, if nothing else, she'd know he was truly a dangerous guy.'

'You don't think she knows that already? You don't think that's part of the attraction? She'll never believe he's dangerous to her.' Hardy dragged a palm down the side of his face. 'Here's what I'm really wondering. What if, purely if, it was Tony who heard about Brittany getting raped and went over and killed Rick Jessup? Because, you know, that's what he does.'

Frannie sat back in her seat, her eyes wide.

'Let's just go with it for a minute,' he continued. 'If he's in love or even lust with Brittany, will he let her father have this trial and maybe even go to prison?'

'Sure. Why wouldn't he? At least it's not him. And, in fact, if Moses does go down, it makes Brittany even more vulnerable, doesn't it? Then Tony's the only man left in her life. Do you really think that's possible?'

'I don't know. Ever since Abe told me last night, the possibility has kind of gnawed at me. Tony was the first one Brittany told about the rape. What stops him, after he drops her off at her parents', from going over to Jessup's right then, or the next morning, or sometime the next afternoon?'

'But he didn't have the shillelagh,' Frannie argued. 'Moses had the shillelagh.'

'Who says it had to be a shillelagh? It could have been the

butt of a gun. It could have been a wine bottle. A wrench from the saddlebags on a bike. A rock from the garden, for Christ's sake. Any hard, blunt object.'

Frannie was shaking her head. 'No, no, no. If somebody brought a gun, especially an ex-cop who supposedly has killed other people, don't you think he'll use the gun? And if he's accustomed to a gun – and you'd have to think that's the professional weapon of choice, wouldn't you? – then he's not going to try something new on the spur of the moment.'

'He might. What if he's really enraged? What if killing gets him off? What if he starts out with a swing at the head and it feels so right, he just keeps going? What if he didn't have a gun at all and just felt like he needed to kill the guy right away with whatever was closest to hand? How have I not once thought of this before yesterday? How come nobody else thought of it?'

'Because it's been about Moses the whole time. Nobody – certainly not the cops – even looked at anybody else, did they? I mean, wasn't that the whole deal with that different warrant? Just go get Moses and get him now?'

'I've got to get Tony back on the stand.'

The two of them sat staring at each other, numbed with the import of what Hardy had spun out. The waiter opened the curtain and cleared away the mostly untouched appetizers. When he closed the booth again, Frannie said, 'You don't want to get him on the stand, Dismas, at least not to accuse him of anything. You don't want him thinking that you have any suspicions of him at all. You understand what I'm saying?'

Hardy's eyes were focused somewhere over Frannie's shoulder.

'Diz?' she asked.

'It couldn't be any clearer,' he said.

They were in Brittany's apartment, in her bedroom, in the afterglow.

Tony, naked, got up to bring back a pint of ice cream from the freezer, and she pulled the bedsheet up around her, tucking it in under her arms, covering her breasts. Through the bedroom door, she watched him padding around in the kitchen, carrying the ice cream over for a short blast in the microwave, grabbing some spoons from the utensil drawer.

Thank God it was all over, she was thinking, her actual testimony. And Tony's. Maybe now her life could get back to some kind of normal. She had to admit that things didn't look good for her father, but she had a lot of faith in her uncle Dismas, who, as far as she knew, hadn't lost a big case in his career. Of course, there was a first time for everything, but he didn't have his reputation for nothing. She wasn't going to worry about her father until they brought in a guilty verdict. And even then, they could appeal.

The most important thing was knowing that her father hadn't done it. She'd picked up enough from listening to Uncle Diz outline the stuff he'd found out about Liam Goodman and Jon Lo. Both of them had serious problems with Rick and every reason in the world to want him dead – maybe more than her father did. They didn't have a timetable for how it must have happened, but her uncle had private investigators working on it, and she was sure they'd come up with something.

The other great thing was that Tony's testimony, as he'd convinced her, had made no difference. If he had been the only one contradicting what she'd said, in spite of her protestations to the contrary, it would have been a problem between them. Instead, there'd been three others. She couldn't believe the number of people she'd told. She felt pretty stupid about that, irresponsible, but she'd learned her lesson. People say they won't tell anybody your secrets, and then they tell their three closest friends. That had been her, too, but not anymore.

Never.

'What are you thinking about?'

'Today,' she said. 'Getting this behind me. I never want to go into a courtroom again. I don't know how you did it all the time as a cop.'

'You notice I've stopped being a cop. Now you know why.'

She reached out for the ice cream container, scraped off a spoonful, and ate it. 'Also,' she said, 'I'm wondering if my uncle's idea of how he's going to get my dad off is going to work.'

'What's his idea?'

'Get the jury thinking other people had motive, too.'

'Did he mention any names?'

'One of them is your old friend the supervisor.' She started to give him some of the details of Hardy's investigation when her cell phone chimed on the bedside table. She handed the ice cream container back to Tony and, reaching over, looked at the display, then pressed the connect button and brought the phone up to her ear. 'Hey, Beck.'

Two minutes later, teary-eyed again, she had her laptop open on the bed. The *Chronicle*'s home page filled her screen. It was a picture of Brittany and Tony approaching the back door to the Hall of Justice that morning. The caption began: 'Sporting a Giants hat and accompanied by a new bodyguard, Brittany McGuire . . .'

'It's never going to end,' she said. 'Never.'

Tony couldn't seem to tear his eyes from the computer screen.

'The Beck said the picture is also on *People*'s daily website, where they call you my "hunky new bodyguard." I don't understand why they can't just leave us alone.'

A muscle in his jaw working, Tony didn't answer her.

'Tony?'

'I'm here.' After a minute, 'The guy got us pretty good, didn't he?'

'We should have gone for his camera and smashed the damn thing.'

At last Tony reached out and closed the laptop. 'This is going to be in the paper tomorrow?'

'That's what it looks like.'

His face set, his eyes dark, Tony nodded several times.

'What are you thinking?' she asked.

'Nothing,' he said. 'I'm not thinking anything.'

36

EYEWITNESS TESTIMONY HAD played a crucial role in identifying Moses McGuire as a suspect, which was why Hardy had gone to such lengths and expense to discredit it. But when the first witness got up and took the stand on Thursday morning, Hardy found that she had little if anything of substance to contribute to the prosecution.

Susan Antaramian was the upstairs neighbor who'd heard what sounded like a struggle in the apartment below that Sunday evening, and who'd looked out her window to see a man in jeans and hiking boots and an orange and black Giants jacket leave the building. Stier, expecting God knew what, led her through the recital, taking an excruciatingly painful twenty minutes, and at the end of that testimony, Hardy – barely hiding his impatience at this all but meaningless nonsense – finished her off in less than five. Could she identify that man as Moses McGuire, sitting at the defense table? She could not. Did she see this person in the building at all? No. Did she see him enter or leave Mr Jessup's apartment? No. After this man left the building, did she go downstairs to see if Mr Jessup was all right? No.

Indeed, Antaramian's testimony was so inconclusive that Gomez invited counsel up to the bench. 'Mr Stier, I don't mean to interfere with how you're presenting your case, but I would hope that if you plan to continue in this vein with your eyewitnesses, they will have something of a little more relevance to contribute.'

'. . . about the most tedious six hours I have ever spent in a courtroom.' Hardy paced between the Sutter Street windows and the coffee station in his office. Wyatt Hunt lounged nearly sideways in one of the leather armchairs. Hardy went on. 'It was exactly as I knew it would be. Yeah, it was him. Yeah, I ran into him in the street that Sunday night. Yeah, I picked him out of the six-pack of pictures and then out of a lineup. Still him. Yep, that's him over at the defense table. Okay, I'll point at him. Yes, that's the defendant, Moses McGuire. Jesus Christ!

'So then I pull out every single discrepancy, uncertainty, and inconsistency from every witness. And if they did see him, so the fuck what? Did they ever see him with the victim? Did they ever see him near the apartment? No? Then what the hell does it matter where else they saw him?'

Hardy stopped. 'And now here I am, haranguing you and making the day even longer, aren't I?'

'I can take it,' Hunt said. 'Spew some more if you must.'

Hardy went over to the counter, picked up his coffee cup, and turned around. 'I should be happy we lost no ground today. That's how I should look at it. But that was the longest day of my adult life. Moses and I started playing hangman right there at our table . . . I know, inappropriate. And if the jurors had seen it. But they couldn't, 'cause they were all sleeping, too.' Hardy leaned against the corner of his desk, sipped his coffee, made a face. 'Okay, I'm done. How'd your day go?'

'Decent. Mr Goodman didn't want to see me again after the other day, but these guys, Lo and Goodman, I'm predicting a sad future for their relationship. You'll remember that Lo gave up the fact that Goodman kept Jessup on, in spite of his bad behavior with Lo's girls, because Jessup was blackmailing him about the Army Business.'

'Got it.'

'But except for Lo's word, I had no proof or even corroboration that the blackmail was actually happening. So I thought it might be productive to ask Goodman about it directly. The Army Business.'

'And how'd he take that?'

'He didn't know what I was talking about, naturally. In his law practice he'd fortunately been able to help place a lot of childless couples with surrogate mothers. What did I suppose Jessup would blackmail him about?'

'What, indeed?' Hardy asked.

'I told him I supposed that was the reason he called it the Army Business. That all the surrogates, or at least a large percentage of them, were still on active duty. That Jessup's job was finding these women and putting them in touch with him, for which he got a big bonus. And that this was all defrauding the U.S. government out of the women's wages and medical expenses.'

'Did he believe you?'

Hunt smiled. 'I think he came to understand my position. In exchange for us not bringing up the Army Business, if Lo denies it, he will testify that Lo told him he thought Jessup had beat up his girls. So Lo will have a motive in play if we need it. Oh, and do you want to bet a buck that if I massage things just right, I can get Lo to roll over on Goodman about the blackmail if we choose to go in that direction?'

Hardy broke a tight smile. 'There you go. Nice work.'

'Thank you, but there's more.' Hunt straightened up so that he was sitting naturally in the chair. 'Just to be thorough, I asked Goodman if he knew what he'd been doing on the day Jessup was killed, and after his usual stab at complete ignorance – he laughed and asked if I was kidding – he got out his calendar. It was Palm Sunday. He had political stuff going on all day. There's no way.'

'If he didn't hire somebody.'

Hunt shrugged. 'Not so easy and not so common as you might think. Plus, Goodman's a slimeball and a hypocrite, but he's not, for example, Jon Lo, who probably has serious muscle on the payroll here in the city. But even muscle . . . I don't know, Diz. A button guy is a whole different can of worms. In the Tongs, they fly some guy in, he does the hit and then disappears forever back to China the next day. I think Koreans, it's the same. Somebody like Goodman, forget it. I just can't see it.'

Hardy had placed his coffee cup on the desk next to him. His arms were crossed, and he was staring at the wall behind Hunt's head.

'It's neat,' Hunt said, 'when you can actually see the gears turning. What just hit you?'

Hardy hesitated. 'You just described the same scenario for paid assassins that Brittany told me about, that she in turn got from our friend Tony Solaia, the protected witness I asked you to look into a couple of months ago.'

'Sure. I remember. Not my finest hour.'

'Don't worry about it. The point is that I decided to take another run at him from a different direction. I asked Glitsky if he would try to go through an FBI contact and maybe hook up with Tony's keeper in the marshal's service that way.'

'How'd that go?'

'Better.'

After Hunt heard about Solaia being a killer for hire, he was sitting at the front of his chair.

Hardy was going on, 'So then this guy goes out of his way to tell my niece how these Asian assassins work. Why? Because he knows she's going to tell me, get me thinking in that direction in the likely event that I'm going to implicate Jon Lo as somebody else with a motive to kill Jessup. This is the same guy – remember, Brittany's boyfriend – who contradicted her testimony and led the pile-on in court that locked in our client's motive.'

'I'm not seeing what you're getting at.'

'Two excellent suspects, neither of them him.'

'You mean Tony? As Jessup's killer?'

Hardy nodded. 'I started liking him last night when I realized he was the first one to know about the rape and had his own motive. I'm liking him a little better today.'

'So Mose has gotten all the way here and he actually didn't do it?'

'Maybe.' Hardy showed off his craggy grin. 'Wouldn't that be amazing?'

Hunt had left an hour ago.

Now, dusk settling outside the window, Hardy sat at his desk in the quiet office, a legal pad in front of him. It wasn't too soon to put in some time on the outline of his closing argument, which would center prominently on his 'some other dude' scenarios – people with legitimate motives to want Rick Jessup dead; not only Goodman and Lo but any of the individual girls abused by Jessup in Lo's places, or perhaps their boyfriends, if they had boyfriends.

He wondered if he was getting ahead of himself with his enthusiasm for Tony Solaia as another plausible suspect. Probably, he thought. From the beginning, he had been all but certain of Mose's factual guilt, and all the evidence still convicted him. So it didn't really matter if he got a little enthused over Tony's possible involvement in the crime, even though he had nothing approaching evidence and no way to go about trying to collect any. If, indeed, any existed. But, he reminded himself, he didn't need proof. All he needed was to create reasonable doubt in the mind of one juror. And if Tony's presence in the narrative, however tangential, gave even Hardy a moment of almost reasonable doubt, it had an excellent chance of affecting a juror in a similar way. That could only be a good thing for Mose's defense.

The other side of his affirmative defense would be an attack on the Ramey warrant and Vi Lapeer's takeover of the case, which she clearly had done for political reasons. Once again, Liam Goodman was to figure prominently.

All this was to the good, he supposed.

He stopped writing, laid his pen down next to the pad, asked himself the big one: if he were on the jury, what would he think?

On trial was a man with a demonstrated propensity for violence who, upon learning that his daughter had just been raped – now firmly established – had taken a handy weapon, driven to the home of the assailant, and beaten him to death.

Did Hardy believe that? Did the evidence support it? Was there any real alternative scenario that answered to these facts for which there was any shred of evidence?

Nights like this one were when he had always come to the solutions that characterized his past successes. In the majority of those cases – in every one that he could recall – those solutions had come with an understanding of what had happened, of what was the actual, literal truth.

What was he missing tonight? What was he overlooking, ignoring, fooling himself about?

He was getting up to go around his desk and throw a few rounds of darts to clear his mind when his cell phone rang. He pushed the button to pick up and said, 'I'm on my way, just walking out the door.'

'I'm not calling about that,' Frannie said. 'I just got off the phone with Susan. Brittany's with her.'

'Is she all right?'

'Not great, no.'

'Did Tony hurt her?'

'No. But it's Tony, all right.'

'What?'

'He appears to have dropped off the face of the earth.'

The last call of the night was a late one.

Hardy had told Glitsky to call him back at any time and it was eleven-fifteen when the phone rang in the kitchen. 'What up?'

'I just got off the phone with Schuyler. Tony's gone.'

'We know he's gone. What happened to him?'

'No one knows.'

'His marshal doesn't know?'

'Apparently not.'

'Do you believe that?'

'I don't think Schuyler does, but that's what he told me. You saw the picture this morning?'

'Who didn't?'

'Evidently, nobody didn't. Schuyler says the cover's blown, which I'd agree with. He's either out of the program, or they're pretending he is.'

'So how are we going to find him?'

'I'd say, offhand, we're not.'

'He just up and left?'

'That's how they do it, Diz. No good-byes. Just poof, you're disappeared.'

37

A PROSECUTOR IN a murder trial is unwise if he fails to establish that someone is, in fact, dead.

To this end, Stier called San Francisco's seventy-seven-year-old medical examiner, John Strout, who, despite his years, was still a very sharp tack indeed. Quite often, Strout's was uncontested testimony, presented pro forma to a jury without objection. With the shock of Tony's disappearance roiling through his guts, Hardy was just as happy to sit through this part of the trial, where, for better or worse, he didn't have much to say anyway.

Thin almost to the point of emaciation, with wispy white hair and wearing a coat two sizes too large, Strout spoke in a deep Southern drawl as he laid out the results of his forensic examination of the body.

'. . . no question as to the cause of death,' he was saying in response to Stier's question, 'which was blunt-force trauma to the head. The only real question was which of the blows did him in, or whether it was some combination.'

'Doctor, can you say with certainty how many times Mr Jessup was hit?'

'Not 'xactly. From those that left impressions on the skull, I estimate about eight.'

'Do you have a professional opinion about what he was hit with?'

'Not with real specificity. I can only say that it was a hard, blunt object. Whatever it was had some distinctive protrusions, and the surface of it also may have been smooth-textured rather than rough.'

'Why do you say that?'

'If it was somethin' rough, it would have abraded the skin at the edge of the blows. There wasn't any sign of that, or very little.'

'Were any of the blows strong enough to leave an impression on the victim's skull?'

'Yes. Three of them broke the cranium, and five left an impression. There were two other contusions on the scalp, one on the upper-left forehead and another just above the left ear.'

'Were there any other bruises on the victim's body that you found significant?'

'Yes. There was a recent heavy bruise and a small fracture on the victim's left forearm, probably from defending himself against the attack. At least consistent with that, anyway.'

'Doctor, you mentioned that the smooth texture of the blunt object caused little abrasion on the skin. Does that mean these injuries did not bleed?'

'No, not at all. Head injuries don't need to have a lot of broken skin to get a lot of blood.'

Next to Hardy, Moses seemed to grow more tense as the testimony went on. Hardy noticed Amy surreptitiously putting a hand gently over Mose's hand, then withdrawing it. Mose seemed to be taking controlled, shallow breaths, almost reliving the moment of the attack. Or at least that was how Hardy read it, and he was afraid the jury might as well. Leaning over, he whispered, 'Relax. Think about something else. Find a juror and make eye contact. Chill out.'

Over the next hour, Strout's dry recitation of injury was punctuated by Stier's presentation of a series of genuinely horrible color photographs of Jessup both at the scene and on the autopsy table at the morgue. Of the fifty available photos, Gomez had permitted Stier to use ten. They were plenty.

Finally, it was Hardy's turn.

Hardy knew Strout well. In his earlier life, when Hardy worked as a prosecutor in this very building, he'd had many dealings with the medical examiner, none of them rancorous. Strout was a character whose office was a mini-museum filled with instruments of death, from a rumored-to-be-live hand grenade that he used as a paperweight to a variety of actual murder weapons and assorted medieval instruments of torture.

Hardy had nothing serious for him now, but he did have a little tiny something; his core belief was that you never let anything pass; you were a duck, bent on nibbling the prosecution to death. Good defense work involved getting the maximum out of the smallest prosecutorial flaw, misstatement, oversight, or lack of specificity.

Standing up, Hardy gave Moses a quick buck-up squeeze on the arm – a bit of spontaneous camaraderie for the jury to witness, good guy to good guy – and then came around and stood in front of the witness chair.

'Dr Strout. Good afternoon.' Hardy, familiar and easygoing, a friend to the court, even to prosecution witnesses. 'You have no way of knowing exactly when Mr Jessup died, do you?'

'There is no medical way to determine that, no, sir.'

'What about the possibility of taking the corpse's temperature? Can't that lead you to fix the time of death?'

'Not really. There are too many variables – temperature in a room can change. This here room had an open window, I understand. Bodies can cool at different rates, depending on the amount of fat in the body. In this case, it appeared the man had been dead at least several hours, so the body was approaching ambient temperature. There's lots of formulas and rules of thumb out there. Practically every pathology book has got a couple, but you can't use 'em in any particular case, 'cause it's entirely possible you'd be just plain wrong.'

'So to repeat, in this particular case, there's no way of knowing?'

'Not medically. Of course, he had to die between the time somebody saw him alive and the time somebody found him dead. Maybe you could narrow that down by other evidence at the scene, but I can't help with that except to say what's possible.'

'Doctor, can you say with any certainty how long it would have taken Mr Jessup to die of his injuries?'

'Not really, no. But they were very serious.'

'But he might have sustained them – that is, the attack on him could have taken place – sometime before five o'clock?'

'Yes.'

'How much time, would you say? What would be the maximum?'

'I can't say.'

'Would an hour be possible? Could Mr Jessup have lived for an hour with these injuries?'

'He could in theory, I suppose, yes.'

'Can you, in fact, Doctor, put any limit on the amount of time that passed between the attack on the victim and his death?'

'Well, as I said, the last time we knew he was alive, I suppose. After that.'

'But it could have been shortly after that, could it not? A few minutes to an hour or two, right?'

'I can't rule that out.'

'Thank you, Doctor. No further questions.'

Next up was the sergeant in charge of crime scene investigations, Lennard Faro. Like Strout, Faro had been at his job for a long time and was good at it. Pretty much the sharpest dresser on the police force, Faro sported a soul patch under his lip, and his hair was carefully groomed. Today he was dressed all in black – slacks, shirt, tie, coat – although it was impossible to say whether in deference to the victim or simply as a matter of personal style.

Faro's testimony was also Stier's opportunity to introduce to the jury more color photographs taken at the crime scene. Usually, for a violent murder, they tended to be graphic and powerful enough to lend an atmosphere of true drama to the proceedings. By now, no one on the jury was dealing with an abstract event. You can talk all you want about concepts such as reasonable doubt and burden of proof, but their meanings differ in the context of a horrible and brutal crime that took the life of a handsome young man.

Moses was again having trouble controlling his visceral reaction. His eyes were glassy and focused on the courtroom's floor in front of the defense table, and he kept his hands clasped tightly in front of him. Hardy wished he could get his client to tamp down his reactions, but in truth, he realized that the photos could literally make a person sick, and the fact that Moses took them so seriously might help to humanize him to the jury.

Finally, with the photos now marked as prosecution exhibits, Stier came back to the witness. As he'd done with Strout, he walked Faro through the details of the crime scene. As the jury could see, there was a lot of blood on the hardwood floor and under the head. There was no other sign of struggle in Jessup's apartment; he'd fallen a few steps inside the door, and that was where he'd died. When they'd arrived, the front door had been unlocked, because the cleaning lady had opened it that morning upon discovering the body and calling 911. The door did not appear to have been forced open. Stier thanked the witness and gave him to Hardy for cross.

This was precious little for Hardy to work with, but again – nibble, nibble – he thought he had a couple of crumbs.

'Sergeant Faro, you've testified that the door showed no sign of forcible entry, is that right?'

'That's correct.'

'Was there a peephole in the door?'

'Yes.'

'Did you happen to notice whether it was working? Whether it was obstructed by anything?'

'No. It worked fine. I looked through it to make sure.'

'So Mr Jessup, inside, could have looked through that peephole and been able to identify the person standing outside his door?'

'If he looked, yes, he could.'

'And the door opened inward, did it not?'

'Yes.'

Hardy longed to make an argument here. If Jessup, knowing that he'd raped Brittany the night before, and remembering his beating at the hands of McGuire two months ago, saw him standing outside his door, how could he possibly be so foolish as to open the door to him? But Hardy couldn't make that or any argument. At least not now.

Besides, he had one other small but decent point. 'Sergeant, the photographs show a great deal of blood on the floor, do they not?'

'Quite a bit, yes.'

'And isn't it your standard procedure for your crime scene investigators to make every effort to keep from disturbing the crime scene?'

'Yes.'

'And was there any disturbing of the crime scene, particularly the blood, that you identified or noticed?'

'No.'

'Were there any identifiable footprints in the blood? That is to say, footprints that could be compared to a pair of shoes?'

'No.'

Hardy needed to pound this point home. 'How about unidentifiable footprints – that is, a pattern that came from a shoe – even if there was not enough detail later to compare to a shoe. Did you find any of those?'

'No.'

'How about a disturbance in the blood that might have been a footprint? Did you see any of that?'

'No.'

'How about any sign that anyone had touched or interfered or come into contact with that blood in any way?'

'No.'

'If you'd seen anything like that, we'd have close-up photos to show it, wouldn't we?'

'Yes.'

'And as an experienced crime scene investigator, you're very aware that it would be important to see and document that kind of evidence?'

'Yes, sir. I am.'

'So you were very specifically looking for evidence like that and did not find any, is that right?'

'Yes.'

'Were you the only crime scene investigator at the scene?'

'No. There were several of us.'

'And they all have similar training and various levels of experience, correct?'

'Yes.'

'So we might think that even if you inexplicably missed such evidence, someone else on your team could have noticed and documented it.'

'Well, I was the one doing the blood, but yes, if another investigator saw anything like that, they would bring it to my attention.'

'So, Sergeant, we may be comfortable that there is no evidence whatsoever that the assailant in this case stepped in that blood or touched it in any way?'

'There was no such evidence.'

'Thank you. No further questions.'

Hardy felt pretty good for the fifteen seconds it took Stier to demolish his argument. 'Sergeant Faro,' he began. 'If the assailant stepped in blood during this struggle, could later bloodshed or blood flow have covered up any sign that he did so?'

'Yes. Absolutely.'

'And do you have to step in blood to get it on you?'

'No. In this case, there was obvious evidence of spatter and spray from the infliction of injuries that could have got on an assailant without him stepping in blood.'

Stier let out a little breath, decided he had all he needed, and excused the witness.

The next few witnesses were a wash. Stier wanted to show that the CSI team had done a thorough job. Hardy pointed out that the thorough job had produced no useful evidence. Had they checked for fingerprints? Yes. Found any? No. Cloth and fiber analysis? Yes. Nothing worth testing. Crime scene reconstruction and blood spatter. Absolutely. And what did it prove? Nothing that made any difference. Somebody had beaten Rick Jessup to death, but everybody already knew that.

38

THE DAY WAS flying by as Stier immediately established the significance of the blood at the scene with witnesses who testified about the hiking boots in McGuire's closet, the testing showing blood on those boots, and finally, the DNA technician who conclusively demonstrated that the blood came from Rick Jessup. Stier did the same with Mose's Giants jacket and the car. There was no doubt about it. Jessup's blood was on all of it.

All Hardy could do was remind the jury that Jessup's blood on those things didn't necessarily make Moses the murderer. After all, they knew that Moses had fought with Jessup before. Why couldn't the blood have come from that fight?

Hardy stood for his cross on Sergeant Natalie Morgan, the blood expert from the police lab. 'Sergeant Morgan,' he began, 'you've testified that the DNA testing you did matched blood from the car, the Giants jacket, and the hiking boots to the sample taken from Mr Jessup at the autopsy, right?'

'That's right.'

'How old was the blood on the boots?'

'I beg your pardon?'

'The blood on the boots. How long had it been on them?'

'I don't know.'

'Is there any way to tell?'

'No, unless it's old and has degraded.'

'And how old would old be?'

'Depending on conditions – for example, if it were exposed

to extreme weather – it could degrade in a matter of weeks, but under normal conditions, the blood would be identifiable for a few months, at least.'

'A few months, at least?' Hardy picked it right up. 'Had this particular blood degraded?'

'No.'

'And the same is true of the blood on the jacket, is that right?'

'Yes.'

'How about the blood in the car? Had that degraded?'

'No.'

'Just to be clear, Sergeant, the blood that appeared on Mr McGuire's hiking boots, and on his jacket and in his car, might have been on these articles of clothing for a matter of months. Is that correct?'

'Yes, I'd say it is.'

'Now, did that blood get directly on those objects from Mr Jessup?'

'I don't understand your question.'

'Well, supposing, for example, that Mr McGuire had gotten Mr Jessup's blood on his hands somehow. Could he have transferred that blood to the Giants jacket?'

'Yes.'

'If he got in his car, could the blood on his hands have gotten into the car?'

'Yes.'

'If he took off his boots, could the blood on his hands have gotten on his boots?'

'Yes.'

'So, for example, if Mr McGuire had punched Mr Jessup in the nose and given him a bloody nose, that could account for all the blood that's been found in this case, couldn't it?'

'I don't know myself where any of this blood came from. I just know that samples were delivered to me at the lab. But yes, blood can be transferred, so if your question is can the blood from somebody's hands be found later on objects that the person touched, the answer is yes.'

Hardy went on, 'And your testing is remarkably sensitive, isn't it?'

'Yes, very.'

'A tiny, almost invisible drop of blood could produce the results that you've testified about, right?'

'Right. Even a sample invisible to the naked eye could give us these results, but we only tested areas where we could see blood.'

Finally, it was time for Stier's coup de grâce. Sergeant Clay Brito from the crime lab was a large man of about fifty, gray-haired, sallow-skinned, and if looks were any indication, utterly humorless.

'Sergeant Brito,' Stier began, 'do you have a specialty in the crime lab?'

'Yes. I am a firearms and tool mark examiner.'

'What do you do in that capacity?'

'As my title indicates, I identify the marks left when one object interacts with another under pressure. This includes pattern injuries and ballistics testing – bullets fired from specific guns make specific microscopic indentations that are unique to each firearm environment. Similarly, I'll look at firing pin and ejection marks and such on gun shell casings, again microscopically. Over the years, I've specialized in the analysis of the impressions that various tools and weapons – hammers, brass knuckles, rings, and so on – make when they come into contact with various other surfaces, such as skin, leather, plastic, wood. Really, whenever one object meets another, there may be some sign of it left on one or both of the objects, depending on their relative hardness, density, and the like. Everything from a key in a piece of clay to a boot mark on a piece of skin.'

'A boot mark on a piece of skin, Sergeant? Does human skin take and hold an impact mark? A pattern injury?'

'Yes, absolutely. The most common one probably being a bite mark, but even if the skin isn't broken, it may retain the identifiable characteristics of the impact weapon.'

Stier walked to the evidence table and turned over a movie poster-sized blowup of a photograph that he introduced as a prosecution exhibit and then set up on an easel so Sergeant Brito and the jury could see it.

Hardy could see it, too, and though it wasn't unfamiliar to him, he wasn't happy about what it depicted. Taken from the Wall of Shame at the Little Shamrock, it was a picture of a grinning Moses McGuire about two years before, holding the shillelagh up as though he were a caveman with, yes, his club, about to brain somebody. The original color picture evidently had been taken with a high-quality camera; even blown up to poster size, the detail of the grain and the small bumps on the knob end of the club were clear.

'Sergeant Brito,' Stier began, 'have you seen this picture, People's Number Fifteen before?'

'Yes.'

'Would you please identify for the jury the object that the defendant is holding.'

'It's a club of hardwood. Judging from the grain, it is probably ash. It is cut at one end, but the other end is a pronounced natural knob.'

'Can you tell us anything else about this club, Sergeant, which is commonly called a shillelagh?'

'I can. By comparison with the size of nearby objects in the photograph – the beer spigots, particularly, but also the defendant's head – we can say with confidence that the object is twenty inches long, about an inch and a half thick at the tapered end, three and a quarter inches at the knob. If it is ash, it should weigh between two and a half and three pounds.'

'Sergeant, do you see any distinctive markings on this shillelagh?'

'Yes. There are four. They are the dark specks on the knob in this picture.'

Stier, well prepared, returned to the evidence table and introduced two other poster-sized photographs as People's #16 and #17, which he set up side by side, each on its own easel.

Hardy, squirming, knew what was coming. It was gruesome; it was compelling.

'Sergeant, could you please identify these two posters for us?'

Brito might as well have been describing mud drying. 'On the left is a blowup of the shillelagh picture we've already seen, focusing on the knob and its four distinctive points, which I've labeled A, B, C, and D.'

Hardy knew those points. Even after all the years and the wear and tear and rubbing away, they protruded slightly enough to feel. You couldn't miss them.

'The other,' Brito went on, 'is a close-up of the victim's shaved head.' Stier projected this picture on the screen next to the shillelagh. The jury had already seen it during Strout's testimony. It was one of the autopsy photos. It hadn't gotten any prettier.

A low groan made its way across the gallery, and Gomez picked up her gavel, then let the reaction run its course.

'Sergeant, do you have a professional opinion about the pattern injury we see in the picture on the right?'

Brito pulled out a laser pointer. 'Well, we can clearly see the A, B, C, and D points reflected in the pattern here on the scalp. They appear to be exactly the same relative distance from one another and assume the same shape when taken together. In my opinion, the shillelagh depicted in the photo here was used to inflict the injuries in the autopsy photo.'

'What supports that opinion?'

'The shillelagh is not a machine-made object, nor does it appear to have a common configuration such as a jack, a tire iron, or a hammer. The injury had to be caused by either that shillelagh or one exactly like it.'

'Thank you, Sergeant.' Stier turned on his heel with buoyant confidence. 'Your witness, Mr Hardy.'

There was no escaping the damaging nature of Brito's testimony. Hardy knew he could bring up technical objections until he turned blue, but he doubted that he would convince even one juror that the shillelagh was not the murder weapon.

That did not mean he didn't have to try.

Getting up from his table, Hardy took a moment to glance down at his legal pad, although he didn't need a reminder of what he was going to say.

'Sergeant Brito,' he said when he arrived in front of the witness, 'the reason you say it was the shillelagh or something exactly like it is because in the photo, the shillelagh has four protuberances that appear to match four injuries to the victim's head. How do you know that those four injuries came from a single blow?'

'Well, I don't.'

'So any object with a knob could have been used to hit the victim four times, and you'd get the same result, wouldn't you?'

'In my opinion, that's extraordinarily unlikely. First, the four injuries aren't precisely the same, just like the four knobs on the shillelagh are not precisely the same. So you'd have to use four separate objects exactly like the four knobs on the shillelagh and then deliver the blows in precisely the same relative positions as if he'd been struck by the shillelagh.'

'So they're not exactly the same, but each of those knobs is simply a rounded protuberance, isn't it?'

'Yes.'

'It is possible, is it not, that an object with a rounded

protuberance like that could have been used to hit the victim four times and left these marks?'

'I can't say it's impossible. Most things are possible. In my opinion, it was the shillelagh.'

Hardy knew that it wasn't much, but it was the best he could do, especially since the experts he'd consulted had all told him the same thing – the murder weapon was the shillelagh or something very much like it.

Hardy took in the jury briefly as he turned to walk to his table – no one was asleep today. Then, as though he'd just remembered something important, he whirled back around. 'The shillelagh,' he said, raising a finger. And then he was at his place in front of the witness, to all appearances newly energized. 'Sergeant, you've described the shillelagh in People's Number Fifteen and Sixteen in some detail. Size, weight, identifying protrusions, heft, and so on. Tell me, where did the crime scene locate this shillelagh that they brought to you for your analysis?'

'They didn't.'

'I'm sorry. Could you repeat that?'

'They didn't.'

'They didn't locate the shillelagh?'

'No, not that I know of. If they did, they never brought it to me to analyze.'

'Well, then, Sergeant, how did you make your analysis of it?'

Brito hesitated and tried to look behind Hardy to get some kind of a clue from Stier. But there was no help from that quarter.

'I analyzed it using assumptions that could be made from the photograph.'

'But you've never seen the actual shillelagh?'

'No.'

'Sergeant, were you present when the picture of Mr McGuire holding the shillelagh was taken?'

The question sent a ripple of humor through the gallery; even the witness seemed to think it was funny.

'No,' he said, 'of course not.'

'So you have never held the shillelagh in that photo or seen it close up or anything like that?'

'That's correct.'

'So, Sergeant, how do you know it's real?'

'What do you mean?'

'Well, you've been calling the object in the photo a shillelagh, which is a heavy wooden club, correct?'

'Yes.'

'How do you know what the object in the photo is made of?'

Hardy knew that the exchange galled the bejesus out of Stier. Try as they might, the police hadn't found a single witness from the Little Shamrock who would admit to even having touched the shillelagh Moses kept behind the bar. They would say it was there and that it looked real, but every other question about the shillelagh was met with an indifferent shrug.

Brito said, 'It appears in the photo to be an actual shillelagh, so presumably, it's made out of heavy, hard wood.'

Sometimes Hardy simply loved the theater of the courtroom. Now he went back to his desk, where he'd left his huge lawyer's briefcase. Opening it to the gasps of the gallery, he withdrew a twenty-inch length of what looked for all the world like Kentucky ash, with a tapered lower end and a distinctive knob on the other end.

When he had shown the exhibit to Stier during pretrial motions, the prosecutor had gone crazy, telling Gomez it was simple fraud, an active attempt to deceive the jury. Hardy countered that it was no such thing; they were not going to claim it was the murder weapon or the object in the photo. All it did was prove that no one could tell from the photograph that Moses McGuire might have had access to what might have been a murder weapon. And Gomez had agreed.

As Hardy walked forward to offer it as an exhibit in evidence, the rumble behind him got loud enough that Gomez lifted her gavel. *Bam bam bam.* 'The court will come to order.' Finally, Hardy was standing in front of Brito as the last of the murmuring subsided.

'Sergeant,' he said, 'do you recognize this club that I'm holding, Defense B?'

'It looks like the shillelagh, the murder weapon.'

'I'm going to ask you to assume that this is neither the murder weapon nor the object in the photo. Would you agree that it looks like both?'

'Yes.'

'And what, based on your analysis of this visual inspection, would you estimate as the weight of this shillelagh?'

'I'd say somewhere between two and a half and three pounds.'

Hardy handed it to the witness. 'Sergeant, holding the shillelagh in your hand, would you estimate its weight?'

Brito was not happy with this development. He glared at Hardy with true contempt. 'Two or three ounces,' he said. 'It's a fake.'

'It's not a fake at all,' Hardy said. 'It simply is what it is. Which, Sergeant, would you agree is an object made out of something like Styrofoam that looks like a shillelagh?' Taking it from the witness, he placed it on the evidence table. 'I'm sorry, I didn't hear your answer.'

'Yes. It's an object made out of Styrofoam that looks like a shillelagh.'

'No further questions,' Hardy said, then, to Stier, 'Redirect?'

Ugly, on his feet, in clipped tones. 'Sergeant Brito, referring to People's Number Seventeen, the photograph of the victim's shaved scalp, did you have an opportunity to see the pattern injury on the victim's head in the coroner's office?'

'Yes.'

'Did you take the picture of it, seen here in People's Number Seventeen?'

'I did.'

'Did you edit the photograph in any way?'

'No.'

'So this was a very real pattern injury inflicted by a very real instrument of exactly the kind you've described, is it not?'

'Yes, it was.'

'Thank you, Sergeant,' Stier said, shooting a withering look at Hardy. 'You may step down.'

39

BY THE END of lunchtime, Hardy knew little beyond the bare fact of Tony Solaia's disappearance. Wyatt Hunt had located his apartment building in the Tenderloin and had talked his way inside. The manager had verified that the tenant had come in with another man – 'some kind of cowboy' – and the two of them had packed up what little goods Tony had and moved out the day before in the middle of the afternoon. They had a small U-Haul into which Tony pulled his motorcycle. He had left no forwarding address, although the manager suggested that Hunt try the post office, which he did to no avail.

For all intents and purposes, Tony Solaia was gone.

When they got back to court, and no doubt in response to Sergeant Brito's testimony regarding the shillelagh, Stier called David Wickers.

The drunk from the Shamrock shambled nervously up through the bar rail. His collar-length hair, today combed straight back and tied into a ponytail, retained a trace of its natural blond, which went with his eyebrows and his powder-blue eyes. He wore Sperry Top-Siders, no socks, tan Dockers, a purple shirt with a black leather tie, and a tan corduroy sport coat.

Stier didn't waste any time. 'Mr Wickers,' he began, 'would you call yourself a regular customer at the Little Shamrock bar, owned by the defendant on trial here, Moses McGuire?'

'I guess I would. I'm there most days.'

'How long have you been a regular there?'

A little laugh. 'At least as long as I can remember.' He turned to the jury, chuckled again. 'Which is about yesterday.'

Gomez gaveled away the courtroom's response. 'Mr Wickers,' she said, 'this is no place for jokes. This is a court of law, not a barroom.'

Dave's head went down in contrition. 'Sorry. I guess I'm a little nervous.'

'Fine. But please answer Mr Stier's questions seriously. Understood?'

'Yes, ma'am. Sorry.'

'Do you remember the question, Mr Wickers?' Stier asked.

'Not exactly.'

Another wave of laughter.

'I'll repeat it. How long have you been a regular at the Little Shamrock?'

'I'd say seven or eight years.'

'On average, how many days of the week do you find yourself there?'

Frowning in concentration, Dave pulled at his collar and tie. 'Pretty much every day, if I'm not sick. And sometimes then.'

'So nearly every day, is that right?'

'I'd say so, yeah.'

'And during your many days there, did you have occasion to notice a club, sometimes called a shillelagh, that the defendant kept there?'

'Sure. It was always there, hanging under the bar.'

Dave described the shillelagh with great accuracy and identified it as the club or weapon held by McGuire in People's #15. 'Have you ever held that shillelagh?' Stier asked him.

'No.'

'Nevertheless, from your observations of Mr McGuire's handling of it, could you estimate its weight for the jury?'

'I don't know. Heavy for its size. Maybe three or four pounds.'

Stier paused for a lengthy moment and then, realizing that he'd gotten about all from Mr Wickers that he was likely to, turned him over to Hardy. Who, because he knew something Stier could not know, bounded up out of his chair like a much younger man.

'Mr Wickers,' Hardy began, 'when you say you are a regular at the Little Shamrock, do you have a regular seat where you usually sit?'

'I sure do, and everybody knows it.'

'And where is that?'

'The stool at the front corner of the bar, by the window.'

'And the bar is L-shaped, is that right?'

'Yeah.'

'And you sit at the corner on the short side, facing the long side of the L, right where it turns?'

'Right.'

'So, just to get this clear; if you're sitting in your regular seat, you're looking straight down the long line of the L along the top of the bar, is that right?'

Dave closed his eyes, making sure, then nodded. 'Right.'

Hardy paused to let the positioning sink in. He crossed back to his table and picked up his legal pad, which, for once, he was going to use. 'Now, you've testified that the shillelagh was, and this is a quote, "always there, hanging under the bar." Is that correct?'

'Sounds like it. That's where it was.'

'Under the bar? It was under the bar?'

'Yeah, down under by the beer spigots.'

'And those beer spigots are on the long L of the bar, too, are they not?'

'Of course.'

'The bartender doesn't have to turn around to pull a beer, in other words?'

'Right.'

'The shillelagh is under the bar, by these spigots? You're sure?'

Dave rolled his eyes. 'Come on, already. How many times do I got to say it?'

'Is that a "yes"? The shillelagh is under the bar by the spigots?'

A weary sigh. 'Yes. All right. Yes.'

'Well, then, Mr Wickers, tell me this. How do you see the shillelagh under the bar from where you're sitting on your stool?'

For an instant, Hardy thought Wickers looked uncannily like an intelligent dog, trying to work out the meaning of some obscure phrase like 'get the ball.' Finally, he said, 'I'm not sure what you mean.'

'I mean you're sitting at the end of the L, looking down the length of the bar along the top of the L. How do you see what's under the L?'

'Well, it's always been there.'

'It's not there now, Mr Wickers, is it?'

'I don't know. I don't think so. We were talking about it being gone.'

'So when was the last time you saw the shillelagh hanging under the beer spigots? A couple of months ago? A year ago?'

'I don't think it was that long.'

'When was the last time you specifically remember actually seeing the shillelagh hanging under the bar or in the bar at all?'

Wickers closed his eyes again, took a few breaths, pulled at his collar and tie, then opened his eyes and shrugged. 'Sorry, but I just can't say. I don't remember.'

Stier's next witness established that when police searched the bar, the shillelagh was nowhere to be found.

After Gomez called the afternoon recess, Amy leaned over in front of Moses and said to Hardy, 'What did you put in your cereal this morning? You're tearing it up in here today.'

Hardy looked around behind them and whispered to her. 'With Dave, it's almost cheating.'

'You know what's really pathetic?' McGuire put in. 'I've talked to that guy like two hours every day, five days a week, for the last five years.'

'That's a long five years,' Hardy said.

'That's a long first two hours,' Amy replied. 'Five times a week for five years. If I knew that guy was coming in every day – no, never mind.'

'I'm trying to remember one single thing we talked about.'

'I don't think that'll turn out to be a productive use of your time, Moses.' Amy was all business. 'Who's up next, you think?' she asked.

Moses asked, 'Doesn't recess mean we take a break from talking about the trial for a few minutes? I mean, we were almost having some fun there with Dave for a second or two.'

'Fun?' Hardy deadpanned to Amy. 'He's joking, right?'

Next up was Inspector Sergeant Lee Sher.

Crisp and professional in her uniform, she took the stand and sat with an air of expectation as Stier introduced into evidence both an original tape recording and the transcript that Sher had vetted.

Hardy had read the transcript in his discovery papers, and it had led to his biggest fight with Moses of the entire ordeal. Because, contrary to Hardy's explicit orders, and more than a little drunk, the client had made the decision to basically spill his guts to his two arresting officers, who'd had the good sense to place a recording device under the backseat of the police car.

That disastrous decision, Hardy knew without a doubt, would be coming back to bite them.

'Inspector Sher,' Stier began, 'please tell the court how you are connected to this case.'

'When Richard Jessup's death got called in to the Homicide Department, my partner, Paul Brady, and I were assigned to investigate. Over the course of the next few days, we identified the suspect and eventually arrested him for Mr Jessup's murder.'

'Where did this arrest take place?'

'At the defendant's bar, the Little Shamrock, on Lincoln Way near Ninth Avenue.'

'And what is your procedure when you arrest a suspect, Inspector?'

'The first thing we do is inform the suspect that he is under arrest, and then we read him his Miranda rights warning.'

'And what is that?'

'It basically informs the suspect that he is under arrest, he has the right to an attorney and the right to remain silent, although if he does choose to speak, anything he says can and will be used against him.'

'And did you read Defendant McGuire his Miranda rights upon his arrest?'

'We did, yes.'

'And what do you do next?'

'Well, if there is no resistance from the suspect or medical issues to deal with, we handcuff the suspect and put him in the back of a police car, after which we drive him downtown to the Hall of Justice for booking and processing.'

'And is that what you did with the defendant in this case?'

'Yes.'

'Thank you.' Stier walked over to the evidence table. 'Sergeant, I'm going to play a tape recording for you, and at the end, I'm going to ask if that was a full and accurate recording of what the defendant had to say on the way to the station after he'd been arrested.'

Hardy spent an excruciating half hour trying to show no reaction while listening to an obviously drunk McGuire do exactly what Hardy had told him not to do.

When the tape was finished, Stier asked Sher, 'Did you tell the defendant he was being taped?'

'No.'

'Were you or Inspector Brady asking any questions?'

'No. We just let him talk.'

'So, during the ride to the station, Mr McGuire said, "He needed killing, and I'm glad he's dead."'

In his ongoing plan to stay on the good side of the judge, Hardy had been trying to limit his objections, but this was too much. He rose to his feet. 'The tape speaks for itself, Your Honor, and is in evidence. It is inappropriate to ask the witness to repeat bits and pieces of it out of context.'

'Sustained, Mr Stier. The jury has heard the tape, and they'll have it in the evidence room if they need to hear it again.'

That was small comfort to Hardy. Gomez was exactly right. The jury had already heard, and would certainly hear again, his client's drunken rave: 'Either of you have kids? No? What do you think you'd do if you had a daughter and found out some little punk had first beat her and then raped her? You think you'd sit around wringing your hands? C'mon, you guys are cops. You'd go and handle things, wouldn't you? Tell me you wouldn't. Because sometimes the law doesn't get it right.'

Hardy decided to let Sher go.

After she had left the courtroom, the judge said, 'Mr Stier, your next witness?'

Stier replied, 'Your Honor, the People rest.'

PART
FIVE

40

HARDY SPENT A great deal of the weekend at his office in the company of Amy Wu and Gina Roake. At issue was their SODDIT defense, upon which they were basing most of their hopes. They were there to draft a response to a motion that Stier had served on them and filed with the court late on Friday afternoon. It was entitled 'People's Motion to Exclude Speculative Evidence Regarding Possible Third-Party Culpability.'

Upon the first quick read-through, Hardy thought it sounded a death knell to their hopes. Stier, no fool at all, had seen where Hardy planned to go with his witnesses and had moved to head him off at the pass.

Both Goodman and Lo had been subpoenaed and were on the witness list and would be available to the court on Monday morning. Both had reason to dislike or even hate Rick Jessup and feel either a threat from him (Goodman) or a passionate urge to punish him (Lo), so both had an arguable motive to want him dead. Similarly, six of Lo's women had been assaulted by Jessup and possibly subjected to who knew what other humiliations; either they or their protectors might be assumed to have a motive to kill the victim as well.

On an entirely different level, the disappearance of Tony Solaia might be played into a major issue. Viewed starkly, Tony was perhaps the best alternative suspect Hardy could present to the jury, assuming the judge allowed it. Tony had, after all, been the first person to hear about the rape. He was Brittany's boyfriend, at least, if not lover. He'd had access to the shillelagh on Saturday night, and he had no alibi for any part of the next day. Add to that the stunning revelation that he was already in the witness protection program – someone who had turned against his former comrades in crime and would provide evidence against them in return for the government dropping charges against him, charges that apparently included murder for hire – and Tony Solaia should certainly be a person of interest in the murder of Rick Jessup.

But there was huge disagreement among his team over how to play the card. Amy and Gina were convinced that they should ask for a dismissal but settle for a mistrial. Clearly, the prosecution had failed to turn over exculpatory evidence: one of their principal witnesses was a murderer being protected by, and getting money from, the feds. Even if Stier didn't personally know this – and Hardy had no way to find out – they would argue that he should have. The bottom line was that even if Gomez wasn't inclined to find it was anybody's fault, a badly tainted witness had testified, and the defense hadn't had the opportunity to confront him about all the dirt in his past. It was simply unfair.

As a second separate issue, Tony was still subject to recall by the defense, and they couldn't call him because he'd gone away, probably with the assistance of the federal government. Again, direct governmental interference with the defendant's right to a fair trial. Even if Gomez couldn't blame Stier, Hardy had a powerful argument that they should get a do-over for this reason alone.

Gina had told Hardy bluntly that she didn't think the trial was going well. Brilliant tactician though Hardy might be, the Big Ugly was eating his lunch on every major issue with every single witness. In Gina's opinion, it couldn't get worse. It was time for a legal Hail Mary, whatever that might be. They'd had a chuckle over the possibilities. In fact, Amy had added, the issues supporting a mistrial were so clear and their arguments so strong that the court of appeal might very well find Hardy and Amy ineffective if they didn't ask for one. Amy didn't know about Hardy, but she planned to continue in the practice of law for quite some time, and it didn't help bring in clients for a court of appeal to publicly label you incompetent.

Hardy wasn't sure a mistrial would be to their advantage. It wasn't like Moses would get out on bail or the case would be dismissed; it just meant a do-over in sixty days, and as bad as the case was, he couldn't think of anything likely to make it better.

In the end, it was a moot point. Moses flat-out vetoed the idea. He wasn't going to start over and endure more time in jail and more expense while his attorneys prepared for another trial. That wasn't going to happen.

Their last problem was with what was formally called the 'third-party culpability' defense. All along, Hardy, Gina, and Amy had known the problem was substantial if not insurmountable: for any evidence related to another suspect to be admissible, it wasn't enough to produce a possible motive, even a great motive. It wasn't good enough to produce a motive and show opportunity. No. The defense not only had to produce a *specific other person* with motive and opportunity, they also had to show direct or circumstantial evidence linking the third person to the actual perpetration of the crime.

This was a high hurdle, particularly in the cases of Goodman and Lo.

Goodman had informed Hardy first thing Saturday morning that he was bringing his own lawyer to court on Monday morning and, if it came to it, he would dispute the admissibility of his testimony with the judge. Liam Goodman was not about to get on the stand and admit to unproved allegations that showed he had hated Jessup and defrauded the U.S. government. Did Hardy think he was that naive? He could prove where he had been during every minute of the Sunday when Jessup was killed, beyond which there was no direct or circumstantial evidence linking him to the perpetration of the crime, words he actually used, which meant – no surprise, since he was a lawyer – that he was prepared.

Lo, for his part, was in Los Angeles over that weekend, so actual perpetration of the crime was an impossibility for him, too. Whether or not Lo knew that, Gomez would, and if Hardy could not convince her otherwise, she wouldn't admit the questioning of Lo.

That again left Tony, whom Hardy had reserved the right to recall, if they found him. Hunt had done a fine job of tracing the U-Haul truck but had lost the trail in Salt Lake City, at which time Hardy called him off.

So of their three 'other dudes,' two might be ruled inadmissible by Gomez, and the third, also possibly inadmissible, could not be found.

Hardy had argued third-party culpability before, and had prevailed, but this time out, he did not have a specific person to implicate in the actual crime, as he'd had with his previous successful arguments. Also, he had the feeling that his scattershot approach – proposing three alternative suspects instead of a single most likely one – might work against him.

And if the jury wasn't going to hear about other suspects, where did that leave his client? Had Hardy adequately refuted any of the prosecution's claims?

Motive? No. Means? No. Opportunity? No.

By Sunday night, he was as close as he'd ever gotten to true panic. This was why you never wanted to let your client talk you into going to trial as soon as it could be calendared. Hardy, after finally discovering the motives of Goodman and Lo, had no time to connect motives to either of them or to any other specific person. He had no time to discover more details about the other case Tony was involved in. He had no time, period, for everything else that needed to be done.

Frannie came into the living room where he was sitting in his reading chair, binders piled around him, reading none of them. She moved his feet over and sat on the ottoman in front of him. 'You ought to go to sleep.'

He shook his head. 'I'm freaking out here. I think I've based my whole damn case on a bad premise.'

'You always feel that way.'

'That doesn't mean I'm wrong this time.'

She rubbed a hand on his leg. 'Come up to bed. It'll look better in the morning.'

'If Gomez turns me down on third party,' he said, 'then all I've got left is rush to judgment – the whole Lapeer situation – and the problem with that, notwithstanding O.J., is that it's not a real legal defense. So the judge looks at me and says, "Fine, Mr Hardy, but why should we care that the police acted as they did? They didn't break any laws, they made a righteous arrest. The evidence accuses the defendant. What's the problem?"'

'She won't say that.'

'She will. She will say exactly that. Unless I can talk her out of it.'

'Which, history argues, you can. As you say, it worked with O.J.'

Hardy barked. 'Hah. There's a precedent you want to follow.' He sighed again. 'This could be over quick, you realize that?' He hesitated, then lowered his voice. 'You should plan on going down and talking to Mose in the next day or two.'

'I will.'

'Before the verdict would be better.'

'Thank you. I'll try to keep that in mind.'

'I'm sorry. I don't mean to nag. I'm tired.'

'I think that's why I came in here. Something about you coming to bed.'

41

As soon as Gomez entered the courtroom on Monday morning, Hardy made his pitch for a dismissal, based on the new evidence about and the disappearance of Tony Solaia. As predicted, the judge refused the dismissal and offered a mistrial, which Moses, on the record, said he did not want and would not accept.

After a forty-five-minute recess to read Hardy's response to Stier's third-party-culpability motion, Gomez reentered the courtroom. It was clear that she was pumped up. The courtroom was packed. She took the bench much more briskly than was her custom, took notice of one and all, apologized for her tardiness, and then greeted the jury by dismissing them to the jurors' waiting room while the court held a hearing about some matters that had come up over the weekend.

After the jury had left, Gomez wasted no time. 'Mr Hardy, earlier the court allowed you to add to your witness list the names of Mr Goodman and Mr Lo, both of whom are presumably outside the courtroom in response to your subpoenas today, and both of whom knew Mr Jessup. The court has reviewed your response to "People's Motion to Exclude Speculative Evidence Regarding Possible Third-Party Culpability" and has a few questions for you regarding the testimony you hope to elicit from these witnesses.'

Hardy got to his feet. 'I hope I can answer them to your satisfaction, Your Honor.'

'We'll take your witnesses separately, beginning with Mr

Goodman. Without going into details of the specific areas of your speculation, you argue in general terms that Mr Goodman had a motive to kill Mr Jessup. Assuming even that your speculation is true in every detail, Mr Hardy, and that Mr Goodman's motive was strong and compelling, do you have any direct or circumstantial evidence you'd now like to introduce that ties Mr Goodman to the actual perpetration of the crime against Mr Jessup?'

'Not in so many words, Your Honor, but—'

Gomez held up a hand. 'Not that it would be sufficient, either, but do you have any evidence of Mr Goodman's opportunity to have killed Mr Jessup?'

'No, Your Honor.'

Gomez nodded, looked down in what seemed to be true disappointment, then came back at Hardy. 'I am assuming that you read Mr Stier's motion, is that correct?'

'Of course, Your Honor.'

'Did you not note the sixteen separate cases he cited that rejected mere speculation as admissible without direct or circumstantial evidence linking the third person to the actual perpetration of the crime?'

Hardy took as a bad sign the judge's repetition of the exact phrasing of the decision in *People* v. *Hall,* the controlling Supreme Court case. 'I did, Your Honor.'

'And in what way, barring the introduction of such new evidence, did you hope to circumvent this well-established precedent?'

'I thought by the time we got here, Your Honor, that my investigator would have uncovered some evidence more strongly linking Mr Goodman to the crime.'

'But your investigator has not done that?'

'No. But I had hoped to question Mr Goodman more about his opportunity to have committed the crime.'

'Although you know that opportunity alone, even in the presence of motive, does not rise to the level of admissibility?'

'Yes, Your Honor. As I say, I had hoped to discover direct or circumstantial evidence.'

'By questioning Mr Goodman on the stand? Hoping for a Perry Mason moment, were you? Am I to assume the same general answers about your reasons for listing Mr Lo as a witness?'

Hardy could choose to brazen it out and debate each separate part of the discussion, but Gomez was making crystal-clear her unhappiness, even disgust, and if he wanted to stay alive to fight another battle – at least two more of which were coming – he could not risk incurring any more of her wrath.

'I have no direct or circumstantial evidence linking Mr Lo to the murder of Mr Jessup, if that's what you mean, Your Honor. And none to introduce.'

'That is exactly what I mean, Mr Hardy. And given that' – she tapped her gavel – 'I'm granting Mr Stier's motion to exclude the testimony of these witnesses.' She turned to the bailiff. 'Call in Mr Lo and Mr Goodman. They will both be excused.'

The judge called another recess, and Gina, sleep-deprived and anxious nearly to the point of distraction, made her way up to the bar rail within seconds. Bushwhacked by the speed and decisiveness of Gomez's ruling, she needed a few minutes of postmortem to put this devastating defeat into some kind of context. And then, having pretty much failed at that for the first ten minutes, she moved on to their next possibility, their next strategy. 'Do we have evidence on Tony?' she asked Hardy. 'Anything remotely serviceable?'

After reading Stier's motion the past Friday night, they had from the start been skeptical of their success. Because of that, Hardy, Gina, and Amy had decided not to include any mention of Tony in their response on third-party culpability, which would only exclude him out of hand, as Gomez had done with the first two. When, in fact, there were significant differences about Tony's situation.

This meant if they ultimately decided to go there, they'd have to duke it out in court without a written motion to prepare the judge and opposing counsel for their argument. 'We've got new information,' he told Gina, 'or at least information the court hasn't heard—'

'But here comes the judge,' Gina said. 'Put on your dancing shoes, Diz. You're going to need 'em.'

'Mr Hardy,' Gomez began, 'are you prepared to call your witnesses? Should I call the jury back in here?'

Hardy rose to his feet. 'Not quite yet, Your Honor. There is another third party whose behavior and personal situation – of which the defense only recently became aware – meets the standard of admissibility, we believe.'

Stier wasn't inclined to let this pass. He pushed his chair back and stood up. 'Your Honor, the People strongly object. Counsel has filed no motion with respect to this latest individual, so the People will have had no time to prepare a response. Meanwhile, we have no facts, no offers of proof, nothing upon which to base admissibility.'

'Your Honor,' Hardy countered, 'as I mentioned, we've only recently become aware of some of these facts, which I now intend to present to the court and which I believe the court will find compelling.'

Gomez didn't like it one bit, but she didn't want to give Hardy grounds for appeal because she hadn't allowed him to present all of his evidence. 'All right, your objection is noted, Mr Stier, but the court is inclined to let defense counsel make its case and then make a ruling. Mr Hardy, who is this latest third party?'

'He has already appeared before the court as a prosecution witness, Your Honor, and I have reserved the right to recall him. Tony Solaia.'

Gomez frowned in concentrated memory. 'The gravamen of whose testimony, if I recall, contradicted the defendant's daughter's statement that she hadn't told the defendant about her rape until after Mr Jessup was dead. Do I remember that correctly?'

'Yes, Your Honor.'

'And why should I not include Mr Solaia in my earlier ruling about the admissibility of third-party culpability?'

'Several reasons, Your Honor. First, unlike Mr Goodman and Mr Lo, who both had alibis for the period while the crime was being committed – and therefore could not have been the perpetrators of the crime – Mr Solaia had no alibi. Second, he was romantically involved with Brittany McGuire, and she told him about the rape right after it happened, so his motive is every bit as persuasive as the defendant's purported motive. Third, as the bartender at the Little Shamrock, he had access to the shillelagh, which the prosecution proposes as the murder weapon.'

'All this is well and good, Mr Hardy, but I think I've already made it clear that you've got to get beyond the mere possibility that some third party might have been involved in Mr Jessup's murder. Without a show of actual evidence . . .' She picked up her gavel.

'We do have information rising to the level of evidence, Your Honor, which the jury needs to hear.'

'And what is that information?'

Hardy paused only an instant before he plunged in. 'Tony Solaia is not his real name. His real name is unknown to the defense. He is in the federal witness protection program, where he will be testifying against his former colleagues in a human trafficking ring in exchange for pardon of his own crimes, which include murder for hire.'

'Oh, for the love of . . .' Stier couldn't restrain himself, slapping his hand down on the table and almost knocking over the chair in his haste to get up. 'Your Honor, just when you think you've heard it all, Mr Hardy's imagination seems to know no bounds. How does he expect the court to believe any of this nonsense?'

Hardy shot back immediately. 'What I think the court should find unbelievable, Your Honor, is that the prosecution flagrantly violated its constitutional duty to turn over this obviously exculpatory evidence about one of its key witnesses. This is a clear violation of my client's fundamental right to a fair trial, and if Mr Stier didn't know about this, he absolutely should have.'

'Both of you, stop it. We've done this. Mr Hardy, I've already told you, I'm not giving you a dismissal. You and your client have said that you don't want a mistrial. Do you have any proof to put before this jury directly connecting Mr Solaia, or whatever his name is, to the murder of Mr Jessup?'

'Flight is clearly established in the law as a sign of consciousness of guilt, and it rises to the level of circumstantial evidence. And unusual as these events may appear, they are all true, and I can and will call witnesses to testify to their truth.'

Gomez was shaking her head in either frustration or wonder. 'I admire your pluck, Mr Hardy. I really do. And leaving aside the question of whether you could in fact produce a witness to corroborate any or all of it, I have heard nothing that links Mr Solaia, or whatever his name is, to the actual perpetration of the crime.'

'Your Honor, the man is a paid assassin with motive and opportunity to have killed Mr Jessup. The jury needs to know this information.'

Gomez nodded a few times, perhaps internally phrasing her response. 'Mr Hardy,' she said at last, 'I'm sorry, but case law doesn't agree with you. And neither do I. Your motion to include this line of testimony is denied.'

After lunch, where he couldn't force himself to swallow a bite of Lou's Special, whatever it had been, Hardy was down to his last round of ammunition. He was fighting the unassailable feeling that it would turn out to be a blank.

He had San Francisco's chief of police on the stand. Stern, formidable, humorless, and articulate, Vi Lapeer cut an imposing figure of authority and rectitude. She sat back in the witness chair, one leg crossed over another, arms on the chair rests, relaxed and comfortable.

Battered by the morning's results, Hardy nonetheless had to summon some feeling of confidence that Lapeer's involvement in the case had weakened it for the prosecution. But if it was weak, then why was he so worried? On the other hand, if the evidence convicted Moses, was it his intention to criticize Lapeer and her inspectors for gathering it as quickly, legally, and thoroughly as they could?

As he approached his place in front of the witness box, all of these doubts – legitimate questions about what he was trying to accomplish with this witness – came tumbling down around him. He thought it had been clear enough in the run-up to this moment, but now suddenly the clarity with which he'd viewed his entire strategy seemed to have become muddied.

Worse, any talk of a conspiracy to obstruct justice between Goodman and Lapeer might inadvertently lead to a similar accusation against him and Glitsky. It might lead to a discussion about their collaboration, their long-standing friendship, past cases in which they had both been involved. Hardy knew that certain rumors, even after all this time, had underground currency in some parts of the legal community. It was for this reason that Hardy, working on his interrogation of Lapeer, had decided not to call Abe as a witness after all.

Once people started pointing fingers, it could get ugly.

And now these were the waters he was about to wade into with Lapeer, right after his every idea had been shot down, just when he felt that the tide of his energy was at dead low.

But there was nothing for it. He was here. He had to begin.

'Chief Lapeer,' Hardy began, 'are you directly involved in the running of the Homicide detail?'

'Not usually, no.'

'But in this case, you did take a hands-on role, is that correct?'

'Yes, it is.'

'Could you tell the court briefly how that came about?'

Lapeer, ostensibly only too happy to oblige, said, 'Certainly. I got a telephone call one afternoon from Supervisor Goodman, who was the employer of the victim in this case, Rick Jessup. He was concerned that the investigation wasn't producing any results, and he supplied me with the information that the defendant here, Mr McGuire, had come to their offices a couple of months before and had beaten up Mr Jessup. This seemed relevant to the investigation, so I brought it to the attention of the then head of Homicide, Lieutenant Glitsky, who brought in the two inspectors working the case, Sher and Brady, and passed it along to them.'

'Did Sher and Brady already have the information that you gave them?'

'Yes. Essentially. They had identified the defendant as a possible suspect.'

'They were actively working the case, is that right?'

'To all appearances, yes.'

'They had put together six-packs of photographs to use in eyewitness identification, had they not?'

'Yes.'

'With Mr McGuire's picture as one of the six?'

Lapeer nodded. 'That's how we do it.'

From behind him, Hardy heard Stier's chair creak and the familiar 'Objection. Relevance of this line of questioning?'

'What is your point, Mr Hardy?' Gomez asked.

'The point, Your Honor, is that because of the actions of Chief Lapeer, all of the eyewitness identifications in this case are fatally tainted.'

'All right. The objection is overruled. You can try to make your point, but be careful.'

'Yes, Your Honor, thank you.'

Buying himself some time, Hardy walked back to his table and pretended to read from his legal pad. He shot a quick look at his client's face, at Amy Wu's waiting for him expectantly, and in that instant he couldn't shake the feeling that it was all falling apart. Coming back to his spot in front of the witness, he started again.

'Chief, you've testified that you got involved in this case because of a telephone call from Supervisor Goodman. Did he tell you why he was interested enough to call the chief of police?'

'I presumed it was because the victim worked for him and he wanted to make sure that the investigation was moving forward.'

'Could he have called Inspectors Brady and Sher with the same information?'

'Yes, I presume so.'

'And yet he chose to bypass them and come directly to you?'

'Apparently.'

'In the aftermath of that phone call, you went to Homicide to convey the information, did you not?'

'I did.'

'Did you specifically discuss the defendant, Moses McGuire?'

'Yes.'

'After Mr Goodman put pressure on you to show some tangible

results, didn't you urge the inspectors to proceed by investigating Mr McGuire as the prime suspect?'

'At the time, he was the only suspect.'

'It's a yes-or-no question, Chief. Did you not tell the inspectors you wanted results with the identification of Mr McGuire as soon as possible?'

Lapeer waited, obviously hoping for an objection, but none was forthcoming. Shifting her position in the witness chair, she nodded. 'Yes.'

Feeling he was about halfway back to solid ground, Hardy wanted to keep her in a rhythm with easy 'yes' answers. 'Chief Lapeer, do you believe that you conveyed to your two inspectors your sense of urgency about identifying Mr McGuire?'

'Yes.'

'To the exclusion of all other suspects? Yes or no.'

Lapeer broke a deep frown, looked again at Stier, let out a breath. 'Yes, but—'

'So your inspectors went out to show their six-packs of photographs to these purported eyewitnesses, knowing full well that Mr McGuire was the only right and acceptable answer, isn't that true?'

'Objection.'

'Sustained.'

Hardy said, 'Let me rephrase. Chief, you've just said that Mr McGuire was the only suspect, correct? And you told your inspectors that you expected them to make an arrest, right?'

'Not in those words.'

Though it wasn't a direct answer, Hardy let it pass. 'So when they went out with Mr McGuire's photos, they knew you expected them to get an identification.'

'Objection. Speculation.'

'Sustained.'

'That's okay, Your Honor, I think I've made my point.' Hardy knew he wouldn't have to remind the jury about Dr Paley's testimony on this topic: a whole body of evidence that police can influence witnesses simply by knowing the correct 'answer' to a test, equally applicable in a six-pack identification or a physical lineup.

Hardy had gotten basically what he wanted out of Lapeer. But he wanted more, felt – especially after the disastrous morning – that he needed more. So he took a breath and asked, 'Chief, do you know a San Francisco businessman named Jon Lo?'

Stier nearly yelled in his disgust and fury. 'Objection! The court has already ruled on this issue.'

'Not in this context, Your Honor,' Hardy shot back.

'Close enough,' Gomez said. 'Sustained.'

Hardy took another tack. 'Chief. You know how to obtain an arrest warrant, do you not?'

'Yes.'

'And typically, that involves running the case by the district attorney, who agrees that the case merits prosecution and goes to a judge to file charges and order the arrest of the defendant. Isn't that the way things work?'

'Sometimes.'

'And by "sometimes," Chief, you mean far more than ninety-nine percent of the time, don't you?'

'I can't give you a number.'

'Out of the hundreds of arrest warrants that get issued in San Francisco every year, you know for a fact that all but a handful go through that process, don't you?'

Lapeer had to admit that she did.

'But that's not what happened in this case, is it? Here, you bypassed the district attorney and had your inspectors go directly to a judge so they could arrest Mr McGuire with no assurance whatsoever that the DA would file charges against Mr McGuire based on the evidence you'd gathered thus far. Isn't that true?'

'You could say that.'

'Yes, I could, Chief. And outside of the desire to get your name in the paper, appease some powerful local politicians, and have Mr McGuire spend a couple of days in jail, there was no reason to do that, was there?'

'Objection. Argumentative.'

'Sustained. Mr Hardy, you can probe this area, but please control the tone of your questions.'

Swimming against the current, Hardy went on in the same vein for another five or six minutes. By the end of the questioning, he had not made a dent in the evidence – the blood, the eyewitnesses, the motive, and the shillelagh that formed the core of Stier's case. However, he was at least reasonably certain that no juror doubted Lapeer had pressured her inspectors to make an arrest for political reasons.

Maybe, Hardy told himself, maybe that was something.

42

As soon as Hardy excused Lapeer, the judge called the early-afternoon recess, and Gina Roake got up from her seat in the back of the courtroom. She walked up the center aisle until she got to the first row, where Susan Weiss had been sitting day after day since the beginning of jury selection, the very picture of the steadfast wife, hanging in there in support of her husband, while Moses was in the midst of deep conversation with his two attorneys, all three of them apparently buoyant after Hardy's handling of the chief of police.

Gina, despite herself, was impressed that Hardy got in as much as he did. She'd spent the entire weekend in the office with him and Amy. After receiving Stier's motion to suppress the third-party-culpability question, they all knew they would be in deep trouble when court reconvened this morning. Hardy had been hoping against hope that Wyatt Hunt or blind fate would pull a rabbit out of the SODDIT defense hat.

Maybe they'd be able to identify one particular bodyguard among Lo's entourage who seemed plausible as a true suspect in the murder. Maybe Goodman, under the pressure created by Hardy and Hunt that had impelled him to call his own attorney, would crack and confess to the crime. Maybe Tony Solaia would be found and brought back to testify and possibly incriminate himself.

But, of course, none of those things happened.

This morning, Hardy – against Gina's prediction that the judge would not allow him to call Lapeer, as she had disallowed any mention of Lo and Goodman – had not only gotten her onto the stand but done a creditable job of demonstrating the pressure that Goodman had brought to bear on her and that she had in turn passed on to her inspectors. Hardy had given the jurors a clear reason to believe that the eyewitness testimony was tainted.

Long shots all, but a vigorous and creative defense.

And one, Gina believed with all her heart, that had no chance.

Now there would be nothing left but the closing arguments, and then the jury, having no real alternatives to consider, would come back with a guilty verdict.

Yesterday afternoon, late, after Wu had gone home, Gina and Hardy had shared an Oban in the solarium, kicking around their options. Finally, Hardy sat back, his feet on the huge round table, upended his glass of Scotch into his mouth, and – joking around – said that if they got shut out on the motions tomorrow and wound up with essentially no affirmative defense, there was only one last thing that could be done. And Gina would have to do it. Except for the minor flaw that the idea was insane. They'd had a laugh about it.

But then afterward, back home, Gina got to pondering both the flaws and the enormity of Hardy's insane idea, and she hadn't slept one minute.

Now she was up to where Susan sat in the first seat on the center aisle of the gallery, eyes glazed and forward, hands crossed in her lap. Tapping her gently on the shoulder, Gina felt the need to introduce herself again. After all, they had barely met. Then Gina whispered in a tiny voice, 'I wonder if we could talk for a minute outside.'

Even when working a case as sensational as the Jessup killing, Homicide inspectors never ran out of other work.

Now Paul Brady sat in one of the interrogation rooms just off the Homicide detail with a suspect named Leon Brice.

Leon was nineteen years old. He was in the stolen-cell-phone business generally, but he had run into some bad luck with his latest victim, a twenty-three-year-old Stanford Ph.D. candidate in mechanical engineering named Jason Eichler. Actually, it had been worse luck for Jason, who was now dead, but things didn't look good for Leon, either, who, when he'd been apprehended, was in possession of no fewer than six cell phones, one of them belonging to Jason's girlfriend, Lily Faraday.

The way it had gone down – Lily's testimony – was that she and Jason were at Rome Burning on Saturday night. Lily had put her brand-new four-hundred-dollar phone down on the table for the time it took her to turn her head and order another drink, and when she turned back, it was gone. Later that night, Jason had run the GPS app to locate the phone and texted a message to it, offering a reward.

Yesterday at around eleven A.M., Jason had gotten a call from Lily's phone offering it in exchange for the reward, which was how much again? Jason said a hundred dollars, and the voice on the phone described himself: 'Black, Afro, five-ten, one-sixty, nice grill on my mouth, black tennies, camo cargo, black T-shirt, standing at the corner of Leavenworth and Ellis. You won't miss me.'

Rather than making any attempt to notify the authorities, who Lily believed would do nothing anyway – 'For a cell phone? I'm sure' – the chivalrous, brilliant, and utterly clueless Jason drove down to the meeting place, one of the most godforsaken intersections in the city, with Lily; saw Leon standing in a small posse of guys; then pulled over.

After telling Lily to take off in the car if there was any sign of trouble, Jason got out, waited for her to get in the driver's seat, then crossed the street to conclude the transaction. When Leon produced the cell phone, before Jason gave him the money, he said he wanted to make sure the phone worked, so he stood there, surrounded by gangsters, punching in apps and phone numbers, waiting for answers from a couple of his friends, including Lily, who screamed at him to give the guy his goddamn money and get the hell out of there.

Next – Lily had rolled the window down and heard the entire exchange – Jason decided that since he had the phone in his possession and Leon had no rights, since he had stolen it, he was in a good bargaining position. Reaching for his wallet, he pulled out a twenty.

That led one of Leon's confreres to grab at the wallet, after which things got out of hand quickly, with punches being thrown and cell phones clattering out onto the street. Jason, a triathlete as well as a scrappy and skilled fighter, kicked at a couple of the guys, swung at a few more, then went to grab for his wallet, which they'd torn from his hands and was now on the street.

Leon leaned for the wallet at the same time, Jason pushed him and he went down, Jason went to punch him, and then there was a shot, and another shot, and the brave and foolish Mr Eichler went down and did not get up. Lily, following Jason's instructions, slammed on the accelerator and fishtailed the BMW down the street.

Now Leon was regaling Brady with his version of events. 'So I'm walking down the street, minding my own business, I see like six, eight phones just lying there. That's where I got 'em. What am I gonna do? Leave 'em sitting there? I don't think so. Leon Brice's mother don't raise no fools.'

'There wasn't a body – a dead body – anywhere near these phones? They were just sitting there in the street?'

'I never seen no dead body.'

'How about the witness who described you and what you were wearing, by your own description, and has picked you out of a lineup with a positive identification?'

'What? She white. I'm black. That ain't likely holding up.'

'What about the gun you had on you when they picked you up? You find that too lying in the street?'

'It *was* in the street.'

'Where you'd just thrown it, Leon. Where your arresting officer saw you throw it.'

'That just ain't true. I ain't never carryin' no piece. You can ask anybody.'

Brady knew it was going to be a long couple of hours before he got anywhere substantive with Leon, and it wouldn't hurt to let their suspect sweat for a while in the tiny booth. Besides, outside the window, Lee Sher had come over with a very pretty woman of about his age and was giving him the high sign to come out.

'You keep thinking up things you think I'll believe, Leon,' Brady said. 'I'll be back in here with you in a little while.'

'Hey,' Leon said. 'How about a Coke? I could use a cold Coke.'

'I'll see what I can do.' Brady opened the door into the blessedly cool main room, turned, and made sure he'd closed and locked the door.

'Paul.' His partner looked a bit sick to her stomach. 'This is Gina Roake, one of Dismas Hardy's law partners. The McGuire case. She's got a statement she wants to make.'

For a long moment after Sher turned off her tape recorder, the two inspectors on either side of their back-to-back desks were silent. Until finally, Sher said, 'I'm a little appalled here, Ms Roake, by how sleazy this is.'

Brady nodded in agreement. 'You expect us to believe this?'

'I don't care whether or not you believe it. It's the truth.'

'I don't think so,' Brady repeated.

'Well, you're welcome to that reaction, of course.' Now that Gina had told her story, her fatigue rose up and almost turned her legs to jelly. She all but held herself up against the side of

Sher's desk. 'But whether you believe it or not, you are obligated to convey it to the district attorney.'

'I don't think so,' Sher said.

Brady added, 'It's a little late for discovery. The trial's almost over.'

'"Almost" is the operative word, Inspector. I've just come from the courtroom, and they haven't delivered closing arguments yet, probably won't until tomorrow. You have new evidence in this case. It's not my place to tell you what to do, but you know as well as I do that you've got to give this to the DA, and the DA has to give it to the defense. Under *Brady*' – here Gina broke a small smile – 'and with your name, I know you'll be familiar with *Brady,* you don't have a choice.'

Gina was referring to *Brady* v. *Maryland*, a Supreme Court decision declaring that the defense had a right to any *prosecution* evidence that might cast doubt on a suspect's guilt. The DA had to hand over absolutely everything – evidence, testimony, background, interviews – that might serve to exculpate the defendant.

'You know,' Brady said, softening his tone, hoping to reason with her, 'if you testify to this, it would be perjury, ma'am. You could go to jail.'

'It wouldn't be perjury.' Gina remained calm, resolute. 'It's not perjury,' she repeated. 'Because it's the truth.'

Sher leaned toward her. 'And you haven't mentioned this until now? How could you, a lawyer, have done that?'

'Being a human being,' Gina replied, 'I kept hoping it wouldn't be needed. But today the defense case pretty much blew up. As to why I wouldn't want to bring it out at all, that's pretty obvious, isn't it? It's going to cause severe pain and suffering to his family, on top of everything they've been through.'

Sher turned to Brady. 'This is unbelievable.'

He nodded. 'You realize we're going to go back and check your phone records for that date. And McGuire's. We're going to know where both of you were every second that afternoon and evening.'

'I'm telling you where we were,' Gina said, 'and you're wasting time.'

At her desk outside of Wes Farrell's office, Treya Glitsky was wearing a telephone earpiece and whispering into it. 'I don't know what it's about, Abe, but they're screaming bloody murder in there. It's got to be about Moses.'

'Who's doing the yelling?'

'Mostly Brady.'

She could almost hear her husband break one of his rare smiles. 'Gee, wouldn't it be awful, if in their rush to find something on Moses, they didn't get around to something else that might have been important?'

'That's what this seems like. Whoa!' She looked over at the closed door. 'Somebody just hit or threw something.'

'Is anybody screaming in pain?'

'Not yet.'

'You say it's Gina in there with them?'

'Yeah. She looks terrible. Well, for her. Still better than the rest of us.'

'I doubt that,' Abe said, 'but what do you think she's got?'

'No idea. But it's got to be huge.'

'Is court still in session downstairs?'

'I'd assume so. I could check and let you know, get back to you in five. You thinking of coming down?'

'It might be fun.'

'Where are you now?'

'Believe it or not, I'm with Bill Schuyler in the Fed Building. I'm working with Wyatt Hunt, trying to get some kind of line on Tony Solaia.'

'After this, maybe you won't need him.'

'Your mouth to God's pretty little ear. Meanwhile, if you could find out whether they're still in court . . .'

'I'll get right back to you.'

If not bona fide arrows, Hardy thought he had at least a couple of darts left in his quiver. He had the theory about how the blood came to be on McGuire's boots, and the jury had heard it. The entirely plausible possibility was that Moses had inadvertently stepped in Jessup's blood while beating him up back in February outside his office in city hall. The blood had worked its way between the sole and fabric – indeed, that was where it had been found. Of course, Stier had established the beating in his case in chief to show Moses's animosity toward Jessup and Moses's potential for violence. But given the importance of the blood evidence, Hardy wanted to reinforce it now. The only problem was that his witness was Joseph DiBenedetto, of Liam Goodman's staff, who had not witnessed the beating. So to get anything, what Hardy needed was not just that there had been a beating but that Moses had drawn blood, and to get that, Hardy was wading through a sea of hearsay objections from Stier, most of them valid and most sustained. The young man had been on the stand for the better part of forty-five minutes, and Hardy had just about decided to let him go and concentrate instead on Goodman's admin, Diane, who had at least met Moses and witnessed the opening minutes in the exchange that led to the beating. Then a chorus of murmurs from the gallery made Hardy stop and turn to see Wes Farrell coming down the center aisle, followed by Inspector Sher, then a stone-faced Gina Roake, followed by Brady.

'Your Honor,' Farrell said as he got to the rail, 'please pardon the interruption. Permission to approach the bench?'

Gomez looked the question down at Hardy, who was technically in the middle of the examination of his witness. He said, 'No objection, Your Honor. In fact, I'll excuse this witness.'

'Mr Farrell,' Gomez said, 'you may approach.'

Farrell, with unaccustomed fury in his eyes, pushed open the low door in the railing. Coming abreast of Hardy, he slowed down and punished him with a flat and hostile glare. Turning his whole body away from the jury, he brought his mouth close to Hardy's ear and whispered, 'This bullshit is beneath you.'

In the judge's chambers, havoc and anger had been the order of the day. Gomez had no choice – Gina Roake's testimony had to be heard. Everyone knew that if any evidence were ever discovered or came to light, Farrell would prosecute her for perjury to the fullest extent of the law. Hardy stood, most of the time, mute and in shock. Whatever this was felt and smelled like disaster. He knew that he had joked about the scenario with Gina the night before, but never in his wildest imaginings had he envisioned her coming forward this way, with this story. When at last the meeting in chambers broke up, the principals began moving back toward the courtroom, where court would reconvene in fifteen minutes.

Hardy stood just outside the door to the women's restroom and met Gina as she was emerging. She gave him a tense and trembling smile. 'Are we having fun yet?' she asked.

He couldn't dredge up any kind of response. He motioned with his head, and she fell in next to him. They both were intimately familiar with the back rooms of the Hall of Justice, and Hardy, gripping her arm tightly above the elbow, quick-stepped her along to an empty interrogation room down by the elevators. Leading her inside, he turned and closed the door, placing his foot against it so it couldn't be opened. Whirling on her, he said, 'Now what?'

'Now you get me on the stand and I tell my story.'

'Gina . . . Jesus Christ.' He ran his hand through his hair. 'This can't work. This is insane.'

'What is?'

'Please. What are you doing?'

'I'm telling the truth.'

'You can't—'

'I can. I most certainly can. You've lost, Diz. Stier has won with every witness. If Moses goes to jail, you and Abe and I might not be far behind him. Don't you realize that? Are you willing to risk it? Doesn't it matter to you?'

'Of course, but—'

'No "buts," Diz. They've shut down every affirmative defense. This is the only chance.'

'But it's perjury. It's a lie.'

'It's not a lie. It's the truth.'

'You know it's not. It's an idea we laughed about last night. It never really happened.'

'I'm telling you that it did.'

He shook his head. 'Gina, please. You can't win this way.'

'You can if it's the only way. And none of us can afford to lose.'

'We don't know that. We don't—'

'We can't take the chance.'

'This is no chance. The jury won't believe it.'

'Yes, they will. I'll make them believe it.'

'And then I'm supposed to argue it in my closing?'

'You do what you've got to do. I do the same. You're the one who always says it: we're all grown-ups here on this bus.' Gina stood facing him, feet spread, arms crossed. 'This is happening, Diz. You're going to question me, and I'm going to tell my story on the stand.'

'I can't do that.'

'You have to. I'm swearing to you right now that it's the literal truth, every word. Let the jury decide.' Gina checked her watch. 'We've got three minutes. I'm not changing my mind. What's happened has happened.' She stepped toward him. 'Let's go,' she said with a sudden gentleness. 'It'll be all right.'

Hardy felt in many ways that nothing would be all right ever again.

The attorneys, the judge, the court recorder, and the district attorney had returned to the courtroom, and now Gina Roake raised her right hand and swore that the testimony she was about to give was the truth, the whole truth, and nothing but the truth.

Numb, Hardy stood in front of her. He was Moses McGuire's attorney, sworn to give his client the best defense allowed by the law. And here he was, about to solicit testimony that might convince a jury to acquit.

Even though he knew it was a lie.

She could swear forever that it was the truth, and he would always know it was a lie.

The plain fact was that she had told him, as she would swear in court, that it was true. It was neither his job nor his moral obligation to expose flaws in her testimony but, rather, to solicit it. He could not prove she was lying, he told himself. And even if he could, that was not his job.

He hated the rationalization, knowing that it, too, was false; nevertheless, there was nothing else he could do. As he would have to do for any other client, he was obliged to put on this evidence. 'Ms Roake, what is your relationship with Mr McGuire?'

'We have been friends for six or seven years.'

'Has that friendship included physical intimacy?'

Gina looked away from Hardy, over to Moses, out to Susan at her place in the gallery. 'Yes, it has.'

A low buzz ran through the gallery. Somebody said, 'Holy shit.' Susan brought her hands up to her mouth at about the same instant as Moses lowered his head and covered his eyes. Several of the jurors, already alert to the fact that something extraordinary was afoot, exchanged glances, coming forward in their seats. At the defense table, Amy Wu leaned over and whispered something in McGuire's ear, her hand resting possessively on his forearm.

'Ms Roake,' Hardy continued, 'did you recently come forward to the police with information about this case?'

'Yes.'

'Where were you on Sunday, the first of April of this year, the afternoon of Rick Jessup's death?'

Gina, dark shadows showing like bruises under her eyes, took in a deep breath. With a series of questions and answers, Hardy had her put her account in front of the jury. 'I was at my apartment doing some writing in the late afternoon, four or five o'clock, when Moses – Mr McGuire – came and knocked at my door. He was very upset. He told me that his daughter had been raped the night before. He was beside himself with rage and helplessness. He didn't know what to do. He knew who his daughter's assailant was and where he lived because he'd had occasion to look up the address earlier, when he'd sought out Mr Jessup and gotten into a physical confrontation with him. Now he thought he wanted to go to Mr Jessup's apartment and kill him. I tried to reason with him and got him a little calmed down. After a while, he started crying in his helplessness, and I came and sat next to him, hoping to comfort him.' She let out a breath, took in the jury, and then quickly looked away. 'In any event,' she went on, 'one thing led to another, and we . . . we became intimate. When we got up several hours later, he took a shower, and then, just as it was getting light outside, he left.'

The courtroom had become dead silent. Susan Weiss stood up, turned her back to the court and her husband, and walked down the center aisle of the gallery and out the door.

Hardy stood without any movement. Finally, he nodded. 'Thank you, Ms Roake.' And to Stier, 'Your witness.'

The prosecutor took his time rising from his seat and moving to the center of the courtroom where he would face Gina. Before turning to her, he stood before the jury for a moment with a completely neutral expression, somehow conveying the notion that he was inviting them to share his skepticism and disdain.

But the wind was gone from his sails.

In all the time Hardy had known the Big Ugly, this was the closest he had come to feeling sorry for the man. He seemed confused and disorganized and did himself more harm than good in what followed.

He made the last quarter-turn toward the witness and began. 'Ms Roake, what is your profession?'

'I'm an attorney and a writer.'

'You write fiction, do you not?'

Hardy stood and objected. Somewhat to his surprise, Gomez sustained him.

'All right, let's talk about the attorney side of your profession. Are you affiliated with a firm?'

'I am a partner with the firm of Freeman Hardy and Roake.'

'And is the Hardy in the name of that firm in this courtroom?'

'Yes. Dismas Hardy is Mr McGuire's attorney.'

The courtroom broke into tumult. Gomez wielded her gavel, called for order, and eventually restored it.

'In other words, you are Mr Hardy's partner, is that right?'

'Yes.'

'Well, now, Ms Roake, might we assume that you are on Mr Hardy's side, as it were, and want to help him in any way you can gain an acquittal for his client?'

Gina shook her head. 'No more than I am on Mr Farrell's side. He was also my partner in the same firm, and he is your boss, is he not?'

Hardy caught Gina's eye and gave her a solemn nod. Stier, in his enthusiasm to take her down, had just made an unforced error, perhaps a costly one.

Clearing his throat, Stier took a different tack. 'As a lawyer, Ms Roake, I'm sure you realize that the testimony you've just given comes rather at the eleventh hour. Why did you wait so long to bring this apparently crucial evidence to light?'

'For obvious reasons, I was hoping it wouldn't be necessary, that we wouldn't have to involve Mr McGuire's wife or children, or that Mr McGuire's other defense options would prevail. But the judge ruled against almost all of them just this morning, which didn't leave the jury much if anything to consider in the way of alternatives. If I didn't speak up, they might convict him, and that would be a travesty.'

'All right.' This was a losing argument, too, and Stier seemed to realize it. 'Let's go to another point,' he said. 'Where is your home located?'

'It's on Pleasant Street on Nob Hill.'

'That's nowhere near the Marina District, is it?'

'Not really. Maybe two or three miles.'

'Ms Roake, we have heard three eyewitnesses tell the court that they saw the defendant walking through the Marina District in the late afternoon on Sunday, April first, carrying a clublike instrument. Can you see any way to reconcile your account with theirs?'

'No. They must have seen somebody else. Because he was with me from about two or three o'clock until the next morning. That is my sworn testimony, and it's the truth.'

Stier, shaking his head, let his shoulders sag in disappointment with Gina and, by extension, with humanity in general. 'I'm through with this witness,' he said.

Hardy stood up. 'Your Honor,' he said, 'the defense rests.'

43

FOR ALL THE heat and bombast of the trial, on Tuesday morning, the closing arguments from both sides were more or less methodical and anticlimactic.

Stier, going first, laid out the evidence that he'd presented – the eyewitnesses, the blood, the shillelagh impressions, the backstory between McGuire and Jessup, the immediate motive on the Sunday of the crime. He barely mentioned Gina Roake's testimony except to dismiss it as a feeble attempt to mislead the jury in a last-ditch effort in a losing cause.

For his part, Hardy spent the first chunk of his time talking about the blood on McGuire's boots and jacket and in his car, which simply had to be dealt with. He segued from that into a lengthy riff on Dr Paley's identification issues, arguing once again – the third time the jury had heard it – that if officers administering identification procedures knew or thought they knew the 'right' answer, they could and would unconsciously cue an eyewitness to guess the one suspect out of six 'correctly.'

Clearly, the officers in the case had been under undue pressure from their chief to identify McGuire and only McGuire as the prime suspect. Their urgency and certainty that Moses was guilty had no doubt conveyed itself to the eyewitnesses, fatally tainting their testimony. Hardy spoke about the physical evidence that the prosecution had not provided: there was no sign – no fingerprint anywhere, no DNA evidence, no fabric evidence, no nothing – that Moses had ever set foot in Jessup's apartment. This was no small thing, especially considering the violent acts that had gone on there that afternoon.

Finally, he came to the trump play: 'Ms Roake came forward on her own, under great duress. She knew that her testimony, especially its eleventh-hour nature, would subject her to torment and even ridicule. Only when events in the courtroom had forced her hand did she reluctantly come forward, knowing that the damage she would do to herself and the defendant's family would be significant. Still, she was willing to pay that price to prevent the conviction of an innocent man.

'Moses himself, meanwhile, had been the victim of his own guilt.

'But it wasn't murder he was guilty of. If you are to believe Ms Roake's sworn testimony, it was adultery. He had made up his mind that he would rather spend time in prison if that meant sparing his wife the pain of learning about his betrayal, or sparing his daughter additional pain about the rape she'd endured and the inconstant, perhaps even evil, nature of men.

'Rather than a coldly calculated trial strategy, as I'm sure Mr Stier would have you believe, Ms Roake's decision could not have been more agonizing to her and to everyone else it affected, and she will have to live with its consequences for the rest of her life. She has accounted for the whereabouts and activities of Moses McGuire on that Sunday afternoon and evening last April. The plain fact is that if you believe Ms Roake – and remember, this was testimony given under oath – then the absolute truth is that Moses McGuire did not kill Rick Jessup.'

Hardy considered sitting down, but there were a couple of last arguments he felt the jury needed to hear. 'Who did kill him, then?' he asked. 'We don't know. What we do know is that Mr Jessup was a despicable human being whom any number of people might have wanted to kill. Do you seriously think that Brittany McGuire was his only victim, the only woman he ever assaulted? A man who lures her to a bar with drugs in his pocket, coldly planning this most brutal of crimes? What about his other victims? Could not any of them have killed him? What about their lovers? Their brothers? Their boyfriends? Did none of them have a father who became as angry, as upset, as potentially violent as the prosecution claims Moses McGuire became?

'That reaction is a natural one. Any one of us, any one of you, might have had it. But the prosecution in this case never tried to find any of those other people who had the same understandable, if not justifiable, motive to kill this very bad man.

'But that vigilante, the man who killed Rick Jessup, was not, could not have been, Moses McGuire. Moses McGuire was somewhere else at the time the murder occurred, and now you have heard where that was. Let us remember one last time that there was no physical evidence implicating Mr McGuire in Mr Jessup's apartment.

'Finally, who did those witnesses see walking on the Marina sidewalks, holding something that came to be called a club, the more it got repeated?

'The answer is that they saw a man of average height and average weight in a Giants jacket, jeans, and hiking boots. As you have no doubt noticed sitting here in the same room with him during this trial, Mr McGuire is of about average height and about average weight. He has brown eyes and brown hair with streaks of gray and no visible distinguishing marks such as tattoos or scars.

'So the eyewitnesses who testified in this trial saw some man who looks like Mr McGuire, wearing the most popular jacket in the city of San Francisco. We don't have to know who that man was. We simply have to know that it was not Moses McGuire. And it could not have been. He was not there at that time.

'Remember, it is not up to us, Mr McGuire's defense team, to prove that he was not the killer, although we have done precisely that. Rather, it is up to the prosecution to demonstrate beyond any reasonable doubt that among Mr Jessup's other victims and their boyfriends and yes, fathers, there was not another man of average height, of average weight, wearing a Giants jacket as common as any garment in the city, with the same motive, who could have – indeed, who must have – committed this crime. They didn't do that.

'Sadly, because of the politics that have tainted this case at every juncture, they never even tried to do that.

'And that is why, for all of these undeniable reasons, because of all these reasonable doubts, you are obliged by law and your oaths as jurors to find Moses McGuire not guilty. Thank you.'

About forty minutes later, Hardy and Glitsky were sitting out in the main room at Sam's. Hardy had brought his martini over from the bar, and Stephano had just served him a glass of cabernet and a veal chop wrapped in bacon. Glitsky, Mr Low Cholesterol because of his past heart attack, was having grilled petrale with a side of steamed spinach and iced tea.

'You ought to go wild,' Hardy was saying, 'and ask Stephano for a lemon wedge.'

'I don't need it.'

'Who said need? We're talking pleasure, flavor, good stuff. Lemon goes great on spinach. It's great in iced tea. It's great on petrale. Nothing on your plate has any kick to it.'

'I don't need kick. I'm high on life. Ask anybody.'

'You want, for a buck, I'll give you a sip of my martini.'

'I don't want a sip of your martini. How long have we been friends and you keep trying?'

'Friends? We're friends?'

Glitsky drank some tea. 'Better than you and Farrell, I'm guessing.'

'Wes will get over it. What's he gonna do?'

'I don't know. Throw you in jail. Have Gomez cite you for contempt or perjury or something.'

Hardy sipped his martini. 'Gina's a very serious woman, I'll give her that.'

'She or somebody she works with.'

'You're saying I had something to do with her testimony? You don't think she's telling the truth?'

Baleful, Glitsky raised his eyes. 'Please.'

'I'm serious.'

After pushing his food around for a second or two, Glitsky put his fork down. 'Here's my concern, and it's a real one. You think they're going to let this go, and they're not. Sher and Brady not only look like fools, you've accused them of being sloppy slipshod cops. That's not going to go away. To say nothing of Vi Lapeer. So they're going to find something that proves Gina's lying.'

'Her phone was off that entire afternoon,' Hardy said. 'She checked.'

'There! That's what I'm talking about, that little detail. The bare fact that you know she checked that. Why did she do that? And what about Mose's phone? Did they have a GPS on that for the day?'

Hardy shook his head. 'He didn't bring it with him that day when he went over to Gina's. It was at his place all day.'

'You're sticking with that? Really?'

Hardy popped a bite of veal. 'Got to. As far as I know, it's the truth.'

'It was slick how, just when Gina admitted they'd gotten together—'

'I think she said they'd been intimate.'

'That, too. Right then Susan gets up and leaves the courtroom, right when Moses hangs his head in deep chagrin. It was almost like it was choreographed. To your credit, I think the jury noticed it.'

'The choreography?'

'No. The actual display of emotion.'

Shrugging, Hardy said, 'Natural reactions. I hope Moses and Susan don't break up over it.'

'Just for fun, I'm going to keep at this until I find a crack. But Sher and Brady and Stier, they'll be at it in earnest until they stop breathing.'

'Well, I wish you luck. Them, too, while I'm at it. But how can you argue with the truth?'

'You're not giving this up, are you?'

Hardy drank a little more gin. 'Probably not. Not that there is anything to give up. But even if there were. No.'

Behind his closed office door, Hardy in his shirtsleeves was throwing darts.

There was no point in pretending that he was going to think about, much less concentrate on, anything else until the verdict came down, which would happen when it happened – today, tomorrow, a week from now.

He was playing a solitaire game, twenty down, and was now on 'eleven,' having thrown only four rounds of three, which meant he'd missed twice. He was locked in, a thin current of adrenaline pumping through him, keeping him focused and alert.

As he was pulling his darts from the board, the phone on his desk – his direct line to Phyllis – buzzed, and he went over to pick it up. 'Yo.' Phyllis always hated when he did that, which was why he almost always did.

'Mr McGuire's wife and daughters are out here to see you.'

'Give me a second and I'll be right out.' Hardy straightened his tie, put on his suit jacket, and dropped the darts into their place behind the cherry-wood closet that hid his dartboard. Opening his door, he stepped out into the lobby area, across to his in-laws, and hugged them each in turn, making appropriate noises, leading them into his office, where they could sit and have some space to relax – Susan, Brittany, and her younger sister, Erica, whom he hadn't seen since the whole thing had begun.

When they'd all taken seats, Hardy offered them water, coffee, tea, wine, anything, and after they all turned him down, he boosted himself onto his desk. 'I'm glad you came by. It's so good to see all three of you hanging together. And this is really the hard part,' he said. 'The waiting.'

'This is nothing,' Susan said. 'The hard part's been the last three months. Now it seems that no matter how it comes out, we're going to be in the middle of more controversy again, Diz.'

'You don't need to be.' He looked at each of them in turn. 'None of you need to be. Are you being hassled by reporters?'

Brittany spoke up. 'Only every minute of every day.'

'We just tried to have lunch at Lou's,' Susan said. 'We finally decided maybe we needed to hide out up here. I hope you don't mind. It was crazy in there.'

'I don't mind at all,' Hardy said. 'That was a good thought, although it might be a while until the verdict comes in. If it drags on, you can all come over to our house and stay with me and Frannie, then come on back in here and hide out more tomorrow, no problem.'

'Well,' Susan said, 'actually—'

Her younger daughter cut her off. 'That's not the main thing. The main thing is if Dad really slept with that woman.'

Susan cleared her throat, waited until she had everyone's attention. 'I already told the girls, Diz, that they shouldn't concern themselves with that. Gina pulled me out of the courtroom and told me what she was going to say, and also that it was a lie.'

Hardy's eyebrows went up. 'She told you that?'

Susan nodded. 'Trying to spare my feelings.'

'Right,' Brittany said, 'but you know what the problem is with someone who tells you they're lying?'

Hardy knew. He nodded. 'They might be lying about that, too.'

'So what's the truth?' Brittany asked him. 'Do you know?'

'What do you think, Uncle Diz?' Erica asked. 'Did he tell you? Do you know for sure?'

'I know what I believe, but I can't know for sure, Erica.'

'And what's that?' she pressed. 'What you believe?'

But Hardy refused to be drawn into this discussion. 'The point,' he said, 'is not what I believe. It's that you don't need to say anything.'

'But they keep asking . . .' Erica continued.

Hardy nodded, understanding the great vulgar maw of the media and what these women were going through. 'Let them ask,' he said. 'That's their job. Your job is not to respond. I'm afraid you've got to decide what you believe for yourselves.'

'But,' Erica said, 'if Dad didn't have this relationship with this woman, that means he went and killed Jessup.'

'Not necessarily,' Hardy said. 'Maybe somebody else killed him. But listen up. You're all laboring under the impression that you have to say something, that you have to explain things or even have an opinion. Well, here's the easy answer: you don't have to say a word to any of these people. Just say, "No comment." Whatever they ask you. "No comment." Not even "I don't know" or "I couldn't guess" or anything else. Just "No comment."' He broke a tight grin. 'You guys want to practice? It takes practice, believe me. It's weird and unnatural, but it has to happen. If you want, I can ask you questions all afternoon, and you can tell me "No comment."'

'But that seems like we're actually hiding something,' Erica said.

'Like what?' Hardy asked.

'Like we're covering up for this lie. Gina's lie.'

'How do you know it's a lie? Or which part of it is a lie?'

'Dismas,' Susan said, 'come on. Am I supposed to tell my friends that the reason I know my husband didn't kill that man is because he was being unfaithful to me at the time? And I'm okay with that? Hey, it's no big deal?'

'No,' Hardy said. 'You're supposed to say that it's none of anybody's business. Let them wonder and speculate all they want. It's a family matter, and you and Mose and you girls are dealing with it as best you can, and you'd appreciate a little respect for your privacy. But even better would be if you just said "No comment" to everybody. If they're your really close friends, then I can give you a special dispensation to say, "I'm sorry, but really, no comment." But don't even feel like you have to do that. Privacy, I realize, is a little out of fashion, but it's a real concept.'

'But what's the truth?' Brittany asked.

'Let's say that the truth is what Gina told your mom. She and your dad never had the affair she told the court about.'

'If that isn't true,' Erica said, fighting back tears, 'then that makes my daddy a murderer.'

Hardy took a moment to reply. 'Your father fought in Vietnam, sweetie, where he killed people, and so did I. That doesn't make us murderers. Homicides aren't always murders. Sometimes they're justified.'

'Do you think,' Brittany asked, 'if he did it, this one was?'

'Nobody can answer that except your father, Brit.'

A long silence settled. At last Brittany let out a heavy breath and said, 'I've got one that maybe you can answer, Uncle Diz. Do you know what happened to Tony?'

Again, Hardy paused. 'We know he packed up and left town.'

'But why? Do you know?'

'I do know.' And he told them. 'He was a charming guy, Brit,' he concluded, 'but he was basically in hiding, so when his cover got blown by that picture of the two of you, he had to go. If it's any consolation, he wasn't what he seemed to be. To any of us.'

'I could have helped. If he'd trusted me more.'

'Some people,' Hardy said, 'maybe most people, you can't change. I truly believe you can't save anybody. So it's probably a better idea to choose to hang around people who don't need changing or saving.'

Susan laughed with a bitter edge. 'Except all these years,' she said to her daughters, 'you've seen me putting up with your father, who often needed changing or saving, and loving him through most of it. But still.'

'You picked good, Susan,' Hardy said. 'You girls are in pretty damn good shape, too. We get over this last hump, things will straighten out. You just wait.'

He'd barely finished speaking when there was a quick knock at the door. Amy Wu pushed it open, breathless, her eyes shining with excitement. 'The court just called,' she told them. 'They're coming in!'

At 3:22, the jury filed back into a courtroom overflowing with reporters, spectators, various denizens of the Hall of Justice. Out in the gallery, Hardy saw Wes Farrell, whose visage remained stern and unyielding. Also from Farrell's office, Treya had come down, although she was sitting with Abe in another row on the defense side. Wyatt Hunt was there, too, along with some of his staff, all the McGuire women, and much to Hardy's surprise, his wife (who, unbeknownst to him, had made her 'be aware and stay quiet' pitch to Moses in the jail an hour before) and their daughter, Rebecca. Gina Roake was nowhere to be found. All four eyewitnesses and Jessup's mother sat in the second row directly behind Stier and Gunderson's table. On that same side, right in front of the eyewitnesses, sat Lapeer, Brady and Sher, and the crime scene supervisor, Lennard Faro.

Hardy, Amy, and Moses sat at their table, the tension almost unbearable as the jurors took their seats – far too slowly, it seemed to Hardy.

So slowly.

Hardy's hands were sweating, his stomach in a knot. He loosened his tie, which had begun to choke him. Picking up his glass of water, he realized that the water's surface telegraphed the tremor in his hands, and he put it back down.

The stone-faced jurors were taking their seats one at a time. Not one of them met his eyes or even glanced in the direction of their table.

Next to Hardy, Moses seemed drained of blood except for his eyes, which were deeply bloodshot. His breathing was audible. Amy Wu sat on his left, holding his hand and rubbing it.

At last the bailiff came to his feet. 'Department Twenty-four of the Superior Court of the State of California is now in session, Judge Carol Gomez presiding. All rise.'

Gomez appeared through the courtroom's rear door and, in a swirl of robes, took her place at the bench. 'Please be seated.'

Blessedly, Hardy thought, at least she appeared ready to move things along. He found himself putting a hand on Moses's arm.

Gomez turned her head and spoke to the jury. 'In the matter of the People of the State of California versus Moses McGuire, has the jury reached a verdict?'

The foreman, Philip Waxman, one of the fathers of a daughter on the jury, stood at his seat. 'We have, Your Honor.'

'And is that verdict unanimous?'

'It is, Your Honor.'

'Please give all the verdict forms to the bailiff.'

The bailiff took the forms to the judge, who examined them to make sure they were appropriately filled out, signed, and dated. Gomez then gave them to the clerk. 'Madam Clerk, would you please read the verdict?'

She began with the caption of the case, including the defendant's name, case number, and what court they were in. And then at last.

'Count one. We, the jury in the above entitled cause, find the defendant, Moses McGuire . . .'

44

WHEN MOSES FIRST went on the wagon, he'd listened a lot to a Collin Raye song entitled 'Little Rock,' whose lyrics referred to the fact that the singer hadn't had a drink of alcohol in nineteen days. It hadn't sounded like much of a deal, not such a long time, but Moses had found in the living of it that it was nearly an eternity.

I won't have a drink today. I won't have a drink today. I won't have a drink today.

One day at a time. Forever. Or nineteen days, whichever came first.

In reality, he hadn't had a drink in a lot longer than nineteen days, since the day of his arrest. In jail, they didn't serve wine with the meals. But since the not-guilty verdict, since he'd been back behind the bar, he'd had easy access, and not drinking under those conditions made all the difference. So today was a kind of personal milestone, his nineteenth day back at the bar. He'd been crossing off dates on the calendar, and now that he'd made that magic number nineteen, he decided he could start to let himself think that this time he might just make it.

Now, on a relatively balmy late-summer Tuesday evening at 5:30, life was almost back to normal. The Little Shamrock had a good crowd going. Regular Dave was back in his usual spot, on his third beer since four o'clock. One of the dart leagues was having a tournament in the back room, and there were twenty or so players, whooping it up and spilling out into the hallway that led up to the bar area proper.

Four couples sat at eight of the ten stools at the bar. Back by the bathrooms, a group of six or eight college-age kids – legal, as Moses had made sure – was on the first round, and everybody was into drinks made with premium-call liquors. If Moses could keep them happy, that would turn out to be a nice profit center.

This, too, gave him some small hope for the future. Only small, because he was not as solvent as he once was. He had relinquished another 24 percent of the bar to his brother-in-law as payment for Hardy's representation. He couldn't really complain, since he was free again, and Hardy had made that happen. Despite a definite cooling in their friendship, Hardy was still a good guy, and their deal left Moses as the majority owner – 51 percent to 49 percent. Further, when Hardy's share of the profits reached the sum total of Moses's legal fees in about a hundred years, Hardy insisted that he would return the 24 percent to McGuire. They shook on it.

On the home front, things were not so positive, although he held out hope that he and Susan would get back to where they once were. Clearly, she was – both of them were – trying. They would start formal counseling next week. In the meanwhile, Susan couldn't come to grips with the person he was, with what he had done. Even though she thought she believed he was not an adulterer, Susan had never directly asked Moses to deny it, and he had never done so. Because to deny the truth of the affair all but admitted the alternative – that he had in all probability, as the evidence suggested, killed Rick Jessup. That, too, was unacceptable to her. So she was living – they both were living – in a no-man's-land of ambiguity and distress.

In all, he'd come to the belief that, like everything else in life, it would take time, maybe a lot of time. All he could do was stay sober and faithful and hope that they would reconnect.

Down at the end of the bar, he brought Dave his fourth beer, refilled a couple of cocktail orders from the couples, pulled down a Guinness stout glass and added ice and a lime wedge and a good blast of club soda from the gun.

Turning around, he dialed up 'Little Rock' and three other oldies on his playlist.

He checked his watch.

The song came on.

Tony's backup person – Moses's longtime Sunday/Monday bartender – Lynne had taken over most of the night shifts. She'd gotten used to making more money and was game for all the shifts Moses could throw her way. She was due in twenty minutes, after which he was going home to have a barbecue on the roof with his three girls.

When he got home, he'd also announce the nineteen days, the great psychic barrier that they all knew about. They'd know he was on his way, holding up, doing as well as anyone could hope.

He pulled a couple of Bass pints. The guy with the girl down to his right said, 'Hey, Mose. What's the only word in English that sounds the same when you take away its last four letters? I don't think there is one.'

'Yeah, there is,' his girlfriend said.

The front door swung open, and a middle-aged, gray-haired woman came in alone. Though it was an unusually warm night, she wore a heavy coat that went to her knees. Standing still for a second, letting her eyes adjust to the slight dimness, she saw the free stool at the bar directly in front of him and walked over to claim it, then swung her large purse off her shoulder and laid it on the bar, nodding at Moses in a familiar way. There was something familiar about her, but he couldn't quite place what it was. Close up, she was a nice-looking woman, he thought, although at about his own age, maybe a little old for the Shamrock's typical customer base.

'Moses McGuire,' she said.

Though the bar didn't need it, McGuire out of habit was wiping down the area in front of her, never completely unaware of the divot he'd made with the shillelagh so many months before. He put down a napkin and said, 'That's me. What can I get you?'

Next to her, the girlfriend said, 'Queue. Take away the last four letters, still "Q."'

McGuire pointed at her, said, 'Good one,' and held up his hand so they could high five each other.

In the split second while he was looking away, the gray-haired woman put her hand in her purse. Now, as he came back to her, she was withdrawing it.

She said, 'I'm Penny Jessup.'

When her hand emerged, it was holding a large silver handgun, which, with no hesitation, she held in both hands as she fired three shots point-blank into McGuire's chest.

After the funeral at St Ignatius and the burial in Colma the next Friday, the Hardys invited people over for an informal celebration of Moses's life. In spite of the crowd of perhaps two hundred that had attended the services, they expected only about thirty or forty people. But about double that number showed up – Wes and Sam, Abe and Treya, Gina, Wyatt Hunt, Amy Wu, and many Shamrock customers, as well as folks Hardy didn't know from his brother-in-law's A.A. meetings. More surprising were the several beat cops from the Shamrock's neighborhood and two members of McGuire's jury.

Hardy was surrounded by guests, pulling a cold Beck's from one of the coolers in the kitchen, when Wes Farrell appeared beside him. 'I'll take one of those if you can spare it,' he said. When Hardy handed him the beer, he continued, 'Quite a turnout.'

'Moses was a popular guy.'

'For the record, I'm just sick at what happened.'

Hardy nodded. 'Somebody should have thought of it, kept an eye out, something. She was always out there. I should have thought of it.'

'Why would you have? Her son was already dead.' Farrell hesitated. 'I guess she didn't believe Gina's story.'

'That's a fair assumption.' Hardy sipped his beer. 'For the record, since that seems to be the phrase of the day, nobody's disproved it.'

'If you don't mind,' Farrell replied, 'I'd rather not talk about it in those terms. It was a fair trial, and you won it. By the way, Sam tells me you haven't RSVP'd to the wedding.'

'We thought you might be regretting having sent us the invitation.'

'Are you kidding? I've only got like three real friends in this town. It would be nice if some of them came to my wedding.'

'I heard even Sam was pissed off at me.'

Farrell chuckled. 'Treya finked.'

'She might have.'

'The funny thing about that? Remember how she was going to try to take my side on all of these moral arguments we get into? At least see things from my point of view, if she could? That was her first effort.'

'How's it been going since then?'

'She's kind of come around to thinking you did the right thing. Moses should have killed that guy, since rapists deserve to get killed. This from my liberal fiancée.'

'The jury said Moses didn't kill him,' Hardy said. 'But I'm impressed with the way she's thinking. The DA's wife ought to be in favor of the death penalty, don't you think?'

'She doesn't like the "penalty" part. Just go take out the rapist.'

'Your own little vigilante.'

'I know,' Farrell said, 'it's special.' He squinted into the crowd. 'I don't believe this.'

Hardy looked. 'What's that?' Then, 'Wow.'

Farrell nudged him on the arm. 'I'll let you take care of this one on your own.' He moved off to the back door and outside.

In another moment, Paul Stier was shaking Hardy's hand. 'Sorry to barge in on your party, but you said everybody was invited.'

'Sure,' Hardy said. 'Can I get you something?'

'No. I'm good.'

'You were at the funeral?'

'In the back. I didn't want to cause a fuss. I think it's terrible, you know. What happened.'

'Farrell just said the same thing.' Hardy, uncomfortable with the conversation, let out a breath. 'He who lives by the sword and all that. If he did, of course.'

'You really doubt it?'

Hardy gave him a tight smile. 'That'll be a "no comment."'

With a sense of surprise, Stier said, 'You think I'm trying to trick you.'

'I wouldn't say it's outside of the realm of the possible.'

'Man,' Stier said, shaking his head with regret. 'Sometimes we are in a shitty business. I'm here because I sincerely wanted to pay my respects.'

'All right. But might I remind you that if you'd gotten your way, he'd be in jail right now.'

'That's better than where he is now, wouldn't you say? I took him to trial because that's what I get paid to do.'

'What's that supposed to mean?'

'It means I play the cards I'm dealt, and I'm morally obligated to try to win with them.' He paused and leaned in closer. 'Also, I always try to pick a fair jury. A fair jury.'

At first Hardy didn't grasp what he was saying. A fair . . .

Then it hit him. Five fathers of daughters. My God, Hardy thought, he had done it on purpose.

With that, Stier took a quick breath. 'I've got a daughter, Diz. She's twelve years old. She loves soccer and baseball and music and dancing. She's the light of my life. If anybody did anything to her, there is no doubt in my mind, I'd kill him in a heartbeat.' He extended his hand again. 'Anyway, nice working with you. Until next time.'

He turned and made his way back through the crowd.

45

HARDY TURNED ON the light and stood in his daughter's former bedroom at the back of his house. They'd left it the way it was when she moved out for college. Recently, Frannie had been talking about turning it into a home office for her marriage and family counseling business, save on the rent she was paying on Balboa Street. But for the moment, it was as it had been.

The Beck had kept up a corkboard with photographs of friends, her brother Vincent, her cousins, going back to her early childhood. Here she was on a horse in Golden Gate Park; body-surfing with Vincent at Santa Cruz; with Brittany covered in mud on a riverbank somewhere; in the role of Eeyore in a grade school production; with her backpack on, hiking with her Girl Scout troop; at Heavenly Valley, skiing with her mother; reading in the front window; dressed up for her first formal dance.

Hardy took his cell phone from his belt, saw the time, and realized that it was too late to call. He didn't like to intrude on her too often. She was busy, studying all the time, or doing whatever else she did that he didn't need to know about. He didn't have anything specific to say to her anyway.

Just that he loved her. And he could tell her that tomorrow. If he remembered to call her.

Well, no.

This was why, he thought, they invented texting. He got his phone again and punched in and sent a message: 'Just thinking of you. 143.' Their code for 'I love you.' 'Dad.'

He realized that he was opening himself to good-natured ridicule by including that 'Dad' at the end. Of course it was Dad. The message came from Dad's phone, so who else would it be? Still, he left it and pressed send.

Frannie's footsteps sounded on the stairs, and in another moment she was standing in the doorway, barefoot in her demure cotton pajamas. 'I thought you were coming upstairs in five minutes.'

'I am.'

'Yes, but that was fifteen minutes ago.' She gave him a searching look, reached out and touched his arm. 'Have you been crying? Are you all right?'

'I don't know.' He was silent for a couple of breaths.

'What is it?' Frannie asked.

It took him another second or two. Then, 'I keep thinking about Mose, and then that leads to Brittany and the Beck. I don't know what I'd do.'

'Let's hope you never have to find out.'

His eyes went to the corkboard, came back to his wife. 'I don't even know what it is nagging at me, except if I wasn't so goddamn clever, he still might be alive.'

'How would that be?'

'She couldn't have got him if he was in jail.'

'Well . . . okay, true, but he didn't want to be in jail. Nobody blames you, Dismas. You got him off, and that was what he wanted.'

Hardy chewed on his lip.

'Anyway,' Frannie said, 'my understanding was that it was Gina who was so clever.'

Hardy hesitated. 'Not entirely.'

'It was your idea?'

'It wasn't even an idea when I said it. But I said it first.'

'And she ran with it.'

'Right. Brilliantly, I might add. But I keep asking myself . . . I mean, this is large-scale perjury, there's no other way to spin it. Or fraud. Or both. Take your pick. It's playing a little havoc with my self-image as a guy who tries to do the right thing.'

'Mostly, you do.'

He shrugged. '"Mostly" doesn't cut it, though, does it? Everybody can do the right thing when it's easy. This wasn't, and I didn't. Moses was going to roll over on me and Abe and Gina, and I, in my fatal glibness, somehow persuaded Gina that we couldn't let that happen, no matter what. Because I convinced her, Moses got out, and because he was out, he got killed. You see why this might be guilt-inducing? And then I find out he probably would have gotten out anyway . . .'

'How would that have happened?'

Hardy paused. 'Stier packed the jury,' he said at last. 'He let on five guys with daughters. I didn't have to do anything but play by the rules, and I would have won, or at least maybe not have lost. But I didn't, and now Moses is dead. Okay, I'm not saying it's my fault. I did what I was supposed to do and had no control over the outcome. But I had something to do with his death, Frannie, a big something that I've got to live with.'

'But you've just said it. He would have gotten out and gotten killed anyway. You didn't do it. Nothing you did made that happen. Moses did it to himself because of what he did. That's the final truth of it all. It breaks my heart, Diz, it really does. And I loved him, but that's who he was. Aren't you the one who always says that character is fate?'

'That was André Malraux, but I've been known to quote him from time to time.'

'Well?'

'Well, yes,' Hardy said. 'Turns out he was right.'

Epilogue

THEY PUT BRITTANY up at the newly renovated Hotel Bel-Air.

The whole thing felt surreal, but every step of the process had proved legit. The men and women with whom she was dealing weren't a bunch of flakes.

Daniel, a perfect gentleman, thirty-two years old, married with two children, had come up to San Francisco to meet with her mother and make sure everybody was comfortable with everything they were proposing. This was a serious production. A network had picked up the series for the first season, and they wanted a new face to play the part of Ophelia, the damaged femme fatale. Daniel, remembering the tabloid fodder from the trial days, had sought her out and found her.

Both Brittany and her mother thought that her part read well; there was intelligence in the writing, real drama in the plotting. Yesterday, Daniel had come up to San Francisco again to accompany her on the flight to L.A., then stayed with her in the limo to the hotel, which was every bit as beautiful and serene as she'd imagined it – the swans in the lagoon, for some reason, nearly brought her to tears.

Was she really here doing this?

At nine A.M. this morning, the late-September weather perfect, the air soft and scented, they were eating breakfast to the strains of a live harpist on the outside patio when Daniel, in a low-key gesture, half-pointed to a nearby table. Brittany looked over and saw Frances McDormand absorbed in what looked like a script, studying her lines. Brittany, realizing the competition that she would be encountering – real professional actors with years of experience and a lifetime of immersion in acting – suddenly felt an almost overwhelming jab of insecurity.

She brought her napkin to her lips, placed it carefully back on her lap. 'You know, Daniel—' She stopped, shook her head, tried again. 'You're not going to want to hear this.'

'I bet I will. Try me.'

She scanned the patio, taking in the setting. 'I'm so grateful for the opportunity that you people are giving me, but I'm not sure I can do this.'

Daniel tilted his head to one side, his expression both sympathetic and amused. 'Of course you can. Look at yourself. You belong here.'

'I don't. I did look at myself this morning.' She brought her hands up to her head. 'I mean . . .'

'Your hair?'

She nodded. 'My not hair.'

He remained smiling, patient. 'Did you happen to notice that every single conversation out here stopped when we showed up? Here's a hint. That wasn't because of me.'

'That's because I look like a freak.'

'Perhaps freakishly lovely. But actually, perfectly lovely.' He leaned in toward her. 'Give me your hand.' After he took it, he said, 'Can you really not be aware of the perfection of your face? I wish I were a sculptor so I could capture it and have it with me all the time.'

'Now you're being silly.'

'Not at all,' he said. 'Not in the least little bit. If you want to know my opinion, six months from now, half the young women in America will be walking around with their hair cropped, all in homage to you. The Ophelia cut.'

She lowered her gaze, felt some pressure in his grip. All but unconsciously, she returned it.

'Then there's that other thing,' he said.

'No.' She shook her head again. 'Stop.'

'I can't,' he said. 'You're doing it right now. The sense of vulnerability you project, the wounded innocence. Every man in America is going to want to protect you, be near you, be part of the magic you create without even trying.'

'Now you're embarrassing me. Really.'

'I don't mean to. I'm telling you the truth that you can't seem to see for yourself. But I'll stop on one condition.'

'Tell me.'

'Give me a real smile.'

He stared, locked in on her eyes, holding her hand, his expression evolving from nearly angry – gradually, gradually, turning to conspiratorial, playful, intimate, playful again. She held her pouty frown as long as she could against this onslaught of easy charm, until finally she broke and her face lit into her stunning smile, accompanied by her lovely, tinkly laugh.

'There you go,' he said. 'Beautiful.' In the next instant, Daniel went serious. 'So damn beautiful.' He brought her hand to his lips and kissed it. 'You're going to be a star, Brittany, a major star. You don't have to worry about a thing. It's all going to work out. And if something does start to go wrong, I'm going to be there to protect you every step of the way.'

A faint undertone, an echoing thrum of dread at these words, tickled somewhere at the furthest edges of Brittany's consciousness, threatening her smile.

But they were, after all, at the Hotel Bel-Air. The day was soft and sweet; Daniel was powerful and handsome. Brittany was going to be successful and happy.

484

The harp's music swelled over the patio, and the minor notes she had almost heard lost themselves in the rhapsodic melody.

Her smile rekindled itself. She brought his hand to her mouth and kissed it chastely. 'All right, then,' she said, 'I'm going to trust you.'

Acknowledgments

Books do not get written in a vacuum, and this one is no exception. This one started out to be a different story altogether. Once it became clear to me that I was pursuing a plotline that did not work too well, I began peppering a group of friends and colleagues for their opinions and suggestions about other ideas and concepts that I hoped would grow into a better book.

For their good humor, flexibility, feedback, and patience as I worked through this process, I'd like to thank my agent, Barney Karpfinger; my great friend and collaborator Al Giannini; the brilliant novelist Max Byrd; perennial best man Don Matheson; and writer/lawyer/bon vivant John Poswall. My assistant, Anita Boone, deserves special praise for her daily infusion of optimism into what sometimes must have seemed a slightly uptight environment.

As a non-lawyer writing books with a lot of lawyer stuff and courtroom action, I am doubly indebted to the aforementioned Al Giannini, who serves as my very first 'editor' and vets everything from police procedure in San Francisco and environs to the actual ballet (with lyrics) that occurs within the courtroom scenes.

Although we did not speak personally, I would like to acknowledge the contributions of Dr Robert William Shomer, an expert witness in the field of eyewitness identification, and whose testimony in another (actual) trial was extremely enlightening and informs a significant section of this book. Likewise, a multipart article by Meredith May on sex trafficking, published in the *San Francisco Chronicle,* provided essential background material. George Q. Fong was helpful on the subject of U.S. Marshals and protected witnesses, and the wonderful author and friend Robin Burcell gave me a tremendous boost with critical information on forensic artistry. My friends Dr John and Lesli Chuck provided an important plot point that turned out to be critical. Finally, I'd like to thank Daniel J. Simons, professor of visual cognition and human performance at the University of Illinois, for the fascinating video referenced in *The Ophelia Cut*.

Several people have generously contributed to charitable organizations by purchasing the right to name a character in this book. These people and their respective organizations are: Wayne and Leslee Feinstein (Gastric Cancer Fund); Vic Sher (San Francisco Jewish Community Center); and Paul Brady (Yolo County CASA).

For all things cyber – my webpage (www.johnlescroart.com), blog, Twitter (www.twitter.com/johnlescroart), and Facebook – I'm grateful to Eager Mondays (Andy Jones, Briony Gylgaton, and Mary Stewart). I truly love to hear from my readers, and I invite one and all to stop by any of the sites and join these lively, interesting, and fun conversations.

My two private editors, Doug Kelly and Peggy Nauts, continue to find and correct mistakes that keep trying to make their way into my books. Thanks to both for their keen eyes and critical intelligence.

I am absolutely thrilled to be publishing with Atria Books, and I'm immeasurably grateful to my new publisher, Judith Curr, and editorial director (and my own editor!), Peter Borland, for their boundless enthusiasm and the decision to add me to the imprint's impressive roster. Thanks also to the tireless efforts of the marketing department, especially David Brown.

I have already dedicated this book to my wonderful wife, Lisa, and our great children, Justine and Jack, but I'd like to acknowledge them here once again – you guys make it all worthwhile. Thanks for being who you are and for continuing to share your lives with me.